ANTERIOR SKIES VOL. I

EDITED BY C. F. PAGE

CONTENTS

IV | EPHEMERAL ALCOVES

INTERMISSION | ESSAY

V | FORM AND BEAST: AXIOM

VI | THE COSMICISM OF THE FALLEN

VII | BALLAD AND CODAS

INTRODUCTION

Pipe dream or not, I had contacted Thomas Ligotti to see if he could write the introduction for *Anterior Skies: Volume I.* You may deduce from having written the introduction myself that Ligotti said no. You wouldn't be wrong. (Although he was very kind and intelligent about it.) But he did plant a bug in my ear—pretty directly, in fact—when he told me, "[Writing the introduction] *is really the task of the editor, that is, the person who chose the stories for certain reasons and who should be the one to introduce them to the reader.*" I suppose I was merely trying to keep up with other anthologies, ones who have *this* bestselling author or *that* award-winning writer for their introductions; but after absorbing Ligotti's advice, I feel like slapping my forehead.

Because *duh.*

Of course it had to be me.

I'm the one who picked these stories and who understands the reasons for picking them and their meticulous arrangement.

So what is *Anterior Skies*? The simplest answer—although perhaps not the most accurate one—is that it's an anthology of Lovecraftian and Ligottiian short stories and poems and everything in between. The more complex (but honest) answer is: I haven't the slightest idea.

Is it horror? Mostly. *I think.*

Fantasy? Sort of. Probably. Kind of.

Science fiction? *Yeah?*

Anterior Skies was conceived on vacation in Gatlinburg, Tennessee, in the summer of 2022 (*way* too hot), on the porch of an

Airnb-rented cabin, with a too-fancy cigar dangling from my mouth. A few minutes after finishing reading Matt Cardin's essay "Gods and Monsters, Worms and Fire: A Horrific Reading of Isaiah," and a few minutes before seeing a bear skitter past the porch—in which I immediately dropped my cigar and *What the Daemon Said* (an essential read for all aspiring horror writers and horror enthusiasts, in my humblest opinion) ~~and ran inside like a frightened child~~ and bravely walked inside and shut the door behind me—I knew I had to helm an anthology of the weird and cosmic. I was so unnerved by an almost . . . *cosmic trepidation* of merely an analysis of an Old Testament book—in fact, just a few passages—that I craved to find more unconventional horror experiences. Let me reiterate: Cardin's *essay*—emphasis on the word "essay"—goes toe-to-toe with my favorite *fictional* works by King, Lovecraft, and Ligotti. (Of course, I could write my own collection; but I'm not a short story fella—I have a hard enough time keeping a novel under 200,000 words.)

Anterior Skies is divided into seven parts (and an intermission, because, considering *Native Fear* has one, I guess that's my "thing"). We start off with *Theses and Ode*, and *The Fallenness of the Cosmos*, which contain more of your traditional Lovecraftian tales. Then we stumble—quite abruptly—into the nihilism and weirdness of *Tohu: Phantom and Void*. Following that, we enter into *Ephemeral Alcoves*, or what I call "the Ligotti zone." It's past this section, starting with the intermission, that I gradually take you home. *Form and Beast: Axiom* is the inversion of *Tohu: Phantom and Void*—these stories are less nihilistic and, contrary to traditional cosmic horror (although I hesitate to paint all the *Axiom* stories with such a broad stroke), have objective morality; cautionary tales; Good Vs. Evil. Then *The Cosmicism of the Fallen* mirrors *The Fallenness of the Cosmos*, and *Ballad and Codas* (mirroring *Theses and Ode*) concludes the anthology.

I don't want to overexplain my thought process (H. P. Lovecraft did famously say "don't explain anything"; and I fear I've explained too much as it is), but only to let you, dear reader, understand that, as the saying goes, "There's a method to my madness." I will, however, say I'm grateful for the short stories and poems I received from all these fantastic authors, and I hope that you, dear reader, will let the experience wash over you as it was meant to be: from beginning to end.

Again, I ask myself: What is *Anterior Skies*? But that's the wrong question (mostly). A better question: What

(should)

does *Anterior Skies* make me *feel*? To reutilize and paraphrase an excerpt from my upcoming *The Last Feast of Harlequin*-inspired novel, *Nocturnium*:

On some nights, in some portions of the overhanging cosmos above your hometown, are refracted obscurities from some faraway but unreachable horizon. These extracosmic flashes are brief—blink and they're gone—except, of course, for around the latter months of autumn. Then these ether images linger like superimposed psychedelic parasites of megalithic proportions. It's beautiful, it's scary, like caravans of wandering spirits, or an ectoplasmic miasma of celestial decay. Glitching astronomical bodies blanket across this gloomy yet many-hued pane of seemingly extraterrestrial firmament of an uncomfortably low-hanging impression. That which were spattered across its bleak horizon are dead stars, pale suns, blood moons, and blots of strange black that if one were to gaze too deeply upon, well . . . never you mind that, Dear Reader. And yet these are only placeholder words: one speculates that the sky-stained pictures of cosmic anomalies are a few clicks greater than the third dimension. The ones whose psyches haven't yet turned to mush by mysterious night terrors—and other, *stranger* forms of paralysis—call this night sky spectacle "Anterior Skies."

C.F. PAGE

I

THESES AND ODE

LITTLE MOTHER

by Heath Mensher

CAN YOU READ THIS?"

Rachel didn't want to tell Parker what the inscription said. "*Shrey nit*" was Yiddish for "*don't scream.*" There was a smell that stung her eyes, and the bedroom was a blur of tears, the fox stoles, the dolls.

"We should go, Park."

Rachel had let Parker draw her into the excitement of seeing the legendarily obese Mr. Bleich's house from the inside. She watched Parker filling his pockets with nesting dolls. "Matryoshka dolls," her father called them. "*Little mother.*"

They turned to leave but Mr. Bleich stood filling the doorway.

"Have a seat. Let me show you."

The terrified children sat crisscross on the floor. Mr. Bleich unbuttoned his shirt. A look passed his eyes like he was about to sneeze, and his skin split down the middle. Thin streams of blood leaked down as his scalp cracked like a rind of cheese. He whined as he removed his clothing, his butter-white fat spilling onto the rug. He rubbed his body as the skin came off, globs piling at his feet.

"You see?"

Standing before the children was a naked woman. Brown hair slicked salmon-red, skin shiny wet.

"Another?"

Her chest ruptured, spitting blood onto the children like warm rain. Some pooled on Rachel's upper lip as the woman sloughed off her form again, the head deflating and falling backward onto the floor. Beneath, a small naked girl smiled.

"Another," the little girl whispered. "*Shrey nit.*"

ADRIFT EBON TIDES

by Pedro Iniguez

IKE A LILY PAD DRIFTING helplessly down a river's currents, soft waves rocked the liferaft deeper into sea. Leandro turned to look behind himself until the light of the flames engulfing the ship finally vanished behind the dark horizon, leaving only a dome of glittering stars above. He looked back at Paul Mahoney, who had now taken to wrapping his arms around his chest.

Leandro stuck a thumb in his mouth and chewed on his nail. "I had no choice. You saw it, too, right? Whatever that was?"

Mahoney looked down at his neoprene boots and nodded. The young fisherman looked like a corpse in the darkness, his lips purple, his face blue.

"Maybe some of the guys are still alive," Leandro said.

"Maybe," Mahoney said softly. "I hope not."

Leandro nodded and leaned over the side of the raft. The moon's pallid reflection was round and bright upon the surface of the ocean, breaking its endless ebon monotony. He inhaled a whiff of briny air and wished so desperately to be back ashore, holding his grandson on the docks as the waves crashed against the rocks.

What he'd witnessed tonight had no place in this world. Any world. He'd burn the whole planet down if it meant never having to see that thing again. Then, he thought about the rest of the crew.

His heart started to burn a hole through his chest. He tried to push the guilt back down into his belly and told himself he did what had to be done. Though the more he dwelt on it, the less sure he was of what exactly had happened. Everything transpired so quickly, his mind was struggling to grasp what he'd seen. Impossible things. Horrible things. Things that made him want to gouge out his eyes.

Yes, it had to be done. There was no other way.

The surface of the water broke and the moon's reflection began to phase in and out of existence. He leaned back inside the raft and watched as a swell of sargassum swarmed the dinghy like flies over a carcass. A shudder ran up his spine at the sight of the tangled mass of seaweed, piling higher and higher around the raft, like long, wet strands of hair.

Leandro's teeth gnashed against his thumb until it had numbed completely. "We won't last long like this. Any idea where we are?"

Mahoney shook his head.

"Me neither." Leandro sighed. The skin on his arms erupted with goosebumps as the frigid air nipped at his body. "Any family back home?"

"Two kids," Mahoney said.

"Great. What are their names?"

The man in front of him bit his lip and remained silent for a long moment. He began to rock back and forth, clutching his shoulders as if something was going to whisk him away into the night. Perhaps he wasn't wrong. "I can't remember."

"You can't remember?"

"No," he said, looking around. "Why are we here?"

Leandro opened his mouth to speak but stopped himself. He plumbed the depths of his mind, sifting for a piece of something that was now missing. He looked up at the man who was now a stranger. "I don't know."

Something moved in his peripheral vision. An unexplainable blur. A flash of light. He looked up at the sky. The stars were now bending in peculiar ways, their light twisting into impossible ribbons. He turned to his companion, curious if he'd been seeing the same thing, but the man's head had been smoldering, his pink flesh partially melted. Small things wriggled in the dark of his eye sockets. Leandro leaned forward, hoping to make out what it was. He fought the urge to vomit when the maggots spilled out onto the floor of the raft.

Leandro rubbed his eyes with his palms. When he opened them again, the man's face had been restored, but his own hands were now coated with blood, the warm, viscous fluid pooling at his boots. His thumb had been gnawed off, leaving a large chunk of exposed bone. He spat out a wad of blood and cursed under his breath. What the hell was going on? If it was a dream, he wanted nothing more than to wake.

He eyed his masticated thumb again. He was lucky the cold had numbed the pain. Not knowing what to do, he tucked his bleeding hand into his armpit and clenched his teeth. In this cold it was only a matter of time before his organs shut down. Soon, they'd both die of exposure.

For what seemed a lifetime neither man said anything, each nestled in his corner of the raft as wisps of vapor crept out their mouths and faded into the night sky. "I'm cold," his raftmate finally said.

"Me too," Leandro said.

Leandro's raftmate pursed his lips and reached into a compartment by his side. He slung an emergency kit at his feet and sorted through its contents. Gauze, bandages, mylar blankets. Shrugging, he tossed them into the ocean.

"No point," his raftmate said.

Leandro nodded.

His raftmate's hand trembled as he retrieved a flare gun from the kit. He ogled it in wonder for a moment, turning it this way and that in his grasp. When he'd spent enough time looking over the thing, he stuck the barrel in his mouth and pulled the trigger. There came a resounding *pop* and a geyser of blood spewed out the back of his head. In the darkness, the man's maw flickered a jack-o'-lantern grin, the fire crackling like a scrambled television channel. The man's limbs dropped limply at his sides and in moments his head was completely ablaze.

Leandro sat there and gazed at the beauty of it all. The way the flaming tendrils lapped up the man's head like a torch, the way the fire's aura lit the endless black ocean. The heat felt immaculate on his face. Leandro shuffled across the raft and embraced the man and his gracious heat. The flames began to spread over his clothes, his flesh, even catching on his beard like tinder. Before the fire enveloped him, he offered the sky one last glimpse. The stars ceased their twinkling, their light now suspended in animation as they watched him like unblinking eyes. It was the last moment he ever knew fear. For that, he was thankful.

THE SINGING OF OLD HOUSE

by Godwyn

THOU SEEKETH OLD HOUSE, Traveler. Yea, I am vaguely aware—via traversing and probing the bookshelves of the sooty, cobwebbed passageways of mine overlong memory—that ye denizens of Cromledge call it a name different to mine. The Obelisk Under the Mountain: is that not the name thou art familiar with? Ah, well, close enough I'd say. And yet I've heard stranger and more verbose names for *Old House.* The Bogeycastle of Blood and Bones and Blackness, the Shivering Bone of the Fallenness of the Outer Darkness, and—perhaps the most frustratingly anticlimactical, vague, and *suggestive* of all the names I've heard over many *great-turn-stones,* but certainly not as longwinded as the aforesaid—the Red Tower (are we talking red masonry, furniture, flowers, blood, or something else entirely? A mad name it is, and I'd squelch it under heel if a name of a thing had shape to squelch).

By the looks of thine inequitable getup, I'd say thou knoweth very little of the art of killing. I mean not to offend thee, Traveler, but it's only that thy helmet—an obsolete relic of an olden epoch—isn't sitting properly upon thy spoilt breastplate (don't meddle with it with those oversized, mismatched gauntlets, neither, for there be nothing to be done for it); thy pauldrons seem peasant-rigged, made of reforged sleekstone; a rerebrace is missing on thy left arm, a vambrace on thy right; and I pray not a blade fall anywhere near thy merely leatherbound legs.

Ah, I see. Thine uncle being a blacksmith fills in *some* of the outline of thine aenigma, Traveler. Although, by the look of that ashen dismay smeared across thy face, coupled by thy taut but blemished skin having seen somewhere shy of twenty *turn-stones*, mayhap thy kin's skill—or utter lack of (mine apologies)—may account for thy half-protectedness, but thine *agency* accounts for the other half. The unshielded half. Yea.

That's it, isn't it?

Suit and skin.

Thine overall frail form.

The ever-so-slight crackle of thy voice.

Thou could be traversing to *Old House* in search of a kin. Mother or sister, mayhap. Nay. Not kin. Look at the flush about thy cheeks, dear me. The love of thy life, a sweety pie—erroneous, am I? Of course not. Read as easily as a childhood tome, thou art; and seldom on the matter of the heart am I wrong as it is. And thou hath come to take her back from that Wicked Old Thing which prowls *Old House* and its surrounding grounds. And what art thou carrying for steel, Young Traveler?

Dagger.

Mace.

Both fine.

I suppose a greatsword, even a shortsword, would issue strain from thine embryonic gristle and meat. What I'm telling thee, Young Traveler, is that thine age and thine overall poor breeding has disallowed something which is mostly inherent with an age greater than thine own: the strength to wield the necessary steel which may hath enough reach and weightiness to slayeth the Wicked Old Thing lest you stumble upon IT; for IT, I warn thee, is cunning, enchanting, and terrifically precarious. In plainer speech: thou art too young, too feeble, and a dagger and a mace may be fine and fine—for, mayhap, an expert who's seen twice or thrice as many *turnstones* as thee. A breadknife may hath suited thee better, for the Wicked Old Thing may hath deemed thee unthreatening and thus cast a blind eye upon the fleshly stain in ITS acreage—meaning thee, of course, with a dull breadknife and mayhap a chamber pot for a helm; haha heha ho; alas, a mace and dagger, as thou art armed with, is just threat enough to receive not *meticulous scrutiny* from the Wicked Old Thing, nay, but scrutiny just the same.

I digress, Young Traveler. Slacken thy circumspection a moment and enjoy this warm *godbreath* smoldering below and betwixt us and forget thy looking over thy shoulder, straining thy neck, to gaze upon that impressive vista of death and stranger, *secreter* things nestled against the mountainside. *Old House* won't waltz up behind thee in the middle of the night if thou were to looketh away for just a spell, will it? Looketh towards me, Young Traveler, and mayhap thou be *green* enough to prattle with a friendly old man.

I thank thee kindly.

Thou hath heard of Lord Manager Reed and the Obelisk Crusade, I presume? O! I'm surprised thou hath not. Do ye lads and lasses not study respectable history in the Kingdom of Cromledge? Although, I suppose if thou had, thou would *not* hath ventured into this starkly ominous, darkly charnel country. Other than Lord Manager Ivæn the Weak, who'd been slaughtered by Ubon Halfman—*what?* Is that what they teach, that he'd been slaughtered by his own guards? Thou talketh very little, and then thou talketh too lavishly; let me finish my point, Young Traveler. As I was *saying:* only two Lord Managers had ever been killed—at least, brutally (Tren the Quiet *did* die of a mysterious illness, but it was quick and painless and he went out very—no pun intended—quietly)—during their Managerial terms. Ivæn the Weak by the will of ye catacombs-kept thrall, Ubon Halfman, and Reed the Gentle by *the Song of all Songs*, a strand of *Endlessness*. (Hark, now! Sense enough will unknot itself from mine enigmatic words, but only at the end of things to come.)

Both stories are dark and twisty enough for one speaker and one listener sitting in the night country, feeling the warmth from the broiling *godbreath* greedily gobbling *godbones* in the pit before them—but I'll lecture only of the relevant latter, of Reed the Gentle. I of course am the speaker, and thou, Young Traveler, art not merely a listener but mayhap a passenger on this yarn, a note or lyric in this *Song*. Haha heha ho. But before I begin, unsheathe thy dagger and thy mace. Get cozy near me. Yea, very noble. Leave them be—close enough to reach them *if* the need is rudely borne, but I'm just a friendly old man, so what need there be to feel terror and to shiver in this lukewarm, breezeless dusk?

Look out that way into the night country, Young Traveler—yea, I give thee consent to crane thy neck once again. See how the graylight shines thinly and redly around *Old House* (mayhap that's why some lazily call it the Red Tower); see how the mountainside crawls up its backside like a hungry mouth; see that lush, vibrant, pristine land which sits from where we sit here to where it—*Old House*—stands there; and see that—despite its splendor, mayhap *because* of it—something seems *off*. Disordered, diseased, and decayed; a breed of fog ye folk can't see but only feel. Mayhap there be a *Song* which ye can see but not heareth; and it draws ye in . . . over and over . . . throughout however many *great-turnstones* since its, shall we say, *wicked conception* . . . with its harrowing beauty . . . and because of that, because of seeing and not hearing, it drives ye men into utter madness.

By the way of any—or, as ye folk say, "*anyway*"—that is only my notion. The truth of the matter is beyond even the wisdom of an old thing like me. Where was I? I thank thee, Young Traveler, for the constructive skull-nudge—

Yea. Lord Manager Reed of many *great-turnstones* agone was of immense beauty. Mayhap he even looked like thee, Young Traveler—just a tad, anyway—although he was thrice thine age, and broader of shoulder and thicker of arm, for he *could* carry steel. Appropriately dangerous steel, I should say. And, too, he could swing it. Slice it. Cut through the flesh of foes and savage beasts. He was strong and skilled, as well as beautiful, and the women of thy kingdom were infatuated with him. And why not? A chin like that. And eyes like warm seawater. A trimmed torso, also. Long of leg, strong of arm, deep of voice. Well-read and well-spoken, too.

That's right, Young Traveler; a Manager takes an oath of celibacy. Lust can be a crux of a man fallen; even love—noble as it seems—can be a catalyst for very great calamity. And I mention his allurement not for any narratively superfluous and -ficial reasons, or simply to hear mine own tongue trot, but that a lady like the daintiest of flowers—some may even hath described her demeanor as *simple*, yea, but not dull, nay, never dull, for she shone brighter than Sol the Great Sky Ring—well, she'd found herself in the favor of Lord Manager Reed. Mayhap that be why he adored her so, for many adored him but she wasn't so easy. A challenge. Prior to their not-quite-secret mutual love, she had never once spoken a word to him, had never gawked nor glanced at his fundamentally flawless form. She was a humble maiden, a charitable healer, a giver to the Church, an honorable daughter, sister, and friend, an endless dancer. She was pure, a True Maiden. He sought her for those reasons, would hath chosen her over the greatest jewel in all the kingdom of Cromledge and the lands which spill out from its bowels, and the farther lands yet discovered. There were even whispers of a marriage once his term was ended.

That's well-put, Young Traveler.

That had never come to past; for several days from his final day as Lord Manager, Reed's love—o sweety pie Rebeka, as I had called her—had vanished.

Thou don't say? *Thy* lover's name was Rebeka, also?

I meant to say "*is.*"

I imagine that's only coincidence. A common name, mayhap. And thou were to marry her, as well? *O.* Now that may be the core of the pattern, would thou agree not? Certainly. Think on it, Young Traveler; the missing girls are always in love and are deeply, richly, *sickenly* loved by another, and mayhap *all* their names be Rebeka. But let's continue the yarn of the Obelisk Crusade . . .

———

Reed was forlorn. Raggedly unshaven, hair unkempt, smelly even. Thinner, for he was unwilling to eat. Uglier, for he was unable to smile. And he sat in the Great Hall which overlooked Cromledge. But his gaze was limited to a small spot on the black marble floor. And the well-armored Ringguard, adorned in cloaks of blazing golds, radiant greens, and rugged grays—and at equal intervals on either side of the red carpet leading to the immense entryway—were veiled monochrome blurs in his periphery. What may be greater than ten but certainly less than twenty days after lovely Rebeka's disappearance—and precisely three days before his term is ended, and ergo would be lawfully permitted to marry her—Wiseman Gorget entered into the great hall wielding a staff nearly twice his height. If Lord Manager Reed was aware of his councilor's presence, he showed nary a sign; and when the brittle, unimpressively epicene Wiseman Gorget spake in a reedy, thin voice of news (whether "good" or "bad" is in the eyes of the beholder—but considering the eventual outcome, one could argue "bad"), of a sighting of Lovely Rebeka, of her wandering the starkly ominous, darkly charnel country surrounding the Under-Mountain Obelisk, "with a basket, m'Lord, and picking fruit and flowers and singing a lovely song," he showed no sign of hearing. Or understanding the revelation even if he had heard. He just sat there, a lowly, grayed, dejected husk of his former self. O, certainly, Wiseman Gorget—unable to stand silence, and whom the whores of the brothels would concordantly agree loved to hear his own voice—prattled on about the history of the Under-Mountain Obelisk (although I'll call it *Old House* from now on), about how over the many, many *great-turnstones* there had never been—not once—a maiden who had been rescued, "and, Lord Manager, not once has there been a rescuer or rescue party survived the journey. I advise thee only to mourn and let Rebeka be lost to the Will of the Outsiders."

Blue snapped up and pierced into ugly brown, cold ice instead of warm seawater; Wiseman Gorget was stunned into a rare spell of muteness by Reed's hard stare. As aforesaid, they called him Reed the Gentle (although the women may hath a different name, a name their husbands only heareth whispers of), and the very ungentle, uncharacteristic gaze would silence anyone. *Anyone.* How long had that silence lingered was altered of course by the span of *great-turnstones*, for the yarning of tales from one tongue to the next hath a way of inflating even the smallest of details. But at least twelve *clicks* had passed (impressive nonetheless, considering Wiseman Gorget's tongue-trotting, silence-fearing nature).

"We leave on the morrow." Reed's words shattered that silence, and Wiseman Gorget jolted and opened his mouth to cast out a wise warning; but Lord Manager Reed's tongue danced quicker and he quoth, "Find thirty of our fastest steeds and twenty-eight of our strongest men and one experienced guide—mayhap an herb-picker. We leave as the Great Sky Ring rises and the black about the country turns gray."

"Thy will be done, m'Lord," quoth Wiseman Gorget, his disapproval hardly secreted.

And thus it was so.

Lord Manager Reed, and twenty-seven of his best Ringguard, and one man who was not a knight but a stout blacksmith and a relative of sweety pie Rebeka, and not an herb-picker but a deaf but proficient scavenger (and, may I mention, the only surviving member of the somehow-forgotten Obelisk Crusade; Tobyn or Tobyk his name may be) verily took off across the Cromledge drawbridge as the Sol the Great Sky Ring rose in the east and the darkened world turned ashen; and up and out from the earth dirt and moss and grass churned as their steeds' great hooves pounded and volleyed and crushed the cockcrow plains; and they made camp hither and thither—sometimes smartly below plain-crested mountain ridges, sometimes wherever Lord Manager Reed demanded (whether it be foolishly on a hill for the Old Hunters and other beasts to gaze upon, whether with curious intent or malicious desire, or in a valley for the Old Hunters and other beasts to come stumbling down in an ambush and devour them), sometimes near a pond, and sometimes not; and many times did the Great Sky Ring rise in the east and settle in the west before Reed the Gentle and his strong men and Rebeka's relative and the cunning deaf scavenger had come upon the place where thee and me presently convene and discourse.

"Hark!" the Wicked Old Thing heard Lord Manager Reed shout to his posse from where IT, on ITS haunches, drank the blood from a song-slew creature near a spring in that very grove behind us. IT stood and moved to a shrub-and-flower-veiled sightline just over yonder and watched the drama play out with ITS primordial eyes. And listened. The steeds halted, save for Tobyn or Tobyk's; it, a black stallion, danced and neighed one too many *clicks*, receiving stares like daggers from the Ring-guard. It settled finally. Reed waited a beat before speaking. He looked off toward *Old House*. Its silhouette foreboding, its shadow long and windy, its cockcrow-mist about the starkly ominous and darkly charnel lands pregnant with trepidation and wonder . . . and a territorial foe besides.

(Come closer now, Green Traveler, as I paint to thee the end of all things.)

"The time is now," quoth their Lord Manager, as if written by a clichéd, hack of a scribe and had been given to Reed to remember and recite; "to test the burden of legend" or "lore" (I recollect not which, but something to that effect; it was dully but passionately spoken, regardless the word spoken); "and to slay," quoth Reed, "the Wicked Old Thing."

It's at this point that the Great Fool requested to cleave his modest but able—but not able enough, I'll soon reveal—posse. Half and the blacksmith to what ye Cromledge-folk call "the"—what was it again?—"Under-Mountain Obelisk," yea, and the other half and the crafty but deaf scavenger (Tobyn or Tobyk) to search every inch of the surrounding acreage. "Look for fruit and for flowers," he dazedly, stupidly quoth. "And listen for her song" (a *Song* they indeed found, yea, and lucky for Tobyn or Tobyk for his deafness).

So it was then that half the host and the stout blacksmith-relative rode their steeds to *Old House*, with equitable getup—a miasma of golds, greens, and grays from where Lord Manager Reed sat watching—and with much more knowledge in the art of killing than thee, and broadswords and greatmaces and -axes, and lances thrice the lengths of their steeds, for mayhap they encounter a hard-skinned Old Hunter or some such beast about the ominous, charnel country (what happened to them, there is no memory of, alas—but none returned home); and the other half and the soon-to-be only survivor spread out across the stark, dark realm, where they found fruits aplenty, flowers abloom, and a *Song* indeed.

They perished all, so they did. Reborn into notes and lyrical twaddle in the ode of *Old House*, except for Tobyn or Tobyk who heard not a song with his deaf ears but saw only a moving portrait of doom which had befallen the half-host of the Obelisk Crusade. What sights had he seen and dreamt darkly thereafter, one can only guess—mayhap close-ups of terror-infected faces, mouths perfect O's of agony; blurred and jittery phantasmagorias, mayhap in black and white and red red red, of tortured effigies atop four- and three- and two- and one-legged steeds, all flopping and wailing and singing—o, they sang like sweety pies— about the midmost spring in the grove over yonder, as *the Song of All Songs*—the *Endlessness*—inhaled their limbs and heads, blood and bones and all, living or dead . . .

. . . or mayhap Tobyn or Tobyk never got far enough to dream, for he was met with a terrible fate with a length of vine which he'd found not even three *bits* to the west from here—o, thou knoweth the land I speak of—and maybe, Green Traveler, that ruined, deaf scavenger wound about his neck the length of vine and knotted the other end to a branch of a huge *godbone* and dropped and slept dreamlessly: a dangling ornament for the bugs and the birds and the beasts, one that if that ornament at all dreamt then it dreamt black and bleakly.

And several *clicks* before Tobyn or Tobyk found his Lord's lifeless fragments and ran and dreamt blackly, do thou knoweth where Lord Manager Reed sat as he listened to his half-host dance? Very good, Green Traveler—right there, or a few *smidges* over, and on that very slab of sleekstone where thee sitteth.

Lachrymose and wet salt smeared his face. If not for his sniffling like a babe, he too may hath heard *the Song of All Songs*—the *Endlessness*; but nay, he heard only the stomping feet of the dance but not the *Song* itself, and not yet the *End*.

The Wicked Old Thing—definitionally well-fed but never quenched, always vacuous, and eternally rapacious—came down from its ode, the one of many connected doorways that none of ye discern dancing across the twilit firmament, and stepped into the pulp of what might, to some, appear to be a friendly old man.

And like thee and me, Green Traveler, the friendly old man had come and gallantly sat across from Lord Manager Reed, the *godbreath* eating away at *godbones* betwixt them. "Thou seeketh the *Old House*, Traveler," quoth IT. Except he—Reed the *at-the-moment-not-so-Gentle*—acted quickly, for the crimson evidence of the friendly old man's *Song* was smeared sloppily across ITS face. Reached for a shortsword, he did, which lay propped against thy sleekstone—at arm's reach, of course—and he stood, ready to slayeth.

Alas, for him it was too late.

The friendly old man had discarded ITS man-flesh, revealed ITS unfathomable boundlessness, opened ITS true mouth, and sung.

Shortsword dangled and thudded into the smoldering *godbreath*.

Flames hissed and cast across the landscape contorted stains of fidgety shadow.

He saw his sweety pie Rebeka, the hem of her dress trickling down to a stunning abyss; and, too, his half-host he saw, somnambulists dancing across the superlunary sky; saw everything in that most rapturous *Song*, he did; and then at the cessation—at the very *End*, Dear Traveler—he wedded Rebeka, and they consummated their vows at the outer brink of true annihilation.

Thou, too, can dance with thine own Rebeka as I sing to thee . . .

> *. . . bloated fog sang. Dark wings and songs even darker than the wings and the fog inhabited the House of axiomatic disorder, organic disassembly,*

and metaphysical decay in the fog. And the fog was Old—a biosphere for that which were connected to those dark wings; that which sang those opaque, blasphemous psalms; and that which could be seen in the not-considerably-dark—but disordered and diseased and decayed—Old House in the fog of some dreamer's song. Only on black nights across the starkly ominous, darkly charnel acreages does the singer dream . . .

II

THE FALLENNESS OF THE COSMOS

SPIRE

by Marcus Hawke

S PROFESSOR KEANE OBSERVED THE feeding habits of a particularly large angler fish, she thought to herself, *This never gets old.* Two-thousand feet straight down, tracking wildlife through an endless expanse of pitch-black sea, where not even the sun could reach. The midnight of the ocean. One of the most remote places on Earth.

It was something she had prepared for all her life. Ever since reading *20,000 Leagues Under The Sea* and the explorations of Jacques Cousteau, this was all she had ever wanted to do. All those childhood years poring over anything and everything to do with the ocean, even darker works like *The Call of Cthulhu*, led to this. Even having to cram herself into *Nemo*'s three-meter-wide cockpit, with nearly six thousand pounds of pressure all around her, for hours at a time, did nothing to stifle her zeal. Every moment of it was one wonder after another.

Down here were sprawling ocean plains, underwater mountains as tall as any above—perhaps taller—and forests of kelp that rival any found on land. Down here she had no one to impress or look good for; she could wear her biggest Coke bottle glasses instead of contacts, hair done up in a bun and covered with a wool cap à la Jacques if she wanted. Down here she was free from the noise of the city, from traffic, from the *buzzing* or obnoxious ringtones from her mother calling to ask when she would get married and finally give her grandchildren. Free of bills and neighbors and the vast majority of the rest of the world. Down here it was just her and the sea.

Down here she could be alone.

And yet not alone. Desolate as it may have seemed, it was full of life. Everything from jellyfish to giant squid. During her first expedition, she watched for hours as an entire host of sleeper sharks and hagfish devoured a whale carcass. It was worth weeks upon weeks stuck on a ship without people. All things considered, though, she would rather examine the individual chromatophores of a cuttlefish than engage in small talk with Professor Nowitzki about his kid making the hockey team.

It was incredible. Everything about it was.

Well . . . there was one thing.

She had been surveying a seamount off the coast of Ireland and spotted what she thought was a deepstaria enigmatica specimen, one of the rarest jellyfish a marine biologist could ever hope to see.

It turned out to be a plastic bag.

No matter how remote the terrain, none were far enough to go untouched by the wastes of humanity. It broke her heart a little. More than a little.

Somewhere off in the deep blue yonder, a whale sang a somber tune.

Keane watched as the angler drew in a gullible shrimp but missed seeing the little creature caught in its jaws when . . .

She heard something that forced her eyes to stray.

"What is that?" she said to herself, straining to hear over the hum of the equipment. Something other than the sub nautical tone that sounded all throughout the deep. High at first, then suddenly low, ebbing and flowing like the tide.

"Is that . . . ?"

Singing?

Less like singing than the collective moan of countless throats. Though in a way it did remind her of a song, whalesong in particular. But this was eerier. Sadder.

"Topside, are you picking up any other frequency down here?"

No response.

"Topside, this is *Nemo*. Come in."

Her field of vision was filled with four screens, three for the external cameras and one touch screen instrument panel. Nothing showed on any of them, and nothing through the cockpit's glass viewport in front of her. Nothing on sonar. She listened for a voice on the end that never came; and, as she did, the peculiar sound died down, faded away altogether, and was replaced once again with the aqueous babble of the ocean that had preceded it.

Communications with the ship had been lost somehow. It had been choppy when she dove and imagined the eleven mighty tons of steel that was the *Opal Siren* now battered by whitecaps as it was caught in huge Atlantic swells rolling high above her. With that in mind, she thought it best to return.

Professor Keane began to nudge the *Nemo* back toward the ship, simultaneously moving forward and ascending very slowly so as not to strain the exterior pressure by changing it too quickly. The outer lights cast a hazy yellow cone ahead, making visible every bit of marine snow—floating bits of debris and dead matter. But what was 20 feet compared to the untold fathoms in every direction?

The yellow eyes of the sub saw nothing but empty sea. And then it appeared. A massive, gloomy silhouette.

A spire.

At first, she thought it might be an inert thermal vent. But, as she slowly neared, its features became more clear. Twisted in a helix of what appeared to be dark coral, it rose up before her, invisible in the abyss except for where the exterior lights touched it. There were no crabs or tube worms or vegetation of any kind. Not even any fish swimming near it. No sign of life anywhere. The temperature readings weren't elevated at all. Just the opposite. In these waters it was as cold as the grave.

Keane angled the *Nemo* down sixty degrees and then tilted back up toward the distant, invisible surface. No end in sight either way.

No top.

No bottom.

But surely there must be, Keane thought. Since it was on the way to the surface anyway, she decided to find out.

The *Nemo* began to ascend the massive structure. Fifty feet wide, at least judging roughly from the comparative size of the cockpit. A realization dawned on her; actually it had occurred to her when the shape of the spire first appeared out of the darkness, but now she was sure of it. When you lived your life at sea, the vast and varied shapes, sizes, colors, and combinations thereof become second nature. But nothing, absolutely nothing, in the sea could form something like this. There was no way it was natural.

This was made.

But by whom? Or . . . what? For what purpose? The very thought made her cringe.

Images came to mind of things in the untold depths of the sea. Things with imperceptibly alien intelligence prowling every body of water, ready to swallow you whole. Great eldritch beings that call the subterranean their home, not only tolerating the crushing dark but thriving in it; things which spent eons crossing the stars from the ocean of one world to another, whose fathomless psyches allow them to touch the minds of seafarers and mariners through their dreams, promising them knowledge and prosperity if they agreed to do their bidding and offer them worship. So that once they shuffle off their mortal coil their souls descend into the deep, making them their slaves, who in turn are forced to make towers such as this one. Things which never truly die for they are never truly *alive.* And so they remain.

All this and more lurked just below the surface of every thalassophobe's conscious mind. She knew them, but she didn't fear them . . . not until now.

As the nearest sea shelf was another thousand feet down, she wondered what its base could be attached to. Below a featureless stretch of water, the flat monotony that was the abyssal plain was broken only by this gargantuan monolith.

Five minutes into the climb, when the dark had just barely given way to darkest blue, Professor Keane noticed a change in the dimensions. A slight narrowing in the width. Very gradual. Indicating that the sides would be coming to a point.

And finally it did. The top was not much narrower than the rest of it, leading to an opening of approximately thirty feet wide. No exhaust, thermal or otherwise. No shimmer of heat. The exterior lights did what they could shining down the hollow interior but showed nothing more than the same dark murk found everywhere else.

There was more than enough space for the *Nemo* . . . but there was no question that to do so was dangerous. Stupid, even. Doubly so being out of contact with the ship.

But she had to know.

It may be too dangerous for her, but not for N.E.D.

So named for Nautical Exploration Drone as well as Ned Land, the master harpooner in her favorite book. Keane tapped at the controls that powered up the drone, detaching it from the *Nemo*'s underbelly. Its LED light blinked as the propeller whirred to life and carried it through the opening. As it disappeared into the dark ahead, the fiber optic cable connecting it to the *Nemo* trailed behind it, cast out like a fishing line. It sent back images that fed into a monitor to Keane's right.

So far there was nothing much to it. Black within black within black. Not even the blur of plankton darting in front of it.

Then she noticed something. At first it just seemed like a trick of the light, the human brain finding coincidental patterns in inanimate matter. But as she angled N.E.D. down to the lower side of the spire, she clearly, unmistakably saw the shape of a skull. And not just the one but many. Lined up one after another, forming the winding grooves of the spire, as if they were carved into or out of the stone. The skeletal forms of fish of all kinds, dolphins, eels, sea lions, walruses, and whales appeared with them. Meshed together in a single current of lifeless rock.

Keane's view through N.E.D.'s eye changed slightly as it continued forward; the light, doing its best to creep along the inner perimeter of the spire, no longer touched it as the passage widened. This must have been where she saw the width change, she realized as the path ahead opened up.

Even down here where every bit of oxygen was precious, what she saw took her breath away.

An endless torrent of the dead churned languidly but smoothly, orbiting nothing in particular. A swirling spectral vortex made up of ghostly squid and octopus with milky white eyes. Seals and narwhals—even otters, which she had never seen look cheerless before. Human faces appeared, wave after wave of them, swirling around with all the rest. Bones caught in the tide. Some with clothing, some without. The togas of Roman antiquity, frocks and petticoats, naval uniforms from all periods of history. And many, far too many, wore little more than rags. Had death been as cruel as life, she was sure chains and shackles would have bound their wrists.

Thousands of them—no, *millions!*—all those claimed by the sea. Making this not a tower but a mausoleum.

She wondered if they were aware of N.E.D., but they didn't seem to be aware of anything out of the ordinary. They just continued to swim around and around.

Professor Keane stared rapt at the monitor. It was miraculous. Sad, but miraculous. But amazing. *Unbelievable.* Easily the greatest discovery ever! There was life at this depth, but there was also death. In forms previously unknown anywhere.

After about ten solid minutes just watching and recording the phenomenon, two of the most frustrating words in the English language began to blink on the monitor: LOW BATTERY.

Keane brought N.E.D. back to its dock. It securely clicked into place. A part of her didn't want to leave—not that she ever wanted to leave, but even less so now. She easily could have stayed and watched all day, but her common sense prevailed and she steered the *Nemo* back toward the surface.

"Oh man," she said, practically beaming. "Can't wait to show them this!"

"*And then what?*" a voice asked.

She screamed at the cavernous baritone that echoed through the deep, causing the bulkhead itself to rattle. Close, as though it were coming from right over her shoulder. It may well have been her imagination, a heightened dose of adrenaline making the innocuous rattle of an overhead panel seem like something more, but she sensed that it had come from behind her.

Slowly, cautiously, she craned her neck to the left and peered behind her.

Nothing but the sub's hatch that had been sealed shut since she entered through it.

Her view through the front of the cockpit hadn't changed. Aside from the drifting marine snow, there was nothing but dark, featureless sea.

She didn't want to do it. But she had to know.

With one rickety hand, Keane reached out and maneuvered the *Nemo* around laterally one hundred-eighty degrees so that it was pointed back toward the spire.

There, halfway between her and the opening, a figure floated in the water. Frock coat with wide cuffs, boots, no hat atop his skeletal head from which thin strands of long gray hair hovered around it. The eyes were pale as dead squid skin, leeched of its color. Had they not been wide and fixed on her, she may have been unable to see them. A soul adrift in dark oblivion.

"Too much of the sea already belongs to the Shallow World," came the voice again. from nowhere and everywhere at once. *"They will come. They will desecrate our resting place. This . . ."*

At first there was nothing but the vast dark of ocean.

". . . we cannot allow!"

Then the *Nemo*'s lights reached just far enough to fall on the opening of the spire as a storm approached.

All of the dead within came pouring out and barreling toward her. Dead eyes hurling forth like a gust of bubbles from so many last breaths, before finally they blasted right past the ghost and engulfed the sub.

Lost in a vortex of swirling souls, the *Nemo* was tossed like a bottle in a squall. Each second that passed in this maelstrom put greater and greater force on the hull as it was squeezed tighter.

Metal whined.

Glass cracked.

Suddenly Keane didn't feel so safe. For the first and only time ever, she wanted to leave the ocean and never return.

"Wait! No! Stop! Please!"

This couldn't happen. Not like this.

"I'll erase the footage . . ." She began frantically tapping at the monitor, which had shown her what N.E.D. saw. ". . . No one will ever see it. I promise."

DATA ERASED . . .

The tornado of drowned dead didn't stop. As it continued to compress the *Nemo*, some of the nastier ghosts focused their attention on the glass before her. Schools of sharp teeth and tentacles swarmed her. A shark with those lifeless eyes of theirs, teeth jagged as a breach in a ship's hull, clamped down on the glass before her. One chip appeared. And then another. An octopus, far larger than normal, *schlorpped* its gray, undead tentacles across another third of the porthole, intent on finding a way in. An orca, bearing the wounds of the harpoons that took her life, angrily butted at the ventral side of the sub. Then, suddenly, they all fell back.

A moment later, she understood why.

The *Nemo*'s bulkheads began to groan in protest as trickles appeared where there should be none. The ocean's raw force took over, now that the seal had been broken, no longer resilient to the extremes of the deep.

"Please! NO! I've erased it!" she shrieked, hysterically tapping at the monitor to confirm it. "I've erased—"

Something wasn't right. The file was gone, but the Trash icon showed otherwise. She clicked on it and sure enough, the video file was still there.

"Oh *come on!*"

She clicked the EMPTY button. Papers began to fly out of it.

30% . . .

. . . 60% . . .

. . . 80% . . .

Each moment that passed, the sub shrank. She could feel

the walls pressing in around her. She began to cry, tearful and fearful. Hugging herself. A prayer nearly escaped her lips. There was one colossal noise like a crack of guilty thunder, and Keane hugged her head with her arms, bracing herself for the end.

And just like that, it stopped.

She didn't budge or breathe.

Just stayed fetal for a while, afraid to open her eyes even to see the welcome sight of the words TRASH EMPTIED she knew would be waiting for her on the monitor.

It was cold now. *Wet.*

Hesitantly, she opened her eyes.

There was the sea before her again. Thankfully devoid of the hurricane she had found herself in moments ago. The vortex and all the souls in it retreated back toward the spire. She saw all of this, yet there was no light to show it.

There was also no sub.

No longer confined to her tiny cockpit, the *Nemo* had been crushed and rent apart. What remained of it floated in the water all around her, surrounded by the turbulence of spent oxygen. And there, in the middle of the bubbles and shattered debris, was her body. Broken and crushed. Killed on impact. It almost looked peaceful. At one with the sea.

After all the time and dedication she had given to the sea, all the care and consideration, it had done her in. She couldn't help but feel betrayed by this.

But of course it was no betrayal. The sea did what it does, nothing more.

She looked back toward the spire to see that the ghost of the sailor who first appeared to her was there again.

Waiting.

No gashes or wounds. Nothing to suggest how he had died. And so she decided that he must have drowned. He took one look at her—something akin to remorse washed across his dead face—and drifted back toward the opening of the spire before finally disappearing from view.

It took her a few moments, just long enough to watch the remains of her former self and the vessel that housed it slowly sink down into the deep. With a final glance upward, toward a world she would never see again, she followed.

And so the secrets, the sanctity, and the silence of the deep were kept.

For now.

PRODIGAL

by Derek Austin Johnson

COCKTAIL OF GRIEF, exhaustion, and highway hypnosis made Jake slam on the brakes and twist the steering wheel so he could make his exit. In the sudden deceleration, the dingy white plastic bag slipped across the passenger seat and tumbled to the floor, spilling the trip's detritus all over the passenger floor mat: Styrofoam coffee cup, empty chip bags, crumpled hot dog wrapper flaked with dried ketchup and stained with grease. The car crawled to a stop. On the other side of the road, a rat darted along the shoulder. A snake chased, its large black body quickly overtaking the rat. The rat squealed as the snake sank its fangs into the bloated stomach.

Letting out a slow breath, Jake cursed at the mess on the passenger side, then checked his Rolex and pressed his foot on the accelerator.

Not late. Not yet.

The car passed unkempt green fields and murky pools, both abruptly giving way to a subdivision. The neatly trimmed but treeless lawns fronting houses of bright-red brick and expansive windows obviously had been built after he'd left more than a decade ago, when Jake took a bus to Dallas and swore never to return. There had been many reasons to leave, but he couldn't remember the one that finally caused him say "enough."

He twisted the radio knob looking for a station. Static crackled through the speakers, so he pushed the cassette into the player and adjusted the volume. It was a mixtape, one his dorm mate gave him on his twenty-first birthday, the first song a fusion of gospel and funk that had been popular the previous year. The song was a favorite of a woman he dated in college, though she changed one word of the lyrics every time she sang along. When he asked her why, she said the song went against the teachings of her congregation's minister, but she liked the singer's voice. He stopped dating her shortly after that.

As he approached a convenience store, the low fuel indicator pinged and glowed. Jake pulled up to a fuel pump and filled his car, then went inside. The cool air plastered the white shirt beneath his black jacket to his back and arms. He'd forgotten how hot and humid it could be this time of year. It was likely he'd be a mess by the time he got to where he was going. He thought it might not matter.

He handed his credit card to the young woman behind an electronic cash register. Her Faith No More tee shirt was so large its short sleeves came to her elbows. A name tag identified her as DANIELLE. On the counter behind her rested a state history textbook—odd, if only because he was sure classes ended in May. *Summer school,* he thought.

"I don't need saving."

"Sorry, what?"

"No one wears suits around here, not on a day they don't have to. Not unless they're selling salvation. And I don't need it. I'm doing all right. Best that I can, anyway. You get that black absorbs heat, right?"

He brushed his damp hair off his forehead. His hand came back clammy. "Your shirt is black."

"Yeah, but it breathes. You off to a wedding?"

"Funeral."

Color drained from her face. "Oh. A friend?"

He felt very tired. "Family. My younger brother."

"I'm sorry, mister. I thought you were just passing through. I knew you weren't here for the festival because that was a couple of months ago." She pushed his card and receipt across the counter. "Younger brother? You don't look all that old so he must have been young. Did he just move here?"

His mouth tightened into a line. "He was born in our parents' house. It's near the old church. We grew up here." *And there may be some unfinished business,* he thought.

Danielle nodded in understanding. "Old Town. Near the swamp, right? I've lived here since I was eight and I've never been. No reason for me to go. Nothing there anymore. All the buildings are abandoned, and the electric towers are sinking. Not surprising when you try to build on marshland."

A headache spread from behind his eyes and down his neck. "Do you have a payphone?"

She gestured to the front of the store. Outside, the heat was oppressive and cloying. Sweat trickled between his shoulder blades.

The pay phone stood to the right of the convenience store's entrance. He dropped a quarter into the phone and dialed his home number, then pressed four digits on the keypad. A monotone electronic voice told him he had no new messages. He fished a slip of paper from his jacket, then entered another quarter and dialed.

It picked up on the first ring. *"Hello?"*

A woman's voice, low and neutral.

"Is this Evelyn? It's Jake. Clark's brother."

"Oh. Yes." Her tone didn't change. *"I was hoping you would call. I tried your apartment last night but got your answering machine."*

"I left after work last night. Just got into town."

"Okay. Good. We were hoping you'd be able to make it. I know it was a long drive."

Evelyn had been Clark's roommate or girlfriend or fiancé. Jake couldn't tell from Clark's letters. Even still, Jake was led to understand she had known Clark better than anybody over the past several years. It sounded intimate, however Clark described it. A week ago, Evelyn phoned Jake to tell him Clark had died. She provided no details except that Clark had been in poor health and that his death appeared to be from natural causes. "So, he wasn't bitten?" Jake had asked, but she evaded the question.

It was how their father died. That's what he understood, at least.

"The drive wasn't bad," Jake said. "The town's grown a lot since I've left."

Evelyn's chuckle was low and without humor. "*They built the subdivisions and a new civic center after they finished construction of the freeway. You can drive right past without seeing an exit. The pine trees hide just about everything. But it's booming. People are moving here and commuting to work in Houston.*"

Jake leaned against the store wall. The brick felt rough against the back of his head. "Did you talk to our mother? Do you know if she'll be there?"

A pause. "*I spoke to her. She sounded fragile. Your uncle Howard has been looking after her. Clark once told me she'd been that way ever since your dad died, and that Howard was, well, fond of her.*"

It didn't surprise him. On the occasions he thought of his childhood, he never pictured his mother as being young. "Did the coroner's report ever come back with a cause of death?"

"*No.*" Almost too quickly. "*No heart attack indicated, no stroke. They've sent blood to a toxicologist to see if drugs were involved, but it could be months before we see the results.*"

It sounded true, even if it didn't sit well with him.

"*You remember how to get to the church, don't you?*"

"I know."

"*It's still being held this evening. So if you need to grab a bite to eat you should do that beforehand. And don't worry about pallbearer duties. We have that under control.*" Another pause. "*I really wish we were meeting under different circumstances.*"

"Yeah," Jake said, his soft voice drowned by the roar of an eighteen-wheeler speeding down the road. He hung up and went back to his car.

It didn't take much time for Jake to become lost. No matter which street he took, he seemed to face the same houses with the same lawns. Regularly he found himself in a cul-de-sac and was forced to turn back. At one intersection he unfolded a map, but sunlight glared across the green street signs, making them impossible to read. He squeezed the steering wheel in frustration. His mixtape taunted him with a song whose abrasive vocalist couldn't drive fifty-five.

Eventually he came to a shopping center. A full parking lot fronted a grocery store and was surrounded on either side by boutiques selling cheap clothes and cheaper shoes. A garish red-and-yellow sign hung over a Mexican restaurant. Jake's stomach growled.

Inside, the smells of roast chicken and grilled onions hung onto metal chairs surrounding heavy tables tiled in colored ceramic. Conjunto music blared through speakers nesting in the corners. Jake's mouth watered. It was the kind of place Clark would have loved.

A waitress led him to a booth whose stuffing billowed like dirty clouds from cracks in the imitation leather. His frozen margarita was almost thawed, the outdoor summer air seeping through the tinted window overlooking the parking lot. Jake dabbed at his head with a paper napkin as he crunched tortilla chips and finished his drink in two gulps.

Questions buzzed through his mind.

He examined them, but they either eluded answers or spawned new questions, like cells in mitosis.

"Can you tell me about the festival?" he asked the waitress when she brought him the check. She held the plastic tray over his table and stared at him.

"I heard there was a festival last month. Do you know anything about it?"

She continued to stare as she set down his check. He tried again as he reached into his jacket for his wallet. "Do you know where they hold this festival? It's not anywhere near the swamp, is it?" He rummaged through his wallet. Bills, business cards. A photo of someone he'd dated during his first year at the agency, her name now lost to memory.

His credit card wasn't there.

He pulled a ten out of his wallet and asked for the pay phone. She motioned to the restrooms near the back of the restaurant.

He lined up two quarters next to the edge of the pay phone. First, he called his home phone number again. His answering machine stated he had no messages. Then he dialed Evelyn. The line rang eight times before he hung up.

He dialed again, this time more slowly.

No answer.

A slim phone book rested beneath the phone. Jake flipped through it before dialing.

Two rings later, the call picked up. A woman's voice. "*Stop 'N' Shop.*"

Jake cleared his throat. "Yes, I stopped for gas earlier. I don't know if this is the same person I talked to, but you asked if I was a preacher or something."

"*That was me,*" Danielle said. "*You know you left your credit card here, right?*"

He checked his watch. "Can you hold it for me until this evening? I won't be able to pick it up until later."

"*Sure. That's right. You were going to your brother's funeral, right. I'll keep it here but my shift ends soon.*"

He pressed the receiver against his ear so hard he could hear the dull roar of waves crashing in the folds of a seashell. "You said something about a festival."

"*The Serpent Festival? Yeah. The chamber of commerce and the mayor started that shortly after the developers began building. The developers tried getting rid of all the snakes, but there were too many. There was a loony religious group in Old Town that celebrated or worshiped them and convinced the developers to start a preserve. Then the developers needed an event to draw people in, make them think everything was safe, so they looked at the religion's beliefs and just took out all the weird teachings, kept things like masks and music. I mean, it's kind of cool. They'll set up booths in the parks, showcase a few snakes,*" *make a bunch of fried food and funnel cakes. The musicians are local, but they aren't bad."*

More waves crashed against his ears. "When did they start?"

"Definitely before I moved here. The last one was maybe the eleventh or twelfth annual festival. They used to behold them in autumn, but more people visit in April."

They were holding it earlier than the real one, he thought. "The religious group. Do they participate?"

"Oh no. Nobody from Old Town comes here."

"Do you know if there are many of them still there?"

Danielle took her time responding. *"I really don't know. I don't go out by the swamp. Or anywhere near Old Town. It's too weird. Too country. Like some* Deliverance *shit."* She paused. *"Were they people you and your brother grew up with?"*

He hung up, almost slamming the receiver in its cradle. The quarter clattered as the phone swallowed it.

The weight of his past pulled at him.

It was the last place he wanted to go.

Outside, the sun was too bright, the heat so great he felt like a frog slowly boiling in a pot of water.

He glanced at his Rolex. It would be enough time. When it was done, he would get his credit card, find a hotel outside of town, and catch some sleep before he drove back to the city.

He pulled out of the parking lot and headed toward the swamp, toward Old Town. Toward his old house.

A place where he'd sworn he would never return. But had to.

So many new houses and shopping centers crowded the road that he wondered if the oldest buildings had been torn down to make way for new development. The civic center gleamed with white columns and pink granite, palm trees from California shading walkways. It put to mind an Art Deco vision of the future; Roman influences given a modern twist. Better than the Old Town square, at least, which had looked ancient even before he left home.

Eventually green fields spaced the houses at greater intervals. Pine trees replaced them, becoming so tall they occluded the late afternoon sun.

And then, on his right, he saw the old gas station.

Two rusted gas pumps with round orange heads reading GAS in faded blue letters guarded a decrepit wooden house with shattered windows and a sagging porch. The white paint had chipped away, revealing dark splintering waterlogged panels. Every Saturday, when Jake was barely in his teens and Clark just ten, they would walk here for Dr. Peppers and Twix bars, treats their mother allowed one time a week. Clark always expressed concern that the snacks would harm them—"Dad says they rot you from the inside," Clark said, citing the passage from the Book of Teeth that read, "A Pure body is a Strong body"—and Jake always reminded him that Dad's teachings, yes, were good for pure mind and body, but that Mom said an occasional indulgence was good for the soul.

Past the gas station, the road curved. Despite being away for so long, he recognized overgrown patches of land where houses once stood, grain silos stained with rust, barns leaning so far to one side they might topple with the next strong gust.

He knew exactly where he was and turned onto a dirt road once the paved way ended. The car's tires crunched gravel as he entered a canopy of oak trees, and abruptly ended as he approached an unkempt lawn overgrown with weeds. Behind it loomed a dilapidated two-story Victorian house. A shutter on the second floor clapped against a window.

Jake nosed his car onto the gravel driveway, behind his parents' old Chevy Nova. He got out and climbed the steps. Dirty lace curtains obscured the windows, making it impossible to discern what might lay beyond.

No one answered when he knocked. The screen door screeched when he opened it and entered the living room. Immediately his eyes watered from the dust swirling through slats of sunlight. He fought a sneeze.

"Mom? Are you here?"

Between a decrepit sofa and a worn rocker stood a small table topped with so many framed pictures it resembled a cityscape. He picked one up. It was a black-and-white photograph. A man in his mid-fifties glared at him, a pair of trifocals magnifying intense eyes that seemed all pupil. A bolo tie hung from his collar, with a round polished stone sitting at the center of the upside-down triangle of heavy silver. He shuddered and placed it back on the table.

"It's me, Mom. It's Jake. I came back for . . . I came back."

The shutter clapped against the windowsill, the sound fading as he walked through the dining room. As he walked, something bumped beneath the pine floors: most likely an armadillo or opossum.

His footsteps clicked on the kitchen's amber linoleum. At the sink stood a thin woman in a threadbare baby blue sundress, curls of gray hair spilling down her back. The window over the sink provided a view of the backyard, the large oak tree obviously dead and denuded of leaves, the branches still in the humid afternoon air. The kitchen door stood open; its screen door fastened by a hook. The faucet dripped, and water splashed against a pile of plates dried with the remnants of a meal served long ago. He gagged at what smelled like rotten eggs. It was from the water. He hated drinking it when he was a boy because there was so much sulphur in the wells. It made the water they drank milk white, even when they boiled it.

"Mom? Hi. It's Jake. I didn't know if you'd heard me."

She turned. Her face was drawn and weathered, the crow's feet radiating from the corners of her eyes catching shadows to make them look deeper. The straps of her dress dropped to the edge of her slumped shoulders, exposing prominent clavicles. "You made it." Her soft voice was no louder than the clapping shutter upstairs.

"I got in a little while ago." A small laugh. "I almost forgot the way." He sat at the small kitchen table next to the tile counter and ran a finger along a crack in the ochre tablecloth. The crack resembled a shed snakeskin. "Mom, what do you know about Evelyn?"

"How did things go at the church?"

"I haven't been there yet. There's still time before the funeral begins."

"Was it full? Was the congregation engaged? I know quite a

few have stopped attending. They've fallen out of favor, the old ways. Soon it will only be the devout who pay obeisance."

"Mom, I'm not . . ."

"Those who fail to obey the Book of Teeth will meet the same fates as those who never believed. They'll never Shed."

"Mom," he barked and stood, the chair scraping on the floor.

She started, and for a moment clarity filled her face. "Jacob," she said, eyes wide with surprise.

"Jake, Mom. I haven't gone by Jacob in a long time. Since before I left. Mom, I have to ask you about Evelyn. She said she'd tried to call me but got my answering machine. But she didn't leave a message. How well do you know her? How well did—"

"You look like him."

"I don't think so, Mom. Clark had darker hair and was heavier."

"Not him," she said, blowing a wet raspberry. Saliva bubbles swelled from her lips. "You know, it disappointed him that you never wanted to lead the congregation. He was sick after the Serpent bit him, which you probably didn't know. He never Shed, but something was growing in his head. I know it was scary, the outbursts. The sudden movements. The screaming and croaking. But even if he didn't Shed, it was the True Voice. He could speak the Call of the Serpent right up to the end."

Upstairs, the shutter's muffled clap. "I had my reasons for leaving. I knew there was a world beyond this one. It wasn't right to ask . . ."

He stopped.

Through the window, the dead oak's branches remained still. They hadn't moved since he got here. He couldn't remember there being a breeze since he'd gotten into town.

Clap.

Beneath the dining room floor, bumping grew louder. Closer.

Ceramic dishes clattered in the sink.

His mother held a large piece of curved ivory in her small hand. It had been carved into something resembling a blade. Its serrated edge glistened with fluid.

"I am grateful," she said, her voice louder, the words intoned like the opening of a hymn, "that you have returned to us."

Jake ran, rounding the table and pushing the chair in her direction.

He shouldered the screen door. The hook rattled in its eye latch. Behind him, the chair scraped on the linoleum. He fumbled at the hook. It was stuck.

His mother crashed into his back, the thick knife slashing through his jacket, its blade biting into his arm. For a moment he lost his footing and slumped into the screen door, a metallic rip near the top. Jack pushed away from it, sending his mother across the table.

Footsteps thumped down the stairway. Too many to count. A chorus of shouts.

Whatever was under the dining room floor bumped again, clouds of dust puffing from between the boards. It growled.

Jake pulled at the door, unjamming the hook, and the screen door swung wide, and he ran, stumbling down the back porch's steps. His ankle twisted and he cried out, but he kept moving, losing one of his shoes in the overgrown grass. Tall weeds scratched at his clothing as he ran, as if attracted by his arm's open wound.

A forest of pine trees bordered the back yard. When he was close, he turned.

Men and women, at least half a dozen, waded through the tall grass toward him. The men wore thick canvas overalls the color of a snake's belly. Dresses of green and light brown billowed on the women.

All six had faces painted green, with a streak of red at their eyes.

And all held blades of ivory.

One of the men spoke. Even with the makeup, Jake recognized him.

"Jacob, you are being summoned," Uncle Howard hollered in a deep baritone. "The Serpent needs you."

Blood trickled from his soaked sleeve and over his knuckles.

He ran into the forest. Tried to. A lack of a shoe hobbled him, as did his bad ankle. Twigs and pine needles bit at his feet.

A depression in the soft earth captured his shoeless foot, sending more sharp pain through his ankle and up his leg. Something spat at him and rasped. He bit his lip to keep from crying out, the teeth sinking in deep. Blood welled from his lip and dribbled down his chin. Trying to breathe as deeply as possible through his mouth, he gasped. His chest and stomach expanded, straining his shirt buttons, but he couldn't fill his lungs.

Holding onto the smooth trunk of a pine tree, he pulled himself to a standing position and walked, carrying as much weight on his good foot as possible. He flexed his fingers and realized they were growing numb. He pushed a low branch out of his way. Writhing snakes tumbled around him and slithered through the grass. The branch caught the clasp of his Rolex's metal band, and it slid off his wrist and onto the ground.

As he walked, trees crowded him, as if they were attempting to block him.

"Jacob." Howard's baritone again. Jake couldn't tell if Howard was gaining; the woods absorbed his voice. "This is silly. How long has it been since you've walked through these woods? How long has it been since you hiked to the lake from here? The paths are gone. You'll lose your way. You know this. You've been lost for a long time."

The voice was closer. Jake was sure of it. He turned away from it and limped to the nearest trunk. The numbness radiated through his arms and across his chest and down his stomach to his legs. His body felt as if it was swelling, and hot.

"Don't run, Jacob." A woman this time. A familiar one. "The Serpent calls for you. Just like it did for Clark. You must come."

Evelyn. He was sure.

He tried to run but couldn't make his feet move and began to twitch. His body curled into a ball as his muscles squeezed tightly, pain roaring from his wounded arm and through his body.

He cried out as they surrounded him. The red at Uncle Howard's eyes hid any emotion, though he panted from exertion.

"You really should have just come with us. Or just gone on

to the church. It would have been easier that way." He motioned to the other two men, who picked him up without effort.

Jake's mouth contorted to say something but only managed a few sibilants. The men carried him through the rest of the forest and the pines appeared to move out of their way, became more evenly spaced. He spasmed, his back arching to the point he was certain it would break, then suddenly he was limp, a sack of flesh. Then pain surged through him again, and he felt as if his skin would split and his entrails would spill from his body. Throughout, they carried him with no more effort than carrying a bag of laundry.

The group came to a clearing and approached the back of a wooden building, its white paint worn to mother of pearl. Over a tin roof stippled with rust peeked an onyx steeple, its top resembling the triangular head of a venomous reptile.

Next to it was a pit.

It was a place he knew far too well. He and Clark once played near here. Their father spanked them when he found out, explaining that this sacred place was not a playground.

A car's engine growled on the opposite side of the church, brakes squealing as it stopped. Jake tried to scream, to warn whoever was inside. No sound escaped his lips.

Gently the men placed him next to the pit. The grass sloping down it felt cool on the side of his face, blades rough against his skin. He tried to make another sound but could not even manage a small moan. Saliva dripped from the corner of his mouth. Around him, snakes curved through the grass.

His mother approached. The car had been her old Nova. She knelt beside him and took his hand. "I know you're scared, Jacob," she said. "This is easy for none of us. But things have not gone well since your father died. The Serpent bit him but he never made the Change. Neither could your brother. He wanted to leave but Evelyn convinced him to stay. She'd left, too, but came back." She smoothed the hair from his head. "And so did you. And for that I cannot thank you enough," she continued, squeezing his hand. "The people who built outside of town, they don't understand. To them, this is all silly. A joke. They won't kill the snakes because the Serpent will punish them, but they'll hold celebrations and take money from tourists. They don't care about what any of this means."

A growl rose from the pit, and then a hiss. His mother squeezed his hand, her grasp tight against his fingers.

He could feel her hand on his.

She ran her fingers through his hair and kissed his head. "It will be all right. The Serpent wants you. He will make us strong again." She rose and strode to the other side of the pit. It was surrounded by the others, who all joined hands and raised them. The sun disappeared behind the front of the church. Jake's eyes followed it as shadows seeped into the sky.

He could move his eyes.

A flex of his fingers, then his toes.

The hiss grew louder.

Jake's arm flopped in front of him, his hand nudging something hard and curved.

His mother's blade had fallen from her dress.

Jake tried to pick it up but couldn't make his fingers work. He rolled forward, and his hand curled around the carved hilt. Then he rolled backward as feeling spread through his legs and arms. He sucked in air and continued to roll.

Behind him, chanting began, all sibilants. It grew louder, and the group backed away as a powerful scaly arm clawed from the pit and landed onto the grass.

Jake pushed himself onto his hands. The feeling in his legs was returning, but he still didn't have enough strength to fully crawl or stand.

Behind him came another thump.

From the corner of his eye Jake saw the thing pulling itself from the pit. It was large and green, with slitted red eyes over a wide mouth lined with serrated, unnaturally white teeth. Thick ebony claws tipped two sets of powerful arms and a pair of thick legs. Its tail whipped the air, mere inches from the worshipers around the pit.

It towered over everyone and set its eyes on Jake.

Jake screamed and continued to crawl, clutching the ivory

blade tighter.

The Serpent caught up with him in two strides and plucked him from the ground with ease. Jake struggled, ineffectually slashing at the Serpent's forearms. It brought Jake up to its mouth and opened, its eyes narrowing. The smell of sulfur overpowered Jake; his mind reeled as he fought the urge to vomit.

Jake felt he had enough strength, and barely enough reach.

He thrust the blade into the Serpent's eye.

It shrieked and let go of Jake, who had not released his grip on the blade. He slid down its scaly body, clothes ripping all the way. At its stomach Jake stabbed and sliced, the Serpent's thick, coppery ichor and foul organs spilling from the wounds. It staggered and fell backward, and Jake continued stabbing until it gave out a final cry and was still.

Jake rolled off and shakily stood, rubbing blood from his eyes.

He heard screaming.

Beside the pit, the worshipers wailed and writhed, clawing at themselves. It was getting dark, but Jake made out clearly the snakes slithering up legs, around waists, across chests. They were biting arms, faces. Bodies swelled and skin split like sausage casings. Soon the worshipers were still.

Jake dropped the blade and rushed to them. They were dead. All but one.

His mother pushed herself on her elbows, wriggling across the ground. He rolled her over. Bites marked her face. Her eyes stared beyond him, into a sky with stars winking to life.

She choked and vomited. He turned her head.

"Honey," she said. "I think Jacob might be in trouble. Did you get him out?"

Jake closed his eyes. "It's Jake, Mom. Jacob isn't me." He raised the ivory blade and thought. "Not much of me." And brought it down.

He sat for a while. The day's heat dissipated, replaced by a cool wind that buoyed the rising half-moon. After a time, he dragged his mother to the pit and dropped her in. He surveyed the other women, thinking he should give Evelyn a burial, but he had no idea which one Evelyn was.

Returning to his parents' house was easy, now that he knew he was close to the old church. He navigated the woods with ease. When he got to the house, he stood beneath a cool shower, scrubbing with an old washcloth until his skin was red. Afterwards, he bandaged his arm with gauze and pads in the medicine cabinet and examined himself in the mirror, running his tongue along the teeth, feeling the ridges and points.

He slept until sunrise.

Hunger groaned in his stomach as he took a pair of jeans and a tee shirt from Clark's old room. The shirt was too big, and the pants were too short, but they would work.

He changed the bandage before he left. The wound was healing. But an ugly rash radiated from it, rough and dry and peeling. It itched so badly he scratched until the rash was bloody.

When he pulled off the tee shirt, he saw more red patches.

His ears itched. He rubbed one. Skin flakes dusted his finger.

It was starting.

He went downstairs to the kitchen. Behind limp celery and liquefying spinach, a dozen eggs sat in a deep ceramic bowl. He cracked each one and slurped the yolks, the whites running down his chin. The milk white water was there, in a pitcher caked with calcification. He drank greedily.

There was a knock at the front door. He wiped his mouth and opened it.

Danielle frowned at him. "You look like hell, mister."

"How did you get here?" He coughed, cleared his throat.

"There are still people around who could tell me how to get to the church. You said you lived near it, and this was the only house I could find." She held something out to him. His credit card. "You said you'd be by last night. I checked with my manager, and he said you hadn't picked it up. I started to get worried."

He looked down at the credit card. It was green and white, and stood in contrast to her pink nail polish. Already he had trouble making out what the black lettering said.

"I don't think I'll need it."

Her eyebrows shot up into her bangs. "Are you serious? Plastic is identity, it's like personal money. You can't . . ."

"Do you go to school here?"

She started. "I'm taking a summer course, but I'll start at Rice in August. At least it'll be out of this town."

He closed his eyes. Now he could feel the snakes approaching the house. He heard them in the grass, the blades rustling.

"Listen," he said, "when you leave town, stay away if you can. You're right when you say there's no reason to come here."

Curiosity showed in her face, and suddenly was replaced by fear. "I don't understand."

"No, you don't. Trust me."

He closed the door and leaned against it until he heard her car start and drive away.

In the kitchen, he sat at the table. He'd left the ivory knife there. His fingers brushed the serrated edges, pressed against the sharp point until blood dotted his finger.

He picked it up and lay on the floor, then pressed the tip of the blade against his chest. Closing his eyes, he heard everything beneath the house, the snakes slipping beneath the walls and slithering over each other, awaiting their first command. He thought of the rat he had seen when he arrived in town, and the snake that attacked it, and, as he slowly pushed the knife into his chest, realized what it meant.

IF ANYONE COULD CATCH THE MOON

by Chelsea Pumpkins

THE SONG OF THE PEEPERS kept Andy company as she put the finishing touches on her night sky. Cricket legs and the vocal sacs of frogs stretched thin like bubblegum—there weren't sounds like this in the city. Mom made her keep the windows closed in the city. Closed, locked, and drapes pulled shut. Andy had to sneak the sunlight in when Mom was out, to charge the glow-in-the-dark stars on her bedroom ceiling.

But Mom wasn't here now. For the first time in a decade, Andy was set to spend summer in Stratford, with Dad.

She had been counting down the days since Hanukkah, when her parents, who normally never spoke to each other, had jointly proposed the idea. On the eighth night, Andy unwrapped her gift from Dad: *The Astronomer's Guide for Kids*. Inside the cover was a picture of a shiny black telescope set up on a tripod in her bedroom-to-be. A note on the back read: *You're going to love the stars here, Peanut. They shine brighter than you've ever seen.*

She looked from her guide to the ceiling and back, making sure she got the placement exact. She had to admit—these re-stickable stars Dad found were much better than the ones Mom bought. She could remove and reposition until their distances and angles were *just* right.

"There," she said, stepping back to admire her arrangement of Ursa Major.

"And just in time for the moonrise." Andy jumped. She hadn't heard Dad approach, but his smile was warm as he leaned against her door frame. "It'd be a perfect night to head down to the lake. Clear skies, bring the telescope down—what d'ya think, Peanut?"

A grin shot across Andy's face, and she nodded enthusiastically.

Andy's eyes were as wide as the sky and just as clear. They sparkled with reflections of ancient gaseous bodies—ghosts of elder gods and the phantoms of physics. She didn't even need the telescope to see the Great Bear.

"Dad, look! It's the Big Dipper," Andy said, her voice hushed in awe.

"Sure is. Wow, look at that."

He put his arm around her shoulder and pulled her to his side—the two of them, their own Ursa Major and Minor, sharing a silent love language with letters made of stars.

Andy squirmed after a moment.

"You all right, Peanut? Bugs gettin' ya?"

"No," said Andy. "It's the Dipper. It's missing a star, do you see? In the middle of the handle." She pressed her face to the eyepiece of the telescope in front of them. "Huh. I still can't find it."

Dad tried, too. "Think it could be covered by a cloud?"

"But there aren't any clouds out tonight."

"Yeah." Dad stepped back. "You're right."

"Maybe it got swallowed by a black hole."

"Don't ya think it would have swallowed the others, too?"

"Yeah," Andy said. "Maybe."

Although they could have gazed for hours more, Dad suggested they pack it in. He slung the equipment over his shoulder, Andy bunched up the unzipped sleeping bag in her arms, and they headed back to the house, their path lit by Dad's headlamp.

"Night, Dad," Andy yelled, after brushing her teeth. She padded down the hall in slippered feet to her room.

"Huh." She picked up a plastic star from the middle of her floor, sticky-side-up. Looking up, she saw a faint adhesive silhouette where the star once stuck. She pulled her desk chair out, climbed atop it, and pressed the star back into place.

Content with her complete constellation, she turned off the light and fell asleep under their glowing phosphorescence.

"How about that sky last night, Peanut?" Dad shouted over the crackling of bacon and the ratcheting whistle of the tea kettle as Andy entered the kitchen. She darted to the stove and turned off the gas. "Ha," he said, "I need more hands, don't I?"

Andy giggled and grabbed plates, mugs, and forks to set the table.

"I made pancakes." Dad placed a plate covered in foil on the table. "In the shape of full moons."

"Aren't pancakes always the shape of full moons?"

He just laughed in response.

"Chocolate chip?" she asked.

"Chocolate chip."

Andy flung off the foil and stacked them onto her plate. Dad poured coffee for himself and peppermint tea for her and sat down for breakfast.

As Andy shoved strips of chewy bacon in her mouth, she perused the Sunday funnies from the back of The Stratford Sun.

Dad was similarly engrossed, scanning all the other sections. "Hey, speaking of full moons! Did you know there's one next Sunday?"

Andy gasped. "There is?"

"Yeah. They call it the Sturgeon Moon."

"What's a sturgeon?"

"It's a kind of fish. We've even got 'em in the lake. We could go fishing one of these days, if you want."

"Eh." Andy dismissed that offer. "Can we go down to see the moon, though? What time will it be full?"

"1:03 AM. You up for it?"

"Yes!"

"All right then. It's a date."

One week later, on Full Moon Day, Andy awoke to an empty house. Dad was probably doing errands in town. That didn't bother her. She had her books of stars and the lake across the long yard filled with freshwater mysteries waiting to be discovered. But those things were for later. At this bright hour, she was on the hunt for breakfast. Her eyes alighted on a box of Cocoa Crisps. That was one great thing about living with Dad— he bought her all the junk food she asked for.

She collapsed into a kitchen chair with a bowl nearly overflowing. Dad's handwriting caught her eye on a napkin across the table.

> *Thought you could get a head start*
> *on the Full Moon celebration.*
>
> *Love, Dad*

She unfolded the paper bag beneath the note and pulled out a new package of glow-in-the-dark stars. In big blue letters the package read: *Now with moons and planets!*

Andy deserted the cereal, rocketed upstairs, and skidded into her room. In a flash, her new celestial bodies were scattered on the floor and she was flipping through the pages of her guide.

"Sturgeon moon, sturgeon *moooon.*"

The kids' guide mentioned the moon but didn't provide her with a constellation atlas. Slamming the guide with a huff, Andy decided to abandon the rules and use her imagination for once. Ideas came soaring—new astral designs and planetary configurations. She pressed each plastic piece onto the ceiling with care and opened all the shades and curtains to charge them up. Showing Dad after sunset would be her big surprise for him.

Dad crouched to use the telescope instead of adjusting the tripod up and down between him and Andy. Their excitement got the better of them after dinner, so here they were, posted up at the lake four hours early. They brought candy, chips, soda, and sleeping bags for the night out. The sky, the lake, and each other's company would provide the entertainment.

"There are a few things out tonight I don't recognize," he said.

"Oh, let me see." Andy wiggled between Dad and the eyepiece.

"That bright one, to the right of Orion—think it's the space station?"

"Can't be," Andy said. "It won't be visible here for another week." She adjusted the angle of the scope. "It almost looks like another moon."

"Could it be Jupiter?"

"Maybe . . . I guess it *could* be. But look! There's another one way off in the distance." She moved aside to let Dad back to the telescope.

"You're right. I wonder what it is."

They passed the hours like this, making up stories for newfound objects in the sky. Around midnight they got a bit tired, so they indulged in a sugary picnic and rested on the ground, waiting for the clock to strike 1:03 AM.

"Has a way of making you feel small, doesn't it?" Dad was laying back on the sleeping bag with his knees bent and hands clasped behind his head. Yards away, the usually still lake lapped at the shore. The rhythmic *whooshing* of its current over the rocky beach complemented the voices of the peepers— together, their song was sublime.

The deep red Sturgeon Moon hung low and bright above them. It was so perfectly round and full that Andy worried it might actually burst. It was like a water balloon filled to the very brink.

"Actually," said Andy, "it makes me feel like a giant." She was sitting up with her arms wrapped around her knees and her chin tilted all the way up.

"Oh yeah?"

"Yeah. Like I could reach out and pluck it right out of the sky. It's closer than I've ever seen."

"If anyone could catch the moon, Andromeda, I'm certain it would be you." He leaned up and kissed the top of her curly head.

Andy was disappointed to smell nothing but the fabric softener of her pillowcase the next morning—neither sweet nor savory fragrances wafted from the kitchen. She trudged downstairs and found Dad in the den instead, standing in front of the droning television with his hands in his pockets.

"What's for breakfast?" She rubbed her eyes.

"Sorry, nothing big today. Can you just grab yourself a Pop-Tart or something?" He was hypnotized by the news. She couldn't be bothered—she was too hungry.

As she tore open the silver cellophane of the s'mores-flavored pastry, the headline on the front of The Stratford Sun screamed in red from the kitchen counter: *TIDAL WAVES DECIMATE COASTAL CITIES WORLDWIDE. DEATH TOLL PASSES TEN THOUSAND.*

The chocolate flavors in her mouth turned to ash as she flipped through pages of photos. Faces covered with mud and blood, striated with tears, contorted in anguish. People wading in waist-high water holding up signs in numerous languages— SOS or lost names, she couldn't tell. Probably both. Limp bodies—so many limp bodies—facedown, bobbing in the brackish water left behind. Floating just offshore like a flock of pelicans.

Andy shuffled into the den and tucked herself under Dad's arm.

"It's up to thirty thousand now," he said, without looking at her.

The marquee scrolled endlessly with names of cities: Los

Angeles, Lima, Cape Town, Mumbai, Perth. Entire island nations: Singapore, Philippines, Cuba, Faroe Islands.

There wasn't a hemisphere these waves didn't touch.

The newscast split into two as the host welcomed a new expert to the show. Dr. Toomajan from NOAA started to answer questions about tidal waves. She described the gravitational interactions of the solar system and their effects on the Earth's tides. As with any information about astronomy, Andy soaked it in. As more details flooded her brain and mixed with the memories of the night before, her mouth dropped further and further towards the floor.

At the end of the segment, Andy ran out the back door and sprinted down to the lake.

It was a graveyard.

The tide had receded at least a hundred yards out, and the remaining shoreline was littered with twitching fish bodies. Their flared lips frantically gulped at dry air as birds yanked out their entrails. Lake algae lay prostrate on the slimy mud, shriveling in the sun. The air reeked with pungent rotting flesh and the mineral scent of secrets long buried in the bed of the lake.

Andy crouched down, in the muck, next to a spiny-backed fish with whiskers on its chin, and cried—huge, wracking sobs.

Dad caught up to her, huffing and wheezing. Then gagging.

"Oh my god," he spat.

"The tides," Andy said, breath hitching. "Our lake." She pointed at the fish next to her feet.

"That's a sturgeon," Dad said.

She sobbed harder.

Dad picked her up, and she curled against his chest, shivering. He held her tight and lumbered back to the house.

That afternoon, Andy awoke in her room to find that Dad had tucked her in. She must have cried herself to sleep.

She stared up at her ceiling, trying to erase the scene from the lake that was still playing back in her mind. Her artistic pride slowly smoldered into hot shame as she recognized patterns on her ceiling—the strange orbs from last night.

The sky that made the waves.

She threw back her covers.

The chair howled as she dragged it across the wooden floor. She ripped down her entire constellation with all the fury of a supernova. When her ceiling was clear, Andy stood panting in the middle of the plastic fragments, choking back sobs, again.

She heard Dad hurrying to her room.

"Andy! Peanut, what *happened*?"

"It's my fault, Dad." Andy tilted her head back, trying to force escaped tears back into their ducts.

"What? What's your fault?"

"The tidal waves! I changed up my stars. I didn't follow the book. I—"

"Andy, slow down. What are you talking about?"

She took a deep, shuddering breath. "My stars, Dad. I made my own designs of them. I added a bunch of moons and planets, and the next day—after the full moon—this . . ."

"No, Andy. No, no, no." He knelt down in front of her and grabbed her hands in his. "You had nothing to do with this."

The sky was empty that night.

Empty of clouds. Empty of stars. The moon.

The peepers were nowhere to be heard, and the black night's silence was heavy, as if it had its own gravity.

Andy was hunched on her bed, cornered in by the walls, reading a book, when Dad marched in through the half-open door.

He dropped an armful of square packages on her bed and gently pulled the book from her hands.

"C'mon," he said. "We're putting your stars back up."

"No, we can't—"

"We can. And we are. Peanut, the tidal waves, the low tide— they were *not* your fault. It was just a coincidence. A terrible, awful coincidence." He stroked her hair. "Let's put your ceiling sky back together, and I'll prove it."

And so they did. The two of them covered the entire ceiling.

Shooting stars. Neutron stars. Ringed planets. Shadowy moons. Everything they could find in the piles of plastic galactics—even a rocket ship.

All of it was Andy's design. She orchestrated new orbits; she invented a galaxy.

"Andromeda's Galaxy." Dad winked at her.

"Yeah, right." Andy rolled her eyes, holding back a big smirk.

"You gonna be able to sleep with all this light?"

Andy pinched her chin between her thumb and the knuckle of her forefinger. "Actually, I hadn't thought of that."

They both laughed so hard they had to hold their cramping stomachs.

Dad was right—the bedroom was luminous in the dark. A nebula of green, white, and yellow radiated onto her face while she lay nestled in bed. Their glow reflected off the windows and made it difficult to discern which starshine came from inside or outside. The night sky was shimmering, too; the symphony was in tune again, and Andy fell asleep happy.

"What we're witnessing is known as the 'Andromeda-Milky Way Collision.'" An expert from NASA was on their TV. Dad and Andy had already been up for hours. Distant sirens woke them around dawn.

"Is this a normal phenomenon? Was it to be expected?" the interviewer asked.

"Well, yes and no. The collision has been a certainty for years, but it wasn't predicted to collide for another four or five billion years. This has really come as a shock to all of us."

"Billion," Andy whispered, her eyes teary from not blinking.

Dad changed the channel.

"So far, the Coast Guard has confirmed thirty-seven shipwrecks in the U.S. waters. At least fourteen of those military vessels and another dozen are cruise ships. We've confirmed six hundred forty casualties so far—"

Click.

"—plane crashes around the world, from cargo aircrafts to small private planes. The FAA is reporting deaths in the thousands—"

Click.

"—wildfire on the move after a horrific pile-up on I-87 North—"

Click.

"It seems that navigation systems are all on the fritz, Jan. Experts are pinning The Collision as the cause."

Click.

Dad turned off the TV and slumped into his armchair, his face expressionless. Andy went to his side and held his hand. The two of them stayed like that for a while, staring at the blank screen before them, making eye contact through their darkened reflections.

"I'm—" Andy sniffled. "I'm going to take a walk. To the lake."

She released Dad's hand and walked out the back door onto the dewy lawn, in her slippers. An obelisk stood on the horizon, from the lake.

She ran.

When Andy got to the lake, there was no tide. There was no lake. There was only a vast field of glistening mud and the desperate flapping of dying creatures.

The lake water had been pulled into the center, standing upright in a swirling liquid tower: a gargantuan lighthouse without its watchful eye.

The vertical currents threw the air around it into a whirlwind. Andy had to lean in to brace herself against its gusts. It whipped her hair against her face and pressed her thin pajamas to her clammy skin.

She pushed herself, against the forces, closer and closer to the looming prominence of the column. The muck swallowed her slippers, and the velocity of the wind ripped her breath from her lungs, but she had to get closer.

"Andy," Dad yelled faintly—still far away. "Get back from there!"

She reached the water's edge, now a vortex—a wall that stretched eternal, into the dark sky. An elevator to the cosmos.

She pressed a hand to it and felt its current, thrumming like a pulse. It drew her like a magnet. Closer. Closer.

Andy thought of the lives her power had destroyed. The faces from the paper and the TV were vivid—the suffering she had caused, with her tiny acts of ingenuity. She imagined how many more lives it could ruin.

She thought about leaving everything behind—to save them. A simple exchange.

After all, she was just one girl. They wouldn't miss her. Well, Mom and Dad would. But one girl, for all humanity? It would be so easy—to save them.

All she had to do was—

She held her breath and stepped over the threshold.

Perhaps among the stars was where she belonged . . . perhaps she was just another celestial body.

The lake pulled her body upwards, as if she jumped into a waterfall in reverse. It carried her onward, into the galaxy.

Perhaps she was a god.

It had been a long time since Dad looked up at the stars. They reminded him of her—how could they not? And when he thought of her, the fragments of his shattered heart ached.

But tonight, Comet Swift-Tuttle was going to be orbiting close to Earth, and this was an event he couldn't miss—Andy would be disappointed in him if he did. He'd never see it again in his lifetime.

He'd do it for her.

Dad packed up her telescope and walked to the lake, alone.

The night wasn't as clear as when Andy had been around. He couldn't tell if it was the atmosphere or the gloom he wore like a cloak, but nevertheless he could make out the constellations through the lens.

Hours passed—full of memories, full of tears—until he saw it. The comet flew through the black-blue sky overhead, its tail a blinding flare. He stopped breathing, could have sworn his heart stopped beating.

"Has a way of making you feel small, doesn't it, Peanut?" he said.

The comet continued its orbit, retreating from Dad's sight. He took a deep sigh and looked up once more before heading in.

The Big Dipper shone back at him, and he remembered the missing star. It was back now. They never did find out what happened to it that night long ago. He pressed two fingers to his lips and kissed them, then outstretched his hand, offering the kiss to the star.

The star disappeared. And then returned. It blinked at him two more times.

"I love you, too, Andromeda."

SHIPBREAKER

by Aaron Beardsell

INTERSTELLAR SPACE BETWEEN SOLAR SYSTEMS.
DAYS SINCE ENGINE FAILURE: *UNKNOWN*.

HADES LIMPED THROUGH THE SUNLESS void. The ancient vessel bristled with cannons that would never be used. The warship, now barely more than a mausoleum, was a lump of metal snaking across the skeleton of an asteroid. Generations had passed since the glory days of the destroyer.

The hull was pockmarked from thousands of micro meteors. Ragged sections of *Hades* had been exposed to the darkness. From these holes, damaged electrical systems sparked, the glow of electricity revealing the wounds inflicted upon *Hades*.

The Traveler saw all this and was happy. It had searched for so long, hungry for new followers. It had out called to the faithful across untold ages, spoken to them in vision, dreams, and nightmares. They had heeded the call.

Memories of dead civilizations reminded the Traveler of what it had been before the old enemy had sundered it: a God. It hungered to return to its rightful place. The old enemy had faded into extinction. Shards of it remained hidden deep beneath the skin of planets and scattered through the universe like seeds.

None could oppose it.

The Traveler ripped into the weakened skin of *Hades* like a needle, crumpling the old metal before bursting through. The ship rumbled under the assault.

In a fit of agony, the engines stammered to life with haphazard energy, going dark again almost as soon as they had awoken.

Hades drifted onwards; a graveyard cursed to wander forever.

The ship jolted under a massive impact.

Leo's head smacked into a doorframe. "What in the Holy Light was that?" He winced and rubbed at the red welt growing on his forehead.

The ship groaned from some unknown pressure as metal vibrated. Mildewed corridors surrounded him, a dark maze that spread in all directions. The vibrations slowed, then stopped.

Leo breathed in to calm himself. He scratched at his stubble, annoyance creasing his forehead. His once-black uniform had faded to a pallid gray. Like all aboard the warship, Leo was a squat block. Generations of poor nutrition had stunted his people's height.

Leo stood before the rusted entrance to the warrens. *I just wanted to stay in bed, not waste my time neck-deep in filth.* Once, they'd been a web of storage areas, filled to the brim with supplies. They had been converted now, providing spaces for families. The supplies were long gone.

The entrance was guarded by fellow Inquisitors and militia. *Why would the Order bother to send us down here? The last of the heretics were executed years ago.* He sighed and then pushed onwards.

Wails and snatches of conversation drifted up from the filthy tunnels ahead of Leo. Almost by instinct he blocked out the wretched symphony. The smell, however, was impossible to ignore.

"Once more into the fray, may you guide my way. Praise the Messengers. Amen," Leo mumbled the prayer, fingers touching the rusted crucifix pinned to his uniform's breast pocket. It had been a gift: the only inheritance he'd gotten from his father.

Leo didn't know how old the crucifix was, but he guessed at least three generations. *I wonder if it's as old as the mechanical beast that we call home.*

"Jesus Christ that sti—" The militia soldier shut up upon seeing Leo's uniform. He turned pale.

The stench of poverty assaulted Leo's nose. He strode through the corridors, inspecting the troops. Stifling his gagging, he almost vomited before even reaching the first level of the warrens. He breathed through his mouth, hoping it would help. It didn't.

Leo whispered a prayer, thanking the Messenger Church for their wisdom in segregating the classes aboard *Hades. I guess even a broken clock is right twice a cycle.* The stench of over-crowding would never breach the military sector of *Hades. Hopefully.*

His nose itched from the dusty generations of dead skin cells fouling the air. *Oh, how I wish we still had rebreathers in the Inquisition.* The last one had broken down over a decade ago, possibly longer. *If only the mechanics had bent the knee, they could have fixed it.*

The Holy War had ended with the destruction of the engine. The mechanics claimed to have done it to save them all.

They'd claimed humanity was not meant to follow the Message. *Maybe they were right.*

"Inquisition, open up!" a militia soldier shouted, banging on the thin steel door to a dwelling. The door squealed as it was opened.

A bone-white face appeared, gaunt and malnourished. It was a woman, judging from the greasy strands of hair dangling past the shoulders. Leo stepped forward to enter.

Wait. What the hell is that? He raised a strip of fabric to cover his mouth and nose. *Better than nothing.*

Her skin was covered in ocean-blue marks. They reminded

Leo of mold. He'd never seen the ocean, but he'd seen photographs in the history books.

She slumped forward, her frail body sagging against the door. *Disgusting; it must be an infection of some kind.* Leo grimaced, fixated by the rotten blue holes pockmarking her skin and oozing creamy yellow pus.

"Search her room." He kept his distance from the woman. If it was a new disease, he certainly didn't want it on him.

A militia man pushed the door open further, shoving the woman out of the way. She stumbled and collapsed. He left her there.

"Search every room. Go into every nook. If you find books, bring them to me or the other Inquisitors," he called out to the militia.

The ability to read—rare among *Hades'* passengers—told Leo to avoid going into the homes. The smell discouraged him further. Signs above the doorways announced:

DANGER! CHEMICAL WEAPON STORAGE

The paint was peeling in places, and rust-eaten metal peeked through gaps.

It explains the short life spans of lower-deckers. No one knew the original purpose of *Hades*, but Leo figured he had a good idea. He assumed the weapons were intended to serve the same purpose as fire and chemicals onboard *Hades* served. *To cleanse. But how did the Church obtain such a vessel?*

A wave of dread washed over Leo as the ship creaked like shattering ice. He suppressed a shudder. The thin shell of *Hades* protected him like the yolk of an egg. He had been born in the warship and knew he would die in the warship.

For a moment Leo felt something watching him. He looked up at the jumble of wires hanging from the damaged ceiling.

Something the color of storm-riven oceans chittered away. Lanky and gangrenous limbs flashed behind the cables and disappeared into the walls.

Blue mold clung to the walls of the lower decks. *It's growing. Spreading further the longer we stay here.* Leo wondered if ordinary mold could pulsate like a newborn's lungs. *Probably not.*

Flakes of rust floated through the air, stirred up from the search. Rust-lung was alive and well these days, in stark contrast to the skeletal dregs living on *Hades*.

Leo hoped they could find a heretical tome so they could flee this pestilential maze. According to the archives, the books of an Earth author, Karl Marx, had been banned not long after the engine failures. He'd heard rumors that reading was once a universal skill before the Holy War onboard *Hades*.

The militia man exited the room of the gaunt woman, shaking his head. He stepped over the dead body. "Nothing banned, sir."

Leo sighed and shook his head. "Then move on to the next; we wouldn't have been sent down here without good reason."

"As you command, sir."

Lights flickered like candles in the hallway, giving the horde of militia the impression of ghosts and ghouls. The dozens of hovels that formed the first layer of tunnels were soon ransacked and cleared. The catacombs echoed with footsteps.

A handful of bodies had been collected by a second inquisitorial group. Over half the bodies were covered in the blue mold which clung to the walls. The corpses would be recycled. *Hopefully the mold gets removed before meal preparation.*

Leo motioned the militia to form around the stairs leading down. The strange mold was thickest here. The once-bright lights overhead had been broken, filling the stairs with shadows. The bulkhead was a pit of darkness beckoning them forward.

The cold thrummed around Leo. Frost crackled in the air. It shouldn't be this frigid. We're not even a third of the way to the hull. Something must be interfering with the temperature.

"Holy Stars, it's cold in here," someone muttered.

"Stow the whining," Leo snarled to no one in particular. "We aren't dealing with just heretics anymore."

The militia clustered around him like scared children. Many of them were mid-deckers and hadn't seen ice before. It was a luxury only available for upper-deckers.

They hadn't seen any lower-deckers in the last hour. Five floors had been searched, and not a single soul found. *How do hundreds of people just go missing?"* The empty rooms were filled with strewn rubbish, dirty clothes, and signs of battle. But no people.

They heard scratching, clawing, whispering noises as they searched. It came from behind the walls. In the ceiling. Around a corner. But whatever it was could never be found, the creature vanishing as soon as they drew close.

It's hunting us. Leo could feel it in his bones, an evolutionary warning from the grassy savannahs and lush jungle days of early humans.

"Form up and close ranks!"

They obeyed, for he was the kelpie and they were his flock.

The door to the next level glowed, despite the broken ceiling lights; the eldritch illumination came from further down.

Leo edged down the stairs. Rounding the final corner, he stepped into hell. "Lord, have mercy."

He would receive none.

The floor glowed with the colors of an oil spill. Tendrils of flesh pulsated along the ceiling. The rhythm was intoxicating. *Almost . . . musical.* The putrescent flesh hissed and gurgled with vitality, releasing clouds of spores which glued themselves to the walls, the ceiling . . . the men.

Leo wished he had a rebreather. It smelled of excessively fermented cheese and fruit. The sound, however, was the worst. Awful moans echoed from the growth spreading through the guts of *Hades*.

Human eyes buried in the mound watched the inquisitorial squad. Limbs twitched, their hands reaching out, begging to be pulled from the river of flesh. Mouths formed at random, crying in anguish and exultation before dissolving into the chaotic heap.

Leo crept forward.

"Hold position," he whispered, the order rippling through the ranks.

The flesh twitched. The mass flung a tsunami of tendrils at Leo, and he dived sideways. The fleshy appendage smacked into a militiaman. The soldier was dragged beneath the surface. Leo watched him scream as he was dragged into waves of stinking meat.

"Full retreat!" Leo waved his arms, urging the remaining soldiers to flee towards the upper decks. He sprinted, his lungs burning from the filthy air.

Soldiers were dragged backwards by the abomination. Impaled by the tentacles. Begged for help as they drowned in the folds of flesh.

Leo suddenly itched. He clawed at his arm, a fever-warm pain burning across his skin. His lungs felt heavy.

The airlock door welcomed him, a bastion of safety. He reached the door, slamming it shut. With a heavy thud, it sealed. His surviving squad reached the airlock, pleading for him to open the door. A thunderous crack silenced them, except for the sound of their shattered bones echoing through the walls.

Leo bit into his knuckles to stifle a sob. He had fled to his quarters and barricaded the door behind him. Then he backed into the far corner, squatted down, clenched the sword hilt in his clammy, mold-stained palms, and prayed. His eyes ached from staring at the door for fear an appendage prying itself through the seal.

The ceiling *screamed*, and he jerked his sword in that direction, sweat dripping against the floor. It screamed like the men and women whom the monster had consumed. Their guttural, desperate cries echoing in his skull. Screaming while it *digested* them, screaming while he ran and ran. Before reaching his quarters, where he now cowered, he'd passed a group of priests muttering malignant prayers from malformed orifices.

"*We finally found God we finally found God,*" one priest chanted like a mantra. Red evidence of botched suicides marked their wrists.

The ceiling quieted.

"Not my fault, it wasn't my fault," he muttered to the musty air. Dust motes danced like asteroids.

Am I the only one *left?*

It had been silent for quite some time *since the wailing in the walls.*

Not long ago, his arms had started weeping infected pus. Leo had to cut away his mold-tainted skin only to discover the spores had dug deeper than a knife could reach. His blood burned; his body itched.

Rustling in the air vents.

Couldn't lift his sword. Slipped from bloody fingertips and clacked against the floor.

The walls creaked and groaned and pressed inward.

"Please," Leo pleaded dryly.

Blue light leaked from the vents. "*No one should be alone,*" a myriad of voices whispered.

Leo had always believed he would go out fighting, that he was a brave man, but this cancer eating through *Hades* had revealed his hollow conviction.

"*Please, just leave—*" he started to say until the metal vent buckled and the beast exploded into the room, smothering everything, suffocating him in its blue, moldy oblivion.

Waves of awareness washed over Leo, crashing into him with thunder and fury. *There are so many voices.* They whispered, whimpered, and wailed. One voice commanded the others, moved flesh, and distorted reality: the Traveler.

Leo could feel his bodies. Their flesh stretched the crumpled shell of *Hades*, through the decrepit tunnels, across dozens of floors. His nerves spread throughout the crypt-quiet ship, sensing the rest of his body. *It's everywhere, in every galaxy. Death.*

Memories which weren't his own smothered him. Worlds and stars and aliens which he'd never seen. He was assaulted with a range of senses he couldn't understand, far beyond the pathetic handful that humanity had evolved.

It was everything. It was nothing. It was bliss.

The Traveler hungered. It would consume and spread its cadaverous greed through the cosmos. Leo would share in the joy of feeding. Countless systems had already been drained and discarded like rotten fruit.

"What are you?" Leo implored. Was this the Message? Was this what our faith heard? Is this what our God was, nothing more than a dark hunger from without and within?

The Traveler prepared him for metamorphosis. The bloated converts wriggled like maggots from a putrefying carcass. Leo felt his consciousness flayed apart. He was riven across multiple bodies. The pain was a caress; gentle and loving. *The warm itch of a fresh scab.*

Hundreds of ravenous spores hurtled off into the darkness, stygian wolves slavering for new planets to devour. *I belong to the wolves. I am the wolves.* The *Hades* would become a new womb for the Traveler. Millenia would pass, alone in the darkness.

But new worlds could always be found.

III

TOHU: PHANTOM AND VOID

THE BLOOD ACT

by Andy Gehlsen

THE TELEVISION SCREEN BULBED OUT of the wooden frame like Freddy might come through. It hadn't been on in days. We had long since let go of the promise. The demon horns that ripped through the earth surged into mountains. Plumes circling about. Black halos. Red streams cutting through red earth. The screen cut out, then returned, crawling with static bugs that fell off and into the carpet. Their little mouths screeched, limbs flailed until they starved or were eaten. The film ended with:

A hand's giant wart into which everything swirled, plummeted. A drain, hardened with fleshy, mildewy coral. A rough-hewn strata, reverse-spiring, inward, mutating into something darker, redder, titillated. The center's mighty black spore widened into a vast gape. A volcano's rim into plasmatic black. It sniffled like a nostril before sucking in all of existence, the walls in a furry and phlegmy spiral all the way down. Black hole, wormhole, asshole, somethinghole. Corresponding with the unconscious. A carnivorous slathering of the mind.

I remember hearing stories about how everyone in the old world talked about this part. Last water cooler moment. But then we realized none of us knew if anyone had ever kept their mind to the end.

There was a tiny grunt. The wart exploded yellow-brown all over the screen. That generation's *Un Chien Andalou*. An extended edition. The epic last film of the old world. When it ended, scholars wrote how the planet mutated. The film's title stayed up onscreen until the body flowed and swallowed it whole . . .

The Blood Act.

From across the room came a knock on the door. Up. Clasp. Squeak. Scrape. Ssshh.

The boy's cauliflower ear unclogged in a dribble of translucent brown juice. He wore sweatpants and spandex underneath. His gristly meat-horns protruded from his greasy, pulsating face, which seemed to dilate in some hallucinatory maneuver. He swayed. Too-high irises. A soldier awaiting assignment. I trembled.

I felt like Ebenezer. On my way out. This boy was called a ghost.

Oh yes, I had heard about this part.

The boy danced awkwardly. A truth, and a parody of life. But I felt him—just as he saw my flesh as spirit. He didn't know everything, and he didn't act like he did. He'd been taught scorn, not communication. I dripped pity from my leaky nostrils. A stream of thick mucus extended. Two gelatinous limbs. They gripped the floor. Two thick hunks formed at the bottom. Horse hooves.

The soft-hard something splat-thudded like a mound of pudding. My own fashion show. The boy cackled. *Was this a jester or a demon?*

As if in answering, horns slowly rose out of the seething split of gaseous fissures in his head, steaming out, heaving breaths from the yellow-green slime springs. It provoked the wrestler-boy into groans that made me wonder if this was his first orgasm. A heap of writhing limbs squeezing from the cracks, like melting cement between a brick building. The building folded, groaned, and fell with momentous moaning.

It would still be called Splash Mountain. I smiled, feeling my memory slide down the sides of my head like warm summer rain.

An orgy of freed workers. Droplets never to be seen again.

But their songs echo:

> *Up and down these old paved streets*
> *—quasi-umbilical,*
> *Kick the Bucket, Capture the Flag, Hide-and-Go-Seek,*
> *—branch off bulldozed remains of rotted-out skeletons,*
> *a modern family tree,*
> *now covered by entangled mossy comb-overs.*
> *Our one-room rental properties*
> *run by demonic landlords*
> *who reside on the Embankments of Existence.*

The yards extended their rubber gutters along, having emitted the exhumed remains of those whose choices could not accommodate what were deemed as failed lives. Debts had to be paid. Core first. Never the other way around. The ghosts went straight for the middle. Stuck their fingers into the creamy center, extended the caramel-like goo about their fingers and slurped.

Through the bone marrow, a shot right into the soul. Fracking the plasmatic oil of being.

The yards were wretched bogs, of intestinal tendrils and hemorrhaged blood-hunks, bones and floating parts from various regions. Of present and past worlds. Little ponds and lakes winding into an ocean of death. Teeth and tongues sailed like lily pads. Language may gather itself into an order all its own—perhaps one day understanding and being understood.

After our party was divided, we all succumbed. Everything else was pillaged, scourged, expunged.

Why not keep the party going?

The boy beckoned me. The sidewalk that led up to the garage and around back formed a cement jetty, overlooking the blood-lake, stretching out into the ocean. Dark and light in the distance. The factory's concoction, an ichor-eggnog cocktail.

I remember the static, the unconscious vileness of the world's now conscious state. This was what they called the Bay of Bava.

The culture-like strands of former life braided along the

surface. The boy's veins then opened up, protruding like one of Cronenberg's scanners, entrenched in a mental battle. They yanked out like barbed wire. He rippled slowly, in reverse motion. The veins poured the boy out over the dock of the Bay of Bava. His body drained, swaying like a burning building, until toppling, splashing.

My trunk feet helped drive the remains over the edge like a push broom.

Oh, I thought.

Upon the bank of the Bay of Bava rested a museum sign. Under the glass, the crimson-stained scroll paper read:

> *Here strings along inside a portrait*
> *Of yolky, banjo-narrated summer:*
> *After bulging in the open throat of a floating mass*
> *It spews forth from a gaping socket*
> *Whose lost eye would float on for miles.*
> *The skull gathers fungus, moss, and more holes.*
> *Little nests for little worlds.*
> *Life surges on with the bones.*

A factory horn whistled. Bureaucratic worshipers collected about the banks, squatted over the embankments, and secreted brown urine, excreted tar, carved graffiti along the surface that bubbled spores of flame. They then ran upstream and cupped their hands and filled them with the bile-blood acid, slurped the elixir. Their deteriorating maggoty surfaces moaned. They looked up to the sky with yellow eyes, groaned and gyrated, heaved improvised sermons.

A spinal cord, jawbone latched to it, snaked along like a car pulling a U-Haul along a weaving highway. A child's train set. Bones collided, clacked. An instrument whose note was never meant to be discovered.

I thought I was different. I looked up to the sky.

I thought it was my turn.

I reached down with cupped hands. And as if in answering to my plea, the factory world groaned, plumes wavered into towering intestines, turned the sky brown.

Hiccup. Tug. The scourge of the acid. A dry-and-wet gag. A wormy salivation heaved from the cavern. The iron chunks roared in my throat.

Scholars said it was written how this would be our ending. I felt the war coming. I waited for static, but there was nothing. The world was changing.

THE WARDROBE IN APARTMENT SIX

by Samuel M. Hallam

THE DOOR YAWNED OPEN, revealing two slim silhouettes standing in a bland, yellowing, nicotine-stained hallway.

"Steph, are you sure you will be all right in this place?" Amy asked her daughter, following her into the empty apartment.

There was something about this place which was tolling a distant bell in the back of her mind. *Crowley House*. Whenever she heard the apartment complex mentioned (hadn't the notorious serial killer, Bernard Noble, lived here some years ago, claiming that this was his hunting ground? And in more recent times, a spate of home invasions and a car crash seemed to center around this place like it was a beacon for the unlucky, cursed, and unfortunate), goosebumps would sprout on her arm, and there was always this lingering sense of this place was somehow *wrong*.

Steph sighed and felt for her ring, forgetting she'd locked it away. Before, it had been one of her tics, and fiddling with it brought a strange sense of grounding, but not now. That ring, now a tan line, along with the black eye, represented an episode of her life that she really didn't want to repeat. *Ever*.

And Amy had that same feeling about Crowley House as she

did about *him*. Right off the bat she knew there was something off about him; a drug-addict, a violent streak lurking beneath the surface, an alcoholic. Something that didn't add up about him.

Ultimately, her daughter's determination won out against motherly intuition. And here she was, helping Steph hide from the wrong man in the wrong place.

"I'll be fine," Steph said. "Gary isn't allowed within a hundred feet of me, and he knows what'll happen if he tries anything."

"Hmm."

"Mom, don't worry. That's all over now. Let's just, you know, move on."

"Look at the state of this place!"

"Mom, please, we've been over this. If renting out this rundown apartment means getting away from Gary, I'll do it in a heartbeat. Anyway, the people who lived here before were desperate to move out, I needed a place of my own, and you know . . . the planets aligned. Here we are."

Amy walked around the apartment, moving from the all but bare kitchen cupboards, barring a rogue tin of SpaghettiOs. She looked up and spotted a patch of what she hoped wasn't black mold stretching across the ceiling and heading towards the bedroom and bathroom, where she walked over toward . . . and was greeted with a foul stench. It wasn't human waste, nor was it bleach. It was something else, something *off,* but she couldn't tell what. Unable to discern where the origins were, she backed out of the room, noticing the cracked tiles and slap-dash patches; her stomach knotted.

Is this really better than Gary? Amy wondered.

"You should've asked to look at the place before putting down the deposit," she told her daughter. "I would have helped pay for a nicer place."

Ignoring her mother, Steph stepped into her new bedroom for closer inspection. She noted the blue geranium wallpaper weeping away to reveal ugly patches of yellow paint underneath;

noted a cold draft, its source unobvious; noted how the drooping ceiling stains were uncannily face-shaped, mouths lopsided circles of agony; how the floor around the perimeter of the wardrobe in the back left corner raspily moaned when stepped upon; and how the wardrobe itself—with intricate hand-carved designs, and nearly flawless brass fixtures and fittings—was so stunning, so magnetic, and with such fine and devoted crafts-manship, that once she saw it, once it *pulled* her in, nothing else mattered.

The wardrobe doors were padlocked.

Written on the front and covering the doors in big black letters:

DO <u>NOT</u> OPEN

"The bathroom is a mess, and you need to get a plumber in, and an electrician, and a—Steph, what is that?"

"A wardrobe."

"No, no. Not that. *That.*" So mesmerized by the wardrobe Steph hadn't even noticed the messy black scrawls covering the wall behind it, reaching out like an eldritch and blackened spiderweb.

Footfalls echoed as her mother crossed the room and stood next to her.

"No wonder this place was so cheap. Scummy landlords love to exploit places like this. It honestly looks like a child had scribbled all over the wall in a tantrum."

"But what about the wardrobe?"

"What of it, hon?"

"Look at it. It's old, probably Victorian era, or earlier. So why did someone leave it behind?"

"Steph, it happens all the time." Her mother knocked on the side. "Solid oak. It would take at least four people to get this out of here. And then there's the stairs . . . it wouldn't be worth the time and effort."

"What about the warning?"

"Landlords put it up. Hinges are probably loose. They don't want a hundred-pound door to come crashing down on someone's foot, and a lawsuit. Just don't monkey with it. Or that awful black mess."

Steph's fingers reached out and brushed against the side where, carved into it, was a winged figure with a head of a ram. An angel, perhaps? She looked on the other side—and the same thing, except the angelic form was positioned differently. The details were so fine, its eyes seemed to be looking directly at her.

"Steph . . ."

"Mom, *what*?"

"Don't get snappy with me. I didn't say anything."

Steph sighed. "Sorry Mom. I'm just on edge."

"Don't apologize, I understand. Anyway, I need to get going before the bank closes. I'll leave you to it. Like I said, call a plumber and an electrician and a—"

"—painter and an interior designer and a cleanup crew and an exorcist, I get it; anything else, Mom? It'll all be fine. Trust me." She turned and gave a weak smile. "I think this is the start of something better."

"I'll check in on you during the week. You've got the pepper spray? In case Gary shows up, maybe . . ." But looking at Steph's expression halted those worried thoughts.

"Okay. You have it under control. I'm leaving."

"Bye Mom."

The floor moaned as her mother turned and crossed the bedroom and made her way out.

Steph heard the front door hinges squeal and her mother's voice. But she wasn't talking to Steph.

"Greetings madam, it's a pleasure to make your acquaintance. I am to believe you are the new tenant?"

Amy paused a moment and looked the stranger up and down. His unkempt appearance, with his hair bedraggled, his glasses resting at the edge of his nose, mixed with his tie-dyed shirt, and his loose-fitting jeans, held up with a rope. She noted his slight slouch, wondering how tall he'd be if he stood upright.

"Oh no, I'm sorry. My daughter Steph is moving in. I'm only giving her a helping hand."

"Ah, a *youngster.* It's always nice to have some young blood in the building." The stranger sighed and gave a toothy grin, flashing his yellowing teeth at Amy, who merely smiled politely in return. "Roman Bellamy, at your service. I live next-door, in number five, with my lovely wife Patsy. She's currently busy but I'm sure she'll be glad to hear we have some youth in the building."

Turning her head, Amy said, "Steph, come say hello to your neighbor; I'm leaving."

"*Yeah, yeah, be right there,*" Steph replied.

"She's coming and I'm running late. Nice to meet you, Mr. Bellamy."

"And you, miss."

Finally peeling her eyes away from the wardrobe—there was something about it, something alluring, something *odd,* and she had to know what was inside—she walked slowly to the front door and found her neighbor lurking like a phantom of the night. She stifled a smirk.

"So you must be the lovely Steph? A pleasure to make your acquaintance, my dear. My name's Roman Bellamy."

"Roman Bell . . ."

"*Bellamy.* Like *Salami* but I don't taste as good. Tell me, what do you think of the place? A pity about what happened before."

"A pity, Mr. Bellamy?"

"Oh yes. Didn't they say? The last tenants had an awful accident. Wound up in the hospital. Patsy and I found them, and, well . . . I'll spare you the—"

"What? What happened to them?"

"*Roman! Where are you!*" a voice bellowed from next door, and Roman bolted up straight, revealing his true height.

"My darling, I am with the new girl. I shall be with you soon," he cooed back softly and turned and smiled at Steph. "Come say hello to Patsy. I'm sure she'd love to meet you."

Steph, taking a step back into her new home, shook her head. "I have a lot of unpacking, unfortunately. Maybe another time?"

"Of course. You know where we are. Don't be a stranger."

"I won't," she said, beginning to close the door.

A hand flashed out, palm pressing over the peephole.

"Oh, there was one last thing. I don't suppose the previous tenants left anything behind, did they?"

"Such as?"

"Oh, I don't know. Patsy mentioned seeing a wardrobe once. I don't know if it's still there or not."

"I'll have a look for you," Steph replied, before shutting the door hastily. That one comment had confirmed her suspicions— there *was* something special about it.

He shut the door behind him.

As she sat in the green chair in the living room, Patsy turned her head to the side, her eyes locking onto her husband.

"Well, what did she say? What do you think?"

"My darling, I do believe everything will come up roses."

As the church bells tolled twice, and all the land slept, Steph rolled back and forth, anxiety-derived voices plaguing her mind and leaking into the bedroom. "Help me," it kept whispering.

"Help me, help me, help me." The memory replayed. The last day with Gary. Her trembling fingers dialing 911. Her weak voice saying—

"*Help me.*"

That time the plea was so audible Steph sat up and looked around the room.

"Hello?" Had the floorboard moaned? Was the shadows in the room's corner just shadows or—

Then panic, and the word slipped. "Gary?"

Nothing.

She rolled over. Told herself the first night in a new place was always bound to be a strange experience.

Eyelids heavy.

Sleep so close.

Something moved. *A thump.* Moaning floorboards. *Thump thump thump.* And howling. Her tiredness evaporated and she threw the quilt overtop of her. In the corner of the room the wardrobe rocked back and forth. The quakes became violent and soon the entire bedroom was shaking; yet still she could hear the voice continued to cry out. The pleading voice—not in her head, not from her anxiety, but in the wardrobe—and the vibrating room built to a deafening crescendo, before ceasing entirely. The room was plunged back into a deafening silence.

As she swung her legs out of the bed and started the short walk over to the wardrobe, she realized it had only been the train rattling along the lines.

A sigh of relief.

Steph woke up at 10 in the morning, late by her standards, and slipped out of bed, heading to the bathroom. On her way back from the bathroom, she inspected the wardrobe by caressing it. Suddenly a rancid stench filled her nostrils. To Steph, it smelled like rotten meat.

"Hhhhhheeeelp meeeeee," a voice called out, far away and faint. She suspected it was next door neighbor's TV, and that they were watching a movie a little too loudly.

She jiggled the padlock and wondered where the keys were. The previous tenants had left keys to the apartment itself and to Crowley House, but frustratingly there were no other keys for Steph. How was she to resolve this issue if she couldn't open the wardrobe?

Leaving the wardrobe for the moment, she decided the best course of action was to visit Roman and Patsy. After all, the old man seemed keen she come over and see them, and it always paid to be kind in this world.

Slipping into her jogging bottoms, a faded Batman hoodie, and trainers, she felt ready to visit the couple next door, and maybe get some answers.

Don't mention the wardrobe. He asked about it yesterday. Maybe Roman knows something you don't. Milk him and see what he knows.

She rapped on the door and hopped from one foot to the other. There was no reason to be nervous, but there was something about Roman which left her slightly on edge.

She turned and was about to forget the whole venture when she heard the door creak open.

Steph slowly stepped inside her home. The scent of freshly baked bread filled her nostrils and reminded her of her childhood, only to be shattered by someone grabbing her wrist.

"Don't dawdle in the doorway, honey," said a tall woman with raven black hair and ivory white skin, a passing resemblance to an older Morticia Addams, and led Steph inside. Steph assumed her to be Patsy and examined her. Much like her husband, she looked like she'd been dragged through a hedge backwards and, contrasting her husband, wore starkly black clothing. "So you're the new girl, are you? It's a pleasure to meet you. I'm Patsy, but I'm sure Ro told you all about me."

"Yeah, um, yeah he did." Steph chuckled nervously. Patsy led her to a green chair and all but forced Steph into it. In front of her, an old box TV played a black-and-white horror film with the damsel in distress and a lizard-like creature stalking her.

"Please, sit, get comfortable. I'll make you a cup of coffee. Roman!" Patsy called off into the bedroom. "What are you doing in there?"

"Just sorting something, my dear. I'll be out there soon."

"Fine, fine, never mind. Well, Steph, it looks like it's just us two girls for the moment. So tell me, what drew you to Crowley House? Especially after the accident."

"Accident?"

"You mean to say you don't know? About the previous

tenants?"

"Oh yes, Roman mentioned something about an accident but didn't go into specifics."

"Hmm," Patsy said "It's a pity. They were such a quiet, pleasant couple. I won't be graphic, but let's say it wasn't a nice way to go. So tell me about yourself."

"Well, I don't know what to say. My name is Steph, I live next door, and I'm happily single." She chuckled softly.

"The tan line on your finger says otherwise. Religious?"

"My mom is Catholic. But you know how it is; my generation isn't overly religious."

Patsy fell silent, her mouth hanging slightly open like a goldfish.

"Sorry, I didn't mean it like *that*, Mrs. Bellamy. I wasn't thinking."

"Honey, don't worry. I understand." She patted Steph's hand. "Religion isn't for everyone. Don't worry."

An uncomfortable silence descended upon the apartment; the only thing vaguely audible was Roman's soft mutterings from the bedroom.

"I meant to ask you something as well," Steph said, trying to break the silence. "Did you have your TV on last night?"

"No, I don't think so. Roman? Were you watching one of your late-night movies again?"

He slowly came into the living room, holding an old red tome, its pages yellowed. "Say again?"

"I said, *did you have on one of your movies last night?*"

He paused, putting his bookmark on a page about midway through, and looked at the ceiling. "I don't think so. No, I didn't. I was up till 3AM researching. But no. No films. Why?"

"Oh, it's nothing," Steph said. "I just thought I . . . heard something.

"Probably that punk with the long hair," said Roman. "What's his name, dear? Jack, John, something like that. He's the inconsiderate, noisy type. Always having parties."

"Probably," Steph said. "Or the train," Steph mumbled softly.

"Train, hon?"

"Yeah, a train rattled by the building around the same time."

Patsy shot Roman a glance before turning back to Steph. "Hon, there was no train. The tracks haven't been used since . . . well, since Mrs. Thatcher took office. Is everything okay, Steph? You seem to have gone awful pale."

"Yes, I think so. Just a bad night's sleep. Excuse me. I still have some unpacking to do."

"I tell you what," Patsy said softly, "I'll stop by in a couple of days and check in on you, okay? I might be able to help with your sleep issues."

"Thank you," Steph replied quietly. "I'll see you soon."

She walked out of the Bellamy's apartment, shutting the door behind her, now more confused than she had been. And the truth about last night was even murkier.

For the rest of the day, all thoughts of the wardrobe were driven from Steph's mind as she unboxed her life and tried for a fresh start in her new home. It was only when she climbed into bed that her thoughts—her eyes—were drawn towards the wardrobe. The moonlight lit it up in a spectral shimmer. It frightened her, appalled her, angered her, but all the while she felt drawn into the mystery of it; all at once she wanted to pour petrol over it and set it alight, break it down with a hammer, smashing it into tiny pieces, and tenderly caress it.

She resisted those urges with a deep dive on Facebook, then Instagram, scrolling through the daily noise from her social media to fill the void in her life. Memories of Gary seeped in from the deepest pits of her mind—good memories she'd tried to force down after he—

"Stop," she whispered softly, as a rogue tear rolled down her cheek.

Eventually she slipped into a deep and uneasy sleep, constantly tossing and turning, unable to escape the dreams which flooded her mind. Dreams of great-winged and horned angelic like beings—always in her periphery, vague and ominous—across infernal purple skies.

Dreams of howling beasts thump thump thumping across endless plains, hunting for prey, for worshipers, immortality. Dreams of lachrymose moaning and

(help me)

pleading.

"Steph . . ."

Eyes shot wide open. The room felt off. *Wrong.* Gooseflesh crawled up her arms as she reached for her phone, turned on the flashlight with a sleep-drunken thumb, and slowly sat up in bed. The phone felt too heavy as she shined it across the room.

When she finally rested the beam of light on the wardrobe— it was *always* the wardrobe—one fifty-nine flicked to two AM. The floorboard creaked through the doorway and her light jerked in that direction. A cold draft carried a stench. Had she left open a window? And then thoughts of *him* came creeping back in.

She couldn't help it. She said, "Gary? Is that you?" before even considering what it would mean if it was Gary, let alone what it would mean if it wasn't.

"Help me!"

A scream this time. Not her imagination, not the TV next door, and definitely not Gary; but a bloodcurdling, hair-raising scream; and she fell off the bed, dropped her phone, found it once more before she dropped it again, where it slid too far under the bed.

"Stop it, stop it, stop it!" she screamed while squeezing her body under the frame, arm stretched out as far as possible. A couple inches more.

The room shook. She heard the pictures—of her old dog, Duke, of her graduation, and of her family—tumble off the wall. Shattering on the floor, glass shards finding their way into the carpet. Her bed thumped up and down, metal cutting into her back. The third time it raised, she could reach for her phone. It slammed down, but she was far enough under the bed that the frame landed inches above her thigh.

"Help me!"

The tremors amplified, the bed rising high enough for her to time her escape. It crashed down. Splinters of wooden slats sprinkled the surrounding floor like woodchips. It rose, rearing like a wild stallion; and she rolled; and down it crashed, the quilt flapping down like a giant gray bat.

Two of the wooden legs severed from the bed and skid across the floor, ricocheting off the walls.

The ceiling cracked and sprinkled her with plaster. The windows imploded, shards spewing across into the room, as the giant gray bat fluttered over her body, hiding her from the ethereal horror. And with that, the chaos ceased instantaneously. A soft whisper. Almost apologetic.

"Open the door . . ."

"Steph, I'm sure it was just your imagination. You might have some PTSD after what Ga— Sorry. Why not stay with me? Get away from the apartment and spend a night in your old room. I miss you, chick." The cellular reception made her mom's voice sound almost insectoid. *"Look at the state of the place! It doesn't feel right letting you stay in a potential death trap. That and there's something plain wrong about Crowley House."*

"But Mom, you only feel that way because of the wardrobe! Something bad happened with it and the neighbors have something to do with it!"

"Honey, listen to yourself. Listen to what you're saying. Consider the implications. If you're not making this up, and if my bad feeling has justification, what makes you think this is going to be like a Hollywood film? Like the one movie with Kevin Bacon."

"Please, can you just bring me a set of bolt cutters? Uncle Malcolm loaned you some the other month."

A long paused ensued. Her mother's heavy breathing was all she heard.

"Fine. Fine. I'll drop them off in the morning, okay? Then it's all up to you. Just . . ."

"Just what, Mom?"

"You don't think that you're . . ."

"What?"

"Moving a bit too fast. That you're trying to distract yourself

from the outside world and everything that's happened recently."

"I'm fine," Steph said, a little too sharply.

"Look, chick, I love you and don't want to see you get hurt again. I know things with Gary turned sour unexpectedly. I just want you to be okay again, and throwing yourself into this belief that there is something in the wardrobe. It's not healthy."

"But I have to know. Please!"

Another silence descended.

"Fine," her mom said. She sighed. *"I guess ghost hunting is healthier than drugs or alcohol. Probably. I'll bring over the bolt cutters tomorrow morning."* She paused *Just remember what I said. Don't rush things. And did you call the plumber and electrician?"*

Steph sighed. "No."

"But . . ."

"What?"

"Maybe you should call one of the ones you joked about."

"An interior designer?"

"An exorcist. I think it's kind of funny that you believe there's a ghost in your wardrobe, Steph, but you're not looking at the wider . . . implications of the soul's survival after death—if, of course, you're not having a mental breakdown. No offense."

"What are you getting at?"

"If there's something in there, what makes you think it's a benign spirit?"

As the sun crept across the sky, Steph had researched the strange but seemingly un-supernatural history of Crowley House after she had hauled the broken bed frame to the street (she'd plastered onto it a sheet of paper reading FREE SCRAP); it wasn't until the horizon swallowed the blazing ball of light and shadows infested the corners of the apartment—her mother's words of warning fluttering across her mind—that Steph considered the implications of there being something contrary to benignity. But whether it was good or bad, the fact remained that she was utterly exhausted. If she ever wanted to sleep, unburdened by whatever lurked behind closed doors, she had to open the wardrobe.

She lay waiting for the wardrobe to quake. The miasma of cold washed over the room, but whether from the mysterious (perhaps supernatural) draft or from the fact that her windows were shattered, she didn't know. But no stench came.

And the wardrobe didn't move.

It was as if it was dead and that whoever or whatever it was had given up its crusade of terror, that it had moved on . . .

. . . then, the cold pressing down on her and her pulling the quilt tighter over her, she drifted off—

"—*child!*"

Huh?

Adrenaline pushed out the somnolence.

She was surrounded by purple. She looked around. No buildings, no landmarks; only an endless, plum-hued hell. Spherical clusters of eyes insanely rolled about her feet. She danced away from their too-friendly curiosity. High above her, strange creatures soared. Some were thrashing tentacle-imbedded messes, carried by great, veiny, almost translucent wings. Others were even stranger—neither bird, insect, nor mammal. Not quite reptilian. More like fish, but of the deep-sea variety, which lurked in the zones where humanity was forbidden to dare enter.

"*Child,*" spoke the unseen speaker. "*You must open the door. You have been chosen.*"

Who are you? Where are you? she said, but not with her mouth. Her voice—or non-voice—echoed through the empty, purple land.

"*I am who I am.*"

Before she had a chance to inquire further details, the world trembled violently. A cloven hoof clomped down next to Steph. She stumbled backwards and lay looking at the giant towering over her.

WHAT DO YOU WANT FROM ME? she thought-screamed.

"To worship my glorious name."

A second hoof slammed down less than an inch from Steph's head, and she

woke up in a sweaty mess despite the cold of winter pouring through the broken windows.

The cloven-hooved phantasm was little more than barely remembered dream residue. Maybe her mother was right, maybe she had been neglecting the real world, hyper-focusing on the wardrobe as a form of escapism. Maybe Roman and Patsy were wrong about the discontinued train. Maybe Roman had been watching TV. Maybe the sleepless nights and the separation from Gary had materialized—via a cocktail of anxiety, depression, and deep sorrow—one of life's great mysteries: a Holy Artifact shaped like a wardrobe, one that was likely left behind because the door hinge had broken (hence the note, hence the padlock), and—as her mother had suggested—it was too heavy to lift.

After stepping out of the shower to dry herself, looking into the mirror at the bruising on her back from the bedframe bashing into her, Steph had an epiphany. Maybe it was for the best to leave the apartment and take the financial hit of losing the deposit; her mother did say she'd help pay for a classier place, and what were the chances that Gary would find her?

Steph heard a knock at the door.

"Hang on, Mom," she called out.

For the first time in months, she felt hopeful. She'd ask her mom to call around and find her an apartment. Still damp, she threw on an oversized hoodie and jogging bottoms. She walked over to the door, unlatched it, swung it open.

Gaudy colors and harsh blacks assaulted her eyes as a tall man and a shorter (but still pretty tall) woman stood before the welcome mat. It took half a second to register they were her quirky neighbors.

"Hello hon, how are you today?" Patsy asked, immediately squeezing past Steph, and making a beeline to the bedroom. Roman followed, carrying the same hefty red tome Steph had seen him reading the other day and in the other hand a pair of bolt cutters. He muttered to himself, not once acknowledging Steph was there.

"What's going on?" Steph asked, following the pair to the bedroom.

"The trouble with paper-thin walls is that anyone can hear what you're saying and doing." Patsy sat on the edge of the bed, looking up at the crayon-scrawled walls. "Well, I overheard you telling your mom about the bolt cutters and thought we'd save you the trouble. Good Samaritans, we are."

"So why did Roman bring that book with him?"

"Ah, an inquisitive mind, such a joy to hear there is another of my kindred in this apartment complex," Roman said, flashing his yellow gaping teeth at Steph. "Seven floors of tenants, and yours is the only head which seems to have a brain in it. All will be revealed, my dear. Now if you could do the honors, please." He held out the bolt cutters to Steph and nodded to the wardrobe before darting to the doorway to block her exit.

Steph laughed.

Roman and Patsy exchanged glances.

"I was scared I was losing my mind; now I'm terrified that I wasn't."

Roman's entire face was a smile. "Should we tell her everything, Patsy? Or should we allow her to see it for herself, to revel in the glory of what awaits?"

"Ro, I wish you wouldn't be so fanatical. Normal people tend to get nervous around you when you say things like that," Patsy replied. "What my husband means to say, Steph, is that we believe there is something in that wardrobe that—to the right people—is considered . . . quite valuable."

"Valuable?"

"Indubitably," Roman said.

"Eh?"

"Ignore his fucking five-dollar words."

"Patsy! Such vulgarity in front of our young neighbor? Please"—Roman sighed—"forgive my wife. Just open the wardrobe. We're not getting any younger and there is only so long we can wait."

"Why not you? Is it because . . . I'm chosen?"

Again, they exchanged glances, an entire conversation in little more than the blink of an eye.

"It is. Well, my mom is coming and—"

"Just open the fucking wardrobe!" Roman yelled, his eyes wild; Patsy, meanwhile, remained calm and unmoving on the bed.

"Do it now, honey," Patsy said, her hand brandishing an archaic-looking blade imbedded with jewels. "We're not asking."

Standing upright, she faced the wardrobe with the bolt cutters in hand. She opened them and clamped them around the chain. Arms trembling, Steph squeezed the bolt cutter handles.

She could hear a murmuring coming from behind the door. For the third time, she knocked, this time a little louder. She wouldn't be ignored again.

"Hello?" she called out. "Steph!"

The door creaked open and a familiar face met her.

"Oh, *Roman.* Am I at the wrong—" She glanced at the door number. She *was* at 6. "Where's Steph?"

"Good day, Amy. Oh, what a glorious day it is indeed. We have something to show you. Please, please, come in, come in," Roman said, grabbing Amy's wrist and pulling her into Steph's apartment.

"Who are all these people?"

"Don't you worry," Roman said, leading her through the crowd and to the bedroom, purpling light cutting through the gaps between the closed door and frame. The same rancid stench from the bathroom drifted out profusely from underneath.

"God."

"Yes. She's with Him now."

"That smell." She gagged.

"Just through there. Go on through."

IN THE JAWS OF THE BLACKFISH

by J.A. Sullivan

THE SECOND SKINS OF OUR wet suits swish as we walk from the parking lot toward the marina. I stare at the sweat beading along the hairline at the back of your neck. The scents of fear and excitement roll off you like the tang of salt from the cold waters of the Pacific. You think I don't know what you're planning.

I slow my pace as we descend the gangway to a dock where a teenaged boy sits watching a tethered jet ski bob in the water. A gull screams overhead, her voice echoing off the breakwall. Besides us, the boy, and the gull, the marina is empty.

The boy waves at you and stands. I stop moving and pretend to watch the fish nibbling algae on the rocks far beneath the water's glassy surface.

Yesterday, you told me the jet ski belonged to a friend, but in my sideways glance I watch you slip some dollar bills to the boy who in exchange passes you the keys. A coy foam dolphin sways back and forth on the black plastic lanyard. You don't even pretend you're going to wear the kill switch key on your wrist. Men like you never do. Master of land and sea and everything that calls it home, that's how you see yourself.

You look in my direction and I turn away, watching the gull

land on the breakwall. Her cries are heard and the others join her, all gazing out over the ocean that seems to stretch out forever. Soon they will hunt, together as a family.

I smile and click my tongue, watching you and the boy share another laugh.

Mother would have said something about the money, about the lanyard, about all the little half-truths that live inside you. She's never liked you. Given the opportunity, she'd gut you like a fish and spill your lies on the faded wooden dock boards for everyone to see.

Sometimes when you come home late at night stinking of cheap beer and another woman's perfume, I can almost see the lies ripple through your chest like twisting eels. It'd be easy to pull them out in those moments, your guard down and thoughts fuzzy. But I don't. Playing along is easier. No one ever gets what they really want; everyone negotiates, getting tastes of what they're longing for, and putting up with whatever comes along with it.

"Come on, slowpoke," you shout over your shoulder as you mount the watercraft.

The boy walks back toward the parking lot, acting like I'm invisible as we pass each other.

"Put lunch in the cooler, would ya?" You don't even look back at me when you say it.

There's a rack on the back of the ski. It almost looks like the Canadian flag, a white cooler flanked by two red jerry cans of gasoline. A single fishing rod is also secured in place.

Inside the cooler, the bottom is packed with cans of beer. You didn't even bother to take off the plastic rings that hold them together. I wonder how many turtles your lifetime of alcohol has killed. One time, when you saw me cutting the plastic rings into tiny bits over the trash can, you laughed. Your apathy is almost worse than your cruel intentions.

I place the paper-wrapped sandwiches and fruit on top of the beer. There's no room for my glass water bottle, so I keep it in my backpack.

As I make a move to sit behind you, you turn slightly. "Leave your bag here. It's too bulky and we won't be gone that long."

A black shape swims beneath the dock; a small wave in its wake gently caresses the jet ski.

"It'll be fine. Come on," you say with a flash of teeth. You probably think that looks more endearing and reassuring than it is. I slide the strap off my shoulder and put the bag on the dock. You extend a hand, which I take, and I straddle the seat behind you. Before I have a tight grip around your waist, you start the engine and take off.

I wonder what it's like to be you. Seeing the whole world in front of you, deciding where to turn, or stop, or how fast you go. I feel like a shadow, bound to you and watching life fly by second-hand.

As we emerge from the marina, beyond the manmade breakwall, I'm sure I see a black fin rise from the ocean and a small spray of mist erupt from the water's surface. In a blink, the water is empty and still. I smile and close my eyes. Behind my eyelids I'm underwater watching a jet ski cast waves. Once the whine of the engine fades, my head fills with the sounds of clicks and squeaks. A family discussion I'm excluded from.

When I open my eyes, I see you've followed the coast closer than I would have guessed. You make a sharp turn to your left, directly toward a rocky island. Even above the engine noise and air roaring past my ears, I hear the panicked barks of sea lions. They scramble off their sunbathing posts as we approach. They fear you without even knowing who you are, and you love that.

Your smile wouldn't be so broad if it were you having to plunge into the icy water, leaving the relative safety of land behind. But then again you think there's nothing to fear but fear itself. That's the bullshit mantra you're always selling. You've never seen yourself as potential prey, even when you are.

Glancing over my shoulder I see rainbows appear in pockets of mist above the water. Three orca fins slip back beneath the surface, skirting the sea lions, though only just. They know where you're going, just as much as I do.

At the last second, you steer around the island and into another cove, this one untamed, though you still see yourself as master. With my arms around you, I feel your breathing quicken as you slow the jet ski. This place is holy to you, but not because of the wild beauty. You think you're the only one who knows how to spill blood in nature.

I hear a splash, point, and yell, "There's a whale, starboard."

You cut the engine, and we watch as dorsal fins and blow-holes dip through the waves toward us.

"Actually, that's an orca. Technically they're the largest member of the dolphin family and aren't a whale at all."

As you mansplain, I hug you tighter with one arm so I can reach forward and pull the key from the ignition.

"Don't worry," you say. "They're harmless."

I drop the key into the Pacific and smile as the dolphin keychain dances atop the waves. My teeth pulse and grow. Before I will no longer be able to speak, I say, "Is this what you wanted to show me?"

You chuckle and turn slightly. "Almost." The smile on your face bleeds away as your gaze meets mine.

My lips have hardened to a permanent grin, fixed to a jaw now filled with sharp conical teeth which are still growing.

"What the . . ." Before you say more, your attention is stolen by a hand emerging from the water. Blue waterlogged flesh grips your calf, so she can pull up the rest of her rotting corpse from the ocean.

My arms lock around your torso, holding you in place. You struggle slightly until you notice the two black dorsal fins cir-cling us.

"Did you miss me?" the bloated cadaver says. "You thought you were clever, dumping me here where my body would be devoured without a trace. But instead of death, I found family."

I push your body sideways so you can look down into the water. Beneath the waves my sister retains her new orca form. She's more beautiful now than the day you strangled her with fishing line. The day you decided she'd be more useful as food to the creatures of the deep.

That was the day Mother found her, comforted the soul that hadn't yet left her body, and gave her a chance at a new life, with a new family. Just as Mother had done to me years before and to thousands of other sisters all across the seas.

"We were never here to be your playthings," my sister says to you. "To be beaten, broken, and discarded. But by now you should know, whatever you throw to the sea always finds its way back to you."

I let go of your body as my sister pulls you off the jet ski. Bubbles of your screams crash to the surface as she swims down in her full orca form to the depths with you in her mouth. Just when I can barely see either of you, she turns about, rushing upwards to breach and flings your body through the air. As you sail through space, our sister snaps you in her jaws and the game of catch is on.

The jet ski rocks gently as Mother taps it with her tail. She squeaks and clicks with her approval.

Smiling, I shed the wetsuit and place it in the cooler. The air feels strange against the skin that is not mine. I plunge back into the ocean where I belong and transform into my blissful body once more.

My sisters brush along me, their touch like a loving embrace. They offer me your liver, which I accept hungrily.

Mother squeaks again, telling us to play and have fun. But we know that soon we will tow the jet ski back to the marina and patrol the waters again in search of more sisters; they are out there, we know, just as well as we know there are thousands more just like you.

And one day we will eat you all.

A RETURN TO THE LAND OF SUNSHINE AND BULLETS

by A.W. Mason

A SCREEN.

Like a television. Not a television.

On it: a midwestern city, circa a decade into the 20th century. A town square, housing, maybe a school. Pan out. Store fronts and a small train station. There are men sitting around the town square, eating. Eating and talking.

"Klamst grui hetalpre!"

Only fifteen more minutes!

"Plimnhang hopkrt."

Okay, mom.

Back to the show . . .

Day 73 (I think)

Not much to report other than a new guy that showed up this morning. Same story as the rest of us, filling up at his local Gas N' Go, then next thing he knows he's waking up on a train platform here. Finally remembered his name after we got him calmed down. Dion.

He's been hanging out with the old-timer. The old-timer always seems to get his claws into the new ones. Still gives them stories about this other place—like this one, only it was a western town. A place that rained bullets and the sky looked like an orange oil painting. How he had escaped, overtook some military installation, and deactivated the forcefield. And then chased by some sort of orbs that killed the handful of people he escaped with, bringing him here instead.

I'll give him this: the man's story never changes but I think he probably has dementia or something. No one here is a doctor. And it always freaks out the new people. Although we only get new people when someone else disappears or dies. So it's been a while. The old-timer is harmless but we have our own shit to deal with wherever we are right now.

Anyway, lunch looks like it's coming so I'll stop writing for now. Damn, I miss my family.

The Show:

Ramon set down his pencil and looked up at the station, where smoke trailed a train crawling to a stop. He flexed his cramping fingers, put away the journal, and started off toward the depot.

From a crate retrieved from the first rail car, Gus handed boxed lunches to those lined up to receive them. Always the same lunch: turkey with lettuce and tomato on white bread, a pickle spear, and grapes. Always the same number of lunches, too: thirty-three for the thirty-three people living in the weird, antiquated town.

The old-timer and the new guy sat in the shade of an old oak, Dion staring at the sky. The sun had risen and now it began to set, as it had every hour of every day Ramon had been here. The older residents were just conditioned to it. Ramon eventually got used to it and was certain Dion would, too.

Once lunch had passed, and the sun was almost at its apex

again, Ramon and the others made their way to old billiards hall. There was, of course, no billiards inside nor was there anything else of note. But it was one of the handful of buildings that could actually open up and wasn't just a backlot fixture.

"Where is everyone headed? What's going on?" Dion asked the old-timer.

The old-timer (he ended up finishing Dion's lunch, too) got to his feet, knees creaking like unoiled hinges. He looked at the newcomer and motioned him to follow.

"In the western town, it was bullets," he said, scratching his face. "Here, it's the band, it's the music."

"What are you talking about?"

"Just come with me. Get inside and I'll tell you all about it."

A Rerun, Season 2: Episode 6:

It's the drumroll. Quiet at first. But hearing it will give you a headache. That's only the *warning*—to find shelter, to create a barrier between you and the music.

Ramon and the others hunkered down in the empty space advertised as a billiards room by the sign above its door. It was one single room, large enough for the population of Ramon and his neighbors. Even inside, with the door closed, the group still needed swaths of ripped up tee shirts stuffed into their ears. Not only did shutting out the music lessen their headaches but kept them all alive, too.

It lasted perhaps five minutes, the length of a song. They never saw the band, but through the muffled noise a few could make out the tubas, trumpets, and clarinets marching down Main Street and the town square. And thanks to the old-timer, he of original residency, the men knew to hide from it.

Alfredo, a week-old newcomer, paced by the door. Since his arrival, things had not settled down for him. He sobbed every night, shrieking to be back in his apartment with his dog and his Netflix. Ramon sympathized with Alfredo's longing for his former life. Hell, everyone there did. But Alfredo still hadn't adjusted, and that worried Ramon.

Stopping, Alfredo looked out of the glass storefront, eyes dashing wildly in search of the band. He clawed at his cheeks as spittle formed in the corners of his mouth. His breath became a succession of rapid bursts.

"I can't take it," he whispered.

Alfredo tore the wadded shirt material from his ears and screamed, "I can't *fucking* take it!"

"What's he doing?"

"Is he crazy?"

"Somebody stop him!"

The music—barely filtered for Alfredo, without his jury-rigged earmuffs—was only halfway finished, and the crazed newbie grabbed the door and yanked it open. Every man inside slammed their palms to their ears, trying to stifle the sound that sent pounding waves of pain through their brains.

"He'll die!"

"Oh, my head."

"Just let him go, shut the door!"

Alfredo made ten strides before the door slammed shut behind him. It happened quick, as it always had. His capillaries burst, blood streaking his face like runny red mascara; then his body crumbled to the ground, violently convulsing; and finally his cranium burst into a deluge of gray matter, skull fragments, and eye jelly (Ramon, who couldn't help but squint at the terror through the gaps in his fingers over his eyes, could've sworn Alfredo's head had swelled—*just a smidge*—right before it exploded). Alfredo's sauce slopped in gooey red splotches against the storefront window.

The song continued and the men waited for it to pass.

Day 79 (?):

Dion has been here for about a week now. I guess he'll still be the newcomer until someone else arrives. He's been much better since his first day. I think he's actually taken a liking to the old-timer. The pair sat through the daily song together and Dion listened to the man talk about the first day he arrived here at River City. Back before anyone knew what the music did. How he was lucky enough to have been drug inside the billiards hall, head pounding while so many others left outside died, their minds blown from the song, and how their messy, unintended sacrifices—over the course of only a few days—allowed the others to figure out the song only played after lunch. "We should be thankful for those early settlers," the old-timer said.

Day 82:

Dion tried running away, tried to escape, or whatever you want to call it. I get it. I've seen many men attempt to find a way out. He wore out his damn self. Went at it for, like, three hours. It messed with his head a little, not that anything else here had the capacity of doing that (ha-ha). But he soon found out that no matter how far you went, in any direction, you always ended up back in River City. The old-timer helped him to the boarding house, where most of us stay, so he could rest.

Current season, Current episode:

"What if you got on the train after dropping off food?" Dion asked, biting into a Granny Smith. The sweet juices ran down his chin.

"You end up right back at the depot," Ramon said. He tossed his own apple (part of that day's food ration; everyone else had Granny Smiths, too) in the air and caught it.

"Why do you think it's all just men here?"

"Hard to say. Old-timer says it's all some sort of military psychological experimentation using extraterrestrial technology," Ramon said.

"Yeah, I heard him talk about the western settlement and how he found some control room manned by soldiers. Do you believe him?"

Ramon looked across at the old-timer sitting in the dark next to a horse stable void of horses.

"I believe *he* believes it. But I don't really know what to believe anymore. We're stuck in a town that looks pre-prohibition. We can't leave no matter how hard we try. An invisible band marches up the street playing 'mind-blowing' music, and the only thing we know is that the last thing we were doing was pumping gas. Everything is strange and nothing is real," Ramon said, chucking his apple into a shrub.

"And if he's right? If there is a control room holding us in with some alien forcefield? Shouldn't we at least check?"

Ramon huffed, then said, "We've tried that. Tore into a few of these old-looking shops. Empty save for plywood and paint cans. Brick walls beyond that."

"But you didn't try all of them, right? Every single building?"

"No, we didn't. And you would drive yourself crazy if you did."

"This place is already driving me crazy."

Dion sat up and walked away.

Day 14:

My Name is Ramon Fulci and I've been in this place for two weeks. I found this little journal and a pencil behind a sign in the dry goods store. The store is fake, like we're on some movie set, but there were a few . . . I guess you'd call them props; and there was the journal. Everything is old, too. Like turn of the century old. I don't get it. I don't get any of it, but I wanted to keep this log so—if we ever get out, or if rescue eventually comes along and finds this place—they might have record that I was here. And perhaps they'll tell my family.

I've walked as far and as wide as this place will let me. There's a sign over the road leading into the town commons that says we're in River City. Not sure if that's a real place or not. Hell, the buildings are mostly fake, too. We can go into the billiards hall but it's an empty room. We tore through a barber shop; behind it was a brick wall.

I'll keep writing in this thing until we figure out where we are. I hope someone finds us.

Current Season, New Episode:

Just after the fifth sunrise of the day, a time when new people should be arriving, the train was empty. Two had gone missing: Todd Brown and Simon Westby. The remaining residents of River City combed through the few remaining places they might be. The search concluded fruitlessly.

It wasn't the first time that bodies weren't found, but usually some sort of cleanup crew came in and found them in inconspicuous areas. Like clockwork, new residents would show up the next day, maintaining the population of thirty-three.

However, today the train had arrived vacant; after coming to what hardly qualified as a rolling stop, it immediately headed back to whence it came; and for the first time since Dion's arrival—even the old-timer's arrival—River City housed thirty-one inhabitants.

"That's odd," Ramon said.

"So . . . what happens now?" Dion asked.

"Guess we'll see if they bring any newbies in tomorrow."

"The train's never been empty before?"

"No, but there's a first time for everything."

"Maybe they are still here somewhere. Alive."

"*Maybe.* Let's head over to the pool hall. You know what time it's about to be."

The men meandered towards the billiard room.

Day 99:

Weird stuff. Yesterday, two of the men never showed up for breakfast. Didn't show up the rest of the day either. We looked for them but no dice. Figure they crawled in a hole somewhere and died, or maybe whoever's in charge here took them out under the cover of darkness. But no replacements came. Replacements always come in after we lose anyone. So those assholes are somewhere.

Then today we couldn't find Eric Chalmers, the guy from Duluth, or Reggie Northup, ~~the guy from~~ (No one knew where he was from; he claimed he couldn't remember.) We searched till about lunch. Reggie eventually meandered back to us just after the train came in, but Eric's still missing. When confronted regarding his absence, Reggie mumbled something about feeling ill and staying in bed. Guess the search party didn't look too hard for him. Makes me wonder about the other three missing men.

Day 103:

Two more missing. Five total. No replacements. Don't think they are removing trash regularly, either.

A pause from your regularly scheduled program for this message from our sponsors:

"Are you tired of always needing to feed the family after a hard day laboring in the asteroid mines? Are the little ones picky about what they absorb? Then try Trerqrox, the meal replacement gel you spread on with an easy applicator. Nine out of ten Dhem'oin families prefer it to any other form of nutrition and— that's right, parents—it's kid approved!"

Current season, Season Finale:

It was a discovery none of them were hoping for and left them with more questions than answers. The answers: the bodies of the missing men (now eight in total) were located, and the smell that had begun to spread across the entire town had a source. The bloated and bloodied corpses lay strewn about the roof of the billiards hall, baking in the sun.

"How the hell did they get up here and who is doing it?" Ramon asked to the group of men gathered around him. The bodies had been covered with heavy canvas sheets and a few of them had started to bleed through the thick material.

"It might be some sort of test!" the old-timer yelled to them from the street below. Ramon didn't think he'd be able to hear them up there.

"It was probably the old man," a man on the roof replied under his breath.

Another man said, "You really think the old sack of bones could haul all these people up here? You're mental."

The first man said, "He probably lured them up here then did it. Wouldn't be hard."

While looking at the makeshift cemetery, Dion said, "Everyone's a suspect."

Ramon said, "That kind of thinking is going to turn us into a version of that one *Twilight Zone* episode."

A man somewhere in the back muttered, " 'The Monsters are Due on Maple Street.' "

Ramon was right. Since the onset of their strange gas pump-to-River City transferal, the inhabitants *had* remained civil. But now the rules had changed, and a tension could be felt rippling through the huddled-together men.

The spell of silence was broken by a scream.

Next to the train depot—on the balcony of a building known as The Estate—Reggie Northup had a man in an armlock and was trying to sever his head with a plastic knife. A small crowd had gathered below pleading for him to stop.

Ramon and the others climbed down the access ladder and ran towards the commotion. Before they could reach The Estate, and before Reggie could finish hacking at his newest victim (assuming he was the murderer), a gunshot rang out. A split second later, the upper half of Reggie's head exploded, plastering bits of brain and bone on the glass door behind him.

As soon as Reggie's body hit the balcony floor, the phantom drumming and brass began to start—*way* ahead of schedule. There was no time to run back to the billiards hall. Ramon felt his head swell, palpitating with the music's tempo. The next thing he'd remember had nothing to do with River City or the men he resided with for over three months.

Thirty minutes later, the electromagnetic dome that had maintained the endless loop securing River City had been deactivated. A smattering of men in Army fatigues roamed the streets, corralling the limp bodies of the residents.

"All right, Sergeant Brenton. Give me the rundown. The *full* rundown."

Sergeant Brenton looked at the tablet in his hand and opened a document.

"As you can see here, General Schrute," Brenton began, flipping the tablet over to the General, "Northup somehow got each man to follow him to the pool hall roof where he overpowered them and sliced their throats."

Schrute thumbed through the photos the team had taken from the unsettling rooftop discovery.

"We should have never stopped using the orbs. Or we should have at least convinced the Dhem'oin to let us use drones. With aerial coverage we would have been able to stop this before it got rolling."

Schrute handed back the tablet and shook his head. He knew his role, and that was not to interfere with the Dhem'oin's experiment . . . but things had gotten out of hand. Very quickly. Murder was not part of the itinerary. In exchange for their technology, Schrute and his team were supposed to monitor and maintain River City and its citizens. Now, however, he had a mess on his hands.

"What about the rest of the subjects?" Schrute asked as he watched the bodies being loaded into covered trucks.

"We used a very low dose of the sonic music penetrator," Brenton said. "They'll have pretty bad headaches when they wake up but they'll live. They are being hauled over to processing, where their minds will be wiped and eventually sent back to their homes."

"What about him?" Schrute motioned to the old-timer being loaded into a separate truck.

Brenton looked back down at his tablet and brought up a subject profile with the old-timer's photo. "Subject 019, one of the originals. Alton Elliot. He'll be reprocessed into the next Dhem'oin experiment. They don't seem to care for him too much after he almost escaped in the Deseret Ghost Town location.

"Lucky him. All right. I'll expect the written report on my desk tomorrow. Carry on, Sergeant," Schrute said, did an about face, and headed back to his own vehicle.

A screen.

Like a television. Not a television.

On it: a midwestern city, circa a decade into the 20th century. A town square, housing, maybe a school. Pan out. Store fronts and a small train station. Men are being loaded into trucks and shipped out to central processing. The camera zooms out and the shot fades.

"Pr'eri grui loupen!"
Turn the TV off, dinner's ready!
"Mnb'iouy hopkrt. Hadu j'opli Trerqrox!"
Coming, mom. I hope it's Trerqrox!

The old-timer, Alton Elliot, wakes up in a pile of sand. The buildings around him look like dilapidated Hollywood movie structures from a bad spaghetti western. He sees others not far from him begin to stir. The sky is the color of Georgia clay until the clouds roll in, raining down bullets in pounding waves.

CANDY FOR THE MOUNTAIN DEITY

By L. Acadia

THE MOUNTAIN DEITY WILL FORGIVE our forgotten offering. Three glasses of papaya-blossom-infused rice wine should supplicate at the trailhead, evaporating as we ascend narrow cliff-gouged scars transecting rockface so sheer that Japanese occupiers enlisted indigenous mountaineers to abseil into their gorge—slashing gneiss, then thrusting North into marble, blasting small tunnels that contain apologetically-carved icons of the mountain deity.

Candy gaudily wrapped and credulously placed around the icon draws her eye and laughter at the superstition. The cave almost buzzes. Her fingers tease over the uncannily bright colors in the cave's gloom, selecting crinkly bronze-wrapped alms she won't enjoy. Flavorless, obligatorily sweet candy.

Strange bird calls and bug song drown the crunch of hiking boots on crushed rock that is like drops of blood the mountain spilled for the sun-exposed gash of trail. We squint, missing a muntjac darting downhill, but not a mountain goat's scent as we creep along the narrowest ledge. Tiny bees emerge as though spurting from steep cliff crags, caressing first, then deranging, unbalancing her. Dozens swarm the candy on her unfurled tongue. She cannot fly over the gorge; the mountain deity exacts its offering: this new strange bird.

IV

EPHEMERAL ALCOVES

THE ARCHITECTURE OF DREAMS

by Kay Hanifen

THE THING YOU MUST UNDERSTAND is that my usual dreams are not nightmares. They're not always pleasant, but a nightmare implies that I'm afraid, when that is something I almost never feel as I wander through the dreamscape, acting out the illogical plots invented by my subconscious mind. No matter how horrific the visions, I am not afraid, or, if I am, it is a distant kind of fear, like concern for a character in a movie rather than the mortal terror I would feel if I came across these images in real life.

A few weeks ago, for example, was an exception to that rule. I *did* feel that fear—though even in the dream, I knew it was just my subconscious mind filling in the blanks of a scary movie trailer I watched. Still, the image of four people in various stages of dismemberment being sewn together alive by a giant machine was vaguely unsettling; as was the cannibal cult from a dream a few months back, and the recurring nighttime adventure where I must perform an exorcism despite being as far from a Catholic priest as you can get. With dreams like these, is it any wonder I'm a horror writer?

It doesn't help matters that my dreams are also vivid in a way I've never seen anyone else talk about online. I can taste, feel, even *smell* in my dreams. Scent isn't a consistent ability, but at least once a month my dreams will have this additional and rather uncanny perception. Sometimes they feel so real that I forget whether the architecture I saw—or the adventures I experienced—perhaps *weren't* REM-invented. I'll get flashes of my house, with exaggeratedly high ceilings and connected to a mall. I've dreamt of breaking my arm only to feel it ache until something else conjured by my subconscious made me forget about it, and of tasting my grandmother's chocolate chip cookies, the sugar and butter melting in my mouth. I've smelled roses and awoke feeling nostalgic for a longtime relationship with someone who never existed except in my mind.

Ever since the meteor shower, though, my dreams have changed. For the last three nights, my dreams have picked up where they left off in the ruins of an ancient civilization. The air smells damp, like the moments after a summer thunderstorm, and the vegetation squelches under my bare feet. Beneath the greenery is a stone path that crumbles a little with every step. The sky is a bright red, and the shadows are long as I walk in the eerie silence of these ruins.

I wander past empty looms, broken pots, and abandoned toys, remnants of a people who had to leave in a hurry. The buildings are more proportional than in most of my dreams, but something about them is off. They remind me of the Marc Chagall paintings that inspired *Fiddler on the Roof,* but instead of a snowy European village, the fiddler plays across the ruins of Pompeii. I know I should be walking towards the center of town, but every turn I take appears to be a dead end leading only to more empty and silent ruins. I am slowly getting closer, though, because I know that in the center is a temple, and an eerie, melancholic sound echoes ever louder each night. *Singing.* This is where everyone has gone, although I am alone, and I have no hope of finding them as I walk through the ever-shifting ruins.

Normally, I would find these dreams rather boring. My subconscious mind has conjured far more frightening images over the years. But despite very little happening, a sense of unease pools in my belly, and I can feel the drumbeat of my heart in my chest, and I wake with that feeling of being watched from afar by a terrible predator just out of sight.

Last night, I finally reached the center, and the temple touched the heavens like the Tower of Babel. And like the Biblical city, I could not understand a word of the song the people inside sang, even though it was loud enough to make me wince and cover my ears. The sounds were soothing, mesmerizing, like the ways a cuttlefish hypnotizes its prey. Did you know they can do that? They lure the prey closer by changing colors until they are within snatching distance. This song has a similar effect. It changed sounds and key so quickly and smoothly, singing with *almost*-words that made me come closer to catch some meaning, until I was at the door feeling like a small creature about to be devoured.

The door opened—and *God*, if you could see it. I think this is what Plato must have imagined when he wrote the tragedy of Atlantis. The interior was so impossibly tall that clouds formed inside the building itself, and the walls were carved with intricate hieroglyphs telling the story of life on this world from the moment the first creature emerged from primordial soup, and up and up until I suppose that we reach the present day. Perhaps it even went *beyond* that, stretching to the future and the eventual end of life on this planet.

Here, the singing was at its loudest, and I was reminded of the idea of Musicalis Universalis, the Music of the Spheres. It's the philosophical concept that the earth, moon, sun, and planets all move in perfect harmony. As it turns out, these ancient philosophers weren't far off. The sun and planets all make their own eerie ambient noise. But that's just noise. This was *music*. This was a harmony unlike anything I'd ever heard, resonating through my very cells, and seeping all the way down to the atomical and molecular.

I finally saw the singers kneeling before a massive altar, their hands raised in supplication. They were shaped like people, with robes of white and gold. And with the confidence found only in the safety of slumber, I approached one, going around it to see its front. Though it looked like a human woman, with curves and hair in ringlets on its head, it was not human. Its face was a smooth, flat surface, with no eyes to see, nose to smell, or ears to hear. It had only a mouth, lips curled into a blissful smile as it sang in the chorus of souls.

When my parents dragged me to church on Sundays as a child, the teachers would describe Heaven as feeling eternally happy and praising God. Was this Heaven? When you died, did your soul become some blind, deaf, faceless thing stripped of all personality and meant only to sing the praises of a supreme Creator in a kind of enforced bliss?

The song reached a fever pitch, and the singers bowed their heads, pointing their hands towards the far wall of the tower. There, I turned, and I saw.

Describing this . . . *being* . . . it's like describing the feeling of every nerve in your body lighting up in pain and pleasure, of having yourself made and unmade in your own private supernova. I was overwhelmed with visions of the past, present, and future all colliding and breaking apart, pinging off each other and absorbing one another like atoms forming molecules, forming cells, forming tissue and bone, and forming me. What are we if not the collective dream of a trillion atoms? And one day those atoms will once again be dispersed throughout the universe, the elemental aspects of ourselves constantly taking new shape.

I tore my eyes away, knowing I would be obliterated if I gazed any longer upon the entity that had invaded my dream. It opened its great mouth full of jagged teeth all the way down its gullet; its worshipers walked one by one into its gaping maw until the last fell silent and I was alone in the tower.

I woke with my heart pounding as though it wanted to break free from my chest, and I came straight here. I don't know why. I hope maybe you'll tell me it was only a dream.

I wish I could say that I'd believe you if you do, that the nightmares of the world I saw—the heaven formed by hungry mouths and blissful singers—was nothing more than an invention of my subconscious, but that's not true: I know because I see it now in my waking hours.

You're probably going to diagnose me as having schizophrenia or suffering from a temporary psychosis, but I know what's coming. With each new fall of a meteor in the sky, I can hear the music of the spheres grow louder and louder. I see flashes of the entity as the meteors burn up like fireworks. A tentacle here. An eye there. Sometimes, that massive, gaping mouth. The entity is coming, and it's hungry, and there's nothing we can do to stop it.

Right now, the music is little more than a faint buzz, but I believe that everyone else will hear it, too, by the end of the week. Can you hear it? Probably not, judging by the way you're looking at me. But if we're completely silent, you might hear its harmony, feel it like a tuning fork trying to align all your atoms to the universal frequency. Soon, our eyes might be swallowed by our skulls, our ears and nose closing until all that is left is a mouth to sing the praises of a seemingly benevolent and paternal God returning. One that we had hoped would grant us the gift of eternal life. One that created us in its image.

I don't know why it chose me to deliver this message, to become the prophet of this final age, but it did. I hope that this is a warning from another, *more* benevolent party, but I doubt this is the case. I think it's taunting us with the hope of a final warning before descending upon us. Soon, we will all be like the people in my nightmares.

AURORA

by Solomon Forse

K ADEN FOUND HER ON THE beach, tangled among the spindly strings of cold kelp.

Was it a "her," though?

He could hardly tell. It was only a few inches long, but there was something feminine about the slender beauty of its legs. Something that reminded him of the girls at school, the ones he would sometimes sneak glances at from across the classroom. His heart ached to know they would never look at him in the same way. But this little creature was not one of them.

Kaden crouched down, wet sand squelching around his toes.

The thing was not exactly human. He had thought it was a toy at first. Some first grader's plastic figurine, a character from one of those new Pixar movies—the ones his grandmother had told him he was too old for now.

But then it moved.

She moved.

Kaden reached out with his hand, his fingers trembling above the cluster of kelp.

His breath shortened to gasps as tingling pains caused him to squeeze his legs together.

He was afraid to touch her, afraid that the pearlescent blue skin would feel warm. That it would feel supple and smooth. He feared that her hair, like fine strands of cerulean seagrass, would feel soft and sheer.

He had never touched a girl.

He had not even talked to one. Especially none of the girls at school. In fact, they went out of their way *not* to talk to him. If he'd had a father or a mother, perhaps Kaden would have learned how to talk to girls. He had asked his grandmother about girls once, but she only turned away from him and turned up the volume on the television.

So, fingers still trembling, breath still shaking, Kaden withdrew his hand from the beautiful little thing and rose to his feet on shaky legs.

He did not know what to do.

Kaden closed his eyes, escaping the situation, if only for a moment. He raised his nose to the air, inhaling the salty breeze. The scent carried a note of pine and cedar from the tall trees that swayed on the slope above the shoreline. From the sky, he heard the soaring gulls that cried as their wings caressed the cool currents. The rolling waves stretched over the shore and washed away the sand between his toes.

Exhaling, Kaden opened his eyes. As if waking from a trance, he looked down, expecting that the willowy figurine would be gone, that she would have been nothing more than a dream.

But there she was, still lying before him, her moist skin glistening between the sea-green stalks that crossed over her ethereal limbs.

Yet it seemed wrong.

A creeping sensation prickled at him somewhere deep within. His heart rate quickened, and the itching feeling spread out and slithered across the surface of his skin and down his legs.

She was wrong.

Still, he could not walk away. He had to help her. At least untangle her.

And what then? If she was unconscious, then she would continue to lay there, sleeping upon the shore until the noon sun cooked her dry. Or until a gull came along and pecked at her.

Kaden could not let that happen.

He knew somewhere deep down inside him, somewhere beneath his anxiety, that she was meant for him. That some divine force, maybe God, or maybe something else, had rewarded him for his suffering.

But still, for some reason—perhaps for that aching feeling welling up inside him, the feeling that had made him push his knees together—Kaden felt like something about it was *wrong*.

As he stood there on the desolate shoreline, long and narrow, he felt an uncanny sensation crawling up his spine, as if he were standing in an empty aisle in a grocery store, tempted to slip a candy bar from the shelf and into his pocket when no one was looking.

Kaden had done it before—when his grandmother asked him, when she distracted the grocer and left her grandson alone in the aisle. Later she emptied his pockets in the kitchen at the back of the trailer, giving him a few pieces of candy before hobbling back to her bedroom.

Then Kaden began to steal on his own.

He looked down at the creature, studying her small form with its smooth skin that still glistened with a veil of seawater. He could gather her up so easily, carry her back home, and put her somewhere safe. Was that stealing? Was it against the law to keep something safe?

If it was stealing, then Kaden hated to do it. His face reddened at the thought of becoming just like his grandmother. Just like his mom and dad. Kaden remembered watching them from the trailer door years ago as his parents sat in the back of the police cruiser. His mom had pressed her tear-stained face up against the glass, her palm streaking down the window as the car drove away.

But this was not stealing.

This was saving—saving this poor thing. Saving *her*.

Who knew how she got here? And who knew what she even was? He could hardly believe that she was there. That she was real. Kaden had stumbled upon a secret.

His secret.

And no one could know. Not even his grandmother. She would not understand. But could anyone understand? What if someone else were to see her? What would they do?

They would take her away.

Kaden's heart beat against his chest as goosebumps crawled across his flesh.

He glanced up and down the coast.

Scanning the droves of driftwood and scattered sea stacks, his eyes could not find any sign of life in either direction. Kaden noticed only the intermittent piers and docks with faded wood that sagged and leaned like his grandmother when she tried to stand. No fishermen. No beachcombers. No dog walkers. Just the creaks of tree trunks tilting in the whirling wind above the water. Only the splashes of the smooth surf rolling across the shore, the sea foam frothing and fizzing on the sand near his feet.

He would do it now.

Kaden dug into his pocket. He pulled out his glasses case, the leather container from the thrift store that had worn a faded outline into the front of his threadbare jeans. He flipped it open, retrieving the soft cloth from inside. It was a scrap of an old t-shirt his grandmother had cut out with a pair of scissors. He used his other hand to balance the case on a piece of driftwood beside him. Kaden shook out the cloth, then kneeled on the beach, small shards of shells pressing into his skin.

Pulling back the tendrils of kelp, he pinched away at the fibers, piece by piece, until the delicate body was free. Then, carefully, he gathered the limp form into the fabric. He did it as gently as someone might cradle a baby bird that had fallen from its nest.

With the frail figure resting upon the cloth, Kaden brought the tiny being to his face. He rotated his hand from side to side, looking at it. Looking at *her*. His breath fluttered the strands of her hair, which were now dry from the fabric that soaked up the moisture. Tilting his hand, Kaden studied the impossibly small structure of her brow, the curve of her nose, the slit of her mouth.

Could she speak?

As he leaned closer, he could barely discern her movements. Her miniature chest rose like a swelling wave. And then it fell, soft as a feather.

Kaden looked away. Closed his eyes.

It felt wrong to look.

His heart ached with painful familiarity. He willed himself against something deep within him welling up like floodwaters threatening to burst through a dam. Kaden swallowed, choking back the pain.

He opened his eyes again, trying to focus on the gentle rising and falling of the figure in his palm.

She could breathe. She was alive. So perhaps she could talk. Would she talk to *him*, though?

The girls at school would not. Yet they loved to talk *about* him. He would feel their eyes staring across the classroom, hear their whispers as they leaned across desks. "Pizza face," they would say before snickering into cupped hands with sloppily painted nails in glittery pinks and sparkly purples. It was that very insult Kaden could not stand to hear, especially not today. Not on Thursdays when the cafeteria menu almost guaranteed it. When he had rolled out of bed that morning and looked in the mirror, when he scratched the pimples away with his fingernails, when he wiped away the yellowish pus and bright-red blood with toilet paper, when he left his skin inflamed and irritated—he knew that they would say it again.

And it would kill him.

As Kaden held the little pixie in his hand, he wondered if she would see him like that, too? As a monster? When she finally opened her eyes, would she see him and cower in fear? Try to scramble away? Would it be like the myth he learned about in school when Andromeda saw the Kraken? He winced at the thought of it, his eyes blinking back tears. Kaden did not want the answer to that question so soon. He was too afraid.

Kaden had often avoided this variety of *hurtful* reality, as he had done earlier that morning when he'd crept into the back of the small trailer, his bare feet trudging through the crust and crumbs of the stained carpet; Kaden nudged open the bedroom door, looking toward the bed where his grandmother slept beside an ashtray overflowing with cigarette butts. Bright flashes from the television danced across the bottom of the bed, lighting the lank legs with varicose veins.

"Grandma," he whispered.

The only answer came from the morning newscasters who talked on the fractured screen across from the bed.

She was in a deep sleep. The previous evening his grandmother had stayed up until midnight watching the local station. "Come back here and watch this, Kade," she hollered from her room. But he had been too tired.

As he fell asleep that night on the coarse cushions that wrapped around the trailer's dining table, he heard snatches of the muffled murmurs echoing from beneath the door. It was an interview between a female reporter and an old man. A fisherman, Kaden thought. He sounded like he talked through no teeth, babbling about some light—an "aurora," he called it— shooting across the sky and smashing into the sea. The waves nearly capsized his canoe, flipping his fresh catch of cod over the gunwale.

Kaden had drifted off at some point, saliva drooling down his open mouth and pooling onto the pillow. Only once had he been jarred to consciousness by the loud laughter of the news reporters before falling asleep again.

When Kaden had risen the next morning, he heard the television echoing down the hall. After going to the bathroom, looking in the mirror, and deciding he would not go to school, he went to his grandmother's room and pushed open the door—but not before holding a warm washcloth to his face for a minute. She would check him.

After his grandmother did not answer him, he had moved closer, reaching out to her. His hand lingered over the lump beneath the blankets, fingers trembling.

"I'm sick, Grandma," he said, a little louder.

With a sullen sigh, raspy and bitter, she replied, "Okay, sugar. Come here."

His grandmother reached her hand up to his face, pressing the papery skin of her cool palm against his warm forehead.

"I'll call the school later." She coughed. "Can you make yourself some breakfast?"

Before Kaden had moved out of the room, his grandmother began snoring with an open mouth, her wet gums catching reflections of the light from the television.

Instead of making breakfast—the thought of eating in that cigarette-stinking kitchen made him gag—he had walked back down the hall and snuck out the trailer door, easing back the squeaky steel spring before wandering down to the beach. Down to his favorite spot.

And then he found it.

Found *her.*

With the nimble, fairy-like form still laying atop the cloth that rested in his palm, Kaden wrapped the fabric around her with his other hand. He thought of the ladies at the store, the women in aprons at the checkout counter who packed the little glass angels that his grandmother liked to buy. But unlike the women at the store, Kaden left a small opening for his seraph to breathe. However, he thought *if* someone were to see him, *if* he would have to slip her into his pocket, she would need more protection. He considered shutting her in his glasses case, picturing her fragile body secured in its leather shell.

A warmness grew from within his chest and washed over his limbs.

He could protect her.

But if she needed to breathe, she might suffocate in the case. Kaden had learned that lesson before with a mouse in a mason jar. His grandmother had laughed and tossed it into the grass outside the trailer door. Kaden would not make such a mistake this time.

He set the bundle down on the piece of driftwood, imagining the creature's lithe, blue body nestled in the folds of the cloth, soft and warm.

He paused, nervous to turn his back on her, a tingling crawling across his spine at the thought of it.

After a moment of desperation, he hurriedly twisted around and bent down, peeling off a section of the kelp with a wet ripping sound.

Kaden stood and returned to the piece of driftwood, retrieving his glasses case. As he checked on the little bundle, confirming that it still rose and fell with the ebb and flow of the whispering waves beside him, he wedged the chunk of kelp into the container, testing his design. The clamshell mechanism had shut, although it had left a solitary sliver of space between the two halves of the glasses case.

She would be able to breathe. She would be safe—for now.

But where would he take her?

Before Kaden could slip the bundle into the case, he heard someone behind him.

"Hey there," a cheery voice called.

Kaden turned around to see a man sauntering down the slope, his athletic shoes crunching on the graveled path above the beach. A young man. The stranger waved as he traveled down the trail that cut through the trees and merged with the coast a few dozen feet from the shore.

"No school today?" he said.

Kaden snatched the bundle of cloth from the piece of driftwood.

As the stranger got closer, stepping out onto the sand, Kaden noted his figure—his tall physique, his muscular form bulging beneath a tight shirt. The man's strong jaw was crowned by chiseled features. A sculpted brow, too. Kaden thought he resembled some of the boys from school: the ones who had started to change, the ones whose voices had gotten deeper, the ones who put on deodorant in the locker room, the ones who shamed him into wearing swimming trunks in the shower after gym class.

Kaden placed his hands behind his back.

"What have you got there?" the man said. He smiled as he slipped his phone into a strap around his bicep and unraveled a pair of headphones.

The man would take her.

She would *let* him take her. Like the girls at school who let the boys take them behind the building, behind the tall rows of bushes near the loading dock.

Kaden's breathing quickened as he loosened his grip. Behind his back, his fingers uncurled. The bundle dropped, landing in the sand behind his feet with a soft *plop*.

The man arched his brow. The headphones dangled from his grip. As the wind picked up, the stranger's thick hair flapped back and forth, the gusts of wind stretching his shirt against his broad chest. The waves, now swelling with the tide, smashed against the shore.

"Your parents out here? Shouldn't you be in school?"

Kaden would not share her. *Could not* share her.

Heart racing, legs quivering, Kaden shifted his weight, leaning ever so slightly away from the stranger. If the man got any closer, if he took even one more step—

"Hey, are you all right?" he said, approaching Kaden with a raised palm.

With a subtle movement, Kaden lifted his heel above the sand and pivoted until his foot hovered above the layered lump. Kaden could feel the fibers of the material tickling against his bare skin. He felt something else, too—a struggle, a slight shuffling of limbs beneath the fabric, pushing against the boundaries of the bundle.

Then he pressed the entirety of his weight onto the squirming bundle. Closing his eyes, gritting his teeth, his muscles cringed as he felt the crackling of brittle bones, felt the wet squishing against his skin like the draining of a warm sponge.

As he slowly opened his eyes, squinting through his eyelashes, the beach materialized before him, blurry against his tears. With a look of moderate concern, the man was still standing there.

Kaden wiped at his eyes, then lowered his head, glancing down at the ground where a dark liquid oozed from beneath his foot, soaking into the cloth and commingling with the sand.

Wafting up from the syrupy mess was an odor that turned his stomach. It was sweet but cloying, like a bottle of putrid fruit juice that had been abandoned on the beach and left to spoil in the sun.

Yet, worse than the smell, even more horrifying than the sensation beneath his foot, had been the sound: a muffled noise, hardly discernible above the crashing of the waves. As Kaden had pressed down upon the poor thing within the cloth, upon *her*, a faint voice had cried out and stung his ear—a tiny chirp, as from a cricket or a little bird.

"You're all right, little fella," said the guy before putting on his headphones and jogging away.

After the sun followed its arc through the sky and dipped toward the sea, Kaden—sunburned and parched—lay among the driftwood, wallowing in his crime, until his grandmother found him.

As she hobbled down the path from the trailer park, lighting a cigarette, she cursed him out for playing hooky. "I knew you'd be down here. Always at the beach. Never with friends. Only with fish and God knows what else—" But when she observed his skinny body—her little grandson—lying face down, shaking and sobbing, and lips pressed against some indistinguishable object cradled in his hands, her usually hard eyes softened a bit. "*Kade* . . . what are you doing down here?" She stepped closer, cigarette between her fingers, slippers paddling through the sand. "You okay, sugar?"

She saw that the object was blue. Maybe a flower, she thought. A larkspur or delphinium. Yet as she stepped forward and stood over her grandson, pushing her glasses up her nose, she thought that perhaps it was a mangled sea star. Its dark nectar had splotched her grandson's hands, his fingers dripping dark jelly-like pulp into the sand.

As her grandson raised his eyes, meeting her bewildered gaze, she saw that his shame-trembling mouth was tainted with a violet stain.

THE TOWN LINE

by Kurt Newton

LOOKING BACK, I understand it now. But now didn't help me then. Whatever calling that was carried on the wind that day was bound to find me, and I was bound to answer.

I grew up in a small town in a small house near the end of a long country road. At the end of the road was the town line, an invisible boundary that transformed one town into another. At the age of nine, all my exploring before that day had been toward the town lake—a bright blue oasis; or toward the town center where I attended grade school; never in the opposite direction toward the edge of town; never past the town line. Even the school bus knew to stop at the last house on the road and turn around.

But, one bright summer day, I decided to take a walk. Call it curiosity or a need to separate myself from what was expected, but I felt I had to do something different, something beyond the norm, so I took off in the direction of where I wasn't supposed to go.

At the time, I knew things existed beyond the town line, things down past the last house, down past the woods. There were rumors of another lake and a whole community of people who lived along its shore. But I grew up with the notion that the people of our town should never associate with the people who lived beyond the town line. It was just accepted, the same way one accepts the notion that one should never go out into woods after dark.

It felt odd walking in that opposite direction, as if I were breaking an unspoken rule. The sun was at my back and a distorted cutout of my body preceded me on the pavement. The farther I walked, the more it felt as if I were walking away from something instead of walking toward.

When I passed the last house, my heart beat heavy in anticipation of what I might discover. How far should I go? How long should I stay? These questions were pushed to the back of my thoughts, like every child who has ever explored the woods or swam out past the buoys at the lake, unaware of the dangers present. As humans we are born to take chances, put ourselves at risk, explore, even in the face of hazard. Or the unknown. Children more so than adults, because children do not think of what's ahead, only what's in front of them. Children are innocent. Until the day they are no longer.

There was no sign or heavy stone that marked the point at which the two towns traded places, where the territory became something *other*. It was more a feeling. I knew the instant it happened that I had crossed an invisible threshold that could not be uncrossed. It was here the road began a precipitous decline. The trees rose like thick green walls. The sunlight drained. I remember it being much quieter there than where I began. There was nothing but the trees and their whispering, and the soft tap of my sneakers on the pavement. The air carried an emptiness like a hollow shell. I was alone and felt that aloneness as if it were a living, breathing thing that had latched onto me.

The pavement looked unused, black as the day it was paved, although it may have been an illusion due to the lack of direct sunlight. Also, the road appeared wider, as if there were once great plans to develop the area but those plans had been abandoned. The air was unmistakably cooler, the vegetation more lush.

Gravity drew me forward, downward, along a harshly

sweeping arc that didn't allow me to see what was ahead. But no sooner had the first doubts of whether I should continue entered my mind, I had walked beyond the curve in the road and I could see it: the end. The ever-steepening hill stopped abruptly, butting up against another narrower road that traversed left to right, winding away in both directions, disappearing from view. Beyond this narrow road, pieces of blue filled in the gaps in the trees, a dark blue the color of bruises. Another lake. I also saw the brown squares of rooftops scattered throughout the vegetation. Lake houses. The smell of dampness was in the air.

As I walked down the last bit of hill, there came the gurgle of water to my left. A stream flowed through the woods. Along the stream's descent, miniature waterfalls cascaded in several places. The stream ducked through a culvert beneath the road and continued to the lake. Other than the stream, all was quiet. Not a car, not a human voice could be heard. Not even a dog bark or the quack of a duck. It was as if I had entered a land devoid of habitation.

At the bottom of the road there was a break in the vegetation: a wooden stairway descended through the thick green undergrowth. I cautiously gripped the side rails of this stairway and followed it down, first to one landing, then another, then another, until I reached a dock below that extended out onto the lake like a long, thin finger. At the end of the dock sat a boy holding a homemade fishing pole.

Excited to finally see someone, I remember calling to him: "Hello?"

The boy didn't acknowledge my call. He barely moved as I approached.

The lake was just as big as the lake in my hometown, only it appeared deeper, darker; the waves more choppy. Perhaps it was due to the overcast sky that hung low like a ceiling made of dirty mattresses. To the left and right were many similar docks jutting out into the water like spokes in a giant wheel. Summer cottages lined the shore, the thick clouds above reflected in their large picture windows. There were no boats on the water that I could see. Perhaps the impending threat of inclement weather had turned them away. It looked as if a storm could abruptly materialize. I stopped several feet from the boy and introduced myself.

"Hi, my name is Wyatt. What's your name?"

The boy cocked his head. "*Why*-it? Why-*it*?"

Perhaps he was simple, I thought, or his parents were not from this country and English wasn't his native tongue. I took a step closer. "In our town, we have a lake just like this one. What are you fishing for?"

The boy moved slowly. He put aside the fishing pole. That's when I noticed that the pole was not a fishing pole but just a long stick; one end of it had been whittled down to a sharp tip. The boy got to his feet, all the while staring out across the open water.

"I live just over the town line. How come I've never seen you come up my way?"

The boy turned. "Because it's easier for you to come down here than for me to go up there."

I took a step back. The boy looked so much like me he could have been my brother. He pointed to the neighboring docks. "Look."

I noticed there were now people on the docks. Had they come outside for a special event? A boat race, perhaps? Except all of them were looking in our direction. Staring. Perhaps they had never seen someone from across the town line before, I thought.

What happened next was difficult to piece together. I either lost my footing or I was pushed.

The surface of the lake slapped me. I had never felt water so cold. The world became muffled. The thick liquid anchored me down, disorienting me. I twisted and turned and, when I finally righted myself, I couldn't move, as if I had become stuck to the bottom of the lake. I saw the clouds above the thick veil of water and the boy standing distortedly on the dock staring down at me with the stick in his hand. He was using the whittled down end to pin my body to the lake bottom.

It had to have been a strange dream because things like this didn't happen in real life. But in this particular dream, I knew that if I didn't act, it would be a dream from which I would never awaken.

I felt pressure on my heart, and needed to dislodge it, somehow.

With leaden arms, I reached up and, with a sudden jerk, was able to pull the stick aside, leaving behind it inky streams originating from my chest.

The boy tumbled in on top of me.

In a confusion of arms and legs and bubbles, we wrestled each other until I managed to breach the surface and fill my lungs with air. But when I oriented myself, the boy was gone.

I pulled myself up onto the dock and lay there for a moment, my breathing ragged. The people who had watched what had happened were still standing on their docks, still staring, unmoved by the incident. No one rushed to tend to me or to even look for the other boy.

I got up then, and ran, an unnamed fear inhabiting my body, pushing me forward. I ran up the wooden stairway as quickly as I could, leaving dark, wet footprints in my wake. I didn't know what would happen if I stayed. All I knew was I didn't belong there.

When I reached the road, I began walking. It took all my strength to put one foot in front of the other on the uphill climb. At one point, I heard noises at my back that sounded like cries for help but I didn't turn. I continued walking until I rounded the curve in the road and, at last, the sun was there to greet me.

Only then did I realize I was carrying a stick. The stick was dried but the end was wet with something viscous. I tossed it aside. At some point I crossed the town line and it was as if I had never taken the walk in the first place. It was late in the afternoon by the time I arrived home.

As I suspected, my parents thought nothing of my disappearance. They didn't appear surprised that my clothes were damp, my hair a knotted mess. They told me to go wash up, it was almost dinner time.

I did what I was told. I went into my bedroom and removed my damp clothes. I searched the dresser drawers and put on a clean shirt and pants. I took the dirty clothes and put them in a bag. Then I hid the bag. All the while, I refused to look at myself in the mirror.

As I sat at the dinner table eating the food that was put in front of me, I couldn't bring myself to tell them that something bad had happened, something unforgivable. I couldn't tell them that a part of me had died that day. I just continued on as the child they once knew.

And they barely noticed the difference.

IF THINE EYE OFFEND THEE

M. Halstead

DON'T BE SILLY, of course you can ask about it!" said the woman with the rotting eye. "Don't worry, I'm totally used to it. Everyone's always like, *Oh, that's so crazy, how'd you pick that?* I mean, it's really rare, so I get it. Obviously parasitical bonding is so unique, so it's different for everyone, but I just *don't* get the 'modest' placements or whatever. I'm proud of mine. I want everyone to see it. Have you ever considered applying for one?"

You haven't. The acceptance rate is low, and you're not a fan of the mandatory ten-year lifespan you'd have to agree to.

"Ugh, everyone complains about that. Like, *Oh no, I only have a decade to live!* But it's *so* freeing, you know? Like, sure, you only get ten years to live. But it's a *guaranteed* ten years to live, right? Like, you don't want to sign up to die in ten years, but by not doing it, you could die tomorrow, you know? I mean, can you *really* live life to the fullest with that risk? Plus, retirement accounts are such a waste of money."

Your retirement account is anemic. You are beginning to wonder whether you should use your disposable income to bolster it, rather than using it for dates at mediocre burger joints with women who don't bother planning dates at high-end restaurants despite having less than ten years left to live. You shake your head, a little, imperceptibly, to clear it. You want to know why she chose her eye as the connection point.

"Oh, well, it's like—you know, my whole life, my face was, like, this defining part of me. And it still is, I guess." The woman with the rotting eye laughs softly. A viscous bubble of black sludge bubbles in her tear duct. "My face is why people interact with me how they do, and it always has been. Especially with men. But I guess you understand that, right? Sorry, I don't go out with girls that often."

You consider this, and agree that yes, your face defines your interactions. Your face does not cater to them, though; you do not mimic magazine photos the way she does. She *did*.

"Yes, exactly, that's *exactly* my point. People talked to me because of my face but it was totally out of my control. But *this*—this was in my control. Now people look at my face and they treat me a certain way, but it's the way I *should* be treated. The way I *choose* to be treated. They have all these ideas about me and they're all true. By choosing my eye, I'm in control."

You wonder whether she is in control, or her parasite, but don't pursue that line of inquiry. What ideas do people have about her? How does she know they are true?

"*It* actually allows me to read minds. Didn't you know that?"

Alarm.

"Ha! No, I'm kidding. Don't look so hurt. I'm joking, I swear! I can't read your mind. It can't be bothered with such mundane bullshit. No, no, it's all, like, more *cosmic*, I guess—I don't know how to explain it. The little things are irrelevant. Or I guess, it's me in charge of the little things. But anyway, your question— about assumptions, right? Well, what did you assume about me?"

You'd found her profile on the dating app that specializes in matching introverts and extroverts, so you naturally assumed her to be an extrovert. In her photo, she was looking demurely to her right, with her good eye cast downward. *It* had been front and center, seeping mold over her cheekbone, staring sightlessly at you: the voyeur. It occurred to you that the fantastic is often a mere breath away, and you thought that the woman who bore such a mark would be fascinating to meet.

"Two correct guesses. I *am* fascinating, aren't I?"

You wondered why she'd agree to meet someone like you at a place like this. You thought she must have some better use of her time, you thought she might have an ulterior motive. People like her don't run in circles with people like you; being bonded flings her into a higher class. Not just economically, but physically, mentally. Hosts turn their backs on the people from their *old life*. It's not just giving up everything beyond your next ten years. It's giving up before then, too.

"That's true." The woman with the rotting eye looks pensive. "It's not just the distant past, either. Yesterday has already slipped through my fingers . . . I'm sorry, that was pretentious, huh? Go on, it's *so* interesting to hear about yourself from someone else's point of view."

You don't really understand the decision. You've thought about the application more than you let on before, but it's too much. You have roots, you have a history, and letting go of that history would be severing some vital connection in your heart. That's where the parasite would have to nest in your body: in the ventricles, pouring into your soul with every beat, closing you off to pain and memory. It is projection, then, that you think she must be cold and aloof.

"Maybe. But I don't know, like, that's true about me, too. Even if it's mostly about how *you* would be in my position, it's still about me. Maybe not me *now*, but some me in the past, for sure. It's funny because you talk about how you lose your history when you're bonded—and you *do*—but you get a different history. The parasites don't die after ten years, you know. Just the hosts. And in a way, I'm every host that came before me . . . so even if it isn't true now, it probably was in the past. So anything you think of me is true *because* there's so much in me. So much in *it*."

Is she still her? She has changed, irrevocably. Is there still the *her* that wanted to take control of how people saw her face? You don't ask.

"And it feels so *big*, you know? To be a part of something larger than yourself. I'm me, and I'm also more. Taking the downfall of humanity into my own hands, *that's* what I wanted. I wanted to be a part of that. Part of changing the world forever."

You had thought about that, too, lying awake last night, staring at her photo and her rotting eye. The parasites are not benevolent. Everyone acts like they are, like a bond is a good thing, like trading your life for superhuman powers to ensure that your parasite lives to devour the life force of every human on earth is fine. When you first saw her, you thought she must be a monster to have chosen that life.

"That's true, too." The voice with the rotting eye is soft. "Wanting to destroy it all makes me a monster. Some hosts try to play it cool, don't attack others, cut off other hosts. Yeah, I get that, too. Pairing up so they can 'prevent the end,' or whatever. But you're right, I am a monster; there's no denying that. No matter what I do, the bond is monstrous. I have a demon in my eye, and I'm a demon, too."

If she's not a host that wants to prevent the parasites from taking over humanity, what *does* she want? Her dating profile said she hated other parasites.

"Oh, that's easy! I want to win. Not just over the humans— over the parasites, too. But not, like, in opposition to them as a whole . . . humans are finite resources, you know? Like, they reproduce, but not super quickly. The more that're gone, the faster the Purpose is achieved. The faster the *subjugation.* But fewer humans means fewer hosts, right? And if a parasite doesn't have a host to bond to, they die. Oh, sure, the waitlist is so long right now, there's no danger of it any time soon. But I do what I can. All I have to do is ensure that we have our next host, and I take care of the rest."

She kills them.

"Yes, exactly! Less competition means *my* parasite ends up on top. And picking my own host means I don't have to fight with the others when the waitlist dwindles. It's the long game, but I'll play it till it's time to move on to the next host. It'll be great. You'll really *get* it once we move in."

Your brain skitters for a moment. You'd prefer to be killed. It occurs to you that you came here for that purpose.

"No, sorry, no can do. You're *perfect*. You ask all the right questions. All those boys who've taken me out ask the stupidest shit. I'm *so* glad I went out on a limb here. Don't worry, you have like three years to think about the placement, and my apartment is the *cutest*. I've got everything you could want."

You wonder what would happen if you just walked away, right now. If she'd let you. You reach out and touch the rot on her eye. The flesh caves beneath your fingers, crumbles onto her French fries. You try to pull away, but the woman with the rotting eye clasps your hand to her face. Her fingers are warm, and strong, and you think of her holding you, of holding her. Your hand feels slimy. You wonder why she found a replacement so early, whether she needs something from you besides a future. You can feel the curve of the bottom of her eyeball. She lets go of your hand. You stand, pulling away the soft, wrinkled eyeball clutched in your fingers.

"I'll get the bill," says the woman with the rotting cavern in her face. "You can leave that on the plate, if you want."

HOW TO HAVE A LUCID DREAM

by W. Oliver Hunt

Introduction

S O YOU'VE HEARD ABOUT THIS wonderful thing called lucid dreaming—where you can fly around indescribable landscapes and speak with whomever you want, living or dead, and you can paint the sunrise onto the sky with colors that don't exist but should, and if you reach up to the moon with a butter knife you can spread it over a saltine and feed it to that teddy bear you gave your brother when you got too old for it and haven't seen since you were twelve. The only governor of possibility is the capacity of your imagination, how big you can dream.

Lucid dreaming is the vivid awareness that you are dreaming while dreaming. With awareness comes control: not only control of your actions, but, because the dream is happening inside your bulbous head, control of the very dream itself!

Yes, you too can learn to control your dreams at will. And even better, it's simple—like the beach in the purple light of dawn.

<u>Before We Get Started</u>

First and foremost, relax. Any horror stories you may have heard, forget them. Forget about sleep paralysis and hypnagogic hallucinations. Forget about being stuck in the same dream for what feels like years—that pier and the fish and the waves.

<u>How to Do It</u>

Lie down to sleep. This works best if you are extremely tired. Lie on your back with your arms at your side and eyes closed. Relax and stay perfectly still. Lull your body to sleep while keeping your mind awake. Find a mantra and repeat it in your head, like that prayer you'd say each night, first with your brother and then over and over when you got your own room.

Once you are ready to sleep, your brain will send signals to your body. These signals include: getting an itch, urges to fidget, a need to blink or move your eyeballs, a crippling urge to cry and remember how he'd insist on bringing that bear everywhere even on vacation to cottage with the fiddler crabs. Your eyes must stay closed. You must ignore all these impulses.

As your body relaxes, your thoughts will become more dreamlike and may begin to drift like fishing line in the wind above the pier above the waves. Don't fall asleep. Ground yourself in your mantra. Repeat it over and over.

You are in control.

After about twenty to thirty minutes you will feel a pressure on your chest and your head may feel like it's swelling. You may begin to smell strange smells and hear strange sounds like helicopter blades, or waves beating against wooden pillars, or seagulls, or the phrase *I think my line is tangled* repeating over and over from what feels like behind you and you'll want to make yourself look, or your entire family screaming a name over and over until it doesn't mean anything. Don't panic, this is part of it.

You have entered sleep paralysis. It's perfectly normal and exactly what it sounds like: your body releases a chemical that paralyzes its muscles so you don't get up and act out your dreams. At this point, even if you want to move you can't—like when you tried to move but couldn't and his feet went over after the rest of his body and the rod toppled in after him.

You're in control.

Be aware, if you open your eyes you will begin to hallucinate and you will not be able to move your body. You will be on the pier and see him with the bear under one arm leaning over the edge. He will say something and you will look away. Do not open your eyes yet. Ignore the noises and the smells.

You are in control.

When the sounds and sensations blend into a steady hum, your body is asleep. You are dreaming. Imagine pulling away from your body. It will feel slow and hard at first like passing through cellophane, or being born, or grieving. Keep repeating your mantra.

This is your dream, you are in control now.

Pull away from your body and into the humming and when you feel you have pulled away open your eyes.

You will see you and your brother with his bear—only now the bear's twice your size—the three of you walking in the purple light of dawn and he will say *Race you to the pier, if I beat you you'll have to eat a bloodworm.*

This time you are in control.

And you will watch yourself tell him *no.*

<u>INTERMISSION</u>

ESSAY

THE SEVEN MYSTERIOUS DROWNINGS OF THE CREW OF THE SS *NEPTUNE*

by Aleco Julius

I T IS AN ESTABLISHED FACT that sailing the seas has always been a dangerous profession. The Great Lakes certainly has its own history of tragedy and associated lore. These inland seas are home to thousands of shipwrecks. The stories of these sunken wrecks are often told in conjunction with the men and women who worked on their decks, and whose watery graves pervade the cold, murky depths of the lakes.

In the nineteenth century, many of these ships hauled materials such as lumber and iron ore across the lakes. These resources were needed to support the burgeoning towns around the lakes, the shorelines of which became America's Third Coast. One particular steamship, the SS *Cheval*, ran a circuitous route between Muskegon and Chicago, carrying massive tonnages of lumber. The ship was cursed from the start.

Built in early 1841, it was scheduled to make its first voyage late that year. Unfortunately, a fire broke out on the docked ship on the night of Friday, October 22nd, damaging the port side of the hull and postponing its departure. A man who lived close to the water had spotted a luminous glow while looking out his window. A small band of volunteers saddled a horse with severe posthaste, collected all manner of kettle and jug, and rushed to the scene. Since the fire was isolated to the stern of the vessel, it was extinguished using lake water rather swiftly, and the destroyed nautical equipment was replaced.

The fire left a set of black marks on her hull that together formed the vague shape of a soaring bird. A report of the incident in the Sunday edition of the *Muskegon Register* mentioned that the horse that led the rescue brigade that night was accidentally killed when it slipped on the mossy rocks near the shore. No cause was determined as to the start of the fire. Ironically, the SS *Cheval* was originally scheduled to set out that afternoon, but its launch was postponed by the owner of the ship, Mr. Theodore Falter of Rock Valley, Michigan. He was convinced that a Friday departure was bad luck, in adherence with seafaring lore.

In the next few years, this commercial route made Mr. Falter a wealthy man. By 1844, he had purchased several more ships and was delivering lumber to the rapidly growing Great Lakes cities. In March of that year, the ship suffered another setback during a delivery. A late winter ice storm pummeled Lake Michigan, smashing the deck to pieces and shattering the windows of the captain's cabin. His logbook, housed at Grand Rapids Public Library special collections, reads: "The skies thundered. Sounded like the ferocious growl of a wild beast."

Sometime in the spring of 1846, Mr. Falter, who was then in his mid-sixties, embarked on a river boat holiday down the Mississippi River. The trip lasted more than a month, a luxury he could surely afford. The Falter Commercial Distribution Company, however, was near its end. Alas, Mr. Falter contracted yellow fever while on his excursion to the South. He died from the disease on June 20th, 1846. A physician present at his deathbed noted in his journal that Falter's "unceasing fever and vomiting" heralded his gasping last words, which sounded something like "my feline angel!" He undoubtedly must have been hallucinating. Falter's untimely demise warranted a brief paragraph in the obituary section of the *Rock Valley Journal,* which stated: "Mr. Falter's son, one Emil Falter, is expected to take over his sire's business enterprise."

Emil Falter, an only child at 32, was contacted in Chicago and informed of his father's death. Reputedly a mercurial fellow, Emil never had been interested in shipping or lumber at all. His birth records are lost, but it is thought that his mother died when Emil was in his infancy. Documentation shows that Emil inherited the Falter Commercial Distribution Company, along with its six steamers, and quickly sold them off to eager buyers of the period. His father's first ship, the troubled SS *Cheval,* was purchased by the Chicago-based industrialist Luther Willard Smith.

In the fall of 1846, the ship was repainted and renamed the SS *Neptune.* It is believed that Smith's 11-year-old daughter named the ship after she read about the discovery of the planet in a September edition of the *Chicago Weekly Citizen.* Smith wasted no time in putting his new resource to use, immediately hiring eight seasoned men to crew the ship. Its maiden voyage was to transport a cargo of beef to the growing tourist destination of Mackinac Island, located at the northern tip of Lake Huron.

Shakespeare once wrote that "Fortune showed like a rebel's whore." In the case of the SS *Neptune* and its ill-fated crew, lady Fortune characteristically showed fidelity to no one. The rebel on this occasion was the November Witch, whose early arrival that year manifestly impeded the broadening wealth of Mr. Smith. The ship was to set sail on Tuesday, November 3rd. Curiously, as the crew was preparing to set out that morning, one of the crew members never showed. It was a man by the name of Arthur Cane.

After the catastrophe out on the lake that day, Cane was tracked down by reporters to inquire about his delinquency. He obstinately refused to speak, but his wife Agatha was not reserved. She stated that on the evening of November 2nd, the night before the SS *Neptune* was to launch upon its inaugural assignment under its new guise, her husband had a terrifying vision. She awoke in the middle of the night to find her husband out of bed and at the bedroom window: "Arthur, is everything all right?" He was petrified and couldn't speak. Eventually returning to bed, he whispered, "It came from over the lake. Great furry wings. Eyes that glowed like a cat. It called me awake." Agatha told him, "It was all just a bad dream, dear." These words are taken from the *Fergus Historical Series*, published in Chicago in 1882. Mrs. Cane added that her husband thought he had seen the figure dive into the black waters of the lake.

In the morning, Arthur Cane refused to go down to the docks. The rest of the crew, which had gathered at dawn to prepare for embarking, needed to scramble for his replacement. His position was essential, for he was the cook. One of the deckhands rushed to a nearby tavern called the Pigeon, and banged on its door to awaken the owner, Mr. Asa Lyle. The half-asleep owner, who stumbled down from his upstairs quarters, reportedly stated, "I'm sorry, but my son's taken employment on a ship that's left last week. My daughter, however, is available and a good cook, too." Having no other choice if they meant to depart that morning, the crew agreed. And that's how Ms. Addy Lyle became the cook of the SS *Neptune*.

It was immediately clear that Addy could handle herself among the men. The deckhand who had fetched her from the tavern, Jess Brown, knew of Addy from more than a few whiskey-infused nights in Hardscrabble, an area now known as Bridgeport. She spoke very little, according to patrons of the Pigeon tavern, and her face was a continual hard glare of distrust. She could not read or write but could tally up bar bills in her head. She never married nor had children. One can imagine the 30-year-old Addy striding up the ship's ramp with determined confidence among the small crew. Within the first hour on open water, however, Addy knew she was in trouble in a different way. This being her first time out on the open water of the lake, she was walloped with a bout of seasickness.

Though the skies were mostly cloudy and the winds whipped sharply, Captain Marshall Baptist deemed it no cause for concern to leave at dawn toward their northeastern destination. Soon after departure, the waves grew rougher by the minute, and the going was extremely slow. Captain Baptist was straight away worried that he would disappoint his employer, Mr. Smith, who had demanding expectations. Addy with delirious with nausea in less than two hours of travel. The ship had only advanced an estimated ten miles from the shoreline, perhaps even less. The pilot of the ship, P.J. Malley, noticed Addy's illness and made a joke about it to deckhand Tomas "Tug" Winborn. Just then, a jolt of purple lightning cracked against the sky, shedding a shock of eerie light across the gray churning surface of Lake Michigan.

The vessel's bad luck had indeed not run out. A chilling blast of wind rushed in from the north, a sound like the flapping of monstrous sails, or wings. Moses Reddick, the steamer's fireman, was belowdecks at the arrival of the gale. An intense anger began to swell in him, because he had thought beforehand that the ship should have postponed their departure until after the bad weather passed. He even gathered the courage to approach the captain to suggest that, just maybe, there might be a storm brewing. Captain Baptist replied with a sneer and said, "You've got one job, boy, and that's to tend the boiler." Tumultuous waves slammed into the hull.

The lake sprayed frigid water upon the deck as the crew struggled to stand upright. Hailstones the size of fists hammered the ship, one piece striking "Tug" Winborn on the shoulder. Being a rather stout seaman, he was stunned but still on his feet. The first mate, Henry Low, was the most experienced man on the ship, and thus was the first to realize they might not make it through the afternoon. He was familiar with the swift nature of the punishing Great Lakes gales, and with that knowledge made his way through the howling winds to the engineer, Geth Schillinger. The engineer assured Low that the SS *Neptune* had the strength to withstand the tempest.

It was not to be. Captain Baptist ordered the pilot, P.J. Malley, to turn back toward the shore, hoping to either outrun the storm or to at least hold out well enough to stay afloat. Having made so little headway, this was not an unreasonable decision. By this time, Addy was lying on the deck in a bilious daze. The brief spell of hail had ceased, but now the onset of blowing snow reduced visibility to virtually zero. The extreme pressure of one particularly violent wave cracked the hull, a blow from which the ship would not recover. On its first anniversary, the *Chicago Daily Tribune* ran a story of how this memorable storm, which is memorialized as "The Big Squall," destroyed over forty other vessels of various sizes in the south part of the lake.

At nightfall, the seven men of the crew would be safely on land, albeit drenched and exhausted. Their hair, beards, and clothing were crusted with ice, their mouths filled with a mixture of sand, snow, and mud. But what of Addy Lyle? As the crew crawled out of their lifeboat, there was nary a sign of the cook. The story that the crew subsequently told would be strange and incomprehensible. It was first told to the small crowd that gathered near the wharf. When the storm began to die down, the floundering ship was spotted by a teenage boy out surveying the damage with his dog. The boy, known only as Melvin, told the *Tribune* that he first noticed a ship very low in the water. Then, he described, he "saw a little dot out there. A speck being tossed about by the waves." It took the lifeboat approximately three hours to get back to land. Captain Baptist was the only one who did not help row back to land, as his station precluded it.

According to mate Henry Low, it was the most sudden and swiftly developing storm he had ever experienced in his 27 years on the lakes. After a mad scramble to turn the ship around, and a battle against the elements, the SS *Neptune* hit a sandbar about 300 yards out. Amos Reddick heard the tear of the hull and the water rushing in, which to him was the inevitable conclusion of his own warning. It was said that engineer Geth Schillinger was utterly awestruck at the development. He was so bewildered on the sinking ship that "Tug" Winborn was forced to literally drag him to the edge of the deck, impairing his shoulder even further. At this point, the only lifeboat on the ship was lowered at the command of Captain Baptist. It was designed to hold at least twelve people.

According to the crew members' account, the swirling snow and fierce spray rendered visibility extremely poor. Still, what happened next is puzzling. A long, penetrating wail went up from the deck. It was Addy's call of distress. Allegedly, Jess Brown went to her and took to a knee, hoping to coax Addy to her feet. He later claimed that ice had crusted over her long hair and clothes, but what most disturbed him were her eyes. They seemed to be watching something above the ship, gazing with intense exhilaration. The look on her face was a mixture of revelation and fear. Brown turned up toward the dark clouds just in time to see a shadowy form vanish into the heavy weather.

Brown, admittedly terrified, made his way across the undulating deck to fetch anyone to help with Addy. To his surprise, Winborn, Low, and Schillinger were already in the lifeboat. Captain Baptist and the pilot Malley were still at the helm when Brown called out to them, but his voice was absorbed by the winds. They abandoned their places directly and prepared to lower the lifeboat for boarding. They apparently had forgotten about Addy, or else did not care. As the ship began to sink, Reddick was seen attempting to pull Addy by the arms, but the effort was made arduous by the tossing ship and icy surface. Then he realized that the rest of the crew was leaving without him. Dropping Addy's arms, he quickly trudged his way across the slippery deck and jumped into the small boat.

Before they reached the shore near 31st street, the majority of the SS *Neptune* was already beneath the waves. Only the top of the stack protruded from the dark waters. More locals crowded onto the shore, bringing blankets and hot tea for the men. Several knew Addy from the Pigeon, and as they talked among themselves, the fact circulated that she was hired by the ship early that morning. To their shock, she had not arrived with the men on the lifeboat. Shock turned to alarm, which then turned to fury.

They demanded to know what happened to Addy. Each man deferred to the captain, who stated: "We regret to declare that the unfortunate lady was deceased at the time of the accident." The men, who had been drearily recovering from their harrowing escape from the ship, suddenly seemed a bit livelier. They dodged questions about Addy's fate, citing a desire to return to their homes or to find a doctor. The captain commented that he needed to seek out Luther Willard Smith, the owner of the ship.

Within a few days, each of the crewmen had absconded to elsewhere. They left a grieving father, and a small community, with unsettled emotions and unresolved questions.

The first drowning happened less than a year later. The victim was Henry Low, the oldest and most experienced crew member, age 57 at the time of the shipwreck. He immediately was able to find new employment after the SS *Neptune* calamity, this time on a merchant ship out of Manitowoc, Wisconsin. In August of 1847, he was working on the SS *Menomonee,* when a load of iron ore never arrived at its destination of Duluth. It was guessed that the crew of sixteen were all lost to a sudden and apparently fleeting storm. Strangely, though, no storm in the area was ever reported. The ship was not seen by any other passing vessels, and no wreckage was ever found. It was as if a fracture in the wall of physical reality had opened up and swallowed the ship whole.

Several of the bodies did eventually wash up along the shore of Michigan's upper peninsula. Scavenger birds usually alerted citizens of a new dead body, and for a time buzzards were as common as gulls. The *Door County Gazette* printed a list of crew members over a period of weeks, where Henry Low's name was eventually printed. It was noted that his bare chest featured a burned image of what appeared to be a mysterious flying creature, though the family had never known him to possess a tattoo.

The second man to drown was engineer Geth Schillinger. Only in his late thirties at the time of the SS *Neptune*'s sinking, those around him said he seemed far older after the experience out on the lake, as if he were imbued by an ancient spirit. He was a changed man in other ways, too. Previously known as an intelligent, inventive sort who was always fixing things and solving problems on the job, he was afterward consumed with collecting rocks and shells. Not for geological study, however. He was convinced that there were special specimens that would complete a vast unknown puzzle, a portion of which he kept on the floor of his small second-story apartment on Madison Street.

In the early morning hours of March 30th, 1852, his neighbors reported hearing him roar loudly, swing open his door, and stomp down the stairs. He was last seen near the north side of Michigan Park, where a watchman spotted a man in his night-shirt fitting Schillinger's description walk directly onto the rocky beach and into the lake. The man completely submerged himself but kept on walking, his arms outstretched as if embracing some phantom of the icy depths.

The third drowning took place eight years later. At that time, Captain Marshall Baptist was a wealthy, retired grandfather. On the night of September 7th, 1860, he was on the *Lady Elgin* with his son Claude as it set out from Chicago to Milwaukee. Most passengers were on their way back home, having come to the Windy City for a political rally. The return trip was more of a pleasure cruise, with music, dancing, and drinking. Baptist and his family had built their riches on the shipping industry, and the unjust fate of Addy Lyle was an altogether forgotten thought. But on this night, the memory of the lake would seal his doom.

While the party was going strong deep into the night, storm clouds gathered over the ship. The rain and thunder did not dampen the spirits of the merry revelers. That is, until a shocking jolt portside caused chandeliers to come crashing down and sent dancers sprawling across the floor. The ship was struck by the schooner *Augusta*, and hundreds of lives were lost near Winnetka. Baptist's son survived, but the recollection of his father's death haunted him. He told the *Milwaukee Sentinel* that, the night before the accident, he had a strange dream. He recounted: "A man with a trident was seated at a table, and an indefinable being with long hair served him a platter of writhing crayfish."

The fourth man who drowned was Percy James "P.J." Malley, officer for the Union in the Civil War. His directive was to pilot gunboats up and down the Mississippi River for Ulysses S. Grant's army. In May of 1865, Confederate leader Jefferson Davis was captured in Georgia. As Union forces drew close, it was rumored that Davis and his cabinet were carrying a veritable treasure of gold. Nonetheless, there was no sign of this alleged treasure at his arrest, and thus the legend of the confederate gold was born. P.J. Malley was one of those treasure hunters who in the aftermath of the Confederate dissolution sought to discover the fortune that was unaccounted for. When Malley heard that Jefferson's treasure supposedly made it to the north, and that Union officers somehow lost it on Lake Michigan, he realized that no one was more qualified than he was to recover it.

He hired the schooner *Green Heron* out of Traverse City and enlisted a group of Potawatomi men for the mission. They set out on a cool September morning. The vessel was never seen or heard from again, another apparent victim of lakes. A recovery effort made in 1979 did find a sizable chest at the bottom of the lake, near a depth of about 200 feet. Expert divers of the *Great Lakes Shipwrecks Alliance* were able to pry it open, only to find a very old sailing cap with a simple M monogram. Floating beside it was a golden spoon.

Jess Brown, the youngest of the crew at 28 when the SS *Neptune* floundered, was the fifth man to drown. After his death, a friend confided that he sometimes spoke of that traumatic day. When in his cups, which was often, a dark pall would shade his countenance as he told the story of helpless Addy. As far as can be discerned, he was the only man of the crew to talk about the wronged woman. The source of these remarks is the 1897 book *Amazing Tales of the Great Lakes*, published in Printer's Row by Donneberry Press. He is also the only man not to have left the employment of Luther Willard Smith. He worked the lake's shipping industry as a deckhand for many more years, even after Smith sold his company to a faceless conglomerate. That's why it was bewildering to Brown's friend, known as Floyd H., that he wished to go out fishing the next day after arriving from a back-breaking weeks-long excursion on the job.

So, they launched a little fishing boat on July 9th, 1867. Floyd grew uneasy as Brown rowed the boat out toward the site of the shipwreck. Other vessels of all types were out that fine, warm morning. The two men cast their lines and waited for approximately half an hour when Brown abruptly stood up and pointed: "There's someone in the water!" Of course, there was no one there. Before Floyd could protest, Brown dove into the calm water. He did not resurface. When the devastated friend finally reeled in his line, he found at the end of it an impossibly frozen lake trout.

Moses Reddick was the sixth man to drown when he was taken by a rogue wave on the north shoreline of Rock Island. Although little is known about this bizarre incident, there are a few alleged witnesses who recounted their testimony to the Wisconsin Lighthouse Historical Society many years later. As it happened, Reddick was then working in the fishing industry, casting nets for perch and walleye in the upper regions of Lakes Michigan and Huron. His schooner, called *Pride,* was caught out in a hazy fog on the morning of May 2nd, 1869. Luckily, the captain knew that nearby Rock Island featured a lighthouse that for the previous thirty years had lit the way for numerous boats in that area, which was prone to unexpected fog.

As the *Pride* neared the harbor, visibility was low. There was no rain, but the craft was enveloped by a ghostly white vapor. Just before landing, Reddick looked back out over the lake, when he saw a great sailboat emerge from among the mist, gliding slowly and soundlessly. Squinting, and in a state of disbelief, Reddick saw a woman on the bow, whose long hair was plastered down as if soaking wet. He claimed that the figurehead of this spectral ship was that of a lion with wings. He had barely set foot on the beach when a massive wave came out of nowhere and swept Reddick into the lake. Since he was an expert swimmer, it can only be surmised that a rip current withdrew him toward his aqueous tomb.

The seventh and final man of the crew to drown was Tomas "Tug" Winborn, by all accounts an unjustifiably arrogant man. He got his nickname when he was a brawny teen. For a few pennies, he would single-handedly pull boats onto the lake for families out for a leisurely day of sailing. He was hired and fired from several other jobs since the sinking of the SS *Neptune.* Employers could not stand his lazy attitude or his harassment of coworkers. Winborn also walked off a few jobs when he felt he was not paid enough, or when he just got bored. In the summer of 1871, he got a job on a Chicago Sands lumberyard. On the evening of October 9th, yard workers smelled smoke from coming from the south. Swiftly thereafter, the yard caught fire and spread so quickly that dozens of workers were trapped. The only escape from the heat and smoke was into the lake, so that's where they went.

Little did Winborn know that most of the town was in flames, and therefore help could not be expected to arrive. A reporter for the *Chicago Evening Post* wrote that the city that night appeared to be "the adamantine bulwarks of hell." Up to their chins in the water to avoid the hot sand blowing all around them, the magnificent and terrible glow of the conflagration rose up beyond the burning lumberyard. Directly, the frantic workers heard a distant rumbling, approaching quickly but difficult to ascertain. From out of the smoke leapt an army of horses, some aflame, crashing into the water and screaming in agony. Three days later, with the city in embers, Winborn's corpse washed ashore. It was concluded that he had drowned, but not before being kicked in the temple by a crazed horse attempting to escape the inferno.

Over the years, a few attempts have been made to recover the SS *Neptune* shipwreck. Each time, sustained inclement weather conditions prohibit any success at doing so. Funding is scarce, and the lakes do not give up their secrets so easily. The purpose of this essay is to shed light on some of those secrets. The cruel death of Addy Lyle is but one tale in which selfishness and cowardice break through the fabric of the seamen's pact. The point is not to disparage worthy seamen throughout the ages, but rather to present one crew's fragile desperation, and the tribulation that followed. Why and how these men met their ends can only be known to the spirits of the gloomy depths. Addy's story is forever lore of the lakes. Where ghost ships appear from the fog and the bones of sailors lie within her ice water mansion.

V

FORM AND BEAST: AXIOM

THE SECRET IS IN THE MOUNTAINS

by Jasmine De La Paz

THE RAIN CAME DOWN IN sheets of slate gray the morning mother told me he died. It was late in the autumn of the year 1898—the last year I would spend in my old life, although that was unbeknownst to me. I came downstairs, still in a state of waking, startled to see mother sitting at the kitchen table—a steaming cup of coffee already poured and waiting for me. Her head was bowed in contemplation, and when she heard me enter she looked up. The storm's bluish-gray light dimmed the room, but even then, I could see her red-rimmed, puffy eyes and knew something was wrong.

"Hazel dear, sit down with me," she said, with a forced smile.

My worried heart pounded as I sat and said, "Is it Father?"

"No, no sweetheart, your father is fine. Already left for work."

I exhaled a sigh of relief, but mother reached across the table and clasped my hands in hers. I looked down at her aged hands on mine and back to her face. Her bottom lip trembled as she struggled to speak, and a small tear appeared at the wrinkle of her left eye.

"I need you to be strong, Hazel."

"What is it, mother?" I couldn't stand to be in the dark any longer.

"It's Ed, sweetheart, he . . . he had an accident. He fell off a cliff on that hiking trip of his," she stammered. "They . . . they believe he's dead.

Her words whirled in my head with disbelief. *My* Ed? *My* Edwin—dead? No . . . no, it could not be true. I sat there staring at her sobbing and sniffing, droplets of tears now rolling freely down her face and dampening her robe. For Ed was like a son to her—"the son I never had," she would say when we were young, knowing full well that we would marry someday. Everyone knew.

All at once, the kitchen window blew open with a gust of wind, sending a splatter of cold raindrops into our small kitchen. Mother shrieked. I quickly stood up, my chair squeaking back, and hurriedly closed the windows latch. I looked through the streaked glass, feeling the cold seep through the thin panel and onto my skin. What would have been a view of the mountains— where Ed went on his hike—was a thick blanket of dark clouds charged with harsh lightning. The increasing torrents of relentless rain, filling the yard with little gullies full of mud and debris, had furthermore obscured the vista of mountains from the kitchen window. The path leading to his trail was just a couple miles beyond our land, through a thicket of trees and along a stream.

"Ed knew the trail better than any other," I said, still staring out the window. The tears burned behind my eyelids.

"Yes. But nobody foresaw this damned storm, Hazel. It came without warning, and—"

"No one can predict the moods of the mountain," I finished for her.

"Yes, dear. And I'm so sorry."

Then I crumpled to the floor.

Mother took me back to bed. I lay there for hours until father returned home from work. I didn't hear the knock at my door but felt my bed tilt as my parents sat at the edge of my bed. Father patted my back, as he had done when I was a young girl. All the while the rain pounded alongside my grief-stricken heart.

They gently told me more of Ed's accident: Ed was expected back yesterday, but it wasn't unusual for him to spend an extra day or two in the mountains. When he did not return with the first signs of the storm, his mother had had a bad feeling and sent her husband and their bloodhound out to find him. The dog was able to track his scent. Right as the trail began its descent, the canine's nose discovered Ed's hat. At this particular area, the trail thinned around the shoulder of the mountain alongside a sheer cliff so devastatingly deep that one's stomach dropped just looking over its edge. The rain had loosened the dirt and stones of the path, and his father had feared the worst. He was able to climb a little further down the rocks, and much to his dismay, discovered his son's hiking sticks broken and splayed out like limbs. He tried to climb further down, but it was much too steep. Fearing for his own life, he did not go any further. Father finished by saying, "You know he could not have survived that fall anyway, Hazel. Not from that ridge."

I was hysterical, shaking, and raving—out loud and in my mind. How could they be so certain without even finding my Ed's body? What if he was still alive and needed our help? They assured me they alerted the Sheriff, and a team was willing and waiting to find him—just as soon as the storm dissipated, that was.

When I asked when that would be, all I received were shifting eyes and an uneasy answer. With dropping temperatures, the worst was expected: *snow*.

While in bed that night, I couldn't stop visions of my poor Ed bloodied and bruised in the muck, wet and alone in the darkness. His wheat-colored curls matted and soiled. His piercing blue eyes, now vacant, staring off into nowhere. I felt a black void in my heart; my soul hollow; my whole being completely bereft and without meaning.

I slowly got out of bed, wrapping a blanket over my shoulders. I could see the vapor of my warm breath bloom in the air. My tears felt like icicles clinging to my face. I had let the fire die out in my room; only a small ember glowed in the grate. It didn't seem fair for me to be cozy and warm when Ed was still out there freezing.

I imagined hearing the familiar tap of a pebble being thrown onto my bedroom windowpane as I sauntered over, knowing it was Ed beckoning me to come out, like in fairytales. I would peer down to see his smiling face before tiptoeing out to be with him.

Just as I looked out into the yard, the first hush of snowflakes drifted from the night sky, sticking to the ground, and quickly covering the muddy earth in white. The snow seemed to be luminous, brightening the outside with its silent stillness. To watch the first snowflakes fall from the sky was like watching time stop. Ed loved the snow. Now he would be buried by it.

I awoke to mother knocking at my door and entering with a tray of coffee and breakfast. She tutted over the fireplace as I sipped my creamed coffee. Keeping herself busy and helpful was mother's way of coping with grief. She was saying something as she worked to get a fire going, but I couldn't comprehend anything. I had never felt so numb, dazed, locked in a dream. As I set down my coffee on the tray, something caught my eye. I picked it up to discover a rock, or so I initially thought it was. On closer inspection I realized it was a quartz, but like no other I have ever seen—clear and glassy, smooth to the touch, with a wonderful yellow undertone. I held it in my palm, inspecting its perfect diamond shape, pointed edges and all.

"Mother—where did this come from?"

She stood up, wiped her hands on her apron, and said, "Oh yes, I forgot about that. I found it on the kitchen table. I figured it was one of those rocks Ed must have given you from his adventures." As soon as she mentioned Ed, her eyes averted back to the fire.

It was true, Ed would always bring back a gem for me, or a special rock he would find on his hikes, but he never brought me anything like *this*. This gem was certainly cleaned and evenly shaped. I recalled something Ed had said before this last backpacking trip, as if the gem itself brought back the memory. I thought it so insignificant at the time, but now . . .

It must have been around midnight—our usual twilight rendezvous hour—and we were sitting along the stream, all dreamy and silent except for the rush of the water gliding over stones.

"The secret is in the mountains, Hazel," he said.

Puzzled, I turned to look at him. The moon lit his face in a wonderful soft light. He had never looked so beautiful.

"Whatever do you mean?" I asked, smiling.

His eyes widened with excitement. Then his mouth parted, and I could tell he was on the brink of saying something important. He paused. A slight hesitation. His eyes darted nervously. Then he shook his head, laughed, and said it was nothing, and pulled me into his arms.

In the days leading to his trip, he seemed almost crazed with mountain fever: poring himself over maps, flipping through books about the Paiutes and Shoshones (who first settled in the land), while nervously running his fingers in his hair, sighing, and taking quick glances at the mountain. It was cute that he was so invested, always finding a new undiscovered route, lake, or ledge. I was sure no one else ventured as far as he.

"Hazel?" Mother's voice sounded far away. "Hazel, dear?"

"Oh, I'm sorry," I said, my thoughts interrupted.

"It's okay, sweetheart. I know it's hard for you right now. It's hard for us all, but I don't want you going out at night, into the snow. I know you would meet Ed sometimes, but I don't want you out there alone. It's . . . it's much too cold."

"How so, mother?"

"No need to pretend, Hazel—you dragged snow into the kitchen, dear. Why, you even left the backdoor ajar. Nearly froze when I walked in to make your father's coffee."

I felt my brow crease with confusion. I did not leave the house last night. But before I could say anything, she kissed my cheek, told me to stay in bed as long as I needed, and left me be, alone with my ghost gem and a sliver of hope.

The day was a blur. It turned out I couldn't stay in bed, as we had visitor after visitor, paying their condolences with casseroles and questions. I tried to be sweet and thanked the young women and their mothers over endless amounts of tea but would often get caught staring off into the distance, my thoughts taking me away. Sometimes I would catch bits of bobs of the ladies whispering amongst themselves, in between talks of the weather: "Poor dear, what will she ever do now," ". . . just before their wedding," and the worst: "At least she's still young; there's plenty of good church men out there."

All the while I held the gem in my pocket, never letting it go, squeezing it tight. I was afraid it too would disappear, like Ed. It was oddly warm, and somehow, in its own way, brought me comfort. For the first time since hearing the news of Ed's accident, I felt hope. I *felt* that he was still alive. It *must* have been him who brought this into the kitchen last night. But why is he hiding? What is he trying to tell me? Am I losing my mind, unable to accept his death, and creating some farfetched idea? But something told me I was right.

The secret is in the mountains.

I was so exhausted by evening that sleep came instantly.

My eyes opened.

Tap—tap—tap.

I lay there for a moment, unsure if what I heard was real or not. But it came again. My breath caught in my throat, and without waiting another second I rushed to look out the window.

The snow had stopped falling. Everything was still and silent. It must have been the intimate time when night kissed morning, and a low haze hung over the eerie glow of this in-between hour.

My heart pounded as I looked out into the yard, my face so close that it fogged the frosted glass. And—there he was!—standing below with his usual lopsided, boyish grin, as if nothing had happened. Not the slightest trace of worry on his face.

In all my nineteen years of life, I had never felt so happy, so relieved. Ed was alive! He waved his hand, urging me to come down and join him. I threw on a sweater, grabbed the gem, and quietly went downstairs, as not to wake up mother and father. I was shaking with such uncontrolled excitement that I struggled to put on my boots and coat.

The air was crisp and refreshing as I crossed the side yard. My boots sank into the thick powder, slowing me down, and I almost fell several times in my haste. He was still standing where I last saw him, patient and poised. I must have screamed his name because he put his finger to his lips. *Shhhh.*

I was about ten feet away from my love when I stopped. The cold air stung my heaving chest. Something was not right with him. I could not explain it for the life of me—Ed looked the exact same; in fact, he looked healthier than ever before. There were no visible wounds, no dirt or mud on him. He looked as if he was just coming back from his hiking trip, alert and giddy from his discoveries. Cheeks flushed from the cold.

"Ed, where have you been?" I asked.

He didn't answer for some time, only smiled at me.

"Edwin—my love—what has happened to you?"

His eyes softened, and a glimmer of *my* Ed returned. "Hazel," he said, "please come with me."

My skepticism melted after hearing his soft voice. "Where do you want to go? Everyone thought you were dead. *I* thought you were dead! We must wake the others, let them know you are all right."

"All that can wait, Hazel." He took a step closer and reached out his hand. "I need to show you something."

They say love can make you crazy, and, in that moment, I was in a chaotic spiral of madness for him. I grabbed his hand; it was warm like the gem in my pocket, and I let him wrap me in a sweet embrace. I snuggled my face into the side of his neck, savoring his live, warm, breathing body. He let me go, and, still holding my hand in his, led the way. I already knew where we were going.

We walked silently behind the house, through the tower of

oaks and cottonwoods whose branches hung limp with snow, and finally to the trailhead. Ed must have noticed my exhaustion from this impromptu trek through the harsh country snow; he lifted me into his arms, his strength uncanny, and carried me like a young bride as he began ascending the mountain.

He showed no signs of weariness or delay. His breathing was even and smooth. And when I asked how he could carry me with such ease he only smiled and looked ahead, eyes vacant. Either the snow was more packed than it appeared, or he conjured a power of lightness, as his feet did not sink. In my bemused, dreamy state, I thought it must be an illusion.

Without a glance, he walked past the point where his father had found his hat and sticks.

The sun started to rise, but the higher we climbed the thicker the clouds' vapors became, obscuring the blood-orange rays and keeping the snowy trail murky and damp.

We climbed and climbed for what must have been hours, yet he persisted on, steady and strong with me in his arms. At times I felt frightened, wondering where he was taking me, but I remembered I was with Ed. As long as we were together, everything would be all right. I could not lose him again.

We were almost at the peak of the mountain; I recognized the usual ledge where every climber would stop to marvel at the remarkable view of the valley, where groves of aspen trees held onto the last of their golden leaves before losing them to winter. I expected we would stop as well, thinking perhaps he wanted to take me here on some romantic notion of his. We would watch the sunrise together: his way of apologizing for disappearing and almost scaring me to death. Instead, he turned toward the rock face—a place I'd never thought to go—and as agile as a bobcat, ascended the steep slope, till we were so high that I clung to him in fear of falling. We finally stopped, and he put me down.

I trembled in the cold. I was never one to fear heights, yet I found myself swaying on the small surface we stood on, trying not to peer down below. "Ed," I said breathlessly. "What are we doing here?"

"It's quite all right, Hazel. We are almost there." His eyes had lost their prior vacantness; they were almost warm, like how they used to be. He urged me to turn around to face the boulder. "Look here," he said, pressing his palm onto the side of the mountain.

Sketched into the rock was a strange symbol. There was just enough light to see it. Faded with age, it looked like it could have been a Paiute petroglyph, or perhaps something astronomical: faint coiled lines surrounded a circle, with one straight arrow at its center, pointing up. "Why, what is that?" I whispered as I traced it softly with my finger.

"Your *gem*, Hazel. Bring out your gem."

Even if he had brought me the gem in the night, how was he so confident I had brought it with me?

"You do have it, don't you?" he said, grinning. "You know I never forget to bring something back to you, my Hazel."

I smiled at him in wonderment. Whatever was happening was terrifyingly magical. I could feel it in the air—a pulse, a shift. As if the mountains, the trees, the air were taking on a life of their own. Maybe it had always been this way, and some unforeseen force was unveiling my narrow perception.

I pulled the gem from my pocket. It felt warmer than before. Felt as if it, too, were pulsing. I don't know why I did what I did: I pressed the gem to the center of the symbol. For a breath or two, nothing happened. Then a bright radiance flashed out from the symbol. It dissipated. A rumbling sound followed like thunder. Then the rock shifted, split open, revealing a small slit barely large enough for a person to enter.

"You go first," Ed said.

I hesitated, afraid of the unknown.

"Trust me, Hazel. I'll be right behind you."

That was all it took.

As soon as I walked into the cave, moist cold air caressed my skin, and the pleasant smell of earth seeped into my nostrils. My eyes adjusted to the light quickly, as it wasn't completely dark. Dim flares lined the rounded rock walls with a scattering glow along the edges of the floor. The pulse—oh the pulse—it grew ever stronger here. I felt it in my bones, it chattered my teeth.

Ed grabbed my hand and gently kissed it before leading me forward.

As we went deeper into the cave, I noticed more details. "Why, the lights, Ed—the lights! They are gemstones!"

The subdued gold brightened the cavernous space. A shaft of light just above a fiery sunset.

"Citrine," he added, "is a rare variety of quartz. It's what you're holding in your hand. Isn't it wonderful? See how it glows? Hear what it says?"

I did.

This is home, Hazel. Your home.

The same symbol was etched several times across the walls. Sometimes so large I had to strain my neck up to see it, other times so small it was barely visible.

It all felt mesmerizing . . .

Dreamlike.

Suddenly Ed stopped. He moved behind me. One hand pressed lightly on my shoulder.

I turned to look at him. He stared into the clotted darkness of the cave, expectant and alert. I pressed my back into his body, for I knew something was about to happen, and I wasn't quite sure I was ready.

I heard a faint sound, like the delicate steps of a timid child. Ed heard it, too, as he squeezed my shoulder in acknowledgment.

Slowly, a figure emerged—tall, lanky, and languid. It had a human form: torso, arms, and legs, but they were unnaturally thin and elongated, and its head much too large. Its skin looked like an ill-fitted suit for whatever resided therein, stretched and frayed. With an awkward (almost infantile) gait. And despite its outwardly clumsiness, it silently walked forward with its odd narrow feet. Wraithlike. Its arms were so long that its giant, disproportionated hands nearly grazed the ground. When it drew itself into a patch of light, I looked into its facelessness; there was nothing but a coil of limbs wrapped around each other and protruding forward in a monstrous tangle.

I might have cried out. I stumbled back into Ed. Whatever

mouth was hiding behind its horrid tangle of limbs spoke to me.

This is home, Hazel. Your home.

Except I didn't hear those words with my ears; I felt them in my bones.

The figure stopped, tilted its odd head. Studied me.

"Hazel, there's no need to fear it," Ed whispered. "This is our chance, don't you see? This is our chance for *life*, Hazel. Eternal life. Everything I had been looking for, I found. *Here.* Don't you see? This is home. *Our* home."

I trembled but listened to my love. I knew this was meant to be. This was my escape from my future life of cleaning, cooking, going to church, and chatting with the dull ladies in our small town, of utter mundanity. Of course, a life married to Ed would be a happy one, and it goes without saying that I loved mother and father. But sometimes I felt a weight on my chest when I envisioned the years—*decades*—ahead of me; and *Ed* was here to save me from that dreadful routine, my earthly doom.

"Yes, this is home," I said. "My home."

Ed took my hand and guided me toward the ten-foot-tall, gray-skinned anthropoid. It swayed side-to-side like a tree in a light breeze. But I kept my eyes low until I felt in my bones its *pulsing* presence, and then—slowly—I lifted my eyes.

The tangle of limbs about its face began to blossom. Long, serpentine appendages unraveled themselves, making its head seem even larger as they splayed out and undulated around me. It leaned down till my face was level with the center of what hid behind its limbs. I saw flesh, circular in shape (like a closed eyelid): the same gloomy shade as a thunderhead expectant with storm. Another serpentine appendage shot out from this area. It found my mouth with such force that my head was thrown back and my feet hovered as it held me aloft. Its long, waving tentacles then engulfed my body, suctioning my entire head and torso in an unearthly embrace of powerful darkness.

I could not breathe; I could not see.

As this being planted a part of itself in me—consummating our union—it gifted me a new soul. A rebirth. A life where I would live forever—Ed and me and all those chosen in the past, and in the future.

With this new life came power. *Knowledge.* I knew not only the secret of the mountains but all the secrets and mysteries of our universe.

And soon, dear reader, you will too.

Soon, you will join us.

UNTIL THE NIGHT TURNS OVER

by Kyle Stück

THE NIGHT SKY IS STARLESS as I approach the house. The driveway leading to it is littered with cars, each waxed machine nicer than the last. Dead leaves are strewn about the otherwise neatly kept yard; autumn has come tonight. I take a deep breath. The air is crisp and smells of food and tobacco. I am to join a party, which explains the suit I'm wearing. I adjust my tie, knowing somehow, almost instinctively, that it's loose. I continue on. Gleaming light spills out ahead of me from large glass and I feel myself drawn to it like the cliché moth. Shadow shapes dance through drawn drapes in rhythm to the music managing to escape the large house, which at first glance looks new, pristine too—as if it were just completed, yet there is something old about it . . . ancient even.

I continue towards the enigma, and with each step I realize the driveway seems abnormally long. I look behind me to corroborate this but am met with a *deep* black. I can see nothing. I look down and follow the visible asphalt beneath me as far as I can, about two feet or so, before it disappears into night that I can only describe as "empty," as if nothing existed beyond it. I look up and frown at the lack of stars, the question of their whereabouts and the oddity of it all just catching up to me. It's not right.

The beating of a drum, deep and near, interrupts my contemplation, and my goal resurfaces: I must join the party. Another drumbeat, then another. My brow furrows. I'm walking faster now.

The rhythmic drumming follows me up the rest of the driveway and soon, fear does as well. Have I been out too long? I soon find myself sprinting towards the front door, an inexplicable terror now present on the back of my neck, similar to . . . well, something I can't quite remember. The drumming is louder now, almost unbearable.

I reach the front door and am greeted by a large bronze lion. I grip the ring in the beast's mouth and strike it against the door's dark wood. The hairs on the back of my neck are stretching upwards in dread now. Something is behind me. I can feel it manifesting out of the empty black. *You have been out too long.* The sentence arrives in my head and I beat the bronze ring harder against the door in response, ignoring the question of the words' origin.

I move to strike the ring a third time but am stopped by a sound, an . . . organ. It has merged with the drums and I feel myself turn nauseated. *I took too long. I took too long!* I find myself turning—twisting towards the black when I see it: the game warden, a massive collection of limbs, meat, and teeth. I begin to scream.

Suddenly, the door opens. The drumming ceases. The organ dies. And I find the night's shape, the warden, gone.

"Sir," starts a voice. "Why don't you come inside?"

I turn to face the speaker, my previous horror now, somehow, as distant from me as the night's unseeable stars. In front of me, holding the door open, I find a bald and elderly man dressed in a suit and tie similar to my own. Behind him, a guest, drunk perhaps, stumbles away towards the party. I look back to the man in front of me.

"The butler, I presume?"

The man bows. "One of many, sir."

I nod and enter the house. I move to step past the butler but am stopped. I stare at the man with slight annoyance. He stares back.

"Your tie, sir."

I look down and find the tie to be fine. "You must be mistaken."

"Oh no, sir," says the butler as he shuts the door. "It's a mess, your shirt too, absolutely dreadful." With this, he grabs me by my forearm and guides me to a side door leading to a dark room. "You can clean up in here. I took the liberty of having another shirt prepared for you." With that, he flicks on a light, revealing a small bathroom.

"Is this really necessary?" I ask.

"Absolutely, sir. A loose tie and a cheap shirt simply won't do here," the butler says as he begins to walk away, confident in my future compliance. "And one last thing, sir."

"Yes?"

"Best of luck."

Somehow, I know what he means, and yet . . . I don't. Before I can address this, the butler has disappeared around the hallway's corner. Familiarity washes over me at the sight, along with the tiniest ounce of dread. This has happened before.

BOOM. BOOM. BOOM.

The drums echo in the distance. I enter the bathroom and shut the door, quickly resigning myself to the man's requested task. I carefully remove my jacket and tie before stripping off my "dreadful" shirt. As I do, something catches my eye in the mirror, a message written on my bare chest. "Find the King's mask. Check pocket." Obediently, I search my pants. Nothing. I search my suit pockets and am greeted with the same. I lean against the door, agitated. *I don't have time for this.*

Suddenly, I remember the butler's new shirt. I grope for it instinctively, then reach inside the front pocket. I find a scrap of notebook paper. Opening it up, I am met with another message. "Avoid the King's gaze. Evade the wolf. Don't trust his lies."

Despite its length, I read the note over and over again. Somehow, it's hard to remember—unnaturally difficult. I read it out loud, saying each word as carefully as possible. I shut my eyes, crumpling the note as I visualize the words in my head. Confident, I toss the note in the toilet and flush. I *will* remember.

I exit the bathroom and follow the party's music back to the foyer. Entering the main hallway, I spy my butler hastily leading a woman down the opposite hall. Actually, it is he who is being led. The butler looks back at me, and I expect a grin but am met with . . . pleading? The woman catches the exchange and follows its line of sight back to me. She waves, then smiles. I wave back. The woman—more a girl, really—is young, younger than anyone should be in this place. Looking at her now, I notice her dress' color: a terrible and faded yellow. I try to look away, but it commandeers my vision. My legs totter, and for a second—one terrible second—I see what I can only describe as a face *in* it. It is vast. It is hateful. It is both old and new like the house it inhabits. And it is watching me. I feel a chill caress my spine, while a new dryness occupies my throat.

The butler attempts to wave, join the woman's and my ritualistic greeting, but his hand is stopped by the woman, who proceeds to wrap the butler in her arms. He protests but is silenced as the woman's now abnormally large mouth presses itself against his in a kiss. I move—to do what, I'm not sure.

BOOM!

I jerk back at the sound, heat instantly enveloping me. It comes again.

BOOM!

My head whips towards the source—the front door. I back away.

"Coming!" says another butler, bounding past me as he hurries for the door. I turn back to the hallway but find the previous butler and woman gone. *You have been away too long.* I turn around and clumsily walk towards the ballroom. I must join the party. I will find the King's mask. I will avoid his gaze. I will evade the wolf. I will not trust his lies. The door behind me opens and the second butler speaks again.

"Sir. Why don't you come inside?"

The ballroom is large, larger than what I thought possible of the ancient house. Red curtains, like those of a theater, lay draped in front of and across the walls, circling the room and its countless inhabitants. Almost everything is red, the hexagonal carpet the most noticeable after the curtains, the grandest of which lurk behind the ballroom's raised stage. Draped over this platform is a wrinkled, vinyl banner reading welcome back. Despite the creases, it is beautiful, and yet I feel my skin crawl at its sight. My mind insists it's only a banner—synthetic plastic and metal grommets—but deep within me, deeper than I thought possible, I know it is more.

I ignore the sign and step into the spectacle ahead, yet I feel the banner stay with me, *feel* its eyes follow me. The sensation lessens as I disappear into the room's sea of red, a blot of black now among many. Guests, servers, and those beyond classification, busily move in and out of view. Suddenly, a tray with brandy is presented to me, and it's at this time that I notice the masks, my server disguised as a cat and the woman next to him as a duck. I scan the ballroom and find even more masks, mainly those of animals, adorning each and every face in the room.

"Would you care for one, sir?" asks the cat. "A mask, I mean."

I nod. "One in particular, actually."

"Oh?" asks the cat.

"Why yes," I respond, leaning in closely while I do. "The King's," I add with a whisper.

The cat pushes me away and straightens, as if suddenly prodded. "I'm . . . afraid I don't know what you mean, sir."

"I think you do."

The cat looks around, eyeing the few guests now observing us. "You can think whatever you like, sir."

"Have you seen the King? This is his party, isn't it?"

The cat snickers, nearly dropping his tray of brandy. "You really don't know, do you?"

I glare. The cat chuckles even more. I will need to be more discerning.

"Fine," I say—taking a glass of brandy as I do. "How about that mask?"

The cat motions to a table behind me with his free hand. "You'll have to see them about that, sir."

I lift my glass, "Cheers then," and walk towards the table, sipping brandy as I do.

The walk to the table takes less than a minute, less than thirty seconds even, but I feel myself aged by the time I arrive, as if returning home from the end of a long expedition. I rub my face dismissively, but the feeling persists. My vision swirls. My footing wavers. My breath quickens. *The brandy?* I eye it suspiciously, turning the glass back and forth in my hand as I fight the increasing urge to collapse.

"Are you all right, sir?" asks a woman.

I turn and look down at her. She is, along with another woman, wearing a fox mask and sitting at what looks to be some sort of station.

"A bit . . . dizzy," I admit.

"You've been away too long," says the fox knowingly as she hands me a mask. "This should make you feel better."

I set my brandy down and grip the mask. I expect cheap plastic, but the disguise proves superior. It's made of wood and in some parts, iron. I flip the mask and study its face—my face, which resembles that of a lamb. Donning the mask, I feel the senses return to normal. My vision steadies. My footing settles. My breath lessens. It is time to join the party.

As if reading my thoughts, the fox hands me a name tag with what, I suspect, is my name. "Enjoy the party, Peter."

I sound the words out in my head as I carefully peel my name free from its sticky captor. "PETER."

Both foxes nod in unison. Retrieving my brandy, I return the nod, then turn and face the center of the room: the heart of the old house. I have joined the party. Stepping forward, I disappear into the waves of beasts, combing over all I know as I do: find the King's mask. Avoid his gaze. Evade the wolf. Don't trust his lies.

The party is as vast as the starless sky, an achievement ignorant to even the greatest rulers of their times. Images, sounds, and acts, those decent and those not, spill in and out of view, as if they existed to permeate my vision and mine alone. The room is drunk with life, and yet . . . I feel the touch of death. Illustrating this is a table full of animals, some masked and some not.

"Show us! Show us!" one cries.

"We're starving!" shouts another.

A chef, almost reluctantly, reveals the table's main course. I gag, while the beasts cheer, laugh, and dance as yellow matter custard drips from a dead dog's eye. They dig in, while I continue on.

Placing my empty brandy down on a server's tray, I once again feel familiarity wash over me, not at the aforementioned action but the music accompanying it: a symphonic fairy tale. Brass. Percussion. Strings. Woodwinds. They . . . are telling a story and somehow, and I'm a part of it. Turning, I spy the stage and take a moment to listen to the now dominant strings. It is beautiful and timeless. The entire orchestra is dressed in egg white suits and dresses, along with blank oval masks. The exception to this is the conductor, who sports a walrus mask. He waves his arms with practiced ease, and the melodic light of violins, violas, cellos, and double basses rises vibrantly above and out of the stage. I continue on.

I search the crowd for any sign of the King but find none. There is far too much to see, too much to absorb. Stories, feelings, thoughts, smells—every imaginable thing is in attendance and *in* those who attend. Together, it culminates in what I can only describe as a "loudness," one that stretches beyond mere sound. Stranger even, is its scope. Times, my own and those behind and ahead of me, linger here. So many memories. So much time. So many . . . screams. I continue on.

Eventually, I find myself in the back of the old house, outside overlooking a great garden. Lovers, those true and those not, stand coupled below and around the balcony's several heaters. I approach an empty one and procure my pipe and tobacco. I then search for matches but find none.

"Light?" asks a voice.

I turn and meet the stranger, a woman dressed in a feathery peignoir and bird mask. "Thank you," I answer.

The bird lights a match. I lift my mask and lean in, cupping my free hand around her flame. Smoke fills then exits my lungs. I look up and am reminded of the starless sky. I sigh. *Where is this damn king?*

"Say . . ." says the woman. "I do believe I know you."

"How so?" I ask.

"I suspect we met last year, somewhere similar . . . the gardens at Frederiksbad?"

"I've never been to Frederiksbad."

"Well, then perhaps it was somewhere else, maybe . . . at Marienbad or at Carcosa—or even here, at this very party!"

"Impossible. I just arrived."

"Well, yes, but as I'm sure you've noticed by now, time has a way . . . misbehaving here."

I consider the statement, soak it in like a sponge. The woman's words simultaneously astound and resonate. This house. This place. This "loudness." All so strange to me. I remember everything and yet I remember nothing, my mind caught in a tidal pool of unfamiliar but *understood* residue. Perhaps I know this woman. Perhaps I don't. Perhaps she could be of some help. Perhaps . . . she's the wolf?

The woman stares at me expectantly. I look away, searching for a response amidst the dying glow of my pipe's dottle. Saving me from action are the hurried steps and startled gasps of fellow partygoers.

BOOM! BOOM!

Frantic, I turn to re-enter the house but am stopped by my newfound acquaintance.

"Don't fret, darling," she says, lacking the earnestness of her previous verbal offerings. "I don't believe those are for us."

The woman motions over to the balcony. I approach the railing, joining the gathering of my captivated partygoers as an organ drones somewhere in the dark. I see nothing at first, my eyes ignorant to the night's offerings, then . . . I see it.

A man and woman, both unmasked, are running through the garden, away from the old house. The woman has forgone her shoes, the man his jacket. The drumming is louder now, and the evening's previous dread has returned. I want to look away—retreat back in the house—but my eyes are glued to the man and woman. They continue to run. Something great and terrible follows.

"The warden . . ." the woman says bitterly. She spits over the railing. A few other guests do the same. "You familiar?" she asks.

"Met him on the way in," I say.

Her brow furrows. "Darling, that's not a *he*."

I face the darkness. The man and woman are gone now, nearly nonexistent in the deep black. All that's left, it seems, is a remnant of their screams.

It's nearly midnight, and the guests are buzzing with anticipation. The woman I met outside, whose name I come to learn is "Delphine," joins me on my search through the party. Arm in arm, we walk the bordered grounds of what I soon learn is a château. After what we saw on the balcony, we're careful not to stray from the marked path. Delphine assures me we are safe. I remain afraid.

The grounds of the château are symmetrically arranged, full of trees and plants of every kind, while the gravel, the stone, and marble, are spread in a strict array of mysterious shapes. Somehow, throughout it all, the walrus' symphony is still audible. We continue to walk, passing small to medium gatherings of fellow guests, and yet, like before, I find no trace of the King. With a frustrated sigh, I stop and strike one of the nearby hedge animals, grunting incoherently as I do.

"Darling, what ever is the matter?" asks Delphine, only slightly alarmed.

I adjust my jacket. "Nothing, nothing . . ."

"One does not strike topiary over nothing, darling."

I consider the statement, fully aware, somehow, that my time this night is running out. "Fine," I relent. "I'm . . . looking for someone."

"Well, why ever didn't you say anything, darling? Perhaps I can be of assistance!"

"Perhaps."

"Well then, spit it out, silly."

"I'm . . . looking for the King."

"Heavens!" shudders Delphine. "Why on earth would you want to find *him*?"

"Is this not his party?"

Delphine shakes her head. "Perhaps at some point it was, but no longer."

"What does that mean?"

"It's . . . hard to remember," she says, stroking her head as she does. "So much time has passed, darling. So many nights—just like this one—swimming in my head. I do admit, it's hard to keep them all straight."

"What of a mask? Does that ring any bells?" I ask.

Suddenly, the strings of the walrus' symphony are replaced with three terrible French horns.

DUUUUN! DUUUUN! DUUUUN!

The sound is impossibly close. Delphine jumps, then laughs. "My—that startled me! What a horrid sound."

Movement catches my eye, and I spy a shape moving towards Delphine and me from out of the garden's darkness. It gains clarity, and soon a man with long hair—no, a man with a . . . strange mask—comes into view. Sweat stains my shirt. My breath quickens. The horns blare. The wolf, it appears, has arrived.

He glides towards us, his snout and teeth disappearing—then reappearing from the darkness as he passes under lights strung over and around the garden. *Evade the wolf. Don't trust his lies.* I need to move, run—something—but my legs betray the thought. The wolf draws closer. Simultaneously, guests laugh and hurriedly scuttle past Delphine and me.

"We mustn't miss it!" exclaims one.

"How could we?" asks a second. "The whole sky is *his* canvas!"

As if on cue, the particular hissing and popping of fireworks drowns out the guests' pleased cries as dandelion splotches of color decorate the starless night.

The wolf continues towards us.

"It's midnight!" announces one guest.

"Unmask! Unmask!" declares another.

All around, masks and veils are thrown in the air, briefly joining the fireworks in the otherwise black sky.

Delphine nudges me. "Unmask!" she commands in a playful yet serious tone.

I oblige, following her lead. Our masks fall to the ground with decisive *cracks*.

"Evening," says the wolf, stepping on Delphine's mask as he does so.

Evade the wolf. Don't trust his lies.

I clench my fists and clear my arid throat. "What do—"

"You, sir, should unmask," interrupts Delphine, with an ecstasy-filled giggle.

"Indeed?" asks the wolf.

"Indeed, it's time. We have all laid aside disguise but you."

The wolf laughs. "I wear no mask."

Delphine laughs too. "Charming," she adds, while reaching for the wolf's face. I laugh as well, eased by Delphine's confidence, along with, much to my shock, the wolf's presence. There's a comfort to him. He . . . seems familiar, safe even.

Suddenly, Delphine recoils from the man—terrified. "No . . . mask? No mask!" she screams.

Before I can do or say anything, Delphine is gone, retreating in the black. A few guests, those no longer enraptured with the night's fireworks, look over and join her screams. "No mask!" they cry. The wolf grins before abruptly snarling in their direction. The sound hits me like a train, yet I am again—inexplicably—not afraid. The guests jump back, gasping and tripping as they flee, disappearing from our sight. Only the wolf and I remain in the night.

He turns back to me, squints his yellow eyes curiously. "Why didn't you run, old sport? Not afraid?"

"No," I say, surprised at the response. "Strangely enough, wolf . . . I'm not."

"Good," he says with a smile. "We're making progress then."

"I was told not to trust you," I admit, against my better judgment.

"Yes . . . by the help, I know."

"How did—"

The wolf waves his hands dismissively. "I don't believe this will come as a surprise, old sport, but we've been through this before. The hidden note from the butler, or the King—I can't keep track these days—is a newer addition but not one I'm unfamiliar with. It stands to reason the more we adapt, the more the bastards will do the same."

"Who—"

"Listen, I don't mean to be rude, but we've had this conversation hundreds, if not thousands, of times. We can talk on the way. Agreed?"

"Where . . . are we going?" I say, following as the wolf begins to walk.

The wolf turns, looking over his shoulder, a wild shimmer in his eyes. Fireworks crackle in the distance. "We're going to take the King's mask, old sport! And, if we're lucky," he pauses, then adds, "Burn this blasted place to the ground."

It is hard to keep pace with the wolf. He moves through the party with knowing ease, side-stepping servers, guests, and the now plentiful drunks, with grace and speed—as if every movement was rehearsed with meticulous precision. I follow clumsily, waves of déjà vu cracking through my skull following every bumped shoulder, spilled brandy, and mashed toe.

Soon, we arrive in the kitchen. Besides the sea of dirty dishes and unserved food, it is empty.

"*This* is where the mask is?" I ask skeptically.

"No, old sport." The wolf snorts. "*This* is just a pit stop." With that, he mounts a nearby stool and begins to unscrew an air vent cover with one of his claws.

"You're . . . an actual wolf," I gawk, starting the sentence as if asking a question, then ending with a statement.

"For now," the wolf grunts, handing me a long duffel bag. "We'll see how long that lasts."

I think to inquire but am stopped by the bag's contents: weapons.

"Pick your poison," the wolf says, stepping down from the stool.

Without hesitation, I grab a hammer and pistol.

"Huh . . ." the wolf says.

"What?"

"That's . . . the first time you've done that."

I shrug. The wolf grins. We continue on.

Gasoline swishes back and forth in a rubber container as the wolf and I ascend three stories of stairs. Arriving at the top of the house, we are met with a long hallway, impossible in length given the size of the house. I stand transfixed, overwhelmed by the sight. The walrus' symphony is gone. Only that damn dread remains. The wolf turns to me and speaks, bringing me back.

"Okay, listen here," he says pointing at the hallway. "Somewhere down there is 'the Pallid Mask,' or, 'the King's mask' as you keep calling it. It's behind one of those doors. The house switches up *which* exact one every time, but I've gotten pretty good at anticipating its patterns. I think I've narrowed it down to one or two."

"It's about to get bad, isn't it?" I ask.

"Yes," the wolf sighs. "They'll be on us as soon as the house feels the gas. We'll have to deal with her pawns, maybe agents of the King too, and, if we're truly unlucky, the warden."

"They're not all the same?"

"No," the wolf answers, setting his gas can down on the hallway's crimson carpet. "Unfortunately, you are caught up in something much bigger and older than any man should be, old sport. This is a conflict between the house, the king, and . . . yours truly. I'm afraid I'm the one who started all this unfortunate business. Can you believe it? *Me!* If I had known . . ." the wolf trails off, a slight tremor catching in his throat. "I'd go on, but then again, old sport, I . . . already have." He sets a paw on my shoulder. "You ready?"

"I don't imagine I am."

The wolf nods. "Indeed."

I unscrew the cap to the gas can and begin to empty it, feverishly splashing it across the carpet as I walk backwards in unison with the wolf. He starts on a yellow door with an axe procured from his bag. Dropping the can, I proceed to light the trail of gas. Flames race away from me, zigzagging madly as they consume the floor. I feel the air change, feel my body ready itself for horror.

BOOM! BOOM! BOOM!

"Here we go, old sport!" the wolf announces.

Drums, rushed footsteps, crazed shouting, cursing—screaming. The nightmares, it would appear, are here.

I see the cat first—the server from earlier—madly sprinting at me through the flames. I raise my pistol.

"Save the bullet!" the wolf shouts, huffing as he brings his axe down on the yellow door. "Only shoot when you have to!"

I holster the pistol and, in its stead, brandish the hammer. The cat leaps out of the fire, falling hard on his face after an awkward landing. He squirms and swats at the flames engulfing his body. I raise my hammer and brain him. Hot blood, darker than I've ever seen, sprays me in the face. I hit the cat again.

Crunch!

I look over my shoulder and see a medium sized hole in the wolf's door.

"Nearly there!"

More footsteps. I turn and spy three men with Dalmatian masks rushing through the flames.

"You're gonna die!" one shouts.

I club the head of the first to exit the fire and puncture the neck of the second with my hammer's claw. Blood showers my eyes, blinding me. Regardless, I extract my hammer from the dog's neck and continue swinging. The third Dalmatian seizes his chance, catching me off balance and tackling me to the ground. We fall partly into the hallway's flames. The Dalmatian wraps his gloved hands around my neck, muffling my burning-induced cries.

"You won't ruin this!" he screeches.

Thwump!

The Dalmatian spasms, then stiffens as drool—and blood—exits his mouth. I push the corpse off and find the wolf standing above me, boasting his axe.

"Okay?" he asks, offering a paw.

I take it, grimacing as I stand. Together, we hastily pat away my body's lingering flames.

"You close?" I ask, studying the hallway's growing blaze.

"We're in," the wolf responds, pushing aside the splintered door in front of him.

We enter the room, a small chapel made up of pews, lanterns, and paintings—all of which depict one aspect or another of the house. At the end is one giant and superbly clear window. In front of this sits a pedestal displaying a white and unassuming mask.

"That it?" I ask.

"Oh . . . yes. Yes!" exclaims the wolf, darting forward towards the stand.

Almost immediately, the grand window shatters in a violent explosion of glass. The wolf falls back, howling in pain. An organ groans louder, drowning him out. I gawk, trembling in terror as a collection of limbs and hair shimmies its way through the broken window, the ground crunching and cracking as a multitude of jumbled flesh darts its way over the broken glass.

"Bloody hell!" cries the wolf, scrambling back over to me, his face littered with blood and glass.

I stare, my mouth agape as the monstrosity—the warden—positions itself in front of the mask. It's at this particular image, this particular horror, that I *remember*. The king. The awakened house. The stolen mask. The thieving wolf. The resulting war. The endlessness that ravaged a city. I remember it all.

"We ever beat this thing?" I ask, turning to my newest, and

oldest, friend.

The wolf laughs, a mad and crazed laugh. "Not ever, old sport!"

"Well," I start, while raising my pistol, "there's a first time for everything."

Gripping his axe, the wolf stands, a joyful look of recognition in his eyes. He pauses before adding, "It's good to have you back, Peter."

I nod. And with that, I fire a pistol for the first, and what I pray will be the last, time.

THE MIDDLE

by Elaine Pascale

S EE WHERE THOSE BOATS ARE? You want to hug the coast over there. Don't go toward the middle, just keep hugging the coast." The man at the rental shack winked as he pocketed their signed waivers. "Legend is people don't come back from the middle."

"Is there an undertow?" Kara asked as she grabbed a paddle from the rack.

The man squinted and looked to the area he had just been mentioning. "Nope. Nothing like that."

Brett mumbled to his wife as they were strapping the paddle board leashes to their ankles, "He's just trying to scare us away from the best spots. Probably the best fishing or something. That's what the locals do to tourists."

"We aren't fishing."

"Doesn't matter. They want to keep the best stuff for themselves."

Kara picked up her board and moved to the opening. "I suggest we listen to him. I had that feeling, remember? And then that dream."

Brett hoisted his board and followed her. "I refuse to check under the bed for any of those monsters you dream about."

"I never make you check." Her eyes turned angry, and he could see her revisiting the times that she had needed him and he had disappointed her.

"Not that I would mind checking," he added sheepishly.

He saw her shiver, despite the warmth of the water she had walked into. "It had felt so real though. And that growl . . . I could still hear it after I woke up."

"I understand that it upset you, honey," he said, using words he had recently been trained to use. "Let's try to enjoy our day, though." He walked a few steps past her before getting on his board. He had always liked to lead their trips. He was stronger and if they stumbled upon a rip tide or other misfortune, he believed he would be able to work his way out of it and warn her, if not rescue her. Until recently, he had believed that as long as he was in charge, everything would be okay. Despite the hits that that belief had taken, he still wanted to be the one to test the waters first. As her husband, it was the least he could do.

"Hug the shore," she called.

He nodded and waved for her to follow.

The day was warm, and the water was like glass. Brett and Kara were able to skate along at a speed and ease they rarely experienced.

"This is paradise," Brett mumbled, almost afraid to say it out loud. Kara interpreted her dreams religiously, and he had developed compulsive beliefs of his own. Kara had heard a monster in her dreams; he saw monsters behind every promise.

A boat zigzagged along the channel, trying to either throw off or excite the people laying on the large tube that had been tethered to the back. The boat driver was behaving recklessly, and Brett knew a thing or two about bad choices.

Kara called up to him to *stand down.* She was referring to his temper, which had gotten them in trouble before. She had also made him promise that they would have a good day. His transgression was never completely behind them, but they could smile and laugh and try to act as if they hadn't a care in the world.

He had promised her a good day; it had been the least he

could do. Even though he knew what was behind every promise.

You love me, don't you?

He had truly thought he loved Tonya. He had convinced himself that his unhappiness had been Kara's fault. He had convinced himself that she had needed too much from him, too much *of* him. With Tonya, it had been easy. Excitement and passion. Even though it had been very brief, even though it had destroyed his life.

"Let me know if you want to stop and drift for a bit. Or need some water," he called back to Kara.

He had always taken care of Kara. When they had unexpectedly become parents, he had taken care of all of them. He had blamed Kara for the pregnancy, even though they had both been equally surprised. She had been on birth control, and it had always worked. Yet, he felt like she had trapped him. Their friends had been settling down and getting married and starting families, and he had believed she had manipulated him.

He had gone along with everything to a point: the wedding, the new house, the family life. Eventually the lack of control had gotten to him. It had taken some time, and some therapy, but he had learned to accept accountability. He had made a mistake. He had been selfish. And it had cost him. Financially he had taken a huge loss. He had paid for the scam, and for individual and couple's therapy. It had cost him personally and professionally. It would be inaccurate to say that Kara's family had disowned her for his transgressions, but they had stopped visiting. They no longer called her or included her in events, if it meant that he was part of the package. It was also inaccurate to say he had lost his job, but it had become impossible to work at a place where so many people could no longer look him in the eye because of what they had seen.

"Honey?" Kara's voice had a nervous tone. "Something feels off about my board."

"Do you need to stop?"

"I think so."

They moved closer to the mangroves and sat down on the boards. Brett thought that he was wearing his best poker face, but Kara was sensing something different. When he asked if she were holding the paddle correctly, she became angry. "Of course I am and it's not the paddle, it's the board. I know what it's supposed to feel like, and this feels wrong. Please don't act as if I am some newbie or can't handle the board." She had been the one to introduce him to paddleboarding, but somewhere along the line he had taken the role of leader. "There is a drag. It's almost as if something is pulling it from beneath, hanging on, and weighing it down."

"Let me see." Brett lowered himself into the water and waded to Kara's board. As he was feeling around underneath, something caught—like a fishing line. The boat with the tubers being towed made another pass. They were dangerously close this time, and Brett could see the bodies on the tube belonged to young kids. They looked like siblings: a sister and brother. Both were laughing raucously as the wake nearly shook them loose.

The wake also rocked Brett and Kara; Brett ended up with a mouthful of water. "They are going to get someone killed," he said after he finished coughing.

"There always has to be at least one asshole," Kara agreed.

Brett pointed to the other side of the channel. "There's no one over there. And look at how the water is so still. There's no current."

She shook her head, the extended brim of her hat punctuating the motion. "We can't cross over. That man said—"

"—We can go fast. Really book it through the middle."

"Brett, listen to me." She had been saying that a lot lately. Like when she had protested moving back in with his parents as a means to attack the debt they had accrued. Like when she had pleaded with him to ignore the company that had promised to recover both the video and the "stolen" money. Kara had said it was too late, she had already seen the video and that was all that mattered. She had smelled another scam.

He hadn't listened to any of those petitions, but he would

listen this time. It was the least he could do.

It had started as a friendly flirtation. He and Tonya seemed to share mutual friends from his pre-Kara life, from his life of freedom. He couldn't remember her, but that was not unusual. It had been a long time. The pictures she had sent hadn't jogged his memory, but they had stirred a different type of response. She was pretty and fit and the type of girl that he used to date. The type of girl who could afford to have fun because she wasn't tied down with a child. Tonya could stay up all night talking and texting, she could send him racy photos while he was at work. She found him interesting and funny. She told him he was handsome. She just wanted to listen to him; she just wanted to make him happy.

While they never could figure out how to meet in person, she started to request more private moments online. It began with talk and verbal affirmations of feelings. Then newer levels of intimacy developed.

"I know we can't be together the way I want, but I *need* you, baby," she had said on Facetime. He had liked that she needed him in the way he wanted to be needed. This wasn't the business exchange that his relationship with Kara had devolved to. This was hot and sexy.

Kara and baby Cam had been sleeping upstairs while he talked to Tonya in their basement. He had locked the door and had the night to himself. He was ready for this, and he had told himself that if he wasn't touching another woman, he wasn't really cheating. Tonya had sent him pictures in the past, but her camera usually did not work when they talked. That was okay with him as he could hear her responses to him. Her moans excited him. She wanted to watch him, she *needed* to watch him. She promised she would get the camera fixed so that the next time, he would be able to watch her, too.

But the next time hadn't been sexy. It had been a demand for payment. Then a demand for even more payment, which triggered the video to be released to those he wanted to see it the least.

This was followed by the recovery scam; the promise to make it all go away.

The monster behind that promise had been the same monster who had called itself "Tonya." Tonya had been as real as Kara's nightmares. And just as frightening.

The sun had become unforgiving. The boats were keeping to the shallows and rocking the couple with waves so that standing on the board became an acrobatic feat.

Brett felt his paddle knocking against the compact sand on the floor of the ocean. "The tide is really dropping out on us."

"The boats are making it through. Can't be too shallow."

"Should we head back?" He looked over his shoulder to see her frown. "That's okay, we can keep going. I just don't think it's going to work here. It's a struggle when it's this shallow. I think it's deeper there." He pointed to the center.

"Brett, that man said not to go there."

He tried a different tactic. "I bet we see dolphins or at least big fish out there."

"Brett . . ."

He was growing tired of hearing her repeated argument, but therapy had taught him to listen. It had also taught him to realize that his wants were not always of primary importance and that his perception was sometimes off.

"I still feel that tug," she said. "It's so weird. It's not the current. It's pulling in the *opposite* direction of the current."

"Do you want to stop again?"

"No. I want to have a good day." She laughed. "That is still possible, isn't it?"

He turned and smiled at her. She looked young and happy on the board, the way she had looked when they had been dating. The worry lines on her face were no longer visible, and he couldn't help but take in the curves her bathing suit made noticeable.

"Anything is possible," he replied. He winked, forgetting she wouldn't see it through his sunglasses.

"Let's keep going," she said. "I think the workout will do us both some good."

"Your wish is my command," he said, and he meant it. Giving her a happy day was the least he could do.

Despite the waves from the boats rocking his board, Brett had been able to peer over his shoulder to check on Kara periodically. She had been wearing a bright pink shirt with a graphic of a dolphin that looked like it was composed of stained glass. She also had the extended brim hat that made her easy to spot, even peripherally.

He could no longer see her.

They had always stayed close together. That way if one of them needed help, the other could respond quickly.

"Kara?" He nearly fell from the board as he twisted in both directions, trying to spot her.

"Brett!" He could hear her but was unable to see her, which was impossible given that he could see both ends of the channel. There were no bends; it was a straight shot.

"Brett!" He heard again. This time he saw her. She was in the middle.

"Why did you go to the middle?" she asked when he got close enough to hear her.

". . . Kara, *you* are the one who came out here."

"What?" She looked around and realized what he was saying was true.

"I couldn't see you . . . it was like you disappeared—" Her eyes were frantic. "—I saw you. You were rowing to the middle, aiming directly for it."

"Honey, I promise you . . . I said I wouldn't, that I would listen to you and to that man earlier, and I did. I listened. You were the one who came out here."

"But I was hugging the shore, and it looked like you—"

Brett realized that they were getting nowhere with this blame game. "It doesn't matter. Let's get back to the shoreline. Do you need to take a break?"

Kara shook her head. She looked both sad and confused. The way she had looked after opening the video that had been texted to her.

"How do you want to go . . . ? Do you want to tether to my board, and we can go together?" Brett knew he should take care of her, but he wasn't sure how.

"I can do it. I can manage."

"Wait." He pulled up closer to her board and again put his hand beneath. "Your fin is missing."

"I locked it in."

"That's why you are struggling."

She stood on her board, nearly knocking him off his. *"I locked it in."*

He shrugged. "No big deal, we will pay for it."

"That's how we handle everything," she said, pushing ahead of him and not looking back.

By the movement of the sun, it was evident they had been paddling for close to an hour, yet they were no nearer to the shore. They stopped for a wordless drink, then stood to reattempt progress. Brett tried to move his paddle, but it was stuck fast into the muddy sand below.

"What's wrong?" Kara asked, gazing into the shallow water.

"I'm stuck."

She had been balancing her paddle on her board and lowered it into the water so she could move beside him. It immediately sank as if something below the surface were tugging it from her hands.

"Brett?"

"Can you lift it back up?"

"Barely." She squatted and tugged, nearly toppling onto her back to free the paddle.

"What do we do? We can't paddle out of here." She squinted toward the shore which somehow looked farther away.

"I am going to wave to those boats. Maybe they can tug us

behind or something. Or radio for help." He removed his shirt and began to wave it like a flag.

The boats were so close that Brett could hear the music on their consoles, could see the type of soft drinks the passengers were drinking, yet the boat people did not seem to notice him, Kara, or their distress.

"How can they not see the shirt? Or us?" Kara plopped down onto the board and rubbed her forehead. She dangled her feet over the side, and the water reached to her knees.

"Why is the water deeper where you are?" Brett pointed and she looked down, confused.

"It's not, though."

"It's *deeper.*"

She shook her head sadly. "No. My feet are sinking in. I am just too tired to pull them out."

He wanted to cry with frustration. "Honey, pull up your feet. You have to. Keep them on the board where I can see them."

Kara used both hands to tug each leg free. Her board became brown with the thick rivulets of sludge that accompanied her feet when she pulled them aloft.

The boat with kids on a tube was making another approach. He and Kara began to yell. Brett shook his shirt again, and Kara waved her extra-large hat. As the boat turned, it appeared that the small boy was looking directly at them, but he did not respond to their signals.

After finishing the final drops of water from their bottles and feeling as if their skin was going to burn off their bones, the couple lay down on their boards.

"I am remembering more of that dream now," she whispered. Her throat was dry, her lips chapped.

He was close enough that he reached over and touched her arm, and she was tired enough to let him. "How are you feeling? Are you feeling dizzy at all? We are both in danger of dehydration, so let's be careful and conserve our energy."

"It's pitch black."

"The sun is shining, honey."

"No, not here, not on the surface. Below."

Talking about her dream was not getting them any closer to safety. The boats were waning in number. Brett assumed everyone was heading home for dinner. That idea had never been more appealing than it was now.

"It tried to drag me under."

"It?"

She nodded. She had that thousand-yard stare, as if she were looking at the dream again instead of her actual environment. "It was a living shadow. It came out of the calm sea with a huge head and many arms with large hands. It looks like that cloud up there."

Brett looked where she pointed and saw nothing but blue sky.

"It wanted something from us. A sacrifice."

In therapy, they had discussed their opposing ideas about sacrifice. He was no psychiatrist, but he was sure that conflict was the source of the dream.

"It was just a dream, honey."

"I had dreams about you. I knew what you did before I saw the video."

He couldn't argue with that. She did receive premonitions in dreams, and unfortunately his transgression had been one of them.

"The worst part was you were willing to give Cam to the shadow."

His stomach sank. He believed he would never regain her trust. He wasn't sure he deserved it. "I would never do that."

She looked at him above her sunglasses, her vision now focused. "I know." She forced a smile. "Let's just rest and try again in a few minutes."

It was hard to tell if it were a few minutes or an hour later when Brett stood in the shallow water, grabbing his board and the handle on hers. "You rest. I will pull us to the shore."

She sat up quickly. "You can't pull me; you will give yourself a heart attack trying to work against that sand."

Brett knew she was right, but as her husband it was the least he could do.

He took a deep breath before attempting the first step. The sand vacuumed his feet. It felt as if each grain were alive and attempting to drag him under. He grunted as he pulled his left foot free and pushed it forward. The water shoes he had been wearing were sacrificed, and his bare feet met with shells and other sharp objects as he tried to walk. He knew that in the original *Little Mermaid* story, the transformation from swimming to walking was like walking on knives. This was like walking on knives within drying concrete that had been doused with Sriracha. He had no choice, he had to get them to safety. He repeated this action multiple times, which should have brought him closer to shore, but the promise of his steps was unfulfilled.

Then they heard it: a low growl coming from beneath the sand.

"Brett?" Kara whispered. "That was what he sounded like, the shadow from my dream."

"It could be anything," he suggested, not knowing a logical, optimistic source of the growl off the top of his head. He was drenched with sweat, yet he continued to pull up one foot, followed by the other. The feeling of walking on knives intensified; it was now a bed of hot coals.

The sand was soon covering his calves.

"We won't see him again, will we?" Her voice was an octave above normal. "Cam, I mean. We won't see him again."

He turned to look at her. "We will be fine, Kara."

"No . . . no . . . we won't see *him* again." She was crying but no tears fell; she was too dehydrated.

"It will be all right." He leaned toward her board and put a hand on her shoulder.

"You can't say that. You can't promise that."

The growl was louder this time and directly beneath them.

"Kara, I promise you that you will get out of this." Now that a real monster was in front of him, he no longer feared the monsters of promises. And he would make sure Kara was safe, he had to.

Something grabbed his ankle. Multiple fingers wrapped around him. He could feel individual fingers through the water and the sand. The fingers tightened like a brace. A weight on his feet made it more difficult to move.

He remembered what she had said about the dream. The shadow wanted a sacrifice.

"Climb on me. I am going to throw you into that deep water. Start swimming."

She looked panicked. "I don't want to leave you."

"We don't have a choice. Promise me you'll swim?" The hands were beginning to crawl up his calves. His hand tightened on her shoulder.

She shook her head. "I can't."

"You can, honey. Look at me; look at me." His voice broke through the spell she was under and forced her to make eye contact. She was quivering, but he could tell she was listening. "You are the better swimmer, you know that. And"—he had to swallow to get out the words—"you are the better parent. You have to make it. Promise me. While I give it what it wants, you will swim as fast and as hard as you can. Promise me."

"Brett." She threw her arms around him and kissed his lips, his cheeks, his forehead. The pull on his legs was growing stronger, and he didn't know how much longer he could resist slipping beneath the surface.

"Climb on my shoulders," he instructed. It took a few wobbly attempts before she was able to first kneel on his shoulders and then stand. "When I count to three, I am going to throw you as far as I can. Okay?"

"Yes," she said weakly, but he knew she would do as they had agreed. She had always been the one whose words and actions consistently matched.

"One . . . two . . ." He squatted and then pushed up on "three," launching Kara in an arc that was nearly perfect.

He was able to see her land with a hard smack on the water. She immediately began swimming with long, powerful strokes. He watched her until the hands managed to pull his body beneath the dense sand.

He accepted this with peace, as this was finally more than the least that he could do.

OKRA

by H. W. Taylor

Part One: The Dust

THE WHOLE LAND SEEMED TO crumble beneath his feet. The world was dry. Every step in his field rang hollow and cracked, plants as brittle as clods. Irving slung off his suspenders and fell to his knees, sending a false throne of dirt into the air.

The cotton was long dead and the corn was close. He bowed to form a triangle of shade over the wilted plant. It was slumped and sallow, the cob in its sheath no thicker than his finger. He tried to muster up some saliva to at least knock the dust off a leaf, maybe bless it with a taste of wet, but his tongue was a wizened nub. Working the back of his teeth, the parched stickiness made strange sounds. *Chlock.*

When he failed to churn up any spit, he raised his fist in anger. The sun continued to roll its endless wheel of heat over him and the entire land. The area was rutted deep with its blaze. The beaten and bleached out farm was folded over itself.

"Damn it all, anyway," he said. His voice too was a husk, a broken spiration. He stroked his mustache and then brought his fist down on the plant. He struck it flat and pounded it further, hearing it more than feeling it.

He made a divot in the dust and tried to stand. He pulled in a bone of air so thin it stung his throat and pricked his lungs. He stood slowly, his legs as spindly as the stalks around him.

He exited his fields and climbed wearily into the wagon. He snapped the reins of his old nag Abel. They rode up to the sign demarking his land, but Irving noticed that it had fallen over again. Sunstruck, no doubt. Abel paused as he slid down and picked up the post. EDEN FARMS, the etching read. The green paint had peeled away mere months after planting it, a faithful harbinger for his time at the edge of Eke, Oklahoma.

He held the sign in his hand and surveyed the cup of earth where it once stood. He couldn't bring himself to plant it again. He couldn't stand to have even this crop topple over. He snapped the plank over his knee. The wood smoked like it was giving up its ghost. He tossed the sign away, one last useless sowing.

Abel pulled them into town. The silence broken only by the sounds of dirt being crushed like skulls beneath them.

The other farmers laughed at the trading post. His two bags of okra seed, all that his farm had produced in the last year, weren't worth planting, much less trading. He also put up a jar of pears, preserved from when times were better. When his debts for the year were laid out, even the other farmers dropped their eyes to follow their shoes as they scraped the floor.

In the end, Roy, the shopkeep, let him have a week supply of beans and cleared his debt in exchange for his horse and wagon. He slid the pears back to Irving. "It'll help the beans go down," he said.

Free and clear, Irving thought. Free to go, clear to die.

As he trudged out, one of the farmers stopped him and opened the bag at his feet. From it he withdrew a container of salt and handed it to him. "For your beans, Irving."

Irving nodded his thanks but was unable to form a word. He didn't even have wet enough to get his eyes tearful, though his face was furrowed. He tucked it into his bag of beans, spun the top closed, and slung it over his shoulder.

"We'll all be out of luck by next summer, Irving," the farmer said. "Yer just getting a head start on us."

There was a doleful commiseration from the others.

"I got some corn," Irving offered.

The farmers nodded out of pity.

"Just need a bit of rain."

"Ain't no rain, Irving," Roy said sharply. The anger was directed at the rainless sky, but the tone still struck Irving like an open palm. He flinched and walked away.

Outside he examined the sky. It was a bone plate gnawed clean by the sun. Thicker clouds trailed his shuffling than crawled along the horizon. In the shade of the shop, he saw Harjo, an old Cherokee that trained horses. He was cocked back in a chair and picking his teeth with a knife. He saw Irving and beckoned him with a tilt of his head.

Irving drew near.

"It'll rain," Harjo said in his coarse baritone.

"You already in the drink today?"

Harjo shook his head and tried to hide the bottle on the ground with his boot. "It'll rain tonight." He laid back his head a little too harshly against the wall and winced.

Irving scanned the pale yawn of the sky again. "Yer drunker'n shit, Harjo. Here," he said as he withdrew the jar of pears. "Trade you these'n for the rest a that bottle."

Harjo eyed the jar and stood. Taking the fruit with one hand, he tipped his hat with the other and walked straight off with nary a stumble.

Irving watched him until he slipped off into the alley across the way. He bent down to pick up the bottle and found it almost full of deep brown liquid.

"If it rains tonight, I'll call you the prophet," he said to the departed Cherokee.

His ex-old horse nodded once and Irving gave him a rough salute and began his trek back to his dying farm. He reached into his bag and pulled out the container of salt. The container was blue with a picture of a little girl in a yellow dress. She was carrying an umbrella and smiling. *When it rains*, it read beneath the picture, *it pours.*

Irving sneered and launched it into the ditch. Salt the earth, for all he cared. Burn it all to hell. He'd eat his beans plain.

Part Two: The Green

The bottle hit the dust and the last swig cantilevered itself in the glass heel. Irving's cheek pressed a little bed into the dirt for his face and his fingers took root in the soil to keep it from rocking. He kept his eyes closed and breathed.

On the walk home he asked himself, *Why wait till the food runs out before dying?* The three-hour ride on Abel was a five-hour walk at least. So Irving decided that there was no use carrying a full bottle. He'd tossed the cork into the brush and drank.

The road stretched out, but the sun stretched further. By the time he arrived at dry Eden, the sun still had an hour left of shining. He finished the bottle in the center of his fields, skeletal stalks surrounding him. In the pink and purple of dusk, Irving had cried out in anguish and flung the bottle at heaven. He fell over and lay face down.

His urine was released through his pants and into the earth. He laughed, kicking up a small flurry of dust. Harjo was right, he thought as he sunk into the new made mud. It did rain after all.

The next thing he knew, Irving awoke in the cracking of the sky, a flash that ruptured the dark and seared his vision. Rain had caused his clothes to slump across the boney edge of his shoulders and cling to the curl of his ribs. He sat up in his muddy pool.

His field was sodden, corn stalks slapped and flattened by

wind and rain. He stood unsteadily in the howling storm and spun around amazed. The sky was torn open in fury, racked with bolts of light. The sound of thunder was like a knuckle against his ear.

Nausea coiled up inside him and sprung out like a whip cracked against the air. He buckled and added his own sick rain to the torrent around him. Again and again, he heaved, each time angling nearer to the ground. By the end of it, he was tamed and too weak to move. He rolled over and let the rain break over him.

His vision was slurry and slow, his eyelids flinching against the tapping rain. He couldn't help but smile as his crop was slogged to smithereens.

Suddenly a bolt of lightning hit the ground next to him. He nearly jumped out of the slop he was in. A second struck on the other side and his fear caused him to roll and squeal. He was not conscious of a third bolt, merely the crack of air, a faint memory of fire along his spine, and a long black tunnel that swallowed him.

As his eyesight returned, Irving realized that he couldn't move. His body was rattling in pain, like something was knocked loose inside and trussed up wrongly. He groaned.

The rain still pelted him, but he could do nothing but loll and fight for breath. He felt the mud shift beneath him. There was a rolling in the earth, a festering that bulged before him and rose.

Irving tried to scream and scramble back as a dark head broke through and yawned, but he was frozen dumbstruck. Shoulders and arms emerged as Irving felt himself quiver and fade. The world fell into a pinprick of darkness and even the idea of screaming was lost to him.

Irving awoke in his bed. His head and hands were wrapped, his clothes were clean, and there was a plate of cooked beans on a chair set beside him. Steam was still peeling off the food, waking sharp hunger pains. Irving sat up and scooped the beans with his bare fingers. He scanned the room. The table was empty and there was a pile of dirty clothes by the door, the kettle was billowing, but little else seemed different or disturbed.

He finished eating, sucking the juice from his fingers, and called out. Last night was hazy and his head was pounding, so he went to the stove and poured whatever hot liquid was in the kettle.

The water was cloudy and gave off a loamy scent. Some sort of pale tea, Irving thought. But he took a tentative sip, then tipped the contents of the cup fully into his mouth. The drink was vegetable, like brass buttons and green beans.

He poured another cup and downed it just the same. He was about to find his boots when he heard the door creak.

"Who's there?"

The door stopped moving, but Irving could sense a presence outside.

"Farmer?" The voice was low and husky. There was a rattling like a rainstick.

"These're my fields," Irving said. He projected gruff annoyance. "Who are you?"

"Rusk—"

The sound seemed to conclude in clenched teeth and seizures. The strange response caused Irving to rush to the door and sling it open angrily.

"God's bones!" Irving cried.

Standing outside was a tall, naked man, whose skin was green and covered with short bristly hair. Irving registered his white pupils, the thick knotted curls for hair, the spindly fingers, and the wide bouncing pudendum between his legs, all in a moment. He stepped back in fright and stuttered. "What in hell are you?"

The figure raised his hands peacefully, palms up, and petitioned, "I don't know." His rattling voice betrayed surprise. "I found you lying in the mud, as I was, and carried you here."

Irving's mind whirled.

The creature continued, "Did you create me?"

An unbidden sneer broke out across Irving's face, but desperate logic formed dark designs in his heart. "Yes," he said, "I created you."

Part Three: The Soil

Ruskin, as Irving came to call him, placed a sack of potatoes into the wagon. Irving licked his thumb and rubbed a smudge out of his new boots.

"Don't wait up for me, Ruskin. I'll be back late."

The green man made sure the rest of the load was secure, blackberries, collards, onions, and turnips, and stood back.

"If you've got some time," he said with a flick of the reins. "Go ahead and get rid of the okra. I'm sick of it." His nut-brown mare shook her mane and set off.

Ruskin, it turned out, had a knack for growing things. That first day, after finding him an old pair of overalls, he restored his okra crop with a touch and whisper. Within days they had fresh okra, sweet and crisp. Next he cared for the corn, stalk by stalk, lifting it, mumbling over it as if in prayer, and reaffixing it into the earth. Days later the crop stood green and firm with ripening cobs.

Irving was able to tote in two bags of okra and corn and claim that the rain had revived his crops. The other farmers gave him a jaundiced eye, for their lands stayed untouched of any rain, but the produce was good and Roy accepted it in trade for more supplies.

Over the next few weeks, he and Ruskin had revitalized the farm. Irving left the planting to Ruskin while he restored the dilapidated barn. Rows of cabbage and carrots, watermelons and wheat, rose up. The creature provided the seed himself.

Irving marveled at how fast it came up. "How're you doing

this, Rus?" he'd asked.

Ruskin paused over the new growth, a sprig of a pea plant. He was coaxing it out of the earth with a hum that rattled around the lungs. He squinted into the light as he answered. "Once I plant the seed, I put time right into the heart of it."

"Yeah, but that's my question. I seen you singing or whatever to the seedlings, but where do you get the seeds? Half the crop, ain't ever tried to grow."

Ruskin stood and reached a hand into his overalls, making way to his middle. He began manipulating himself, self-pleasuring with his eyes closed.

"God almighty," Irving called and averted his head. When Ruskin sighed deeply, Irving looked over. Ruskin extended his hand to show a handful of seed in a pool of oil. "Don't ever do that around me again, sick bastard."

Seeing that prompted Irving to spend as much time in town as he could. His harvest was rich and frequent enough to be able to eat out and afford a bottle to fall into. Ruskin did all the labor, but Irving had insisted that he stay behind at the farm whenever he went in to trade.

The other farmers were suspicious that a farm of such weak yield could be transformed into abundance after a single rain. "Where you getting this, Irv," they'd ask. His fruit was too good to come from Eke, Oklahoma. "What devil you cavorting with?" was said with laughter at first, then with brooding suspicion.

"Badger John said he saw you with another man out at your place," a farmer said one night after Irving was deep into his cups.

Irving snapped his head up. "What? That's a cold lie."

The man, surprised by the response, pressed on. "You got an indian living with you?" Others gathered around hearing the sort of tone that beckoned a fight.

Irving stood uncertainly. "You're a goddamn liar, any a' you say that." He swung his finger around indicating the circle of men.

"Sounds like a man that got an indian in his bed," said someone behind him. Irving swung his fist around blindly. He threw haymakers until he was knocked down solidly and tossed out of the bar.

That night he pulled Ruskin out of the cot made up in the corner. He dropped a beating on the soft skinned creature until he coughed up a yellow phlegm and spit up okra seeds.

Irving rose and caught his breath, but Ruskin stayed curled defensively. "Get and go sleep in the barn from now on." Ruskin whimpered but stayed silent. "In fact, stay inside during the day. I don't want to see you no more. Do your work at night."

Irving was sour the next day, but softened when he saw Ruskin limping and bruised, swollen about the face, and leaking the yellow sap. They didn't speak anymore.

The land grew richer toward the end of harvest. Irving began to wonder if they needed to put any food up for the winter or if Ruskin could grow it in the cold. He drank most nights and listened to the wind and the snatches of Ruskin's intoning over the crops. He began drinking all night, pissing off his porch and falling back into his chair.

He slept during the day and ate nothing but boiled potatoes flavored with whatever bottle was open on the table. He let his clothes grow rank and let his mustache crawl into a beard.

The summer climaxed and hints of the ending season began to slip in with the clouds. A bottle ended early and Irving wondered about the green creature that slunk about at night singing to the earth.

Ruskin was doing all the work, leaving a tithe of harvest for him daily. He stumbled to the other side of the porch where his offering was left. It was a little altar of potatoes and onions. Ruskin had stopped bringing anything green once he realized Irving left it to rot. He kicked the mound of food into the yard.

It was dusk and his servant would be rising soon to work

through the night. Irving decided to visit him and stepped into his boots, nearly falling before getting his heels in. He walked circuitously to the barn.

Drawing back the doors, he entered with a hawking to clear his throat and spat. The glob smacked upon the dirt floor and two figures turned toward him.

Next to Ruskin stood a green woman, about the same height but with long tendrils of hair descending midback. Her pupils were also white, she had a wide nose and high cheekbones, and the pink inside her mouth was so bright that it seemed to glow.

"What the devil?"

"Farmer?" Ruskin said, surprise rattling his voice.

"Ain't the farmer, Rus. I'm the creator." He jutted his jaw out. "Where'd she come from?"

The female creature drew back. Irving noticed that she was wearing an old shirt of his, slung off one shoulder due to its size. Ruskin moved himself between her and Irving.

"This is Effie," he rattled out.

"Where'd she come from, I asked."

They glanced at each other. She seemed to smother a smile. "The earth gave her to me," Ruskin said.

"That's my shirt."

They stared at him dumbly. Irving walked toward them, shuffling in the hay. "That's my shirt. I want it back."

Effie placed her hands over the buttons.

"Go on," Irving said. "Take it off."

Effie looked to Ruskin before undoing the buttons. She kept her eyes locked onto her green man as she removed the shirt. She let it drop to the ground but angled her body toward Ruskin.

She was formed like any woman, a weedy thatch between her legs, but green and muscular like her mate. The couple embraced and Ruskin protectively shielded her from Irving's gaze. He felt ashamed and left sullenly. They didn't notice him leave.

Part Four: The Gold

Now that Irving had seen her, Effie didn't hide herself. They both worked in full sight of the sun. She labored as tirelessly as Ruskin, still wearing only his shirt, storing up food for the winter. Irving stayed away as they worked, but occasionally was called into service.

Once Effie sent him out to buy more jars. She had to merely jangle an empty jar behind her back, where she knew his eyes would be. Another time she pointed at a pile of rubbish and swept her wrist in the air dismissively. Irving took her commands silently. After he trucked it out, he decided to stay away from the house, lest he be pressed into more duties.

He found a tree and planted himself in its shade. He set about watering himself with the bottles. The green people were making a home for themselves. He considered his fields. Since Ruskin showed up, the corn crop was in, just a couple of patches, but more than it had yielded in years, and a garden that provided a variety he'd never eaten of. Ruskin was working on a pen beside the barn, no doubt expecting him to buy a few pigs. Already Irving had arranged for Tomlin, his neighbor, to drop off his cows on the way out of state. They'd be here in the next couple of days.

Irving sobered up enough to dismantle the woodshed and cart it out to his drinking tree. As September arrived and the cold began creeping into the state, Irving had closed up the front, mudded up the slats, and made a little bunkhouse for himself. He had a chair and a little fire pit, a rock to piss from and a little pocket in the hill for his shit. Ruskin and Effie moved into his house. No words were exchanged in the swap, just slight nods as they passed.

Effie wore a dress she'd sown out of flower sacks. She wore her tendril green hair back and under a kerchief, but still bootless. Some nights Irving couldn't get her naked form out of his mind no matter how much he drank.

The last time he went to town, all he bought were crates of

whiskey. Had to get it at the tavern since he'd wanted more than Roy could sell. He endured the hard looks of the townsfolk and other farmers. He'd been hinting that a wealthy uncle had passed, which had changed his luck, but rumors persisted. He carried a dark cloud over him and people kept their distance.

One night he crept up to the house. Earlier he'd seen Ruskin playfully chase Effie around the barn and later she pinched him as he passed. That night, Irving snuck up to the old house.

As Irving rested his head against the wood wall he heard the springs of the bed compact and leap. He heard air blown from pursed lips, the groans and hums of pleasure. They each rattled like tambourines beneath quilts, quivering, muffled, and struck.

He walked away sickened with envy, revulsion, anger, and tasseled across that vine was the swollen fruit of sadness. He walked straight into his field and trampled the seed corn. Dry husks falling as he stomped and slapped at the stalks. He circled round and found a hidden crop of okra tucked into the corn.

For the first few weeks with Ruskin, once the beans were out, all they'd had to eat was okra. By the time other crops came in, grown in the mysterious way of the green creature, Irving was so sick of the crooked vegetable that he'd sworn them off and had the remaining plants destroyed. Ruskin must've regrown them.

Irving uprooted them. Every one. Calmly, methodically troweling out the roots with his hands and ripping them free of the earth. The stalks popped in the earth as he pulled. Somehow his hands had gotten cut. A little ditch in his skin ran with liquid. He painted the plants red with his blood.

When he was finished he marched back to the house. He eased his feet out of his boots and opened the door where the green people slept. He crept in, approaching the bed with his breath held.

He watched them. Ruskin was nearest, but curled toward her, an arm thrown over her waist. She slept on her back, her chest rising and falling rhythmically. He knelt down and smelled them. Tubers and salt, dirt and dry leaves filled his nostrils.

He reached under the bed and pulled out the shotgun, a 12-gauge Winchester, and a box of shells. He swiftly left, plucked his boots from outside the door, and ran full tilt into the land beyond his fields.

He was weeping as he ran. He ran until his lungs burned and he was stumbling. He fell. Again and again, rising and falling. He'd dropped the gun, shells scattered behind him like droppings. Tears made slivers of the moonlight, but still he trudged on.

Finally he was slung down and his body told him there'd be no more rising for that night. He slumped to the cold earth and found a flat stone for his head. He continued to cry, spit, and wail, sometimes from fear, sometimes from hate, sometimes for a family lost, far gone with barely any remembrance of love. There were wolves howling, the night alive all over, but he felt forsaken and ignored in his own howling.

The land was gold. The sun laid another layer of richness atop it. Irving awoke and rose up, surveying the hardscrabble around him. Animal skitterings and evidence of life were left among the gold rocks and shrubs. He rubbed his eyes.

Harjo was sitting on a rock nearby, hunching over in the morning cool. His face was a dry creek bed dragged with tines, his simple braid of black hair hanging down on one shoulder, his denim jacket pulled tight to his ribs, hands jacked into the pockets like fire pokers stoking flame. He opened his eyes and gently smiled.

"You, my friend, are living a very rough life, I think."

Irving propped himself up with an elbow and jimmied a grin onto his face. "Gimme a swig a' whatever bottle you toting around."

Harjo swung his solemn head side to side. "No drink, Irving." He said his name slowly, two disparate syllables. "But I have something for you." He reached into a sack that was at his feet and removed a jar of pears.

"You been carrying that around all this time? Whatever for?

Don't you know they's good? Don't you Indians know about canned goods?"

He laughed, brushing off the comments. "It was like you gave me your soul, when you gave me these pears. I could not eat them for fear that I would be eating you."

"Well that's a ton a' malarky, but if you ain't gonna eat, hand'em here." He slid a knee up and crouched, extending his hand to accept the jar. He cranked the lid and dug into the syrup with his fingers. He fished out a half and stuffed it into his mouth, chewing slowly.

"Is it good, friend?" asked Harjo.

"It is bitter—bitter," he answered.

"That is because it is your heart."

Irving looked up at the queer Cherokee. "Why would you say such a damn fool thing?"

Harjo nodded to himself. He rose, taking up the bag, and walked away from him. The sun was too bright for Irving to follow him with his eyes. He shattered the jar, tossing it into a large rock. The pears fell out in the dust.

Irving retraced his path back to the farm. Along the way he found his shotgun and three shells. He loaded the gun and walked on.

Coming up to his fields, he felt an uneasiness strike him. The air was hazy, a low smoke rising, and he realized there was fire. A moment later he heard the screaming, a rattling howl, and the bark of angry dogs.

He ran to the source of fear carrying fear with him.

Part Five: The Ashes

The feed corn was ablaze. Irving had to circle round to get to the house. He emerged into the yard to see Ruskin on the ground in a triangle of dogs. They barked and darted, sinking teeth into leg and arm, Ruskin flailing. The dirt was wetted with his pale-yellow blood.

Irving yelled and charged the attacking dogs, raising his gun. Ruskin turned to see Irving racing across the open field toward him. At that moment a dog lunged and sunk his teeth into Ruskin's throat. Ruskin stiffened briefly as the dog juddered and tore the flesh, sap spurting out.

The dogs scattered as Irving arrived, leaving the limp green man to flop dead in the dirt. Irving cradled him, crying out, "My friend, my friend . . ."

Another scream alerted him to more danger. It was Effie from the house. There were angry voices. Someone had seen the green people and attacked. Effie screamed again. Irving picked up his gun and bolted to the door.

He kicked it in.

Two men turned as he entered, both strangers to Irving. Effie's dress was torn, her long locks were wild and shivered as she pressed herself against the back wall. One of the men, wielding a knife, stepped forward and began to speak. "Us—"

Irving shot three times. The wall fragmented as easily as flesh. The man dropped the knife and fell back. The other man tackled Irving. He yelled, but their ears could only hold ringing.

Irving placidly held onto the man's forearms, feeling the man's fingers close upon his neck. He was bigger than Irving and angry. Exertion caused the man's eyes to bulge, spittle ejected by his rough breathing, and the edges of the world grew dark.

Before Irving blacked out, he wanted to warn Effie about the fire. He wanted to tell her that Ruskin was dead. He wanted to apologize for his life.

Irving released the man's arms and laid back, accepting death. He was surprised when the larger man fell over. Effie put her foot onto the man's back and yanked out the knife that had found his heart from between his ribs. She grabbed the man by the hair and placed the knife at the base of his skull.

Irving closed his eyes as she made sure of his death. "Effie," he said as she stumbled toward the door. He realized she was hurt. Her dress was damp and stuck to her side. "Effie," he said again, but she had left.

He stood up and followed. The fire could be seen now, rising in the field, the smoke going up like a flag of war. Effie was stumbling toward where Ruskin lay. He realized she was screaming, her sorrow pitched against the crackle and roar of fire.

He dropped to his knees and watched as Effie knelt over the body of her lover. She rocked slowly, then drifted to her side, slumped over, and then ceased to move.

Irving wept as his farm was consumed. The crop was a torrential swaying of flame. The heat ushered in high noon early. Then he saw that the barn was catching. Irving climbed to his feet. He could save the horse, at least.

Walking over he realized the door was open. The horse was gone and he'd have to catch her.

He entered the barn to find a rope and stopped to watch the far end burn away. Smoke stung his eyes as the fire climbed the beams, leaping across the hay and eating up the burlap sacks that lined the walls.

Without much thought, Irving took a rope and made a quick noose, tossing it over a beam and affixing the end to the wall behind him. He took a stool and stood on it. Sweat was running down his face, blending in with his tears.

He put his head into the loop and cinched it tight. He tried to take a deep breath, but smoke hooked his lungs. He coughed himself empty and kicked away the stool. His neck was wrenched and his throat was closed off. Panic seized him.

Irving clawed at the fibers choking him, unable to work his fingers within its vise. The billowing flame forced him to shield his face. His strength failed him and he finally found his peace, letting his arms fall to his side.

In his last moments, Irving forgave the land and took upon his shoulder all its failings. He would die a deserving death.

But among the sounds of burning, Irving heard a tiny shriek. Some sputtering cry of a newborn. He wildly craned his neck, again trying to wrench free the grip of the rope from around his neck.

In the corner of his eye, he saw a green melon. It shook as he watched, then split. A tiny green leg kicked free. Another rift was made as a green fist burst out. The baby cried again, a wail of fear and betrayal.

The fire drew nearer. The heat blossomed. Irving dangled and flailed, fighting to stay alive, fighting for a single breath, fighting to do one worthwhile thing with his life. The rope quivered.

BETHEL

by W. Oliver Hunt

LEILA'S MURKY DREAMS STARTLED HER awake in a cold pond of body-whisked sheets smothered in perspiration, the clamorous whispers of a rabid city and the derelict evening baying at her apartment window and rattling her deeply. She had dreamed and beheld a ladder swallowed in tarnish and swollen in abandon set up on the earth, its head feebly probing the heavens, and beheld above a wailing seraph weeping sickly red rivers of rust sniveling before a barren seat.

Leila had choked on the clarity of his song and fragments of bone, for the absconded throne tore the teeth from her gums, strangling her awake, and she whispered like a breathless child:

> *Surely the Lord has left this place*
> *and I knew it not.*

Soberly, she abandoned the warbling city and lighted upon a certain place: a sylvan grove carelessly splattered with moon streams and bleached with the silver plumes of naked astronomy. She lay her crown on a vulgar cushion of stones, she petitioned the pastel moon and her spangled attendants:

> *O foul and immovable song,*
> *humming like some cruel and crackling lightning bug*
> *giggling absurdly to your thunderstorm chorus*

O pseudo-florescent fireflies! Inconsiderate water
stars!
Have you perceived our God?
For I dreamt a heaven asleep
and awoke tearfully shrink-wrapped in sweat
The hollow howl of a vacant throne ringing in my teeth
Arise cosmic vassals
for surely you recall:
tenderly he chiseled you, Sister Satellite
birthed your frame and blessed your form
He doused the earth in constellations
and set fire our celestial canopy
Slow your resurrection 'til our Lord exposed
reclaims his seat or stirs his sleep
to shower and shower and shower
To tip his holy cup

And again Leila whispered like a breathless child:

Surely the Lord has left this place.

The clever sphere, ripened with age and rich with the knowledge of eons, burst adoringly into a fiery ballad of laughter as
her be-speckled orbs glinted in accompaniment:

O dear and troubled child,
my tender fretting fawn
bleating amongst the sharp foliage of
her anxious dreams;
O artless daughter
thrashing before vaudevillian visions
of a nude sky swallowed in ruby tears;
drowning in the tributaries of abandoned angels,
in search of her fickle Father
What fragrant melodrama!
And what foul and tethered beast is man?

Swiftly mounting to her feet Leila arranged her lips to
violence, but the ready moon began before her breath:

Gargle your vanity, foolhardy child
lest you tickle my pale anger
For I am the Governess of Floods
and through my distemperature you
see the seasons alter
Lo, your revelations are not singular
Darling Lamb
For when Adam first embraced
the sprawling nudity of the heavens
with his nascent eyes
he trembled
and he wept
For the universe, though graphically surging
with the starry brilliance of our celestial militia
was infinitely conceived of chaos
And in rebellion to this arctic void
he made of the sky a looking glass
And in rebellion to his wisdom
he called it God
(God! How hotly devilish an exclamation?)
Dreams betray desire;
lucidly their art is shown
but solely when the self be known
Outward and upward forever and beyond the glass
abides only icy truth, lovely as it may be
Turn inward for your God
for heaven and truth are far removed

Leila, overwhelmed at the moon-sung clarity, collapsed to the surface of the clearing illumed and tranquilly slept without dreams. And the antique moon whispered to herself like a vigil mother:

Surely the Lord has left this place
and surely we are better for it.

VI

THE COSMICISM OF THE FALLEN

TREE OF METAL AND DIAMOND

by Nathaniel Weber

1

THE TREE OF METAL AND diamond crashed into a mountain. Far away, a sea of faces turned to look. Together they took the form of one great dark shape, staring into the cosmos in search of their god.

"And what did you see, when the 'great dark shape' came into focus?"

Oliver chewed his nails and bounced his foot. "It looked at us. From all that distance away, it looked at us."

2

He waited in a wheelchair, his bare feet cold. The thin hospital gown made him feel naked and inconsequential.

"Nesdoly, Oliver?" The voice was high and feminine.

"Yes?" He raised his hand.

She continued calling names, and the other psychics around him, all in wheelchairs, answered the role.

A young woman, five chairs down, looked him in the eye. The read washed over him. Her mind touched his and he felt an immediate erection.

"Zamora, Adelia?"

"Aqui," the woman said. He could *feel* her words. Her read was the most powerful he'd ever felt.

One of the directors gestured, and Oliver and Adelia's wheelchairs were moved so they were next to one another. The rearrangement continued up and down the line, as the directors gauged read range and strength, and determined the best pairings. With her mind Adelia reached out and touched his, and in the moments that followed, unencumbered by weak physical communication and the boundaries of language, they fell in love.

3

Oliver and Adelia followed their pairing with coupling.

She lay next to him, leg draped over his. They'd never spoken to one another. Her read was weaker now, a good ten hours since the last treatment. Her mind was only a nudge to him, a bump against his.

Mind-reading was impossible, at least for humans. But feelings, directions of thought, impulses, and convictions—those were readable by the members of the group. Close proximity to the edifice, and a potent cocktail of drugs, made it easier, faster, allowed it over distance rather than touch—but they were limited by their physiology.

Her hand grazed his chest and rested there. He turned his face to her neck and kissed her soft skin. Soon they were making love again. This time they spoke in different languages, but with complete understanding.

4

"It was the face of the enemy?"

Oliver nodded.

"Could it detect you?"

"*They*. And I don't know."

"Were there many of them?"

"A whole crowd, in a stadium or . . . like an ancient Roman arena. Thousands."

"Did you feel pain? Fear?"

"Yes."

"It threatened you?"

Oliver stopped chewing his nails. He saw gray-hulled ships, ancient and powerful, aiming batteries of alien cannon. "It didn't have to."

5

The next stage of treatments involved spinal injections. Oliver screamed—not from his own pain but because he could feel Adelia's.

They put on the news while the subjects waited for the worst of the treatment pains to subside. The *end* was coming. The fleet had been destroyed around Jupiter; twenty trillion dollars' worth of spacecraft and two thousand crewmembers: all gone in a single battle. The alien fleet, which had annihilated the outer colonies, was now nearly in Earth's orbit, its massive, gray-hulled ships unstoppable. The president declared Earth's missile batteries to be operational, but that wouldn't be enough.

This project was their best hope.

6

The building shook again while the nurse hooked cables into the ports along Oliver's neck and back. The aliens' bombardment of Earth had begun. The newsfeed showed Boston-Washington Megalopolis burning, cars smoldering, corpses everywhere; Greater Shanghai cratered, the ocean leaking inland, boats and dead whales flecking the watery streets; and the Central African Urban Zone a smoking wreck. Oliver stared at the far side of the room, where a red exit sign glowed above a heavy steel door.

Adelia sat beside him, a blur in his periphery. When the project was over and the war won, he would never be able to connect with her—*feel* her—again. Without the drugs and treatments, what was he? He would need to learn Spanish.

He smiled at the absurdity of the notion. *Once this was all over.*

The rest of the subjects were arrayed in a circle, running all around the room, facing inward at a huge mechanical edifice, baroque in construction, made of curled metal and spirals of diamond. It hummed and emitted a strange orange glow. The edifice reached up until it disappeared into a ceiling carved from stone. Oliver couldn't see more but knew that it went all the way up to the peak of the mountain, where antennas pointed toward space.

The PA system announced the final, most powerful injections were about to commence.

Oliver closed his eyes and reached out to Adelia. In his mind, she held his hand and kissed his cheek.

The injections hit. The sensation that flowed through him was the most intense he'd yet experienced; a migraine, scalding flash burn, and orgasm—simultaneously.

7

The treatments included heavy doses of psychedelics, hallucinogens, and sedatives: cocktails designed to open tele-sensitive neurons within the brains of the psychically aware. It had taken the project two years to identify fifty test subjects from around the world, of whom Oliver was one, and another year to coordinate the subjects, bring them into the facility, and prepare for the project.

The edifice had been built earlier—*much* earlier—and was ready and waiting when the subjects arrived. Their minds opened by drugs, amplified by their close proximity to one another, and seemingly boosted further by the presence of a hostile alien spacecraft in orbit about Earth, connected to the edifice and flowed through it. Human radio signals transformed into waves of psychic energy.

Dr. Maxwell and the other project scientists believed their psychic power could attack and destroy the central nervous system of the telepathic aliens in control of the devastating spacecraft above, already responsible for the death of billions.

When Oliver opened his eyes, he wasn't in the room surrounded by a circle of psychics; instead, he was atop a great mountain, Adelia at his side. They were naked, pale, shivering against hurricane winds and sharp ice pellets. He grabbed her and wrapped her in his arms. He then looked up and saw the *face*, the one from his dreams, dark and great and staring down at them.

It wasn't only him and Adelia on the mountain. He realized the other forty-eight test subjects were there, too, in huddled pairs, struggling against the brutal cold.

None of it is real, a voice whispered.

His flesh was cold and tight, his fingers and toes numb.

This is an illusion. Your mind is beyond our reality.

Adelia shivered, her breasts against his chest, flesh stiff. The mountain they stood upon—purple and blue, like a frozen bruise—shivered underneath gusting bombardments of ice.

The danger is real but it is not here. Remember the enemy. Remember the ships. You must learn or be destroyed.

He looked up to that face, at its dead eyes and thin mouth, drooling. He saw that some of the others were doing the same, lifting their tucked chins against the cold. He squeezed Adelia and she looked up first at him and then to the face.

Its eyes wavered and the thin mouth twitched.

8

Months before, in Oliver's horrible apartment, Dr. Maxwell, with a shock of white hair and a dull suit, sat at the kitchen table. Colonel Wright, United States Army, was with him, in camo.

Oliver, pouring earl gray tea into cheap ceramic mugs for his guests, shook his head. "It's taken me a long time to get away from the voices. Why would I want them back?"

Dr. Maxwell tapped the newspaper on the kitchen table, his finger on the headline. "Because you can help us fight them."

"How does a delusional who can't even pay rent help with that?"

"You are not delusional."

"Not right now, with the drugs. Without the drugs, the voices never stop."

"You never were, Oliver."

Colonel Wright cleared his throat. "Dr. Maxwell and I represent a special project. You are one of fifty subjects we've identified, who are . . . *attuned*."

" 'Attuned?' Is that even a word?"

Dr. Maxwell smiled. "When did you first hear voices?"

"I was eight." Oliver thought back to the lilting, creaky voice that whispered unspeakable things to him. "An old man told me to touch the little girl who lived down the street from me."

Maxwell nodded and slid a folder across the table. "And his name was Wendell Jackson, aged sixty-eight, a convicted sex offender and, later, child murderer."

Oliver looked at the two of them. "No, Doctor. He was a voice in my head."

Dr. Maxwell gestured to the folder. Oliver opened it and saw police reports, legal documents, and photographs. He read for several minutes while the other two watched.

Dr. Maxwell leaned forward, elbows resting on the table, and hands flat for emphasis. "You are telepathic, Mr. Nesdoly. For the past twenty years, you have been misdiagnosed, medicated without reason, maltreated by the system, and marginalized by your family. But if you come with me and Colonel Wright, you can help us save the world."

A cockroach, hitherto hiding under a bowl of fruit, crawled across the table. Colonel Wright said, "At the very least, we'll get you out of this horrible apartment."

9

Several of the other pairs called out to Oliver.

What do we do?

The face focused on them. Immediately, six pairs fell to the ground, screaming, writhing in the frigid, lilac snow, crimson flooding from their ears and eyes.

Fight, Oliver yelled. He found himself only able to express in single words, his brain apparently refusing grammatical syntax. *Focus.*

Another pair screamed before their faces cracked open, eyes popping like broken egg yolks, teeth shattered in their mouths.

The cold incrementally vanished and was replaced by a painless vacuum. The purple mountains vibrated. The face stared down at them, but it shook and twitched. Oliver thought he saw it weeping.

The remaining pairs joined arms and focused their minds on the face. As they did so, and even while the face above faltered, their bodies gave way—discs slipped out of spines, muscles knotted and cramped, hernias ruptured, and vessels broke.

Oliver wept into Adelia's shoulder as they held on. The ligaments in his jaw *snapped.* He bit his tongue in half.

Above them, the face began to flay apart, as though a fan had been turned onto a pile of sculpted ash. A great scream built around them. But not from the humans.

You must learn, the voice said.

No, stop, Oliver cried out, choking on a wave of blood which crawled from his lungs to his throat.

Soon.

More of the humans died, their flesh sloughing from the bones into a steaming piles at their feet. He felt Adelia shatter in a shower of meat and bone. Forces pried open his mouth until his jaw broke completely and the stub of bloody tongue wagged in the air.

10

Remember what I have told you.

Oliver screamed. Jerked forward in his seat. Pulled at cables. He had been connected to the edifice. The edifice in the control room. He was not on a cold mountain. He was clammy and shaking but there was no pain, no metallic taste; his mouth was unbroken, his tongue whole.

The cable in the back of his head disconnected, and he looked around him. The forty-nine others were all in their chairs, drenched in sweat, shaken expressions on their faces, but intact.

Adelia smiled at him. He tried to reach for her but the drugs were wearing off.

The edifice was silent and dark, brooding in front of him. A growing buzz filled the room.

Cheering.

Medical personnel came streaming from the adjoining offices, pushing wheelchairs, and disconnected the subjects from their seats. The wall-mounted screens switched on, showing footage from space. The enemy ships were immobile, their engines cold and weapons silent.

Dr. Maxwell strode into the room. "We did it!"

A nurse helped Oliver into his wheelchair. He physically reached out and touched Adelia's hand; she squeezed his finger, crying. The nurses pushed them down the hallway and toward their rooms, where sleep beckoned the exhausted psychics. Each psychic passed through the same doorway, above which glowed a yellow exit sign.

11

The President was a tall, dark-skinned woman grinning from ear to ear.

"The project was initiated three years ago, when we first gained knowledge of the enemy. Our scientists realized the enemy's telepathic nature, even though it provided them such formidable advantages, might be exploited as a weakness. The project was only operational hours before the enemy fleet arrived in orbit. We owe our lives, our planet, and the very existence of our species to these fifty men and women."

The room exploded into applause.

Oliver stood awkwardly next to the President. Adelia was beside him. The other forty-eight stretched in a long, single line down the length of the dais. Mostly healthy young adults—Dr. Maxwell told him that psychic attunement typically reached its peak in a person's twenties.

The President walked down the line, hanging a medal around each psychic's neck.

Oliver tried to see the detail in the room but could only make out bright lights and shadow.

"They tell me the drugs have side effects," the President said as she placed his medal.

"Mrs. President?"

"Grogginess, memory problems. Don't worry, our best people made those drugs. You'll recover soon." She smiled and Oliver realized he barely recognized her as the President.

Adelia squeezed his hand, and his memory problems suddenly didn't bother him anymore.

12

The rebuilding of Earth took years. Humans dismantled the derelict alien ships left in orbit, learned their technologies, and commenced a new age in exploration and science. The population rebounded and humanity began a golden era.

Oliver and Adelia moved to a lovely home in southern Africa. She learned English and he Spanish. They worked as consultants to the new Psychic Awareness Program, a multinational effort that searched for the attuned. In their position, they traveled the world together.

Years passed. However, Oliver never fully shook the side effects of the project's drugs. He felt as though his life was a series of disconnected episodes into and out of which he slipped with little or no awareness. Adelia held him during the long nights when he wept, struggling to remember where he'd been or what he'd been doing. Even the lucid times between the blackouts began to blur.

13

The car floated across the rugged hillside, lifted by technology derived from the alien ships. Oliver was in the passenger seat.

Adelia in the driver seat. She did not drive with hands. Her eye movements guided the vehicle.

Oliver asked: "*A donde vamos?*"

She stopped in a meadow, beneath the shade of a tree, and got out of the car. Oliver loved to watch her move, the curve of her hips, the swish of her ponytail. He followed her, taking the blanket and the picnic basket. The wind was cold but pleasant.

She walked all the way to the edge of the cliff and peered over. He joined her, his hand on the small of her back and trailing down to her buttocks. "Nobody out here." He smiled, kissing her neck.

"We aren't alone."

She pointed to the mountain.

14

The alpine wind sharpened and stung Oliver's face, but he turned to see Dr. Maxwell in a cheap office chair, tapping a pad of paper.

"The alien face. When did you last see it?"

Oliver looked back into the precipice below the mountain. The darkness engulfed him.

"I can see it now."

Maxwell leaned forward. His glasses were cracked and blood ran down his face. "Oliver, you must listen to me. The great dark shape is below us. You are not here. You are back in the mountain. Look to the precipice. It is there, below us."

15

Oliver looked down. Tendrils of black grew from the tree of metal and diamond and, reaching for him, crawled up the cliff face.

Panicking, he reached for Amelia. She was gone. He looked back to the car. He saw her. Sprouting black tendrils, she opened her mouth to scream. Nothing came out except for glistening obsidian coils.

Adelia came apart, her atoms splitting. Dissolving. Into nothing. The tendrils reached for Oliver from all directions and yanked him down into the abyss.

16

Oliver opened his eyes.

The edifice glowed like fire.

The other subjects screamed and thrashed.

Alarms wailed.

The room filled with smoke. The floor shook violently. But he couldn't move. He counted the psychics. Half were in various states of dismemberment, some still squirming. The other half were seizing, mouths bleeding from severed tongues. Only Adelia held on, gripping the armrests of her wheelchair, and biting clean through her bottom lip. With difficulty, they locked eyes—and she *nudged* him.

Dr. Maxwell!

From behind him the physician appeared, his face bloody and glasses cracked. "Oliver!"

Dr. Maxwell, I've been gone for years.

"Oliver—you and Adelia flatlined for two minutes. There was feedback of some kind—it killed most of us and put the rest into shock."

Adelia nudged them both: *More drugs. Give us more drugs and we can do this.*

Dr. Maxwell keyed commands into his tablet. "How are you communicating with me?"

It shared with us, Oliver thought.

"The alien?"

It taught us, Adelia thought.

The psychotropic drugs hit them like a wall of color and sound, and he and Adelia went back to the mountain.

17

The great dark face stood in a snowstorm and invited them to tea.

The face was vast, its long arms engulfing the table and chair as it poured rich earl gray into fine porcelain cups. Adelia sat to its left and Oliver to its right.

They sipped and smiled. The face drank from a human-sized cup, which made Oliver giggle, and Adelia giggled in turn. The face did not smile but did not take offense.

"Why are you here?" Adelia asked. It was verbal and somehow English, or perhaps it was Spanish and somehow Oliver, who sat watching, understood.

It put down the tiny cup and communicated to them not with words but of mind-flashing images. Of the limply slumped, mangled test subjects. Of the mighty tree of metal and diamond crashing into the mountainside. Of many sunsets and -rises, in fast-forward. Of oceans rising and falling. Of harsh rain and wind eroding rock, and of human cities rising from primordial goop and climbing to the stars, and of alien ships with cool gray hulls orbiting above a fire-scorched Earth and firing their energy beams into the mountains to extract the tree of metal and diamond—glowing orange, glowing bright—and of the great dark face—and others like it—kneeling before the Tree, praying for . . . *forgiveness.*

Adelia and Oliver exchanged confused glances.

The great face redoubled its efforts, presenting them with more images:

First: The great faces, living in huts, dressed in animal skins, watching a great tree—shining and beautiful—descend from the heavens and settle in a meadow of purple grass near their village.

Second: A great face read an ancient scroll, examining pictograms of a tree, studying pictures of the great faces huddled around the tree, with gifts and candles and prayers, and flowing waves of light passing from the tree to the faces—followed by an image of the tree being hurled from their world, into the dark reaches of space, as they watched helplessly.

Then: Vast numbers of the great faces met in an alien Parthenon at the center of which was a mural of the tree. They spoke and debated and crafted charts and plans of tremendous complexity. They set to work building starships with gray hulls, and then nearly all of them boarded the ships. The ships launched and left their world behind.

Then: The gray-hulled ships slid through space, past planets and nebulae and through the tails of comets, as star charts showed their progress and the sun rose and set above their Parthenon.

Then: Dinosaurs standing in a field, eating grass, and scanning for predators, startled to the sound of a sonic boom. Before they could run, an asteroid of metal and diamond slammed into the Earth and exploded like a fusion bomb.

Then: generations of the faces lived in their huge ships. The stars traveled past. The faces dwindled in number, dying of age and disease. The gray hulls grew more intricate, complex, rebuilding themselves as their automated systems took more and more control.

Then: A few remaining great faces bowed to the ships, whose self-made advancements now put them in command. They were living machines with thoughts and emotions.

Later: The ships have dedicated themselves to the tree of metal and diamond, building representations of the Tree onboard. They see the dying great dark faces as an infestation, whose physical frailty can only delay their search for the Tree, and kill all they can find, staking their bodies atop the Tree-representations. A few great faces survive, hiding in the darkest recesses of the ships. They are unable to overpower the ships, not without help, not without the Tree.

The ships detect a signal—a pulse that draws them toward a small, rocky planet. They have found what they sought and are overcome with rage that others live in its presence. The ships are intent on rescuing the Tree from the things that live like pests in great cities all around the Tree, who caterwaul into their radios and hurl pitiful atomic weapons at the ships.

The great dark faces weep while their vessels slaughter millions.

18

The images abruptly stopped. Adelia and Oliver sat slack-jawed, eyes wet and cheeks tear-stained.

The great dark face took a final sip of tea, and it reached for them. Its oversized arms clumsily knocked over a teacup, spilling it to the snowy mountainside below. Its hands were flat on the table, palms up and open. Oliver and Adelia again exchanged glances before putting their hands in the alien's open palms. They felt like the hide of an elephant.

The great dark face changed, lightened. They could now see the few other faces remaining, gathered behind, joining hands as alien guns hammered the Earth's cities into slag. The face who'd served them tea squeezed their hands, and Adelia and Oliver glowed with the orange light of the edifice.

Through Adelia and Oliver the great faces bonded with the Edifice, their holy Tree of Metal and Diamond, and, in a brief moment of glorious rapture, joined it in eternity. A surge of power flowed over Adelia and Oliver. It whispered thanks to them, before the great faces closed their eyes in unison and turned to ash.

19

When Oliver and Adelia came to, the alien ships had already fallen silent. The bombardment ceased. In the weeks that followed, the humans searched the ships, finding them empty save a few desiccated corpses. After years of research, they would determine that some kind of electronic overload annihilated the ship's computer processors and silenced them.

Thirty-eight of the other psychics were dead, as were many of Dr. Maxwell's and Colonel Wright's personnel. The edifice, which had glowed and throbbed with energies, was now inert and would remain so forever, with two exceptions.

Generations of scientists pored over the edifice, studying it with every conceivable scan and test. They never determined the construct's age nor internal structure, other than to determine that the rock in which it was imbedded was as old as the dinosaurs.

The emergency government, which had funded Dr. Maxwell's project, set to work reverse engineering the alien ships, much as Oliver saw in his visions. The psychic survivors became celebrated heroes.

Adelia died sixty years later, from the usual sorts of things that kill aged humans, and several years later her husband Oliver passed as well. Their children and grandchildren mourned their passing, and, at the moments of their respective deaths, the edifice pulsed with orange light once more, projecting into the cosmos a signal of unknown composition or purpose.

Many eons later, many solar systems away, in a distant corner of the observable universe, an alien Parthenon received the signals and was pleased.

MOONSTRUCK

by Alice Austin

I WRAP MY HANDS AROUND the hot mug of coffee and head out to the garden. It's a cold and cloudless night. I'm not remotely surprised to find Grandpa with his telescope set next to the toolshed.

"What're you looking at tonight?" I ask as I pick my way over to where he stands, well clear of the tall hedges surrounding our garden. I hold the mug out to him but he doesn't take it. He only waves a hand at me without removing his eye from the telescope. It's become a routine: me bringing him coffee and he inevitably forgetting to drink it. I don't mind. It gives me an excuse to come out and join him.

"Just put it down somewhere, I'll have it in a minute." His wrinkled hand fiddles with the focus knob. "I'm looking at the new moon. Beautiful tonight. I've never seen it like this before." I raise an eyebrow and look up. The stars are twinkling but I can't see the moon. Then, I realize what he just said.

"The *new* moon? I thought that was the phase you couldn't see."

"*Usually* you can't," Grandpa says absentmindedly. I wait for him to finish the thought but he says nothing.

"I want to look," I say, because perhaps he can see something interesting through the telescope. I come closer to the telescope, waiting for him to step aside and show me what the big deal is, but he doesn't move. And *still* he says nothing.

"Grandpa, can I *please* look?" He holds up a single finger, and I wait. And wait.

"All right then," I say, when it's clear he's not going to speak. "I'm going back inside." A cold wind blows and I shiver, but he might as well have been standing out here on a summer night. He seems to have forgotten I'm even here. "Don't stay out too long," I press, desperate for a response.

Nothing; Grandpa's focus is impenetrable. I shake my head, trying hard to quell the uneasy feeling in my gut.

"Goodnight, Grandpa. Love you."

When I look out my window the next morning, he's still outside. The coffee sits untouched where I left it. We always joked he'd stay out all night stargazing if we let him, but we'd never expected him to actually do it.

I run downstairs and out the door and grab him by the arm. Terror floods through me as my fingers touch his freezing skin. He's as cold as a corpse, but corpses don't exhale vapor into cold morning air. I almost collapse with relief.

"Were you out here all night? Are you ok? Come on. Let's go inside, Grandpa." I gently wrap my arm around his shoulder but to my shock he pushes me away, eye still fixed to the telescope.

"*Stop it,*" he snaps. And with a softer, more reverent voice: "I'm *just* watching the moon." I look at the sky, perplexed, but there's nothing but the sun and a few drifting clouds. Then I notice he's tilted the telescope toward the sparkly frost-kissed ground. I would've laughed if I weren't so concerned.

"The moon isn't in the sky right now. It's morning. And it's not in the grass, either. Please come in; you need to warm up." I pull at his arm as hard as I dare; whatever it takes to get him to leave that damn telescope.

"You can see it," he insists. "You're just not looking hard enough."

I look down towards where the telescope is pointed, and a wave of nausea sweeps through me. My legs go limp and an odd humming rings in my ears. I shut my eyes until the feeling passes.

"You'll see, eventually," Grandpa says, almost to himself. "It won't be too much longer."

I plead with him some more—threatening him with imaginary snow, thunderstorms, and even a tornado—but he refuses to move, so I drape my jacket around him and run back to the house to fetch my mother. Between the pair of us, we manage to drag him inside. He fights us every step of the way, desperately trying to pull his telescope along with him. We bundle him into the living room and, as I slam the door, he lets out an animalistic scream and starts pounding on the other side. The handle rattles, his strength supercharged by his moongazing-frenzy; I grip it harder until my knuckles go white. "You don't know what you're doing! Just look at the moon, then you'll *understand*! Just *look*!"

Mom shakes her head. I can tell she wants to cry.

"Great grandpa began suffering from dementia at a much earlier age. We should be thankful for the extended time."

"He's just tired and cold," I say. "Maybe he fell asleep out there and got confused."

Mom blinks. Nods. "Perhaps. We'll leave him be until he's calmed down."

I hold the door shut as she wedges a chair under the handle. Grandpa screeches but ultimately gives up bashing at the door. I hear him shuffling around inside, muttering to himself about craters and fissures.

When night falls, I look out of the window with a pang of sorrow. It's a clear night again, and it's strange not to see Grandpa out there with his telescope. The thought of him locked in the living room, all on his own and muttering to himself like Gollum, makes my heart hurt. We tried to call a doctor earlier in the day but all the phone lines were busy and we were scared that wrestling him into the car to take him ourselves would break a couple of bones.

I look up at the sky.

Pain shoots through my eyes.

Heat shivers over my skin.

Then chills and breathlessness.

Flickers of stars cut through deep indigo and swirls of velvet. And the moon—it's not visible, not exactly, but I can sense it somewhere in that celestial miasma and I understand now. I understand why Grandpa—

A car horn.

I stumble backwards, the window frame cutting my sightline of the haunted sky. Only the thought of Grandpa standing frail and frozen in the cold morning gives me the motivation to stay away from the window and keep my eyes averted from the alluring thing in the sky.

When I check on him the next morning, I find the living room door ajar. Since Mom is also missing, I would have considered that she'd taken him to the hospital. Except the car is in the driveway. I check every room of the house and, when there's still no sign of either of them, I head to the garden, dreading what I might see.

It's just as I feared. Mom and Grandpa stand side by side next to the telescope. And they're both staring at the ground, mumbling to each other about how beautiful the moon is this morning.

I try to make them snap out of it, but I have even less success than I did yesterday. They fight me viciously, slapping away any attempt to reach for them. When I finally manage to grab Grandpa by the shirt, Mom places her hands on my chest and shoves me backwards. I stumble, land heavily, stare up at her in shock.

"I'm so sorry, honey. You'll understand once you join us! Just wait till it's dark and take a look." She holds out a hand to help me up, gaze still fixed on the floor.

I smack her hand away and pick myself up to run back into the house.

"You can't hold out forever!" I hear Mom calling from behind me.

I collapse onto the couch and stare blankly at the TV.

Talking heads in suits and ties. News people. Video footage of crowds, each and every head tilted towards the floor. A banner crawls across the bottom of the screen:

. . . INSIDE DO NOT LOOK AT THE MOON STAY INSIDE DO NOT . . .

I haven't been to school since Mom's been outside. The school bus hasn't come, either. There doesn't seem much point when it's the end of the world.

I've taken to drawing the curtains long before it gets dark. But even so, I feel the moon's quiet hum permeating through the walls or ceiling. I feel my bones vibrate. I wonder if the moon has a mind. I wonder if it knows what it's doing.

Once every few days I go to the convenience store not even a quarter mile from the house. Each time I've gone out for snacks and soda, more wrecked cars litter the streets, their drivers staring helplessly through the windscreens; more people stand scattered in the road, staring slack-jawed at the ground. I make Mom and Grandpa (still standing in the garden like statues, their eyes always following the path of the moon) drink water and try to force them to eat, but most of it just ends up on their clothes or the floor.

"It's coming," they say in unison as I bring out fresh blankets to drape over them. *"You can already see the cracks beginning to form. We need to sing to it. It can't do this without our help."*

Their words fill my stomach with burning coal.

At the half moon, the silent lunar hum fills its victims' throats.

The streets are packed with humming people. Their combined stench chokes me if ever I have to shuffle through them, but there are still a few like me who haven't been affected yet. I don't know what they look like, only what brand of sweatpants and shoes they wear. We keep our gaze down as we run to the safety of our homes, clutching whatever food we managed to pilfer from the shelves. Society has stopped.

Last night, maybe a thousand filled the street before my house; all humming the beautiful, melancholic whale song. The moon called to me even in my sleep, filling my dreams with its radiance. In one dream I was staring at the blood red night sky, watching the moon crumble apart into a million shimmering fragments as I sang along with the crowd. When I woke up I found myself clawing at the curtains, pale moonlight filtering into my bedroom. The humming from a thousand dry throats kept taunting me as I returned to bed, tossing and turning, eyes fixed on the window, muttering nonsense phrases through gritted teeth in an attempt to fight the siren's call.

The next two nights are spent in similar torment as the moon grows fuller.

At times I barely know whether I'm awake or asleep as I find myself walking towards the window and snap out of the reverie just in time.

I wake on the morning of the full moon with a deep feeling of dread aching in my belly.

Today is the day.

Silence reigns. The omnipresent humming has stopped, and the people in the streets stand limp and weak, drained of all the feverish energy the moon gave them. As I walk through the crowd, I look at some of the faces and shiver. Some of them might be dead.

After examining the sky gazers, I jog home and look at Mom and Grandpa in the garden with their heads hanging low and their eyes glued to a spot just below the horizon. I wonder what will happen to them when the full moon rises. Certainly nothing good. Maybe if I can get them indoors, using whatever force necessary, I can cut off the moon's influence at the height of its power. They fought me off before, but now their legs tremble and they look ready to collapse at any moment. The combination of malnutrition and whatever the moon is doing to them means I should be able to overpower them.

"Not much longer now," Mom croaks out as I approach. *"We've given it what it needs."*

"Whatever you say," I tell Mom as I wrap my arms around her waist and drag her down the gravel path back to the house. Try as she may, she's too weak to challenge me. I slide her feet attached to stubbornly stiff legs across the hardwood floor; then I have to use momentum to get her into the bathroom, so I twist and toss her like a bale of hay. "Sorry Mom."

Grandpa is next. I barely feel his gnarled fists pummeling me as I take him on the same path as I took Mom, all the while the sun is sinking lower in the sky. He alternates between guttural protests and moonward, worshipful humming. The air feels thick and heavy. There's not even the faintest breeze to rustle the leaves on the bushes. Everything is too quiet. And the full moon is coming.

I toss Grandpa in with Mom, and he slips and falls butt-first—"sorry Grandpa"—but he's still humming as he lies crumpled on the floor, so he must be fine. I block the door with a table. I've convinced myself that if I can keep them inside, just for tonight, they'll be freed from the spell. The world will return to normal, and Grandpa and I can watch the night sky as we used to.

I run around the house, shutting curtains and locking doors. The moon's call has already started. My body doesn't feel right, as if my molecules are breaking down. The muscles in my neck ache from resisting the urge to look up. When I've finished, I shut myself in my bedroom and wait. If I had handcuffs, I would have cuffed myself to my bed and swallowed the key. But I don't have cuffs. Only fear.

When I feel the moon crest the horizon, I know I'm lost. My bones ache. A low hum builds in my throat. My skin flushes hot, then a deep, icy cold. I'm breathless. This room feels like a prison. I grasp feverishly at the door handle, pulling it open with shaking arms.

Downstairs, Mom and Grandpa are clawing at the door. I choke as I realize how much I miss them. I miss bringing Grandpa his coffee, and having him forget to drink it, while standing with him for hours, stargazing. And I miss Mom reminding us to come in and giving us both hot chocolate when we finish, and Grandpa forgetting to drink it, too.

I pull the table away and let them out.

"I'm sorry," I tell them. "I just didn't understand. But now I do."

Mom rests her arm around my shoulders.

"Thank you for letting us out. You've done the right thing."

Smiling, Grandpa says, "I knew you'd come around. Come on now. Let's go look at the sky. The full moon is going to be beautiful tonight."

HĀʻOLE

by Luciano Marano

S TORIES LIKE THIS REVEAL MORE about the teller than subject, in my experience. But I'm an old man, and despite everything that happened I find I still miss my friend. So, as it appears he won't be stepping forth to regale any crowds with this, his last grand ghost story, in whatever time is left, it falls to me to recount it for whoever cares, for whatever good it will do.

For myself, I just hope seeing the words on paper will give me some distance from the memory, like my camera in Vietnam. I was a photographer and, as Hollywood colorfully put it throughout the intervening years, *in the shit.* An overgrown boy eager for the chance to test myself against what I imagined would be the defining contest of my time.

Bullshit, of course. What did I know then about time?

But I'm not one of those still-in-Saigon burnouts you see in movies. On the rare occasion I examined the box of prints I keep in my closet, photos I took, they had no effect on me. I was removed, not only through the passage of time, but, more importantly, by the lens and development process.

But now, after what happened to Gallagher, when I unpack those prints I'm shocked to find sensations coming back to me more vividly than ever—the suffocating wet heat of the jungle, sounds of choppers, gunfire, screams; the smell of mud, sweat, blood—as I recall the hell that brought me here, to paradise.

Hawaii is a strange place. A fascinating mix of scenic and seedy. Even as I stepped off the plane, three combat tours completed and discharge in hand, I knew I'd never leave. My ticket to the mainland went unclaimed. The ghost of a stillborn tomorrow that never had a chance.

Honolulu is the remotest city of its size in the world. The island of O'ahu is barely thirty miles across, the capital city densely packed with the majority of the population. It's like we all washed up on the same strange shore and—faced with the vastness of the surrounding sky and ocean, the terror of our own inconsequentiality—huddled close together.

Hawaii has been invaded, conquered, stolen, and ravaged. The sunsets are beautiful works of art that tempt the most devout atheist. But behind the postcard-perfect tableaus and surfer chic, Elvis and Don Ho, air-conditioned buses hauling sunburnt tourists to sanitized excursions—beneath the pineapples, hula girls, and overpriced tchotchkes—is a mercurial land of war, strife, and death. And ghosts, too.

People think a place has to be ancient to be haunted—like those New England cemeteries and European castles supposedly so popular among the active deceased—but I think Hawaii, being young at least in a geological sense, has yet to be wrested completely from the gods. As every new volcanic eruption will attest, they don't seem to be done with it yet.

Spirits are part of life here. The ancient people knew it. Today's wiser residents believe it. Even the military accepted it (ask the old salts about the Shark Goddess of Pearl Harbor, if you doubt). And Gallagher, he made a great deal of money from it.

Honolulu is a city large enough to hold secrets and guard them well, but small enough so that anyone living here eventually meets everyone else. Stubborn rocks in a constantly rushing river of transients, visitors, and development, we tend to recognize one another.

So it was that I met Gregory Gallagher.

I'd managed to land a job as a photographer at the Honolulu Daily Review. It was weird, for a change, to be pointing my camera at people who would most likely still be alive next year. Otherwise, I spent my time playing tour guide to tourist girls. It was midnight on a Wednesday in August, and I was mourning the departure of a particularly friendly Texan named Becky in a Waikiki bar when, having finished one of his Hawaiian Horror walking tours (back when he actually hosted the tours himself, for he was not yet famous, having only published his first book a few months before), he—already known as the Ghost Guy—sauntered in for a nightcap.

The bartender placed a drink before him without so much as a nod. As we were both young, alone, and clearly no longer on active duty—though my hair was still short, I'd managed a respectable beard; he already sported the ponytail he'd keep for life—we began talking.

We discussed many things, as unaccompanied men in bars will do. We talked *around* Vietnam, as men often do (at least, those of us who were really there—those who'd been *in the shit*).

Mostly, we talked about Hawaii. We were both *hā'ole*, after all—people not from there; a couple of white guys—who'd chosen to make a place for ourselves in this strange state. A sort of invasive species, you could say. We toasted the islands, and I got my first of many Gallagher lectures.

"By saying we had no breath, because the first Europeans here were unfamiliar with the traditional Polynesian greeting of *honi*, they were not only implying we were ignorant but that we literally had no spirit. No life inside us."

"I always just thought it meant we were pale," I said.

"It's slightly more than that. One Hawaiian scholar wrote the label originally indicated an alien creature having no relation to race. An outsider in every sense. One who does not conform to the mores of the group and is absolutely void of connection to the land."

It obsessed Gallagher, this concept of his own otherness.

He'd been born and raised in Hawaii, the son of a prominent military doctor, and he'd never left the islands except when sent by Uncle Sam to spend a few bloody years aboard a brown-water gunboat.

But despite his insatiable appetite for Hawaiian history and folklore, and his respect for the customs and culture, he was never truly *of the tribe,* so to speak. I think part of him always hated the place for that.

It never bothered me, the melding and mixing of peoples and cultures being what drew me to the islands to begin with. But it's no stretch to see Gallagher's compulsive pursuit of Hawaiian legends and ghostly tales, his insistence on recording, documenting, and presenting them anew, as an attempt to make himself part of the narrative. To wrap himself up in the lore of this place for all time.

Now, I guess he finally succeeded.

Gallagher and I met regularly through the years as the landscape of the islands changed around us. Those meetings were, I think, like calibrating anchors for us both. Otherwise, we led very different lives. For him, I was a dose of reality, a sobering relief from specious specters and less-than-probable phantoms. And I found him compelling in his eccentricity and, despite myself, increasing fame.

Gallagher was a folklore instructor at a small university and already a well-known collector of ghost stories. People called him from all over the state to report possible hauntings and inexplicable occurrences, asking him to investigate. His office held an ever-growing collection of artifacts and evidence. The walls were plastered with photos of orbs and auras.

His walking tours became more popular and he hired additional guides. His book was expanded and reprinted. He was frequently invited onto local television shows to discuss the subject, and to pen guest articles for the newspaper.

I left the world of journalism, taking a job back in service of our beloved military industrial complex as a staff photographer at Pearl Harbor Naval Shipyard for exponentially more money. The hours, too, were more stable. Back then, there was a woman in my life: a fiancée who became my wife who became my ex-wife with shocking speed. Afterward, it was just easier to stay where I was, geographically and romantically.

A career's worth of grip-and-grin photos, promotion and retirement ceremonies, and industrial documentation passed unremarkably. The war pictures went into the aforementioned closet and I rarely thought of them.

Time is difficult for a single childless man to measure. Women are more aware of its passage and effects, and children are living calendars. But for a man, *alone*, the reality of his years comes home all at once and late in the game—a merciless ambush. Corny as it sounds, one day I looked in the mirror and found some geezer staring back.

Having witnessed the turning of the century, I elected finally to leave government service for the second time. The darkroom had given way to Photoshop, our interns kept looking younger, and I was glad to go.

The island was different by then, too, though some sordid secrets and occult corners still remained—if one knew where to look. *How* to look.

I'd replaced the tourist girls of yesteryear with vacationing divorcees, enjoyed the company of a few friends and several hobbies. I liked to read, about ancient history in particular, and adored riding my Harley, which one can do almost every day in Hawaii. I was not unhappy.

But a few days after I retired I received an urgent e-mail from Gallagher, now a tenured professor and renowned author, which brought me to a bar in Waikiki for an impromptu catch-up.

"Frankly, I'm worried about you." Two sips into the third round, him looking at his watch like he was late for something, and Gallagher suddenly got serious. "I mean, honestly, what will you do with yourself?"

Raising my glass, I said, "You're pretty much looking at it."

He looked again at his watch. Even angry, he was handsome. A bookish movie star in thick spectacles, stylish tint of gray in his ponytail.

"You, my friend, are only happy when you're unhappy," Gallagher said. "First, it was your dirt-poor childhood back East, which you couldn't wait to escape. Then, Vietnam. Next, your lousy marriage. And a job you never once enjoyed. You love having something to hate. What do you have now?"

"Your lectures, apparently."

"Do you want your gift or not?"

"Can I have it now, or must I answer your riddles three?"

"All you have to do is settle the tab and meet me out front." He fixed me with his about-to-tell-a-story look, the one I'd seen him use it to mesmerize many crowds. "I'm being serious, Seth. We're already late."

Outside, rain had slicked the streets and sidewalks. The garish lights of downtown Honolulu were bleeding all over everything. Far off on the Big Island, Kīlauea was grumbling, as evidenced by the noxious mix of fog and volcanic exhaust that weighted the cool November night.

We quickly found his Jeep and the pretty girl leaning against it. She was young, wearing a cheap convenience store sundress, slippers, and an enormous floppy hat. With a squeal, she threw her arms around Gallagher.

"Katie," he said, "sorry to have kept you waiting. This is Seth."

I was used to Gallagher's rotating cast of girlfriends, but in recent months he'd been exchanging them more frequently than usual. This one was new, clearly a tourist, and obviously very drunk. She hugged me enthusiastically, then offered Gallagher a silver flask from her small purse.

"I saved you some."

"Keep it," he said. "I'll drive. Hop in the back, darling, I need a word with Seth on the way."

Katie did, with a pout she probably imagined was cute.

"I'll follow you on my bike," I said.

Gallagher opened the driver's door and slid inside. "I'll run you back right after. Come on, we should hurry."

"I'd rather not leave it. How far are we going?"

"Not far."

I hesitated. Clearly, I remember the moment now and think of it often. How different things might have been.

Gallagher sped along the H-1, past Aiea and Pearl City, following the coast beyond Waianae and into Mākaha Valley, where it devolved from highway to slim rural road. Winding through the night, Gallagher made seemingly random turns. The houses got bigger, placed farther apart and back from the road. Many yards were gated. I do not think I could find the place again—not that I'm willing to try.

All the while, Gallagher talked. Occasionally, Katie would pass the flask from where she slumped in the backseat. Gallagher would hold it for a minute, but never actually take a drink, then pass it back. He didn't offer it to me.

"I've finally found it, Seth."

"What are you talking about? Where are we going?"

"It's the real thing this time. These people, I can't wait for you to meet them. They *know*. Do you see? They live the old ways and have been teaching them to me. It's exactly what we both need, my friend. Something to live for and believe in. Something *authentic*."

The flask came forward again, and Gallagher snatched it. "Thank you, darling. Doing okay back there?"

Katie mumbled something and burped.

"I think she's had too much, Gallagher."

"Nonsense. She's on vacation."

From the backseat a weak little voice said, "The airport . . . he said . . . bought me a hat."

"I sure did." Gallagher handed back the flask. "Finish up, kiddo. Almost there now."

"Gallagher, really. I think—"

"Katie is from Salt Lake City," he continued. "She was on her way abroad for a . . . what did you call it, darling? A *mission*? Lovely. Anyway, after we met she decided she'd rather stay for a while, go to the beach, and think it over before spending more of her life in the service of a misogynistic sect founded by a failed treasure hunter. Her friends were not happy about it, which only proves the point I was very calmly making about intolerance before they started screaming. At least the cult of Christ has antiquity on their side, right? If one is going to be a believer, choose a doctrine old enough to have proven staying power, that's what I say."

Losing patience, I said, "What the hell are you talking about?"

"Just what I was discussing before, Seth. The source."

"Source of what?"

"Everything I've spent my life studying, they're just side effects. Symptoms of a condition I have thus far been unable to diagnose, to borrow some terminology from my father's profession."

Gallagher's father died years before and he almost never mentioned the man. His mother, who I gather he'd been very close with, succumbed to breast cancer when he was a teenager. I understood the men were then left to simmer in what became a lifelong stew of mutual tension and dislike. The old man disapproved of Gallagher's being unmarried, his decision to forgo medical school. But the casual way in which my friend now invoked the man—almost *fondly*—was odd.

We sped around a frighteningly sharp curve, tires shrieking.

"A few days before he died," Gallagher continued, oblivious, "he confided something to me. Throughout his career, my father resuscitated many people. They were clinically dead, Seth, and he punched into the ether and drug them back to reality. He was not a religious man, but obviously he asked them about the experience. Scientific curiosity, he said. And each told him the same thing: Nothing happened. No tunnels. No lights. No voices. Not a single one floated over their body. There was only blackness."

"Shouldn't that have pleased you? You are a heavyweight skeptic."

"How right you are." His face broke into a strange grin that made me uncomfortable. I'd seen that smile before, looking back at me from photographs on the faces of doomed young men in a jungle far away, many years ago. It was the amusement of someone resigned to something terrible and unavoidable. A man sprinting gleefully toward the grave.

"I was pleased," he admitted. "Positively smug, in fact. Did I tell you I was with my father when he died?"

"You didn't."

Gallagher gunned the engine around another frightening curve. High walls of black trees loomed on either side of the road. Asphalt shone wetly in the headlights. In the back, Katie snored, dead to the world.

"He died screaming. Massive heart attack. Must have been agony."

"*Jesus*. I'm sorry."

Gallagher waved a hand dismissively. "No, it's *what* he screamed that has changed my life. See, all this time I never really believed, Seth. I was just playing along. Now, I finally know the truth. My father told it to me as his heart stopped and his body died around him."

I asked, of course.

"Just two words," Gallagher whispered. "*They lied.*"

Did Gallagher have a favorite legend?

Yes, in fact he did. Gallagher seemed to dwell upon one story most and returned to it often, especially late in our drinking sessions. It seemed never far from his mind, but the story wasn't any of those so popular with paying audiences—not the Menehune, the Nightmarchers, or stories of picking up Pele on the Pali.

In fact, he insisted it was no legend at all.

Though cannibalism was never practiced by the ancient Hawaiians (despite ugly rumors spread by early European arrivals to the contrary), and was considered despicable, it was not entirely unheard of on the islands. Records tell of a giant—a great warrior chief, the historians called him—who came to O'ahu sometime in the eighteenth century with rather zealous beliefs on the subject.

Where did he come from? Nobody knows. Some say he was driven from his homeland because of his awful tendencies. They say his native subjects at last tired of satisfying his voracious appetites and ran him off. Others say it was a simple political coup that forced his exile to Hawaii.

What is known is he came alone, proffering no explanation. According to the stories, one morning the guy was just there, standing on a beach with the blazing sun rising behind him. He had no boat, no supplies. It was as if he'd simply walked out of the sea.

He was a brawler as deadly with his hands and teeth as any weapon, and stronger than four grown men. He preached a strict new gospel of *sacred violence* and immediately began gathering a following. He hosted orgies and mandated the ritual cannibalism of both fallen friend and vanquished foe alike, insisting such practices increased one's strength and extended life. The ancient scholars called him *Ke-ali'i-ai-kanaka*, which I understand roughly translates as the King Who Eats Men.

Supposedly, he was from Fiji, or possibly a more distant island. But Gallagher insisted credible accounts exist which described him as looking more like a Viking with long blonde hair, pale skin, and *startling eyes*. He might have been an albino, but Gallagher was convinced that *Aikanaka*, as the man was commonly known, was hā'ole in the true original sense—having no relation to race; an outsider who does not conform to the mores of the group.

Gallagher went even further, insisting the man had no connection to Earth at all.

The stories say Aikanaka established a small kingdom in the mountains of Wahiawa. Anyone who passed into his territory would be captured. Found worthy, they'd be offered the chance to join with Aikanaka's sect. Found wanting, they'd be devoured—roasted alive in an *imu*, placed upon an enormous flat stone, and carved up. Christian missionaries, so it was said, were his favorite meal.

Nobody knows how many souls met their end screaming for

mercy in those hills before lowland warriors came at last, determined to slay the King Who Eats Men. The battle raged for days before Aikanaka, gravely wounded, was supposedly driven into the sea from a high cliff.

For decades afterward, stories persisted that the valley was haunted by the immortal spirit of Aikanaka, who'd eaten far too many souls to be killed. Even throughout the latter days of the twentieth century, some of the more superstitious old folks would lay the blame for every violent crime committed on the islands on the spirit of Aikanaka.

They said he now simply possessed new bodies so as to sate his terrible hunger.

Gallagher was talking again about the King Who Eats Men as he pulled into a long private drive and parked behind a row of empty cars.

The specifics of the mansion are vague in my mind, but every light inside was on, immense windows blazing brightly against the night. It should have been comforting, even cheery, but was not. There was an eerie silence draped over the place. The wind ceased, even the fog thinned, as if unwilling to venture onto the property.

I retrieved the empty flask and sniffed the opening as Gallagher helped Katie out. The remnants smelled weirdly floral and much too sweet, not like any liquor I knew. Underneath was the vague hint of something rancid. My mind flashed on the image of savaged bodies rotting amidst pungent jungle flowers, but I saw it flat and glossy, like in a photograph. My stomach roiled as we walked, Gallagher supporting the stumbling girl.

We circumnavigated the manor around to the backyard, which was enclosed by a fence of dark wood. The light from the windows mixed with the softer glow from strands of round paper lanterns hung above the gathering.

I remember thinking it was some kind of student-faculty mixer because the ages of those assembled were so varied. Maybe sixty or seventy people were there, but it was hard to guess precisely because everyone seemed to be constantly in motion, as if preparing for something.

Two identical enormous men, shirtless and darkly tanned, their massive arms and chests adorned with bold tribal tattoos, were laying slabs of meat on a low grill above a glowing bed of coals. A pretty Chinese girl wearing flower lei perched on a stool near a table cluttered with open wine bottles, gently strumming a guitar.

Katie was instantly swallowed up and carried away by a giggling horde of women. One of them, very pretty with silver hair, dark skin, and large eyes, took a swipe at Gallagher's shoulder, admonishing him for letting "the poor little dear" drink so much, before fleeing after the others.

They all knew him, waving and calling excitedly to Gallagher as he led me through the milling throng toward a row of coolers to pull slick bottles of Heineken from icy water.

Gallagher was quickly bombarded with hugs and handshakes from people clamoring around him, so I wandered away, trying to look casual despite my gnawing unease. My wife had been fond of entertaining, and she'd remarked often during our fleeting union that it was impossible to love a man so obviously happiest when alone. She left me without so much as a note. Had she considered that a kindness? Distracted by this surprise attack of yet another distasteful memory, I very nearly fell into the pool.

The underwater lights were off, making the water look black. It was outlined with blue tile set into cement and, much like the house, should have been inviting. Immediately, I thought it strange that nobody stood near the pool. They all gathered uncomfortably close together on the other side of the yard. I knelt to look closer—and saw the water really was black.

No. I realized it wasn't water at all.

The pool was filled with inky sludge, something you might dredge up from the bottom of Pearl Harbor—the bottom of the Mariana Trench, for that matter. A primordial muck which had never before seen daylight. It stank, too. The expected salty iodine of the sea, typical low-tide stink of the shore, and something else. Something musky and animal-like. Something rancid. I leaned closer.

The still surface was slick with shiny ribbons twirling and dancing across it. And beneath, for just a second, I thought I saw something. An even darker shape moving amidst the blackness. A small wave rolled across the brackish liquid, as if something big had turned over in the obsidian depths. I thought I could almost see it, something big and with too many limbs.

"Don't fall in."

Gallagher was behind me, a fresh beer in each hand. His smile was too wide, voice too casual—a bad actor attempting something beyond his talent. "I don't think Marsha's had that cleaned in years. You'll probably catch leprosy or some damn thing. Come over here where it's safer."

I moved after him, trying to sound nonchalant. "You have to die of something, right?"

"Maybe," he passed me a bottle, eyes on the pool. "But not that."

The silver-haired woman approached again, beaming at Gallagher. "I like this one," she said. "I really do."

"Me too. Marsha, this is my friend Seth."

She was about a head shorter than me, and when Marsha clasped my shoulders I found myself looking down into her eyes, feeling as if I were falling.

"I'm so glad you're here, Seth. Gallagher's told us all about you."

Her face made me think of ship horns and train whistles sounding in places with names I could not pronounce. The world went gauzy at the edges as I stared. Then, I came painfully back to reality, like a man waking after a drunken bender, as she turned her attention to Gallagher.

"Devout, you say?"

"On her way overseas in selfless service of Jesus Christ. Recently fallen. Very recently, in fact. I don't think the girl ever had a naughty thought until three days ago."

"Until she met you." Marsha's smile vanished. She jabbed a finger into his chest. "Tell the truth."

"Not one finger, Marsha, I swear." Gallagher looked a little scared. I'd never thought him capable of shame on the subject of his young female companions.

"It's not your finger I'm concerned about," Marsha said. "You promised. Not like last time."

Gallagher eyed the pool again, his face gone pale. "Not like the others. She's exactly right, just like I said."

"No, Gallagher." Marsha slapped his face. "Just like *I* said. She has to be *pristine*."

Beyond, the party continued. If anyone noticed what was happening, they gave no sign. The sound of guitar music drifted above the chattering and laughter. The smell of charred meat wafted through the air. I looked but could not find Katie among the shifting bodies.

Marsha whispered, "It's not me who will judge. And if she isn't right, if you've failed again, it's not me you will answer to."

She turned and disappeared into the crowd. I watched my friend struggle to collect himself, finally turning to me and waggling his eyebrows. "Saucy old dame. I always suspected she liked it rough."

"Gallagher, what is going on?"

"We'll know soon enough." His eyes strayed back to the swimming pool. "All I know is what I've seen. What my father said. All legends come from somewhere. The risk, I think, is worth . . . well, everything. It's worth everything if it's true."

"If what's true?"

"Don't you know?" Again the scary smile took over his face. "The second coming. The wolf that swallows the sun. The once and future king. It's the end of the world, good buddy, and I feel fine."

He went on, growing more excited. "And with strange aeons, who knows? Even death may die." Gallagher tittered and drained his beer. "More things in heaven and Earth and all that."

A scream silenced the revelers. I watched Katie being forced across the yard, struggling against a horde of women, their eyes blazing with mindless zeal. She was naked, a thick ring of colorful lei around her neck, strange symbols painted onto her flesh. I moved instinctively forward—still a young man of action, in my own mind, at least—and heard Gallagher say, "Don't, Seth. Please."

Like they'd been waiting for the chance, the Samoan brothers were on me, gigantic hands gripping my arms. I struggled about as effectively as the drugged girl did against the mob that bore her to the pool. Led by Marsha, they sang in a language I did not recognize.

The mire began to stir. It frothed and bubbled as if in anticipation while the crowd hefted Katie, bucking and twisting, eyes huge and rolled back in absolute panic, over their heads.

A collective exclamation of ecstasy was echoed at my sides by the brothers, whose hands still held me fast. And behind me, Gallagher sang out too, seemingly one of the tribe at last, having come through with his terrible membership fee.

I cannot be sure if I screamed. But Katie did. I will never forget that sound: the dying cry of a wounded animal cut dreadfully short by a splash as she struck the bubbling surface of the ooze and sank.

The brothers released me and hurried poolside to stand with the rest, all of them gazing fixedly into the still blackness. Gallagher's hand fell onto my shoulder.

"I'm sorry. It's awful, I know. But it will work this time."

This time. How many girls had been offered to the thing I'd seen lurking in the depths of the pool? What was the horrible master these zealots hoped to appease?

The sound of splashing brought me back to the moment, watching as the congregants pulled Katie from the water. I felt myself walking forward as they laid her on the grass, wiping the symbols and black slime from her skin like nurses cleaning a newborn. Marsha cradled the girl's head in her lap, gently stroking her oily hair, beaming proudly.

The corners of Katie's mouth were split, like her lips had been forced open too wide. Her stomach was engorged, the skin stretched taught and slowly throbbing as if in time with her heartbeat. The level of the brackish fluid in the pool had lowered considerably.

As I approached, the unconscious girl began to cough. She sat up, spluttering out an immense gout of bloody sludge over her belly. Then she opened her eyes—their formerly cheerful blue had changed to a startling shade of gray so light as to be almost clear—to immediate applause.

In a deep rumbling voice, Katie spoke in a dialect that seemed impossibly old. The words of men who threw spears at the sun, I thought. Marsha's face streamed with tears, which Katie reached out one slime-covered finger to wipe away. She slowly licked her finger clean with a smile, then reached forward with both hands, roughly grabbed hold of Marsha's head, and kissed her.

Another explosive cheer went up from the crowd, but the kiss went on too long and Marsha began to struggle. When Katie moved her head there was a wet ripping sound, and Marsha screamed as her tongue came away clenched tightly in the girl's bared teeth.

Katie stood, bulging stomach seeming to grow even as I watched. Her eyes roamed the gathering and fell onto me. I can still recall her smile, the way her eyes lit up like the first flash of dawn on the horizon.

But those eyes darkened as she turned to Gallagher. She spat out the half-masticated tongue and spoke again, just two words, in English this time.

"They lied."

I was surprised to find I'd been retreating without thinking. I was beyond the crowd when Gallagher began to scream. As I turned to flee, I saw them reach for my friend with greedy hands and drag him to the ground. He begged for help.

I ran around the house and—not bothering to stop at the car, for I was certain Gallagher had the keys—stumbled down the driveway until I reached the blackness beyond. All of the tropics seem alike in the dark, and Oʻahu was Vietnam, and I was a young man again as I sprinted through the trees. Chased by the ghosts of ancient bullets, ears full of screams both fresh and faded. I ran until I collapsed and threw up, only then feeling my age. But I forced myself up again and ran on. I ran for my life.

That was nearly two weeks ago.

I found my way to the road and got a ride downtown from a passing car. My Harley was where I'd left it, wearing a necklace of flowers. Possibly, they'd been tossed aside by some tourist, but I don't think so. The lei is a symbol of honor, celebration, and memorial. It's meant to convey the spirit of aloha, which of course means both hello and goodbye. I can't help but wonder which meaning they intended.

I went home to my silent house in Kāne'ohe and locked the doors and windows, drew the blinds. Retrieving my photos from the closet, I waited. Perusing the treacherous alleyways of memory, I awaited the return of the king.

Yesterday, I chanced walking to the store for supplies. I passed a young Chinese girl sitting on the sidewalk, strumming a guitar. She blew me a kiss.

Sometimes, the phone rings. I pick up but nobody speaks. After a moment, a woman will begin to hum. Always the same tune. It makes me think of wind rustling the branches of trees that were ancient when humans first walked erect. Waves crashing against shores that had yet to feel human feet. I think of vast sunken cities where the sun does not shine.

The woman never speaks. I think maybe she can't anymore. Maybe she just doesn't need to.

On the news today, I saw they found Gallagher. It's a big story, a famous local author dying in such a grisly way. His remains were found in an empty pool in the yard of a private residence. The owner lives overseas, they said, and police have been unable to reach her. Identification required dental records, as the body had reportedly been badly burned and partially devoured.

A group of men are repaving the driveway of a house across the street. They've been there for days but have made no progress. Supervising the effort are identical brothers, enormous and elaborately tattooed. When they spot me watching, they wave.

Today, I waved back.

Author's Note: I lived in Hawaii for several years during the 2000s and return often to visit family and friends. Intentional superficial similarities exist as a kind of playful homage between the character of Gallagher and actual Hawaii historian/folklorist Glen Grant, whose writing I've long enjoyed. Narrative liberties were similarly taken with actual Hawaiian geography and mythology for the sake of entertainment. Readers curious to learn more are directed to Grant's work (Obake Files and The Secret Obake Casebook, specifically).

DO NOT BE AFRAID

by Richard Beauchamp

WELCOME TO THE **MIN-SAUK** Caverns Guided Tour!

By now, your Min-Sauk Caverns giftshop attendee should have escorted you to the proper entrance for the tour. You smell that? It's the smell of adventure! (Just kidding, it's actually dissolving limestone!)

Please be sure to watch your step as you follow the tour's instructions. The deeper you go into this wondrous ever-growing cave system, the harder it will be for Carter County emergency services to locate you. Min-Sauk Caverns Land Management™ is not responsible for any injuries that incur on the property or for the duration of the tour. Admittance to the self-guided tour counts as consent of this condition

As you step into Main Shaft-34, you will be greeted with a blast from the past! With funds raised by the Ozark National Preservation Society, our nonprofit organization has been able to restore and maintain many of the old mine structures present during the lead-boom period of the early 1900s. Observe the metal trellises and machine-graded flooring that allowed miners to drive huge ore diggers through. These mining roads go approximately two miles in a slowly descending, spiral formation that allowed the miners to safely expand operations as further lead veins were found and exploited.

> **Did You Know?** *The geographic area known as "The Ozark Uplift" contains one of the densest concentrations of Galena on the planet. Known colloquially as the "Lead Belt," the Saint Francois Mountain region of the lead belt alone was responsible for supplying the US military with hundreds of tons of refined lead for the World War 2 war effort.*

As you continue down this gentle downward spiral, you will come upon a submerged cavern to your left. Notice the rust-speckled mining equipment submerged within the cerulean blue water. These are remnants of the Marquette Iron Works 1945 digging expedition. Since the French originally settled in these hills in the 1800s and opened up the very first mine shafts, newly formed mining companies of the 1930s and onwards had to go deeper and dig farther to find further untapped veins. Unfortunately, some of these exploratory efforts to expand into an already vast karst system ended in tragedy as ambitious foremen, not equipped with the advanced sonar technology we have today, inadvertently blasted themselves into underground aquifers, resulting in mass casualty events, as well as the poisoning of nearby aquifers that supplied townships with drinking water.

> **Did you know?** *The flooded cavern you see before you is part of what's called "Mammoth Spring," and is one of the largest first-magnitude underground streams in the entire country. Due to the acidic nature of the spring-filtered water, the immense limestone "bays" that channel the stream dissolve with time, causing sink holes and natural stove pipe lakes to form. To date, Mammoth Spring only remains 5% explored,*

*with bodies of many miners forever being swallowed
by its abyssal depths. Don't fall in!*

By now you will have reached the bottom of the mining road. If you've noticed a change in the atmosphere around you, it's not just you: You are now approximately two miles below the gentle rolling hills and karst outcroppings that comprise the Ozark Uplift. Nitrogen has slowly increased while oxygen has partially decreased. **Do not be afraid:** this is normal.

You will notice several DANGER signs, along with END OF PUBLIC USE AREA. You can ignore these, brave explorer, for if you have made it this far, then you have clearly committed to seeing the true underbelly of this majestic land.

To your right you will see another flooded cavern, and more beautiful crystalline water. Be careful skirting its edge as you gaze into those perfectly clear waters. It seems bottomless, doesn't it? That's because it is.

When removing the NO TRESPASSING saw-horse, please be sure to move it back into place behind you as you begin the next phase of the tour. This is to prevent children and other unworthy explorers from venturing too far off the beaten path.

This section no longer contains ceiling lighting because Marquette Iron Works went bankrupt (winning wars is good for freedom, bad for the lead business!). It also didn't help that between 1935 and 1941 over two hundred men from the Marquette mining corps went missing in these very caves.

In this modern age of cellphones, we assume most intrepid explorers who've gone this far have utilized their phones and flashlight applications for sources of light, but if you happen to possess neither, please feel free to consult the wooden box to your right. The box says TNT, but inside you will find several neon glow sticks. Take several.

You will need them.

By now, you might have noticed mild tremors shaking the ground beneath your feet. **Do not be afraid**: This is normal. Being this deep in the earth, you are sitting very close to the New Madrid Fault Line, which you can thank for creating this immense cave system in the first place. The fault line remains inactive and has only been known to release small "burping" tremors of up to 2.4 on the Richter scale since the massive 1811 earthquake that so transformed this land.

Look up as you enter this raw-earthed portal, and you will see the ever-growing fangs of limestone stalactites above you. As Mammoth Spring discharges hundreds of gallons of water per minute above you, the highly acidic flow drips from cracks in the ceiling, leaving behind trace amounts of minerals with each droplet, causing these beautiful formations to grow at a rate of an inch a year, like your hair or nails. You may want to seek cover if you experience a tremor in this section, as those stalactites have been known to become dislodged and embed themselves into things like skulls and shoulders (Just kidding! That only happened once.)

You should have come to a junction by now. You will come across many of these. Do not try to remember which tunnels you have gone down, or you will be disoriented. Just follow the instructions on this pamphlet, and we'll get you where you need to go!

> **Did You Know?** *There are over 6,400 caves in the state of Missouri alone. Of these, only 20% have been fully explored. The Onondaga Cave system you're about to enter is one of the least explored systems in the state, with over four hundred miles of untamed tunnels and systems mapped by sonar. According to the US Department of Justice, over 600,000 people go missing in the continental United States alone, and it is believed at least a quarter of those result in misadventure in places such as this. Don't become a statistic!*

Follow the pamphlet's instructions closely.

Take the farthest rightmost tunnel. By now you will have noticed a peculiar earthy smell that has probably overtaken the rich mineral scent of the caves themselves. As you proceed down this tunnel, you will notice white lumps protruding from the weeping walls of the cave. If it looks like a head of cauliflower and seems to be mildly iridescent, congratulations, for you have come upon what is known as "Ivory Angel Cap": an exclusively subterranean morel mushroom species that's highly sought-after and indigenous only to this part of the Ozark uplift. Go ahead, pluck one from the wall. They grow like weeds down here!

(Please collect as many as you can, in the event that you become disoriented and lost. It is the only edible thing that grows down here.)

Note the rich, earthy taste, which is followed thereafter by a nutty crescendo that concludes with a mildly bitter end. Its flavor profile is as complex as the many serotonergic alkaloids found within its pulpy rind. Do not be alarmed as you notice a heightening of your senses and peripheral vision. This is normal and necessary for the next segment of the tour.

By now you should have come to another junction. So many options, yes? Do not be overwhelmed. Go left. Follow the sound of rushing water.

You should have now come upon a large underground river. Once one of the cleanest river valleys in the world, the Current River has, in the last 30 years, been subject to multiple biome collapses due to the toxic discharge from the lead tailings that enters its waters as it meanders through some of the more high-yielding shaft mines in place along the Saint Francois mountains. Your eyes do not deceive you as you gaze into the water. Those strange three-eyed fish you see occasionally breaching the surface are rainbow trout and chain pickerel. Fishing for them is *not* recommended.

Follow the bank onwards until you come to a large atrium. You should see a large scum-covered pool to your left. Notice the neon-orange film coating the water here. These are known as "slime pools" and are another side effect of the lead discharge runoff. If you see the surface rippling for any reason at all, it is strongly advised you move to the next area with haste. We do not know what lurks in the slime pool.

Did You Know? *Long-term exposure to elevated lead levels can result in anemia, brain and kidney damage, and general body weakness. The neighboring township of Poplar Springs, who shares a sister-system with the Onondaga, was forced to relocate its entire population in 1975 after the EPA confirmed the town's many well systems drew off a long-contaminated aquifer and is now on the Superfund PAC list. Move over California, the Midwest has its own ghost towns!*

By now, you should be feeling a profound disconnect from your body. Perhaps only a faint pressure behind the eyes and a tingling of your extremities. **Do not be afraid:** This is normal. If you feel yourself being "pulled" in a certain direction, it's not just your morel-muddled mind playing tricks on you. You are on the right path.

Continue forward. By now you will have come to yet another junction, with even more paths ahead of you. Here is where we leave the choice up to you, brave explorer. Let yourself be guided by the tidal pulling you must surely feel in your bone marrow. There is no wrong decision here. Go where you feel the most compelled to.

Succumb to that ephemeral tugging.

As you can see, human industry has had profound effects on these once beautiful lands and the subterranean bowels that you now explore. As you draw closer to the source, you should notice an increase in the presence of the Ivory Angel Cap. This is not a coincidence; you will soon find out why these unique fungi grow only in the deepest reaches of the earth.

By now you should be feeling an overwhelming pull, perhaps it is even a little bit painful. This is good. This means you are close to your final destination.

You have probably heard the shuffle of feet, the susurration of voices around you. This is not your imagination or a trick of the cavern acoustics. Others have joined you on their journey. Do not be frightened by their appearance, as some have been down here a very long time. They mean you no harm. You are all in this together.

Gaze upon it. The white bulbous mass you see before you is older than even these ancient hills. You will notice the large obsidian boulder the main mass has been transmogrified onto. Carbon dating shows this asteroid to have smacked into our humble hill region some 800,000 years ago.

> **Did You Know?** *The Osage and Pee-Wah Native tribes were the first ones to encounter the Ivory Angel Cap. Several ancient cave paintings preserved by the Ozark National Preservation Society show various depictions of the morel connected to a large, white mass via several finely drawn lines. It seems the brave warriors were trying to warn possible cave dwellers to be wary of the fungi and its wonderful connective properties.*

You might be horrified at what you see, but by now you should realize the pull that has guided you here is too strong for resistance. Do not try to run.

As of now, you have probably come to the conclusion that you have been duped, lied to. Those of us on behalf of Min-Sauk Caverns Land Management™ apologize for this necessary deception, but we find this is the most humane way to maintain what little natural beauty is left of the caverns. Those of us with scientific backgrounds postulate this growth had, at one time, been a benign and somewhat harmless extraterrestrial parasite. Having been embedded within the meteorite seen before you, this wonderful growth has since come into contact with the toxic runoff from the surrounding mines, and the resulting mutation has since caused it to develop a rather ravenous appetite.

You might be wondering why we indulge in such deception to bring this being what it wants. The answer is simple: Sonar readings conducted by the United States Geological Survey have shown this main biomass has penetrated the intraplate seismic zone of the New Madrid Fault Line, and carbon dating of surrounding soil samples corroborate the theory that the catastrophic earthquake of 1811 was a result of this being's agitation.

Quite by accident we have discovered that "feeding" this biomass has resulted in marked reductions in seismic activity in the area. We do not know why or how this correlates with the biomass and its effect on the fault line. We do know, however, that not a single earthquake above 2.5 magnitude has been observed since the feeding practice was instituted.

We believe the Ivory Angel Cap was created as a sort of "bait" to entice early native settlers to explore the cave system in—which this poor being has found itself trapped in—and utilize its physiological magnetism. Not only does consumption of the morel strengthen your bond to the biomass, but it also appears to have profound analgesic effects upon those who are consumed by the mass.

As a token of thanks for your cooperation, we will provide you with this hint to ensure your subsumption into the mass is as painless as possible: Eat as much of the fungi as you can. Go in headfirst. We find suffering to be minimal that way.

> **Did You Know?** *Your participation in the Min-Sauk Caverns self-guided tour directly contributes to the safety of the surrounding region and of the entire Midwest itself. You might find little comfort in knowing that you have saved millions of lives from disaster and suffering, but know your life was given for the greater good. As we are a nonprofit entity, we must rely upon subterfuge tactics such as this to produce the "food" necessary to appease the parasite that grows in our seismic zone. Thank you for understanding.*

This concludes the self-guided tour of the Min-Sauk Caverns. Comments? Questions? Concerns? Please send an inquiry to:

MissouriDepartmentofNaturalResources.Extension2.gmail.com

VII

BALLAD AND CODAS

THE FIRST BOOK OF THE SHADOW UNDER CROMLEDGE

by Godwyn

FESTIVAL. MAIDEN'S GHOST.
DAUGHTER OF MUSIC. DARK
REVERIES. SACRIFICE. MUTINOUS
CONSIDERATIONS. BLACK SPIRALS.

I

SEVERAL TURNSTONES BEFORE THE SUN (or *Sol*) and Moon came into being, a festival raged under the graylight. And in this graylight you could see from afar, and dimly, the outline of the kingdom of Cromledge. This was when they who lived behind the walls of stone and *godbone* contemplated their strange point in time (albeit their *physical formation* and *when they came into being* were only half-remembered; *turnstones* tended to grind collective memory to soot, you must understand).

Godbones, during the festival, were cut to excess, till many slivers were born from the blade. These were cast into the yellow-orange glow of *godbreath*[1] as an offering to their memory beyond the graylight. Around decorative pits of stone fed with *bones*, alive with breath, the denizens danced and sang unknowable ballads, danced and drank the *oldsap*, danced wearing the faces of the Outsiders, and they would continue to dance and sing and drink till the Sky Ring materialized above their masked faces.

Branching off the ghostly hall, one devoid of any *godbreath* or ancient light-emitting orbs, the Lord Manager watched from a little high balcony of the keep. He could only see rudimentary blurs from this height, and scarcely a sound . . .

. . . occasional bombastic music, drunken laughter, indistinguishable clamor.

Above, the graylight shivered. His hairs stood on end. *Did the festivalgoers feel it, too?* he wondered. Unlikely; they were too far below, and even if they were able to the festival surely would have drunk that Outer Whisper. Wiseman Aemis had claimed the rumbles from above were (he'd uttered so on his deathbed) the "stirrings of the True Outsider." But Wiseman Aemis was now dead. Had been for two *turnstones*. He was *godfood*.

"Another one," a voice said from over his shoulder, the speaker invisible in the wide, cold, dim hall. The lightlessness all but swallowed Aemis's great cloaked predecessor, along with his low bow (indicated only by crackling ancient bones). Wiseman Tusk cleared his throat. Saving the Lord Manager from needlessly wasting breath, he said, "The parents were Myris and Wen, the basket weavers. Down in the Blight's Hallow—"

"I know them," interjected the Lord Manager. He tried to know all whom he governed. The previous Manager had told him that if he tried to know some, he'd only know a few; if he tried to know most, he'd only know some; but if he tried to intimately know and to be personable with *all*, then he *might* at least know most—and *that* was as noble as feasibly possible.

"I didn't mean to suggest otherwise," apologized Tusk. He

---

[1] Whether this is an archaic word proceeding "fire," or a word which greatly—through unfathomable leagues of time—supersedes "fire," is beyond our comprehension.

stepped next to the Lord Manager. *Crackle, crackle.* The graylight described a long, wispy beard upon a weathered face. If you were to look upon him straight on (most couldn't because of his profound height), the tip of his great hooked nose would obscure his lips. Except, of course, his mustache concealed his lips, anyway. And he was paler than most, for he never crossed into the graylight. Unless he had to.

"Go on," said the Lord Manager.

"It was a boy. Yordyn, she would have named him. She, in fact, *had* named him as he lay limp in her arms, wholly uncomprehending the blade which had ended its abominable misery."

"Yordyn?" the Lord Manager said, speechless save for that one word.

"Flatter yourself another hour," said Tusk. He laughed raspily, his bones crackled. "She'd named him after a cousin, I believe."

"Of course," said the Lord Manager, pushing down his pride. The previous Manager had also warned him of that. *Pride.* Without accurately diagnosing it and promptly snuffing it out, it would corrupt any who breathed in it.

He stared into the outer darkness. Could he see an outline of an Outsider watching the festival? Or was it his imagination? And was there much difference if they were there or not if the result of the festival was the same? Passover—at least for a while. And why the Outsiders required only *one* festival per turnstone was beyond his understanding. Felt like a game. Felt like They were laughing out there.

"I'd like to see the babe, before it's cremated."

"That could be arranged, Lord." And he turned to leave; but the Manager had whispered something from where he stood on the balcony, which halted Tusk. "Come again, my Lord?"

"Why does it happen only on the festival?"

Wiseman Tusk knew many things but knew not a reasonable answer, except for this: "Because it is part of the festival, my Lord; interwoven into its very . . . *fabric.*"

The Lord Manager had wanted to say, *But maybe we're not supposed to do what we do;* and somehow Tusk had known this and said, "If we don't slay the babes, they'll mature. They'll become just like Halfman Ubon. Their numbers would be too great. We must act swiftly when we see the Mark of the Beastblood."

The Lord Manager sighed, sleuthing the Wiseman's wisdom.

"And what of Yordyn's parents? Has it already happened?"

"You must commence the ceremony, my Lord. As Manager it is something you must do."

The Manager waved a hand, dismissing Wiseman Tusk. "I'll be down shortly."

Bowing low (*crackle, crackle*). Tusk made his exit, disappearing into the lightless corridor. Then the *crackling* prematurely ceased. The Lord Manager knew that he had stopped somewhere in that hazy black. "And Lord?"

"Speak."

"Wen and Myris's midwife—I apologize, but her name escapes me." There was a *SNAP* (whether from Tusk snapping his fingers or shifting his body, the Manager wasn't certain). "I think it's one of the Old Names."

A welt throbbed in the Lord Manager's throat. "What of her?"

"She wishes to speak to you. I've sent her into the Temple to await your answer."

A chill ran through him. Had he felt a skyward teardrop land atop his head? Do the Outsiders look upon this broken people in this broken city with dismay? Do they prefer blood? Or compassion? Again, he sighed, and answering the shape in the dark hall he said, "Tell her to wait a while longer and I will give her an ear."

Crackle, crackle. And silence. And again—this time unmistakable—the graylight shivered, grinding together like mountains, and tilting his head skyward the Lord Manager gazed at the hazy gray and wondered what lay beyond.

II

Sarah stood numbly in the Temple of the Outsiders, blood from when the babe was ended still speckling her face. The beads of blood, now dry and flaky, tickled her flesh, as if living things trying to eat away at her skin. If she was right, then perhaps the babe's blood was doing just *that*.

Eating away at her.

The cleric was gone. Off to the festival. Probably drunk himself halfdead in one of the nearby streets.

She looked around and saw an old man sitting on the middlemost stone pew, hands raised to the heavens, tears streaming down his face. His outward show of sorrow seemed to perfectly embody the storm she felt inside (the welt in her own throat not so different than Yordyn's), but that's all she would allow herself to feel.

Footfalls.

She turned and glanced out the Temple entryway. From around the corner, and slightly winded from the long ascent of stairs, came a black-haired, gaunt man who looked ten *turnstones* her senior, with white at his temples and a prominent wrinkle across his forehead—one which hadn't been there a *turnstone* prior. Although that was a façade; the wraithlike man dressed like the Lord Manager was younger than her.

"Sarah?" Dark shadows surrounded dark pupils and wiggled from the flickering torchlight, as if made of black worms. His voice was older. More regal, more haunted. And behind him—like a gray, twisted shadow—came Wiseman Tusk. While Yordyn came up and put a hand on either of her bony shoulders, looking at her squarely in the face, Tusk waited in the shadowy archway.

"Yordyn" had almost slipped from her lips. She corrected herself. "Lord Manager."

And he patted either shoulder before putting down his arms.

"You became a *midwife*." He'd said this as if to convince himself of the preposterousness.

"I became a midwife," she said.

"Well"—smiling with his mouth, not his eyes—"you wanted to see me."

Does he not see the blood from the babe and the sorrow etched across my face? It had been inward dialogue, but she projected this thought as loud as a scream; when they'd been children they shared a form of . . . *frequency.* But whatever sensitivity to that frequency Yordyn once had had been cauterized.

She sighed.

"I'd like to go to the caves."

He took a step back. Looked at her hard and carefully.

From the Temple entrance: *crackle, crackle.*

"What for?"

"Ghost of the Maiden."

"What?"

Crackle, crackle—"an herb, my Lord"—and somehow the old advisor had weaseled his way next to his master. "Antiparasitic, if I'm not mistaken, m'lady."

"Yes," she said. "It's a very rare herb, one that's been found on occasions in the caves to the north and west, but the northern caves are too close to Under-Mountain Obelisk. So it should be west."

"Okay?" He glanced at Tusk who squinted diagnostically at Sarah, then back at his older sister. "Why?"

For a moment she saw not the Lord Manager, but her younger, snotty-nosed brother. She gawked at him as if he was the densest-headed creature to have been born. Yet she refused to utter the words; instead she slipped her hand into the oversized pocket of her blood-stained robe and fished out the answer (at least, half the answer) and spat it into the Lord Manager's rough hands.

He looked at the instrument as if it were a new disease. Weighed it in his hands. Gripped the handle made of Old Hunter bone, five orbs—depicting the Outsiders—etched into it.

"Five women gave birth this evening, Yordyn"—there, she let it slip, causing Wiseman Tusk to hiss—"so I knew there was a chance that the babe I was delivering might need . . ." But she still could not bring herself to say it. She became a midwife to deliver babes into the world, not to take them out of it.

"This is Father's." Holding up the blade to catch the torch-light. "He gave it to you?"

"Before he died, yes. Imagine him giving it to me *after* he died." She laughed humorlessly. "A *turnstone* ago. When you were apprenticing."

He must have noticed the blood, for he swiftly sheathed it and, not without an instinctive reluctance, handed it back.

"This is the first time I'd ever seen the Mark. At first, I wasn't sure if it even *was* the Mark. If it wasn't for the look of dismay on Wen's face; if it wasn't for the sound of the assigned Guardsman at the door, the bored one who made it obvious he'd rather be drinking and whoring on festival night with his Brothers—that distinct sound of cold metal being pulled from its sheath. If it wasn't for those two signs, I wouldn't have known. And I wouldn't have done it myself until the moment that Myris started laughing and kissing her babe—because she didn't see the Mark, Yordyn. She saw only her son, pure and unblemished. Then Wen looking at the unsheathed shortsword: I saw its deathly gleam in the reflection of his eyes, and I knew it must be I."

She pocketed the blade. It felt heavy in her robe.

"The Beastblood ailment, in its infantile stage, looks almost as . . . indistinguishable as, you know"—shaking her head—"Ringrot or Remington's Twist, or any other parasitic illness."

"Aren't there stores of it in the Infirmary?"

She laughed. "No. You can't store it. Its medicinal effects wane swiftly. That's one of the reasons why it's so rare."

Her brother sighed.

"Sarah, what are you asking?"

"I just told you. To the caves. In the west. Maiden's Ghost."

She now paced back and forth in front of the horned statue representing the Great Shifter, occasionally glancing at the old man worshiping.

"I understand *that* part. But what are you *actually* asking? You get Maiden's Ghost—and then *what*? Wait next festival? See if giving it to the babe will cure the *Beastblood*? But you already said it depreciates too quickly." He shook his head. "Regardless, it's not applicable. You'll just put yourself and the Ringguard in harm's way. You must understand that."

She laughed, briefly stopped pacing, then paced again. "You're wrong in two assumptions. Firstly, I wouldn't need your Knights—I remember the last gory expedition. The surviving members spoke of the Ringguard riling up the Old Hunters; caused an aggravated response from them. Rumor has it that a cub was slayed, and its mother attacked justly."

"You've never been face to face with an Old Hunter, then, sister. They're aggressive—"

She waved off his response. "They're just animals. I'll choose an escort. I just need you to permit opening the gate and dropping the drawbridge."

"And the second assumption which I'm wrong?"

A sound from the pews. She turned. Her brother's chariness hadn't given her pause; but the birdlike cawing—the old worshiper's lamentation which had transitioned into what sounded like mad laughter—had caused gooseflesh to spread about her body, making her rigid.

Yordyn, too, glanced at the old worshiper. Had he felt what she felt? That electric flatness which stole the Temple's tone.

"I won't need to wait till next festival," she said with a shiver. "We already have a host."

III

Outside the walls of the Temple came another Outer Whisper. Some of the singers and dancers and masked worshipers heard the sound this time, despite the festival hullabaloo, and so they sang and danced and worshiped with even more feverish fervor— burning themselves out.

But deep below the streets—in the lonely catacombs meant only for the dead of an earlier Cromledge-folk, whose bones are but meal, and a singular abomination, one that walked alone and talked alone—came another song, this one in a strange tongue known only by *some* living Scholars, not to mention many of the moldering inhabitants of the catacombs (but when they were alive, of course) that were moveless save for the spiders and worms inside their brittle husks. This was a sad song, deep as the depth in which its singer sang. A song full of sorrow and loneliness. But a True Song.[2]

A babe (just as lonely as the singer of the Song, for her parents were masked and dancing atop the roof—all she heard was the whisperings of their feet), in a desolate area of Blight's Hallow, heard the True Song. Was, in fact, the only denizen of all of Cromledge that heard the Song. Her parents called her *Zwey*, which meant *Daughter of Music*; unbeknownst to them, a fitting name indeed.

Zwey hearkened the True Song whisper whisper whispering up out of the cobblestone floor like an ever-so-faint breeze that, like a breeze, was felt (but *in the mind*, not on the skin) rather than perceived by the ear. And then, because of a primordial fear that can only be derived from an imaginative babe of two and a half *turnstones*, she worshiped the Song in a fit of hysterical sobbing.

It was around this time when Wiseman Tusk *crackled* forward and said to the Lord Manager's midwife-sister, ". . . and do you wish your brother to suffer the same fate, and for the same reason, as Ivæn the Weak?"

IV

"Some people have a different name for Ivæn," said Sarah.

"Oh, yes, they do"—*crackle, crackle*—"Ivæn the Compassion-

---

[2] Not to be confused with "The Song of All Songs—the Endlessness," although perhaps of a similar—but lesser—species of ode.

ate, Ivæn the Mother, the Brave, and yet Ivæn had even harsher names than Weak, if you'd like to walk down *that* path."

"His soldiers murdered him for trying to be rational."

The Lord Manager saw and accurately translated the red-pink on his sister's cheeks, and he also knew from the particular posture of Wiseman Tusk that he was going in for the intellectual kill. He raised his hand.

"Sister, I don't enjoy this part of the festival."

"But face it," she said, "you're scared."

"Of rebellion, yes; of Halfman Ubon, yes. You don't know what I know of that *thing* down there. He's unnatural, Sarah. By our standards he should be dead. He's surpassed all our history. Jamie Calbot was the last Cromledgian to have remembered anything of that time, and he died—what was it?—six *turnstones* ago, and he even lived an abnormal length of time—surpassing others even younger than him by many *great-turnstones*. Don't you think the men had a sound reason for stopping him?"

"Stopping him? Jordyn, they took spears—five fanatical soldiers, each wearing a mask representing an Outsider—and rammed them into their Lord Manager. They did this out of irrational fear. They were afraid of Ubon; afraid of the Mark of the Beastblood. But did they ever stop and wonder what good would've come from studying Ubon? Finding a cure?"

The Lord Manager sighed deeply, held in his rib-rupturing breath for a few beats, and released it in a hiss. "Listen, I understand that there might be an admiration toward the legend of Lord Manager Ivæn. He was sympathetic for a thing—a babe, and eventually a child—that had no control of the way it was. He treated Ubon like a son, Ivæn did, and I know that takes a heart unlike anybody I've ever known (except for you, perhaps). But there's more to this tale than you know.

"When my name was drawn for Lord Manager's predecessor, I was given access to secret tomes—journals and reports and other credible documents collected by several Master Curators and Wisemen of renown—names synonymous with trustworthiness, such as Wiseman Callahan the Great, not to mention Yukon the Mindful. Some of Ivæn's other nicknames never survived the vast length of *great-turnstones*. The Master Curators and Wisemen made sure of that."

"You're acting like censoring particulars and actualities is high-minded—"

He held up a hand.

"Let me finish, Sarah. Did you ever stop and think why Ubon survived?"

She furrowed her brow.

"If, as you say, the *zealots* had slain Ivæn because they let a child with the Beastblood survive, then why not finish the job? They'd slain family members of his, his servants, and they had tried to slay Wiseman Callahan—although he was too nimble of mind and outwitted the *zealots*—and when the carnage was over and the *zealots* had all ended their lives with daggers they carried—each meticulously, patiently cutting off the other's head, until the final one jumped off the highest keep"—tilted up his head—"there was something found in Ubon's chamber that not even Wiseman Callahan was aware of. A shrine of some strange, dark blasphemousness; and on this shrine stood, in a circle, five spear-wielding figurines. They surrounded a crowned figurine."

"What are you saying?"

"That there is an inherent darkness in the Halfman."

"You don't know that."

He sighed. That's when Wiseman Tusk manifested between the siblings. "I take it that you're in tune with the denizens of Blight's Hallow and the, as I call it, *Dream Phenomenon*?"

She looked at him again with that furrowed brow. Her unknowingness clearly pleased him.

"Perhaps you might have heard the phrase Dark Reveries, the Nightmare Plague, or the Visions of the Globes?"

Sarah shrugged with an annoyed little shake of her head, and somewhere under the great beard and mustache Wiseman Tusk smiled.

"It doesn't matter, Tusk," said the Lord Manager, without breaking eye contact with his Sarah. "My sister is not superstitious—even if, in this instance, it may be to her detriment. But I will give you access to the Outer Plains; however, allow one of the Ringguard to come, and I will give him direct orders not to interview with the beasts of the plains."

"Without weapons," insisted Sarah.

"With weapons or you won't be going at all. Your decision."

"And what of Ubon Halfman? Can I see him? Because if I risk my life trying to retrieve samples of the Maiden's Ghost and cannot see—"

—holding up his hand, the Lord Manager said, "I understand," and turning to Wiseman Tusk: "Tusk, I'd like you to clear out the servants in the entire West Wing. Having fifty Ringguards stationed there—"

"Fifty? Isn't that excessive, brother?"

"A precaution."

"I don't want your Knights breathing down my neck. Have a few in the room; the rest you can put outside the door."

This festival may as well have been called the festival of sighs, for the Lord Manager sighed again (and hopefully the last time this night). "Very well. Choose your escorts, and you may leave on the morrow—or," he reconsidered, "the day *after* tomorrow. You won't want tired people sick with the *oldsap*."

She nodded.

"And what of Wen and Myris . . . can you wait, before you . . . you know?"

He looked at her long and hard, then at Wiseman Tusk.

"I'm sorry. I must see it through. The festival must conclude." And at that he spun around and made his exit, and Wiseman Tusk followed. But not before stopping and turning toward Sarah. His last bit of verbal wisdom would haunt her all her remaining days.

It was this:

"They all dream of the necropolis under our feet. They see, penned upon the walls, in blood that is not his own, the end of Cromledge. Mostly text, but some rudimentary sketches, too. In their astral dream-forms, they all read the same tale—one dressed in blood and bones, torn skin and terrible sorrow. They say, m'lady, it's written in a language they can't understand—

and yet, somehow, they're able to. It's only in the aforesaid secret tomes that Wiseman Callahan admits having taught Ubon the Old Language. And do you, in these *dreams*, know who kills us all, in the divinations upon the walls? Ubon the Halfman—he slays every man, woman, and child."

Then he turned and crackled and was swallowed by the shade of nocturnal beyond the Temple entrance . . . she didn't hear him walk down the flight of stairs.

She walked aimlessly around the sanctuary in order to release the storm of thoughts raging in her head. She may have walked for such a length of time that Wen and Myris may already have been swallowed by the Outer Darkness by the time she stopped to wipe her nose. There was blood on the back of her hand. Not the babe's blood; her own—warm, crimson, liquescent. And she stared at that blood, seeing in it dark foretokens and apocalyptic bedlam. A shudder coursed through her. How had Tusk heard of this *Nightmare Plague* but not she? She might not have lived in Blight's Hallow, but she knew many from in and around that portion of the city.

"Visions of the globes . . ."

A whisper.

She hadn't known she'd speak those words until they'd already tumbled from her teeth-clattering mouth. *Why does this frighten me so? It's nonsense*, she rationalized to herself as she stood, she realized, in front of one of the Outsider statues. This one had seven fingers for a head. Its only name was THE FIFTH.

Looking at its sculped fingers twisting about like serpents, she swore they moved. And was that sound the beating of drums from the festival or had THE FIFTH slipped inside its stone incarnation? Her neck hairs standing on end, she backed away. When she was far away from the statue and standing in the middle of the aisle which split the pews down the center, she turned and immediately saw a skeletal being crawling toward her, blood on its face, mumbling through laughter. Sound that sounded like: "*The Dragon is bringing me to her at last. He told me so. Ha ha he he ha.*"

Realizing it was the old man from the pews, she bent down

to help him.

"Sir, you're bleeding . . ."

Suddenly the man became rigid. He violently convulsed, his forehead repeatedly smashing against the stone floor. Sarah tried sliding her hand between his forehead and the ground, but at her first attempt the strength of his thrashing was so strong that two of her knuckles were crushed between skull and stone, and she pulled away clutching her hand in her armpit. Her throbbing knuckles abated at the same time as the man's becoming still. A pool of blood, achromatic in the *godbreath*-lit sanctuary, formed around his head—

—something cracked.

Lightheadedness washed over Sarah. She shook her head, not quite comprehending—

—and something else cracked: the stone under his head, then his skull, then his ribs (momentarily his midsection looked like pane of flesh from whatever force pressing on him). Some soot near the man's hand wafted in the shape of a spiral and danced until it dissolved. Sarah scooted away.

The man was somehow still alive. Reached out a long-fingered hand, nails unrefined and jagged. Clasped her robe. One blue eye stared at her as his bloodied face pressed deeper into the stone floor. Fragments of white-yellow and yellow-brown teeth lay nearby.

"It is finished," he said. Then his eye became unfocused and rubescent, and a teardrop the color of *rhódon*-shrooms (picked from the southern forests) skated forlornly down his cheek and into the river of pooling blood around his head.

Sarah trembled where she sat, unable to look away from the gory impossibility which lay twisted and broken before her.

Bum bum bum bum bum, said the raging festival.

Bum bum bum bum, said her racing heart.

Bum bum bum, said something between gray matter and spirit as she looked upward and imagined a seven-legged crea-ture, its legs splayed out, ascending into the undistinguishable darkness of the Temple's upper portions.

Bum bum, said the ground as it released the old man; he

expanded and gave a postmortem moan and passed his last gas.

Bum, said the bell near the Keep. The sound entered the sanctuary and banged about the walls, and she felt the rough stone vibrate beneath her hand. Wen and Myris were being prepared, she realized, and the sorrow of knowing—but also *not* knowing—what would soon happen annulled the trepidation of what transpired in this sanctuary. Already she was rationalizing. The old man had suffered some kind of neural spell, indeed. She knew Cromledgians—some young, fit, and seemingly healthy— who, with certain physical or situational or emotional triggers, would collapse and shake. At the moment there was no name for this[3], but it wasn't incredibly rare. And what happened here wasn't so radically different than the other cases. She needed to take him to a Healing House.

V

Gantron the Strong, the Commander of the Ringguard, stood in front of the festive, wound-up, blood-thirsty denizens like a sturdy, wide-branched tree—albeit an old tree, for he'd seen six *great-turnstones* and had survived sixty Festivals of the Ring. One denizen—a man broad but not as broad as he, wearing a rudimentary Old Hunter mask carved of high quality *godbone* and secured around his meaty head with leather straps—came forward and tried to push past Gantron. Said something, but the words were swallowed by the flock. And Gantron said something with his right gauntlet; the word was "*kunthk*" as it dug into the behemoth's face, and the man stumbled back moaning, but the others in the crowd didn't bother buffering his toppling trajec- tory as he landed face first into the cobblestone street. His mask broke and when he turned back angrily toward Gantron, Gan- tron saw he was a predominant carpenter whose shop was on

---

[3] Although it's most certainly what we call epilepsy.

the corner of Trank Lane and Oin Way, a man named Samuel; and when Samuel—still in his frenzy—clumsily got to his feet and looked into Gantron's cool green eyes and interpreted (accurately so), through that brief locked eye contact, that the face-punch was mere politeness, and if he tried to get past him again he'd use a blade. Samuel's rage fizzled, and like a disciplined child he slipped deeper into the flock.

At Gantron's back was the home of the basket weavers whose babe suffered the Mark and then a blade to silence its suffering.

In all his years as Commander of the Ringguard, the whereabouts of the Marked parents had never slithered into the festival celebrants. And a *turnstone* prior, he wouldn't have believed such a flock could have been molded by half-asleep drunkards. But they'd found out, somehow, and here they were.

A commotion.

Silence.

The masked flock riven and whispered; their eclipsed eyes averted groundward. A tall gaunt man dressed in the finest robes in all the city, made of crimson and alabaster and gold, had appeared. Gantron stiffened and pulled his shoulders back and cast his eyes down to examine his person; having deemed his posture and wardrobe of honorable condition, he straightened and removed his helmet for the Lord Manager.

As the Lord Manager strode through the riven flock, he somberly glanced at as many denizens that he could, making direct eye contact, and giving nods here, nods there, nods everywhere. Whomever the recipients were of his orange-brown gaze had immediately shifted in a fit of uncomfortable shame and backed farther away, crafting a wider berth. And behind the Lord Manager ambled Cromledge's Royal Wiseman, long gray cloak following like a shadow. Tusk looked at no man or woman. Kept his smiling eyes forward.

"Lord Manager," said Gantron with a slight bow. Although it came out as "O Ma'sher," for Gantron had lost his tongue as a child.

"Gantron." The Lord Manager nodded and put a ringed hand upon his shoulder, smiling gravely. Behind him the Royal

Wiseman *crackled* into the doorway and looked inside. The Lord Manager stepped away and stilled and silenced the flock with a raised hand.

It only took the span of ten *clicks* before the flock was calm and quiet, save for the previously unhearable weeping of Myris in the house behind Gantron; he was well-liked, Yordyn was, and their quick silence echoed their respect. The Lord Manager turned and investigated the house. "Tusk," he said. A curt nod. The misshapen old man responded by closing the front door, muffling the sobs, and the Lord Manager turned back to the flock. Scanned the crowd, held brief eye contact with the few remaining jibber jabberers. And when they were as quiet as a Temple during service, he spoke.

"The Outsiders have been good to us this past *turnstone*," he said. A gust of wind threw his long, wavy hair over his face, but he spoke onward. "We have this festival to respect They who've come before us, and as a peace offering; but we need also regard Wen and Myris with more kindness. Yes, their babe had been Marked at birth, as you seemed to have heard already, and this Festival of the Ring must resolve with the final . . ."—Yordyn paused, trawling for the right word—"ceremonial gift to the Outsiders. But," and again he held up a hand, "I need you to all leave their home. They're under enough stress. Congregate now at the Wall of Giving and we will be there within sixty *great-clicks*, and you can then pay your venerations to the Nameless Outsiders."

He stopped speaking, letting what he'd said sink in.

A few conversations broke out. Not unruly, per se—and they quickly died down as a torch of *godbreath* dipped in spring. The masked flock dispersed gradually and would undoubtedly reconvene at the Wall of Giving.

The Lord Manager turned, and from his breast pocket he pulled out a small rag to wipe his brow. Smiling at Gantron, he said, "Aside from my commencement, that was the only time I have spake before an audience greater than the ghosts in my head." He chortled softly.

Gantron nodded with a deep bow.

Then the Lord Manager's face convulsed and glanced at Gantron; his mouth gaped to speak (Gantron knew what about and had thick enough skin to take no offense) but closed his mouth as Wiseman Tusk opened the front door and, with quite some apprehension, said, "My Lord!" While Gantron stood his guard and cast his eyes into the dispersing flock, the Lord Manager crossed to the doorway and peered inside and, after an ominous beat, said, "Wiseman, has this ever happened?"

"In my lifetime, my Lord, no. In another Manager's lifetime, mayhap. I shall at once go to the Tomes and spread myself there, at your say-so."

It took a moment before the Lord Manager responded. He was looking into the house, and then shifted his eyes to Tusk. The way he looked at the old man, Gantron thought he was looking *through* him. Finally he said, "I say so, yes, go now and learn what you can."

At that, the old man

(crackled)

ambled his way to the Grand Archive.

"Commander Gantron," beckoned Lord Yordyn, "find a few trustworthy of your Ring-knights and, I suppose, bring a coffin—two coffins"—he sighed. "And take Wen and Myris to the . . ." He screwed up his face, thinking; it was clear to Gantron that he didn't know where to take Wen and Myris. But Gantron also didn't know why he needed to take them in the first place. Why postpone the ceremony?

"My Lord," said Gantron. *My or.*

The Lord Manager's mind was momentarily lost. He was looking through Gantron as he'd done with Tusk.

"I'm sorry," he said, shaking his head. He put a hand on the door and the door closed enough that the remaining flock could not perceive the implied horror. "Take a gander, Commander Gantron, for I do not want to speak it."

Helmet in hand, Gantron walked to the doorway. The Lord Manager opened it a greater angle. Gantron looked inside and saw Wen and Myris lying in a pool of red. A blade half-clutched in Wen's stiffening hand. And in the arms of Myris lay the

exterminated babe. The way the blood obscured the Mark
. . . well, it looked like just a normal babe.

VI

The flock stood near the Wall of Giving. Swaying on jittery legs evidenced the exhaustion which had rippled through them. A faint glow in the heavens had transformed the pitch-black marble sheet of evening into the dark gray of early morning—and on the horizon came a rumor of the rising Ring. Even Samuel the carpenter—his mask fragmented from the Commander of the Ringguard's gauntlet, but he still managed to haphazardly wear it—was on the brink of forfeiting to bed (he had danced and sung and drunk the *oldsap* all the evening; it was tiresome work) until a murmur grew from the back of the flock. The Cromledge-folk shuffled their weary feet. They split down the middle to give passage to the Lord Manager and his Royal Circus.

A great deal more than sixty *great-clicks* had passed and there had been whispers of the managerial freshman to have gotten cold feet. Mutiny—of a quasi-transient nature, that was—seemed to have been on the table, until the tiredness heavily stole over them all. But the question remained—*what took them so long?* There'd been a point, many *great-clicks* after sixty, that Samuel had a clear vision of *things* in the Outer Darkness. Imponderable beings. Shifting impatiently, *angrily*. Needing their Cromledgian blood paid before the Sky borne the Ring

Royal Instrumentalists from the back of the Circus banged their drums, blending into his throbbing heartbeat. From the rear of the flock came a ripple of shouts and croons. At first, Samuel thought they were of a worshipful quality. But it took not even a few *clicks* for him to readjust his evaluation—wrath.

"What is it?" he asked a man wearing a black mask with an endless bone white spiral.

The spiral-face turned to face him, black pupils harmoniously blending into the black mask, and wordlessly turned away. By then, whispers—variations of "it's not Wen and Myris"—circulated throughout the watching flock; as if to cut the "Wen and Myris" chinwag and cause chaos, the question of "how do you know it was Wen and Myris in the first place?" (and variations of that question) trailed behind like a shadow.

"It was Wen and Myris," Samuel drunkenly, drowsily shouted at the Black Spiral, who was generous or curious enough to heed Samuel's ramblings by offering what may have been eye contact. "I was there. That Outsideblasted mute—the Commander of the Ringguard—he struck me, see? Broke my mask, almost my face." But the Black Spiral looked away. From their vantage the bloated belly of the Circus passed by. The Lord Manager and his Royal Court sandwiched between heavily armored Knights of the Ringguard. Samuel spotted a cluster of Royals dressed like the Manager, except without ceremonial armor over their robes, and, obviously, their heads bore not the Crown.

There was Dumb-arse Tusk, twisted and gray. The Speaker of the Keep—a young, handsome man with a headful of ultra-black hair. The tall, old, bald, bearded man was the High Priest. The short fat man, the one whose head bent forward when he walked, was the High Master Curator. There were also a few men and women whose titles Samuel couldn't even guess upon (some of them he hadn't even seen before). And finally, trailing behind like an afterthought, were the Heads of various districts and factions—High Piazza, Market Town, Ring Junction, Ringguard Barracks, the Hunters, and Blight's Hallow, to name a few.

"Look at their smug faces," Samuel said to the Black Spiral.

The Black Spiral paid no mind, his or her attention solely on the *Royal Circus* and its trained chattels.

Farther back from the Circus, Samuel saw, were two people. His lower jaw unhinged, and he found himself—disregarding this fundamentally deep-rooted custom of the Festival of the Ring—removing his mask. This way his vision wasn't obstructed by the slits he'd cut out for his eyes. The rippling rumors had been true after all, and he voiced this to the Black Spiral (but before doing so, and in order to get the person's attention—which he probably wouldn't have done if sober and well-rested—he placed a not-so-gentle hand on Black Spiral's shoulder). "*Outsiders-be-blasted,* my friend, if they are Wen and Myris, then I'm my own father's father. Look't their wrists. Those black bands they wear on their wrists"—Samuel benched, had enough decency to blow it elsewhere, and leaned in closer to the Black Spiral—"that means they're prisoners. Cerulean bands mean something dumb, like pissing in public; red means an act of violence or theft; but black means *murder*—and they'd be sentenced to death. Trust me, I've worn the blue and red more times than I have fingers on my hand. And they keep the ones with the black bands in small cells away from the common miscreants."

The entire flock broke into babble. He suspected everyone else who'd been the basket weavers' house was explaining and complaining to their neighboring flock-member.

Three chunks of broken cobblestone street were flung in the general direction of the Circus. The first thrown stone was a misfire. It skidded off the ground and disappeared into a city-planted garden. The other two stones, with careful aiming, were thrown true; however, the Ringguard had managed through their insanely meticulous training to deflect these two stones—one stone was going straight toward the High Master Curator's noddle, and a Knight perfectly timed a jump and raised his shield and the stone ricocheted off; and, perhaps more impressively, Gantron the Face Punching *Deofol* used a shortsword to cleave the other thrown stone in two. This one had been headed straight toward Dumb-arse Tusk's, well . . . *arse.* If any other Knight of the Ringguard had done this, Samuel would have applauded; but Gantron broke his mask—the mask he just now realized he wasn't wearing, thus slipped it back around his head and tightened the leather strap—so blast him and his old-man-skill to the dirt and the creepy-crawlies which dwell therein.

"Pompous arse, Gantron is," Samuel said to the Black Spiral. The drunkenness was wearing off, and the thrown stones had carved away his festival-sleepiness.

The flock stirred.

The Knights of the Ringguard circled around the Circus, sidestepping in order to face the flock on either side. How they didn't stumble over their profuse, hefty armor was beyond him. The armor made them look chubby the way the silver and gold and iron pieces were layered. Their bellies were bloated by impenetrable defenses.

Except for Gantron the *Deofol*. The Commander of the Ringguard wore a lighter, more mobile version. And a crimson cape with the Cromledge insignia in the center, and colored globes circling it, representing the FIVE OUTSIDERS.

While his Knights pedantically back-, side-, and forward-stepped around the Circus (as if stones were as lethal as arrows), Gantron threw over the Lord Manager's shoulder a blanket made of mail and fastened it around his neck so it would be worn like an awkward, and probably immensely heavy, cape; then he stayed at the Lord Manager's side like a flamboyant silhouette, looking left and right—even upward, at blackened dormers of the few surrounding buildings.

"Does he really think someone's going to *snipe* the Lord Manager?" Samuel scoffed to the Black Spiral. "Blasted, pompous arse. I mentioned he broke my—"

Trumpets sang sharply.

Drums ceased beating.

The Knights formed into a half-circle as the Circus formed a relatively safe distance away from the Wall of Giving, separating the Circus from the flock.

"Silence!" shouted the Speaker, holding up a hand and stepping forward and cutting through the Ringguard half-circle. Two Knights naturally stayed by his side as he walked forward, and the half-circle shifted to close the man-sized gaps.

The murmurs distilled so much that it was indistinguishable from the high winds clawing up the Wall of Giving.

"The rumors are true," the Speaker said, his four words flowing through the flock. "Wen and Myris of Blight's Hallow had a babe on this day. The babe had the Mark of the Beastblood, alas, and per usual it was dealt with swiftly by a blade." He allowed that knowledge to sink in before moving on. "Many of you of Blight's Hallow must know that the two individuals we have"—nodded toward the black wristbanded prisoners—"are *not* the basket weavers."

An eruption of discourse, and a raised hand to silence it.

"Wen and Myris were private folk. What you may not have known was that they'd been trying many, many *turnstones* to conceive a child. They'd gone so far as to believe either of them were barren. Their son's name would have been Yordyn. They'd made a room for him. She'd been expecting the babe thirteen *turnstones* earlier. Ergo, great and overwhelming dismay struck them when she went into labor this very day, this dark day of ill-omened endings. Wen and Myris could not handle their son being Marked; could not handle the sight of their blameless son being pierced by dagger; could not bear the plunge—" At that, he turned and pointed toward the slanted area on the Wall of Giving where safety banisters were absent, where the fathers and mothers of the Marked were cast into the deep dark below. "And so," said the young buck with thick black hair, his voice somehow very loud and very soft, "they took their own lives."

There were gasps and sobs among the festival flock, and the Speaker allowed these sounds to run their course. Then he said:

"Fear not"—but the flock seemed as though fear had inflicted them greatly and so he said, "Fear not," once more; the gasps and sobs subdued, and as the Black Spiral pulled out something from the front of his or her robe and just stood there listening, the Speaker said, "Our wholly intuitive Wiseman Tusk delved deep into the old histories of previous epochs. This has not been the first time the parents of the Marked have taken their own lives. Some of you may remember that five-and-sixty *turnstones* ago, Mary and Peter had evaded the Wall of Giving and had embarked into the Outer Dark and were never heard of again. The Wiseman of that generation found suitable sacrificial proxies. While it would seem as though any two of opposite sexes would suffice, it also seemed unfair to randomly choose, or to choose from an unblemished, innocent populace. That is why we have chosen two from the bridewell, both sentenced to death for murder. Our Lord Manager has deemed this just and apt."

Conversations broke out. This time the Speaker could not subdue the babble.

"The Outsiders will flay us for this deviation," said Samuel to the Black Spiral, then he moved closer just in case the Black Spiral finally decided to respond. Of course, as silent as ever the Black Spiral stood there. Samuel was typically not the snoopy type, but an arcane magnetism insisted that his eyes drift downward to see what had been pulled from the quiet person's robe. A shortsword made of black steel. It glinted menacingly from the light-orbs lining the street.

Samuel put a hand on the Black Spiral's shoulder.

He laughed to cue that he meant not offense. "You can use a dagger to cut meat, a shovel to dig earth, an axe to cut *godbone*, but swordswords are prohibited unless you're a Knight or part of a hunting expedition. Are you a Knight?"

The Black Spiral responded through movement instead of words. Quite effortlessly the mysterious person shrugged off Samuel's shoulder, making his way through the flock.

Something caught Samuel's eye: from across the street he saw another spiral mask-wearing person in an identical long, black robe, and wielding a blackened shortsword. And to his left, another. And another still farther to his left. They were coming out of the woodworks, these Black Spirals, and Samuel felt the hairs rise on his neck.

"Hey! Stop! This ceremony's sacred."

He reached the Black Spiral, grabbed him by the shoulder, spun him around, and whipped off the spiral mask—

Except he couldn't.

The mask was quite absurdly *stuck* to his or her face by a powerful adhesive. But that felt wrong, too. Samuel couldn't help but to, as if in a trance, raise his hand again (the world seemed to ooze all around him, noise and scent and images blurring into muck). His rough palms almost *romantically* caressed the material of the mask.

There were no eye holes for the stranger to see through.

There was no mask; what his hand embraced was more shell

or bone; and a tingling sensation, quickly spiraling into pain, resided in the flesh of his fingers and palm when he pulled his hand away. He looked and saw that small dots of black on his hand became bigger dots of . . . not black but *red*. The blood was slow at first, and then began to flow. He saw, looking back at the Black Spiral, that strands of his skin dangled from its face. Then it made its way through the flock and to the Royal Circus.

A commotion in the flock. There were screams. Not nearby, but from afar, so none of the denizens around him noticed the man whose face spiraled, whose hand wielded a prohibited weapon. Samuel clenched his fist to drown the pain and stepped through a few drunken, sleep-deprived Cromledgians, and yanked on the Black Spiral's shoulder.

"Hey, you blasted daemon! *AHH*!"

With reflexes like no man or woman (and he knew a few women with unusually heightened litheness) he'd ever known, the Black Spiral had gripped his shoulder-yanking hand and squeezed, causing a series of nerve-searing crackles and pops. Then he was let go of. It took a moment to realize, while beholding his hand, how his fingers went in curious directions. His pinky finger dangled by a thread of flesh.

His gaze drifted to the almost-gentle pressure on his shoulder. It was a hand of profane, perverse flesh. Veins like worms, fingers like serpents—seven in all. Samuel's eyes rose, now transfixed on the vacuous malevolence circumvoluting to some abysm where things worse than the dead dwelled. The seven serpents bit down. But he couldn't look away from the endlessness where the spiral navigated pale flesh.

The Black Spiral turned away, its black cloak thrashing in the strong winds of the Wall of Giving. It effortlessly pushed aside the denizens. An old man (Samuel could tell by his veiny arms and long white hair trailing from his mask) being pushed in a wagon by a son or grandson was cut in half by the shortsword. The son or grandson tried to stop the Black Spiral, but the sword flashed out and spat out specks of red. Samuel collapsed to the ground, his shoulder in a helix of incapacitating agony that kept mounting. Where he lay, the son or grandson's head, masked with the Sky Ring painted over black *godbone*, lay with him; its great pillars of light extended their warmth to Samuel the carpenter, whose role in this tale is over. *Almost.*

Editor's note: *The Second Book of the Shadow Under Cromledge* may appear in *Anterior Skies: Volume II.* Or it may be published in its entirety by Godwyn, whether independently or through a traditional publisher. One of my goals for *Anterior Skies* was to take chances, and to do things other anthologies weren't doing. And to give a platform for ambitious works of weird fiction.

UNCONVENTIONAL METHODS

by Maria Barnes

URING OUR PREVIOUS SESSIONS, my psychotherapist had alluded several times to his upcoming departure. But even so, as I stepped into his office for my weekly dosage of prolonged silences and quiet conversations about weather, I was surprised to find an empty room. The walls were devoid of their usual nightmarish pictures from his other patients. The black settee had disappeared, too. But my therapist's moth-eaten brown chair still crouched under the only window in this tiny room.

A piece of paper with hastily scribbled lines lay on the armrest. It read:

> *After our last meeting, I gathered my things, which are few, and will have left the city by the time you read this. I have big news for you. Wait for my return, and do not follow me.*

I plunged into the chair and used my hand to shield my eyes against the dull morning light. But the radiance pressed through my fingers, making me think of the last time he'd abandoned me. It had been last summer when he had fallen ill. During that time—during his *absence*—I was plagued by recurring dreams, in which faceless phantasms pursued me through a succession of strange rooms. There were signs of violence and desertion in every room: blood smears on the floor, splintered windowsills, and electric wires that didn't seem to be attached to anything.

I wouldn't have spoken to my therapist about the dreams, anyway.

However, he was the only person I conversed with regularly. His absence drove me to self-mutilation and days of chaos with nothing to distract me from my despair.

Venomous sunlight bathed the room.

I got to my feet, looked around, and exited my therapist's office for what I knew was for the last time. I headed home along bleak streets and contemplated my bleak future.

I came home to a blinking light on the answering machine. Though no one ever called me, I kept the red apparatus in the corner of my bedroom where I could reach it at night. I pushed the button, causing the not-unwelcome chatter of my therapist's voice to fill the room.

"In time, I will transmute my ideas into a new system of psychotherapy. But first, I must test these unconventional methods. I designed them to ease mental pain and maybe cure some of my more . . . bleak patients.

"Two days ago, I saw one of them coming out of a movie theater. He was forty when our professional relationship began. Tassels of unwashed gray hair hung from the back of his head. As he noticed me, a scowl turned his face into a disarray of wrinkles. I followed him home and entered his apartment. He said nothing, as if he already understood my intentions and readied himself for my unconventional methods. While he was washing his hands in the kitchen, I used the bathroom. I thought I was going to be sick, for my stomach had been tormenting me the entire morning. I still felt a dull ache in my abdomen when I tied his hands."

The street on the other side of the red apparatus slipped into silent oblivion and I began panicking; but my therapist's labored breath came back with the sound of rain, and relief washed over me.

"It's his dissociative disorder that interested me the most. We hardly ever talked about it. My inability to help the patient bothered me, especially considering the extent of his suffering. I wanted to address such affliction by exaggerating it and pushing him to his limits. I regretted my actions later when, after cutting off his face, skin, and all, I could not stop the bleeding. He died before I started stage two of my experiment. I dug around in his drawers for a diary of some sort, but the drawers contained nothing of use."

The rain pounded with even greater force against the phone booth where my fatigued therapist had called me from, no doubt devising better, safer methods of cure.

"I have big news for you," he said.

After a long silence, the message ended.

Out of habit, I replayed his voiced letter until it towered over my other, *bleaker* thoughts. I wallowed in the brutality with which he attended to and tracked his other patients' progresses, as he drifted from one obscure place to another, never staying anywhere for more than a week at a time.

Frail snow, the first in the fall, perched on the roofs outside my window. It tinted the room with yellow mist as I listened to my therapist. He recounted yet another unsuccessful experiment. This time it involved a patient with a severe case of paranoia. In only one night my therapist told her every peculiar tale he knew—from the luminescence of unnamed worlds that hid among the stars, to big corporations joining forces to enslave unguarded minds. Before dawn, she stepped out the window. As I imagined her damaged body, I mirrored the smile that undoubtedly unfolded on my therapist's face.

The notion of the big news accompanied me during my waking hours and even snaked inside my night dreams. I fantasized about this *big news* since I first read the note on that September morning. It was preposterous to guess the exact plan my therapist had for me. But eventually the outline of his intentions came into focus. And I marveled at his skill and inventiveness.

When the phone rang, sending ripples through the still air of my apartment, it did not alarm or scare me. Without a single tremor in my hands, I picked up the receiver, and the familiar voice announced to me the return of its owner.

"*Have you guessed yet,*" my therapist said, "*what the big news is?*"

I have, but it wasn't what I told him.

"*I always wanted to cure you and only you. Now, after weeks of getting ready, I can start the final stage of the process.*"

These words elevated my mood, and I breathed a sigh of relief.

"*I'm going to cure you, David.*"

THE UNIVERSE'S EDGE

by Katherine Quevedo

HE UNIVERSE HAS NO EDGE,
they claimed.
Not so.

I've seen it for myself,
crouched upon its dancing border
of darkness and dust in swirls
of onyx black and cotton candy pink,
raked my fingers through the cold, sticky
mess, leaned forward until my cheeks
and chin tingled with dread and fascination,
until I licked my chops at its closeness.

How far can you tilt until you fall?

They lied when they said
the universe has
no edge, for
I live in it.

AUTHOR BIOS

L. ACADIA

L. Acadia is a lit professor at National Taiwan University, a dog pillow at home, and otherwise searching Taipei for urban hikes and ghosts. L. has a PhD from Berkeley and creative writing published or forthcoming in *Autostraddle*, *The Dodge* (Best-of-the-Net nominated), *Gordon Square Review*, *Neon Door*, *New Orleans Review*, and *Strange Horizons*.

Twitter and Instagram: @acadialogue;
Mastodon: @acadialogue@eldritch.cafe

ALICE AUSTIN

Alice Austin writes a broad mix of fiction. Her main focus is horror, but she often dips into fantasy, humor, and occasionally sci-fi; anything with a speculative element is fair game. Alice lives with her partner Matt and a naughty orange cat called Leo. She tries to write during weekends, evenings, and any time when Leo isn't sitting on her laptop. Her short stories have appeared in various anthologies from indie publishers.

Find her on Twitter at @Al_Austin120.

MARIA BARNES

Maria Barnes is currently studying Literature and Philosophy online. Sometimes, she writes dark fiction and teaches English.

Her work has appeared in *Variant Literature*, *Samjoko Magazine* and *Phantom Kangaroo*, among other places.

AARON BEARDSELL

Aaron Beardsell is an Australian author who fell in love with writing when they purchased a typewriter from a church in the woods. Some say the typewriter has a soul of its own, and lives through its victims. Others say it's abandoned in a basement. Only time will tell. They are the author of the *Dead Station* series, *Coffinwood*, and several short stories. The *Dead Station* series is a fusion of 80s science fiction horror such as *Aliens*, *The Thing*, *Event Horizon*, and Lovecraftian monsters. *Coffinwood* is a novel of interwoven short stories set in an isolated Australian country town. Perfect for fans of Delta Green or the SCIP Foundation, *Coffinwood* follows the Esoteric Containment Taskforce as they attempt to hold back the madness and monsters that are seeping into reality. The old gods have awoken, and they hunger.

RICHARD BEAUCHAMP

Hailing from the lush, verdant hills of the Ozarks, Richard Beauchamp has been spinning tales of horror that take place in the quieter corners of the Midwest and other parts of the world since 2017. His debut short story collection *Black Tongue & Other Anomalies* was a nominee for the 2022 Splatterpunk Awards, and his fiction has been placed in such esteemed publications as Cohesion Press's *SNAFU: Dead Or Alive* and Dark Peninsula Press's *Negative Space* anthologies.

SOLOMON FORSE

Solomon Forse is the founder of HOWL Society, the largest and most active online horror book club in the Western world. If Solomon isn't reading, watching, or writing horror, you'll find him role-playing horror with tabletop RPGs like Call of Cthulhu—or shredding horror on the guitar in his Lovecraftian metal band Crafteon. Check out his latest fiction appearing in *Howls From Hell, Howls From the Wreckage, Into the Crypt of Rays*, and *Boneyard Soup Magazine* vol. 1, issue 4.

Follow him on Twitter @SolomonForse.

ANDY GEHLSEN

Andy studied writing and film in college while working at a library. He also helped develop scripts and reviews for the college radio station. He has since worked jobs at all hours (that copy shop one might have been the worst). He has been published in *Dark Entries Journal, State of Matter, A Thin Slice of Anxiety, The Place Where Everyone's Name is Fear* charity anthology by Anxiety Press/Outcast Press, Hungry Shadows Press, and elsewhere. Writing has been an invaluable path, helping bring ruin to the most vile of monster-dom: our lord depraver Status Quo. He is grateful for Godspeed You! Black Emperor, goofy friends, and horror movies. You may access more weird on Instagram @midwesterngent3. He currently works at a library in Iowa.

GODWYN

On the outskirts of Carcosa, in an alcove of a ruinous dwelling, Godwyn lives in secret (as not to draw awareness from despondent phantasms, vagabonds, and Hastur zealots) with its chamber pot, mattress, and typewriter. When it wants to write, it writes, and when it doesn't, it doesn't.

SAMUEL M. HALLAM

Samuel M Hallam (He/Him) is a British author who dabbles in horror, sci-fi, and fantasy. He's previously been published by D & T Publishing, Night Terror Novels, and has had a few self-published titles including *On the Trail to Vulture's Gulp*, *Haunted Souls*, and *Project Jotunheim*, which he co-authored with Andrew Jackson. You can find him on Instagram @Still_Reading_Sam

M. HALSTEAD

M. Halstead is a graphic designer and book fanatic who spends her day fighting with Adobe products and evenings reading horror. When creating in her free time, she focuses on book and magazine design, horror writing, and traditional bookmaking and printmaking. She lives in North Carolina with her husband and two cats, and can be found online at mhalstead.com/fiction.

KAY HANIFEN

Kay Hanifen was born on a Friday the 13th and once lived for three months in a haunted castle. So, obviously, she had to become a horror writer. Her articles have appeared in Ghouls Magazine, Screen Rant, The Borgen Project, and Leatherneck magazine; and her short stories have appeared in *Strangely Funny VIII*, *Crunchy With Ketchup*, *Last Girls' Club*, *Wicked Newsletters*, *Fearful Fun*, *Death of a Bad Neighbor*, *Enchanted Entrapments*, *Diet Riot: A Fatterpunk Anthology*, *M is for Medical*, *Terror in the Trenches*, *Slice of Paradise*, *Vinyl Cuts*, *Sherlock Holmes and Watson's Medical Mysteries*, *Beware the Bugs*, *Rockets and Robots*, *Divergent Terror*, *The Siren's Call*, *Wishing Well*, *Hush Don't Wake the Monster*, *The Old Ways*, *Dracula's*

Guests, and *Devil's Rejects*. When she's not consuming pop culture with the voraciousness of a vampire at a 24-hour blood bank, you can usually find her with her two black cats or at kayhanifenauthor.wordpress.com.

MARCUS HAWKE

Marcus Hawke is a writer primarily of horror and dark fiction, some fantasy and sci-fi, and a few things that defy categorization. He was born in Toronto, moved around quite a bit during the dreaded formative years. His love for stories and the written word started with the likes of R.L. Stein in childhood and grew into a full-fledged possession thanks to the works of Stephen King, Anne Rice, Ray Bradbury, and JRR Tolkien. His work has appeared in a number of publications from Dark Pine Publishing, Jitter Press, Lunatics Magazine, Adrenaline Shots, his first full-length novel, *The Miracle Sin*, and most recently his first collection, *Acts of Violence: Twelve Tales of Terror*. He lives with his feline overlord in an apartment building haunted by the type of neighbors that make a person wish a ghost would come to visit in the cold, often gloomy great white North.

W. OLIVER HUNT

W. Oliver Hunt is a writer, experimental filmmaker, musician, and connoisseur of fine Salisbury steak. A graduate of University of Baltimore, he is a former editor at their literary magazine, The Welter, and frontman for the band Treeforts. His writing has been published by Death of Workers Press, Strange City Digest, Pyre Publishing, South Broadway Ghost Society, and Horror Sleaze Trash. He resides in Baltimore, Maryland.

PEDRO INIGUEZ

Pedro Iniguez is a speculative fiction writer and painter from Los Angeles, California. His fiction and poetry has appeared in *Nightmare Magazine, Shortwave Magazine, Helios Quarterly, Worlds of Possibility, Star*Line, Space & Time Magazine*, and *Tiny Nightmares*, among others.

He can be found at Pedroiniguezauthor.com

DEREK AUSTIN JOHNSON

Derek Austin Johnson was born in the Northeast but has lived most of his life in the Lone Star State. His work has appeared in *Campfire Macabre, The Dread Machine, Generation X-ed, Midnight Tales, The Horror Zine's Book of Werewolf Stories*, and *Camp Slasher Lake Volume I*. He lives in Central Texas.

Reach him on Instagram and Twitter @daj42.
TikTok @derekaustinjohnson
www.derekaustinjohnson.com

ALECO JULIUS

Aleco Julius is a teacher, writer of essays and stories, and book collector. His work appears in *Vastarien* literary journal from Grimscribe Press, the folk horror magazine *Hellebore*, as well as Anathema Publishing's esoteric books *Seeds of Ares* and *A Wayfarer's Hearth*. He also has written essays for *Cold Signal Magazine, Fantomes* zine, and the *Holland Files* Swamp Thing zine. Much of his work explores obscure knowledge and lore.

Reach him on Instagram @dagger_of_the_mind and Twitter @DaggerMind. He lives in Chicago, where he is often found in the pit at a crushing doom metal show.

LUCIANO MARANO

Luciano Marano is an award-winning author, photographer, and journalist. His short fiction has appeared in numerous anthologies, including *Year's Best Hardcore Horror, The Best New Weird Horror, Monsters, Movies & Mayhem* (winner: Colorado Book Award), *Crash Code* (nominee: Splatterpunk Award), *Breaking Bizarro*, and *The Nightside Codex*, among others, as well as *Nightscript, Pseudopod*, and *Horror Hill*. A trilogy of werewolf novellas, The Ambush Moon Cycle, is now available from Raven Tale Publishing. His reporting, written and photographic, has earned a number of industry awards, and he was twice named a Feature Writer of the Year by the Washington Newspaper Publishers Association. A U.S. Navy veteran originally from rural western Pennsylvania, he now resides near Seattle.

www.Luciano-Marano.com / Insta: @ghosttowngossip

A.W. MASON

A.W. Mason lives in Florida with his cat Wallace, a retired extreme parkour artist (who looks so dapper in his little helmet and knee pads). He enjoys all the nachos, getting lost in the woods and naps.

He is a graduate of the University of South Florida with a degree in communications with a focus on health.

His first book, *A Haunt of Travels*, is a short story collection with tales of horror, terror, suspense, crime and science fiction. His second book, *The Cleanup Crew*, is available now. Mason has also co-authored the extreme horror story, *The Scampering*, with Alana K. Drex.

HEATH MENSHER

Heath Mensher is an award-winning short filmmaker, playwright, writer, and poet. He has written for various publications and television, most notably two seasons working on NBC's "The West Wing," and has worked behind the scenes in over 40 films and television commercials with directors such as Francis Ford Coppola, Spike Lee, Aaron Sorkin, and Paul Reiser. His fiction writing focuses on imagist horror and his flash poetry has been published in journals such as *Crow Calls V*. His upcoming book of poetry, *Glances Through Waxed Paper*, is slated to release in 2023 and features one hundred eighty horror poems crafted to be read in one glance. He is currently working on a full-length novel, *RIPT*, that will release sometime next year.

Heath writes original horror flash poetry daily on Instagram as: @heathmensherauthor.

KURT NEWTON

Kurt Newton's fiction has appeared in numerous magazines and anthologies, including *Weird Tales*, *The Dark*, *Vastarien*, *Nightscript*, *Weirdbook* and *Cosmic Horror Monthly*. His latest collection, *The Music of Murder*, was recently published by Unnerving Books. He is also a prolific poet with recent appearances in *Spectral Realms*, *Penumbra*, *Bleed Error*, and *Cold Signal*. His ninth collection of poetry, *Songs of the Underland*, was published by Ravens Quoth Press in 2022. His tenth collection, *A Troubled*

Sleep, is coming in February from back room poetry (UK). He lives in the northeast corner of Connecticut.

ELAINE PASCALE

Elaine Pascale is the author of *The Blood Lights*; *If Nothing Else, Eve, We've Enjoyed the Fruit*; and the soon-to-be-released *The Language of Crows*. She is the co-editor of *Dancing in the Shadows: A tribute to Anne Rice*. She is a regular contributor to Pen of the Damned and the Ladies of Horror Picture-Prompt Challenge and is also a reviewer for Hellnotes. When Elaine is not on her paddle board, she is happy to engage with readers at elainepascale.com
Facebook: elaine.pascale
Twitter and Instagram: @doclaney
and TikTok: @elainepascale

JASMINE DE LA PAZ

Jasmine De La Paz is a speculative fiction author based in Bishop, CA. She weaves elements of gothic, psychological, and cosmic horror to her stories, and is often inspired by the surrounding nature and landscapes of the Eastern Sierra, where she resides. When not writing or reading through her endless pile of books, she enjoys bird watching, climbing mountains, or swimming in icy lakes.

You can find her on social media @jazz_delapaz

CHELSEA PUMPKINS

Chelsea Pumpkins is a writer from Massachusetts who stays curious about all things macabre. When she's not reading, writing, or watching something spooky, you may find her hiking in the White Mountains with her husband and sweet pitbull, Moose. You can read her stories in various horror anthologies and in *Shortwave Magazine*. She is also the editor of *AHH! That's What I Call Horror: An Anthology of '90s Horror*, and a co-host of The Cutthroat Queens podcast. Learn more about her work at chelseapumpkins.com and follow her on Twitter and Instagram at @ChelseaPumpkins.

KATHERINE QUEVEDO

Katherine Quevedo was born and raised near Portland, Oregon, where she works as an analyst and lives with her husband and two sons. Her poetry has been nominated for the Pushcart Prize and the Rhysling Award, and her debut mini-chapbook, *The Inca Weaver's Tales,* is forthcoming from Sword & Kettle Press in their New Cosmologies series. Her poems have appeared or are forthcoming in *Asimov's, Apparition Literary Magazine, The Collidescope, Heroic Fantasy Quarterly, Coffin Bell, Honeyguide Literary Magazine, Triangulation: Energy, Boudin* by The McNeese Review, and elsewhere. When she isn't writing, she enjoys watching movies, playing old-school video games, singing, belly dancing, and making spreadsheets.

Find her at www.katherinequevedo.com.

KYLE STÜCK

Kyle was born in the jungles of Ecuador, a magical land laden with mystical and wise jaguars, empanadas, and a cool air that has yet to be matched. After graduating college with a B.S. in Digital Cinema, Kyle found a new home in the Ozark Mountains and began his journey as an author: publishing Weird horror and sci-fi stories, along with some angsty poetry. Most recently, he sold the first volume of a horror comedy comic book titled *Evil Cast* which will be available in early 2023. When he's not writing, hosting podcasts on Ominous Media, or describing himself in the third-person, Kyle busies himself with absorbing all forms of media (mainly spooky stuff) or eating and drinking with family, friends, and other creators.

J.A. SULLIVAN

J.A. Sullivan is a genderqueer horror writer whose short fiction has appeared in several anthologies, including *A Silent Dystopia* (2021, Demain Publishing). As a dedicated member of the Kendall Reviews team, they regularly contribute horror book reviews, as well as writing "Scary's Voices," a weekly column of horror podcast recommendations. Sullivan has spent years as a paranormal investigator, has an insatiable appetite for serial killer information, and lives in Canada with their incredibly supportive husband. Updates on their writing journey, additional reviews, author interviews, and original fiction can be found on their blog (writingscaredblog.wordpress.com).

H. W. TAYLOR

H. W. Taylor was born after *Star Wars*, but watched *Empire Strikes Back* from his momma's lap. He's read sci-fi from Asimov to Zahn, teaches Languages, Astronomy, and Classic Literature. Sometimes refers to himself as a Medieval Futurist, though he isn't quite sure what he means by it yet.

H. W. Taylor's work incorporates his love of classic scientifiction, metaphysical hankerings, and abiding love of adventure. He is the author of *The Unique Miranda Trilogy*, the short story collection *Desolations*, and *SOL* written with D. H. Lawrence.

NATHANIEL WEBER

Nathaniel Weber has been scribbling stories since he was a kid. His grandparents and mom encouraged his interest with a steady supply of genre novels and an electric word processor. His favorite subjects to read and write are sci fi and horror. He has a PhD and teaches college courses in American and military history. During his free time he enjoys spending time with his wife, son, and a great multitude of pets. His hobby is miniature wargaming.

He's s currently working on a short story/novella collection and a gritty sci-fi space opera series called *The Migration*.

THANKS

Duane Warnecke, Cedric Carter II, Maggie Gehlsen-Burnett, Anas Abusalih, Paul Rylott, Ernesto, Chris Kalley, Justin Lewis, Susan Jessen, Trip Space-Parasite, Steve Pattee, Nicole Coster, Luke Rooney, David Myers, Ian Chung, Ken Wisian, Klikke Sietel, Allen Herring, Jenna, Lauren Page, Ethan Pollard, Bruce Baugh, David Zurek, David Scott Hay, Tbone Thompson, Tim Lonegan, Josh Mortensen, Isaac T, Jennifer Finch, Mallory A. Haws, Clive Viagas, Carlin McAneney, Alex Fernandez, John Anuci, Thomas Bull, Kelly Snyder, Laura D'Angelo, Courtney Barnett-Johnson, Heath Mensher, Andy

SPECIAL THANKS

Rebecca Rowland, Tim Meyer, Jon Padgett, Thomas Ligotti, Adam Fall, Kristina Osborn, Jeff Waitkev, Amanda Weidemann, Kirsten Aucoin, and Matt Cardin (for putting together *What the Daemon Said*, which was this anthology's muse).

ALSO FROM

NATIVE FEAR *by* C. F. PAGE

“It’s a beautiful, brutal, complex, terrifying read.”
—Scream Magazine

“Page's *Native Fear* is a blistering and evocative examination of man’s darkness. A harrowing read.”
—Steve Stred,
Splatterpunk-nominated author of *Sacrament* and *Mastodon.*

“Page manages to weave together strong undercurrents of cosmic horror, cult situations, splashes of sci-fi, and even some slasher flavors. There are creatures, mysteries, and creepy characters aplenty. . . . original and engaging, with nuanced characters that aren’t caricatures (and, in fact, mock the stereotypes).”
—Kyle J. Durrant,
author of *Beyond Dimensional Veils*

“One of the most intelligent, compelling, and well-written horror novels I've ever read, full stop. The sophisticated prose is fluid and colorful enough to make every scene, character, and ungodly image vividly cinematic, and there's a richness to the world that gives the story itself both a crushing weight to smash about and a delicate hand to do it with. *Native Fear* blends subgenres of horror so brilliantly that the transition from gnarly folk horror to epic cosmicism feels as natural as the ‘monsters’ in this book are unnatural. Clever, perfectly crafted, and innately subversive, this novel is one you won't be able to put down.”
—Jay Alexander,
author of *Starving Grounds* and *The Lunchling*

“Debut author [C. F.] Page presents an intricate horror novel . . . an inventive take on a rural place filled with unspeakable malice.”
—Kirkus Reviews